REDEMPTION

A Novel by Stephanie Baldi

DANCING CROWS
PRESS

ISBN: 978-0-9704420-4-8– Print

ISBN: 978-0-9704420-5-5– eBook

Library of Congress Control Number: 2018945764

Edited by Jean Holloway and Elyse Wheeler, PhD

Cover Design by Mary Rogers

Dancing Crows Press
306 Huntington Drive
Temple, GA 30179

Printed in the United States of America

Dedication

To my Nick, for always being there to
encourage me.

And to my Mom who always said I could do it.

Nominated for Georgia Author of the Year

Readers' Favorite Five Stars

Five Star Reviews from Amazon

Read in one sitting!
By E. Fuerst on January 3, 2019
Format: Paperback |Verified Purchase
Just finished reading "Redemption" by author Stephanie Baldi. Each page filled me with anticipation for the next one. The characters are built so well that they now live in my mind. It's a great and smooth read as a thriller with a bit of romance. Even though I felt I knew what might happen next, I was often surprised and loved to see how the character acted. I'm already casting movie roles in my head.

GREAT BOOK
By Michael Bilotti on November 1, 2018
Format: Paperback |Verified Purchase
Reading this book was a joy. I couldn't put it down. The characters were compelling. The author took the story to some locations that I had never been to but wanted to visit. It is s quick read and I look forward to her next book. I enjoy suspense stories and this lives up to my expectations. I believe that this a first novel by this author and it is a great opening gambit into the writing field.

It's a thrilling ride.
By Chris on November 27, 2018
Format: Paperback
This is a great read. A good storyline and interesting characters. A real page turner.

Redemption: A must-read page turner!
By Donna T. on September 23, 2018
Format: Paperback
Stephanie Baldi has a hit on her hands! "Redemption" is a hard hitting, impossible to put down book. I read it in two sittings, I couldn't stop reading it! It is definitely a must-read page turner! I'm anxious to read the sequel, the characters really got under my skin. Don't miss this novel with its plot twists and suspense!

Acknowledgements:

Val Mathews, Editor Extraordinaire, who believed in my talent and encouraged me. Claudia Rowe Kennedy, my dear friend, I love you heaps and gobs. My sister, Christine Jetter for her love and support. Leah Brumbelow, who shared my excitement and believed in me.

Lauryn Stewart, whose love and light shines. You make my world a better place. To all my Mexican Train gals at Fairfield, thank you for all your love and encouragement.

My amazing family who never ceases to support me. Lots of love to Christina Jetter, Kim Benjamin & Lisa Forts. To the Carrollton Writers Guild, words cannot express what your support has meant to me. You are the best. To my Brooklyn girls, Marianne, Doreen, & Pat who are always close to my heart.

To Jean Holloway who was always there to talk me down from the ledge. You said, "I got you," and you never let me fall.

TL James, I couldn't have done it without you.

And to the loves of my life, Dominick, Nicholas, and Isabelle. Grandma did it!

Breezy Meadows
CARRIE
1999—Petuma, Arizona

The trailer door hung open. She'd only been gone an hour. Carrie's stomach twisted as she ran up the steps. Heart thumping against her chest, she dashed to the crib. His tiny blue blanket lay in a heap. Frantic, she searched the rest of the trailer for any sign of her child.

Six months of her mother being clean of drugs should not have influenced her decision. Going against her better judgment, she handed the most precious thing in the world over to her mother while she went to get formula. Sixty minutes, one hour. Long enough to change Carrie's life forever.

A commotion outside made her freeze. High-pitched laughter rang out, followed by the slam of a car door. An engine roared as its tires spit gravel along the side of the metal trailer. Her panic spread as she hurried to the door. Her mother stumbled in, her arms empty, her eyes lit with euphoria from crack cocaine.

The knot in Carrie's stomach grew tighter. She grabbed her mother's arm, fingers digging into her mother's flesh. "Where is he? Where is Bobby? What did you do with my son?"

She pulled away, jerked her arm free and slammed Carrie aside. Carrie lost her balance and fell to the floor.

Her mother held up her bleeding arm where Carrie's nails had punctured her skin. "Look what you did to me, you little bitch."

Carrie scrambled to her feet and came at her mother again. "I said, where's Bobby?" Her voice rose in pitch as her hysteria grew.

Her mother stared blankly at her. "Stop your whining. He's in a better place."

Carrie's blood turned to ice. Her legs grew weak, threatening to collapse beneath her. "A ... a better place? What are you talking about? I swear, if you did something to him, I'll kill you. Do you hear me? I'll kill you!"

"Oh, stop your fussing. You ought to be ashamed. Fifteen years old and carrying a baby around. He's fine. Bobby's with good people now. He'll have a better life than you could ever give him."

She pushed past Carrie and flopped onto the brown plaid sofa. Carrie tore across the room and pounced. She reached out and snatched her mother's hair, dragging her off the sofa. They both hit the floor, Carrie on top, pinning her down.

"You tell me where he is right now, or I swear to God, I'll break every bone in your body!"

In the end, there were no broken bones that day. Instead, pain and guilt took hold inside when Carrie learned her mother sold her son to a couple passing through in exchange for two thousand dollars which she promptly spent part on drugs.

The police launched an investigation, but the couple, who so callously bought her child, had disappeared. They charged her mother, and she was sentenced to ten years in jail.

Over and over again, Carrie berated herself. One hour. What she wouldn't give to turn back the clock and undo what she had done.

Leaving her child with her mother that day turned out to be the worst decision of her life. Or, so she thought. Travis Montgomery was about to prove her wrong.

CHAPTER 1

CARRIE

2015—Melbourne, Florida

The first time Carrie Overton committed murder, she did it to save him. The second time she did it to save herself. Trapped inside his Chevy Impala, Carrie sat beside a man she didn't love, a man she had mistaken for her savior.

She kneaded the stiff leather seat beneath her fingertips. The odor of stale cigarettes overflowing in the ashtray stung her nose. Outside the window, slices of sunlight channeled through the trees as the car raced toward its destination.

Frigid air whistled from the vents but failed to evaporate the sweat on Carrie's skin. Underneath her short denim skirt, her thighs stuck together, but it wasn't the Florida heat making her sweat. It was fear.

The engine rattled, strained, and then regained its rhythm. Carrie glanced at the man beside her. Travis's long fingers cradled the wheel. He clenched his teeth, and she caught the click of his jaw. A familiar sound, it put her body on high alert.

Travis punched the gas pedal with the tip of his muddy cowboy boot. The car lurched forward. Carrie braced herself against the sharp turn. The tires on the right passenger side screeched and then lifted off the pavement. Her heart tripped in her chest as the Impala swerved into the oncoming traffic lane directly in the path of a tractor-trailer. The massive truck blasted its horn, veering toward the left just in time to avoid a head-on collision. Travis swore and cut the wheel steering back into the correct lane.

Carrie traced her finger along the door handle, wishing she had the courage to open it and hurl herself out of the speeding car. She turned, eyed the briefcase lying on the backseat, and, out of habit, twisted the gold band on her left ring finger.

"Travis, are you sure you want to go through with this? If something goes wrong—"

"Open the glove box, Carrie." The grit in his voice clipped the air like a pair of scissors, sharp and to the point. Travis never wasted words.

She pressed the latch. The glove box sprung open. Her stomach churned at the sight of the .45 revolver.

"Take it out," he ordered.

"Why?" She asked the question even though she already knew the answer. This time, Travis was determined to push things to the limit.

"For Christ's sake, don't argue with me, girl." He jerked the wheel and parked on the shoulder. "Go on, pick it up."

Carrie bit her lower lip and attempted to steady her hand. She lifted the .45 out. The cold metal sent chills across her palm. The gun felt awkward, heavier than she imagined.

Travis taught her how to operate the weapon and check the safety mechanism. "It's insurance," he said. He finished with his instructions and made his way back out into the mid-day traffic. "If I need you to pull the trigger, you better do it."

At his last words, her body heat soared. She dropped the revolver into her purse and flipped the visor down. She studied her face in the mirror. The violet in her blue eyes intensified. Trying to cool herself, she gathered up her long black hair and tucked it at the nape of her neck.

Travis adjusted his weapon concealed behind him in his waistband, then snatched up his cigarettes from the console. He slipped one out, motioning for her to light it.

Carrie deftly brought the lighter up and touched it to the tip. She took stock of Travis's tall, slim build, a contradiction to the fifty-one years he carried. Only the subtle streaks of grey, running like silver threads through his brown hair, hinted at his age. Travis surpassed her by twenty years, but today, she felt a hundred years older.

He dragged on the cigarette and puffed out. The smoke swirled up and hung between them forming a veil—a moment's division out of a lifetime of inseparable misery. It was difficult to imagine a time when Travis used to make her feel safe. After sixteen years, safety had deserted her, turning fear into her constant companion.

Travis cruised alongside the high chain-link fence surrounding the warehouse parking lot. An opening appeared, and he drove through. He stopped near the front of a red brick building.

Carrie peered out the windshield. Straight ahead, its engine silent, a shiny black Lincoln Sedan with tinted windows sat like a vulture, hunched over, waiting for its prey. The sun glinted off the dark hood, and she blinked to clear her vision. Her heart fluttered and beat against her ribcage like a trapped bird.

Travis parked across from the Lincoln. He lowered the front windows and shut off the ignition.

Carrie touched his arm. "Travis, be careful. Please, just give them the briefcase and get the money."

His dark eyes locked on hers. "Get ready."

She watched two men emerge from the dark interior of the Lincoln, their eyes shielded from the harsh sunlight by dark glasses. They crossed the parking lot. Both dressed in expensive-looking suits yet were polar opposites. The short, heavyset one lumbered toward them. His skin was the color of almonds, and his round face sported a generous mustache. The second one, tall and lanky, moved panther-like, his physique in stark contrast to the other man. His slick, sandy-colored hair lay combed back from his pale skin and pockmarked face. Both men removed their sunglasses in unison and pocketed them.

Carrie focused on Travis as he exited the Impala. He flicked his cigarette butt onto the pavement, crushing it beneath his boot. The men stood several feet apart.

"Hey, Carlos." Travis nodded in the direction of the short one first, and then the taller one. "Eddie."

Carlos's posture stiffened. He fingered his mustache. His lips formed a slow smile that leaked acid below the surface as he held out his hand. "The briefcase, please."

Travis remained stock-still. "You gotta understand, fellas, from where I'm standing, I have to make sure things are right. Hand me the money, and the briefcase is yours."

Eddie glanced at Carlos and then at Travis, but he remained silent.

Carrie wanted to scream. What was Travis thinking going up against these two men? She clung to the slim hope that he would stick to the plan and not get them killed.

Carlos held up his hand. "Okay, okay, there's no reason for things to get crazy. Let's be fair. I'll get the money from the Lincoln, and you get the briefcase from yours." Carlos stepped to the Lincoln, reached in, and returned holding a large plastic bag.

Carrie squirmed as muggy air drifted in the windows. Barely able to sit still in the heat, her insides wound tighter while she waited for Travis's next move.

"I have your money," Carlos said.

Travis shook his head. "Doesn't look like fifty thousand dollars to me. What are you trying to pull, Carlos?" In less than a second, he reached around, drew out his gun, aiming it at the two men. "Toss the bag over here."

Pushing against the seat, Carrie wished she could disappear beneath the leather, be anywhere else except here in this parking lot. Her insides shook, and she tried to calm herself.

Carlos and Eddie remained fixed. "Are you kidding me?" Carlos asked. "Do you know who you're messing with?" He motioned toward the gun. "Don't be stupid. Put that thing away."

Carrie observed Travis's stance. She'd physically endured his wrath on numerous occasions and was all too familiar with his body language. She knew he'd never back down.

Travis waved the gun at the ground. "I said, toss the bag over here, then both of you need to take out your weapons and drop them. Do it slowly, no fast moves."

"Bullshit," Eddie said, breaking his silence. "I ain't dropping nothing."

Travis cocked his revolver. "You have five seconds to do what I say, or else."

"Or else *what*?" Eddie pointed his finger at Travis. "You'll never get away with this. Think again, asshole. You don't want to screw with the man we work for."

"No, *you* better think again," Travis said. "Talk about trying to screw someone." He aimed at Eddie's feet and squeezed the trigger. A bullet burst from the chamber, the sound ripping through the dense air.

The bullet grazed the top of Eddie's shoe, and he jerked back. "Son of a bitch! You almost hit me."

Carrie flinched. Her skin prickled as she clutched the purse in her lap. Any sliver of hope that they'd all end up alive vanished. Her worst fears became a reality.

Travis stood firm. "Do as I say, boys. I ain't gonna repeat myself."

Carlos hesitated and then tossed the bag in Travis's direction. It slid across the blacktop, coming to a stop at his feet. Both men lifted their weapons out and threw them on the ground.

Holding his aim steady, Travis called out. "Carrie, come over, too, darling, and bring the gun I gave you."

Blood rushed to Carrie's head. Her mouth turned bone dry. She fumbled with the clasp on her purse and pulled out the .45. Her legs wobbled as she climbed from the car. She held the doorframe to steady herself. The consequences could prove deadly if she didn't come to Travis's aid. Gun in her hand, arm by her side, she rushed toward him.

"Honey, raise that gun and take aim. Make sure they don't move," Travis said.

Carrie lifted up both of her arms. The butt of the .45 rested between her palms. She aimed the gun at the two men and fought to control the trembling in her body. Travis had given her no other choice but to stand by him. She sensed his confidence grow with her by his side.

Travis bent and reached for the bag just as Eddie dove for his gun. Carlos lunged at Carrie, and she squeezed the trigger the same moment Travis fired a shot.

The crack of multiple gunshots reverberated off the sides of the warehouse. The bullet flew from her chamber and hit Carlos dead center in his neck. Carrie staggered backward from the recoil. Carlos's body jolted from the impact. He reached up and clutched his throat. Blood spurted from the open wound and streaked down his hands, turning them red. His airway blocked, he gasped and choked on his own blood. His arms fell limp, and he collapsed to the ground. Rivers of blood streamed across the pavement, seeping into the tiny cracks.

Carrie looked to her right. Eddie lay on his side. Blood oozed from his head wound. Bits of brain matter and tissue stuck to the hot blacktop. The coppery scent of blood and gunpowder lingered in the air. Her ears rang, and a wave of nausea washed over her.

Travis spun around and faced her. "We need to go *now*."

His voice, muffled from the ringing in her ears, barely penetrated. Her legs threatened to give way.

"Carrie, did you hear me? We gotta go." He snatched up the plastic bag.

Terror consumed her, and she couldn't move. Travis's fingers wrapped around her arm. He steered her toward the Impala and shoved her inside. Carrie took one last look at the dead men lying in pools of blood, not wanting to believe what she was seeing.

Travis got behind the wheel and crammed his weapon underneath the seat. The keys in his hand shook as he started the car. He jammed his foot on the gas. The engine swelled, and the tires squealed in protest across the blistering pavement. The stench of scorched rubber wafted in. He hit the gas a second time causing the engine to buck and falter. The automobile rolled to a stop, and he slammed his hand on the steering wheel.

He cursed under his breath and turned the key. The engine whined, hesitated, and then caught. He nudged the gas pedal, and this time, the car charged ahead.

Her fingers still clamped on the butt, Carrie stared in horror at the gun. She swallowed hard and let the .45 fall from her lap. Her stomach rolled. Vomit surged up toward her throat, ready to spill out. She clamped her mouth with her hand and gripped her middle with the other.

"Pull over, Travis," she moaned.

"Are you crazy, girl? We can't stop now." He pressed the pedal harder and picked up speed. White-hot wind sailed in the open windows.

Her stomach coiled again, ready to pour out its contents. "Pull over. I'm going to be sick." She gulped, pushing saliva back. "Please."

Travis drew the wheel sharply to the right and stopped on the shoulder. Carrie bolted from the Chevy and rushed down the embankment. Her shoulders curled, and she dropped to her knees, arms cinched around her waist. Hot liquid burned her throat as she spewed the contents of her stomach.

Dry heaves surged through her, bitter bile stinging her tongue. Wiping her mouth with the back of her hand, she collapsed onto the grass. She kneaded her temples to ease the growing ache inside her head.

Jumping at the blare of the car horn, she struggled to stay erect, as she climbed up the embankment. She shuddered as her knees almost buckled. At the top, she watched Travis toss the briefcase into the trunk along with the plastic bag. She got into the car, and without saying a word, he drove back onto the highway.

Tears welled up, and she focused on the traffic outside the window. Their instructions from Carlos were clear. Make the drop, hand over the briefcase, and get paid. A simple task. Why hadn't Travis followed the plan?

She weighed her own sanity against his madness and became determined to escape.

As the car sped down the highway, she became sure of one thing. As much as she feared him, her hunger to be free of him outweighed her fear.

Carrie dropped her right arm and grabbed the .45. She slipped it into her purse. Travis was too preoccupied to notice.

CHAPTER 2

CARRIE

Thunder drummed in the distance. Heavy grey clouds were forming in the sky. Sultry air tinged with the scent of rain filled Carrie's lungs as she opened the car door at the truck stop. Travis reached for her hand. "Come on, girl, I'm starved."

Rows of semi-trucks and tractor-trailers lined the lot, most of their engines idle. Outside one of the cabs, two truckers stopped conversing and zeroed in on the two of them. Travis squeezed her hand and Carrie focused on the pavement in front of her. This was his way of letting her know he didn't approve. She sucked in her bottom lip to keep from crying out. Stares from other men always made his temper flare. They reached the entrance, and he released her hand. Carrie shook her fingers to alleviate the pain.

Inside, a series of red leather booths formed an L-shape around the perimeter. A dozen or more truckers sat hunched over, wolfing down food. Cutlery scraped across plates, spoons clinked while waitresses refilled coffee cups and made idle chatter with the customers. They took turns calling out orders at the pass-thru window to the cook.

The aroma of freshly brewed coffee and meat sizzling on the grill threatened to throw Carrie's stomach into spasms again. Images of Carlos and Eddie in pools of blood replayed in her mind.

They sank into a booth, and she pretended to study the menu. Her eyes traveled from the colorful laminated pictures of food to the counter, where a stocky trucker perched on a stool. The rolled-up sleeves of his blue plaid shirt exposed beefy, tattooed arms.

Aware of the way he looked at her when they walked in, she made eye contact. The trucker touched the brim of his red baseball cap and grinned at her.

Pain shot up her leg, and she flinched as the tip of Travis's boot stung her shin. His face flushed red. The lines around his mouth creased and his jaw clicked.

"What the hell are you doing?"

His eyes flashed those danger signals she knew all too well. Nervous knots swirled through her stomach. She prayed Travis wouldn't cause a scene.

"Do you think you can disrespect me?" he asked, leaning across the table. His voice narrowed into a hard whisper. "Killing someone making you bold?"

Trying to appear apologetic, she forced a smile. "Calm down. Let's order, okay." She focused her attention back on the menu.

Travis stretched out his muscular arms and rested them on the table. His hands formed into fists, warning her.

A few minutes later, the waitress set their plates down. Carrie reached for her fork and grew queasy all over again. All she could do was push her food around on her plate while she watched Travis practically inhale his meal. Nothing bothered him, not even someone's brains splattered all over the pavement.

Disgusted, she stared out the window. If she hadn't come to Travis's defense, the two of them would probably be dead now, but it still didn't justify the blood on her hands. If they were caught, she could spend the rest of her life in jail or worse.

The heaviness inside her swelled knowing that murder had made the ties between them stronger. Now, more than ever, she wanted to cut those ties and gain the freedom she craved.

Carrie observed the trucker again as he made his way to the cashier. Travis finished his plate, and they rose to leave right behind the trucker. She made her way toward the restroom, while Travis strolled to the end of the counter to pay the check.

His attention occupied, she bolted out the door and searched for the trucker. Carrie spotted him at the far end of the lot preparing to climb into an enormous red cab. Her pulse spiked. She ran toward him willing her legs to pump faster. She reached the cab, and the passenger side door flew open. The trucker leaned down. A broad smile appeared on his face.

"Need a ride, pretty lady?"

"Yes, Mister," she said between heavy breaths. "Please, take me with you."

He patted the seat beside him. "Hop on up here."

Carrie grabbed hold of the handle on the cab door and stepped up on the running board. The trucker's smile disappeared as searing pain raced up her arm. Travis clamped down hard. Her arm threatened to tear from its socket as her foot slid out from underneath her.

"Look, Mister, I don't want any trouble," the trucker blurted out. "Sorry, my mistake. I ain't about to steal another man's woman." He shut the cab door, revved the engine, and drove off.

Loose gravel spewed up and peppered Carrie's bare legs. She pitched to one side as Travis dragged her toward the car. Her shoe came off and slid along the pavement making her struggle to keep her balance. Lightning flashed, followed by a blast of thunder. Black clouds swelled unleashing a torrent of rain.

Travis shoved her inside. He sprinted through the deluge and slipped behind the wheel. Drenched from the driving rain, his clothes plastered to his body, he gulped air in angry spurts. Without warning, he raised his hand and slapped Carrie twice across her face.

She cried out as the sting ripped through her body like an electric shock. Her skull smacked against the headrest while the soft flesh on her lips stung. Her mind hurled through time, returning to Arizona, and the trailer in Breezy Meadows where she had endured a slap much harder than the ones Travis gave her.

She was five years old again, asking her mother questions about her father. The father she used to dream of, the father who would one day come to her rescue. Her mother's answer came swift and sure in the form of a slap hard enough to knock out her front baby tooth causing it to sail across the green Formica kitchen counter, leaving a trail of blood behind it. She didn't dare mention her father again.

Thunder rattled, cementing Carrie back in the present. Her tears trailed along her bruised cheek and dripped off her chin. Blood oozed from her swollen lip. She tasted its bitterness with the tip of her tongue just like when she was five.

Travis reached out and yanked her face toward him. "You ever try to pull a stunt like that again, and I swear you'll get more than a few slaps." He grabbed his cigarettes from the console and shook out two. Placing them between his lips, he lit both and handed one to Carrie.

"What's gotten into you?" he asked.

Carrie put the cigarette to her lips and took a drag. Ignoring the pain from her swollen lip, she watched the rain cascade down the windshield, the world outside, like her life, a blur.

They smoked in silence while the rain hammered against the glass. Minutes slipped by. The rain slowed and then stopped. Like Travis's rage, it departed as swiftly as it had burst from the sky. Without another word, he drove out onto the highway.

The last of the daylight slipped beneath the horizon as they checked into a small motel. Carrie rolled her suitcase to a corner of the room and then lowered herself onto the bed. Her body sank with the give of the cheap mattress. The simple room held nothing exceptional to distinguish it from all the others they had occupied over the years. She glimpsed the patterned carpet layered with dark muted stains. Paper-thin walls carried the drone from a television in the room next door.

Travis set his suitcase next to hers and then drew the heavy drapes. He tossed the briefcase and the plastic bag filled with cash on the bed. Pulling a screwdriver from his back pocket, he worked it against the locks until they sprang free with a loud snap, and the cover flew open.

"Ooh Wee! Look at this," Travis crowed. He raked his fingers over the crisp stacks of bills. "Girl, we are richer than I thought."

Carrie stared at the briefcase, the piles of money, and understood, whether or not the plastic bag held fifty thousand dollars, Travis had wanted the briefcase all along. His greed almost cost them their lives. His greed left two people dead.

"Finally," Travis said. "We've made it, Carrie. No one's gonna stop us this time. We're this close to heaven, baby." He slammed the briefcase shut and placed it in the closet. After he removed the bands of cash from the plastic bag, he stuffed all of it in the false bottom of his suitcase.

He turned toward Carrie. "We'll lay low tonight and leave early tomorrow morning."

Carrie's stomach pitched, her shoulders tensed. Unable to shake the images of bodies and blood from her mind, desperation outweighed her fear. "Travis, I can't go on like this. I'm sick over what happened today."

Travis let out a chuckle. "Put it out of your mind. Those two bums deserved what happened to them."

Carrie rose from the bed and faced him. 'I mean it. I can't do this anymore."

"Do what?" Arms folded tight across his chest, he waited.

"I'm tired. I want out. Please, give me my half of the money and let me go."

He drew himself up and scowled. "Half? What the hell do you mean?"

Every nerve inside her quivered, but she kept her voice steady. "You don't have to give me half. Whatever you think is fair."

"Fair?"

He moved closer, his warm breath fanned her face, and she took a step back.

"Do you think I'd just hand you some money and let you walk out that door? You must be crazy."

His eyes bore into her skin like braille on a blank sheet of paper. She rubbed her arms expecting to find herself covered with little pinpoint holes.

Travis advanced and seized her shoulders. "Reading too many of those lousy books of yours is putting all kinds of silly ideas in your head. Your leaving is never gonna happen. We belong together."

She'd made a mistake. Possibly a worse mistake than when she tried to run away at the diner. To placate him, she said, "Forget it. Forget I said anything. Where would I go anyhow?"

He fell silent. The uncertainty of her words registered on his face. Slowly, he lowered his hands and moved away.

Later that evening, Carrie lay on her side while Travis leaned his body against hers. Her muscles grew taut, and she hugged her arms close to her body. Her head pounded. She knew what he wanted. His hands traveled over her body as she lay unresponsive. Over the years, Travis had morphed into someone who she hated and feared. His touch repulsed her. She let her mind drift to someplace else.

Travis finished and grabbed the car keys from the nightstand. He slipped them underneath his pillow as always. Opening his flask of whiskey, he took a long swallow.

Carrie lit a cigarette and strode naked into the bathroom. Ignoring the shock of the pale blue tile beneath her feet, she plopped onto the toweled mat draped over the edge of the tub.

Guilt drenched her soul. She could never redeem herself. Not for committing murder and not for the loss of her child. She had found a grain of truth in the words Travis spoke at the diner. Killing someone had changed her. After today, she'd never be the same person.

Carrie took the last puff and tossed the butt into the toilet. In the shower, she let the warm water pour over her body and wished she could wash herself clean of Travis and the murders. She frowned and touched the wine-colored finger marks imprinted on her upper arm. Clenching her teeth, she patted them with the washcloth.

Later, a towel wrapped around her body, she crept out of the bathroom. Travis lay stretched out on the bed, head propped up on one elbow. His flask of whiskey still rested on the nightstand. He motioned to her. "Come, get in bed."

Carrie drew the towel tighter before slipping in beside him. In a matter of seconds, Travis pounced on top of her. His rough, calloused hands squeezed her throat.

Her arms shot up to her neck. She clawed at his hands while his full weight pressed against her. Panic ripped through her as Travis's hands tightened, and dug into her flesh. She twisted her body, struggling to free herself. The odor of sour whiskey bit at her nose. A gasp escaped her lips. Her heart roared inside her chest as the room swam in dizzying circles. She closed her eyes. Sparks of reds, blues, and greens swirled behind her lids. His harsh, heavy breathing rang in her ears.

She wished for death. Knew she'd welcome it. Death was better than enduring one more day with him. Her body went slack, ready to give in when he finally let go.

Low, raspy noises burst forth from Carrie's throat. She fought to inhale. Burning pain gripped her neck. She opened her eyes. Travis towered above her, his face filled with blind rage.

"Don't ever think you can get away from me." His lips curled. "I'll bury you before I let you walk this earth without me."

"Travis, please." She could hardly recognize her own voice. "I can't breathe." Tears formed a path down her cheeks and across her lips, their saltiness stinging her tongue.

He lifted himself off of her and then reached for his flask. Twisting off the cap, he gulped down the whiskey.

Carrie forced herself up into a sitting position and swung her legs over the side of the bed. She managed to stand but her legs gave way, and she slumped to the floor. Her neck throbbed. She got on all fours and crawled into the bathroom. Kicking the door shut, she reached up and turned the lock.

She held onto the rim of the sink and eased up. Her throat ached. Turning the tap, she cupped her hands and splashed cold water on her face. Slowly, she lifted her head and caught her reflection in the mirror. Dark circles marked the skin beneath her eyes. She swept her hair up. Ugly red and purple bruises formed a pattern on her neck. Her fingertips probed the swollen veins underneath them. At that moment, all her doubts and fears dissolved.

Carrie unlocked the door and peered out. Travis's heavy snore dominated the room. His flask lay open. She followed the steady rise and fall of his chest. It meant he'd sleep through the night. She tucked a towel around her body and padded softly across the room and grabbed her purse. She opened it and removed the .45. Firing a weapon had empowered her. Made her believe she could stand up against him.

Today, she experienced firsthand, the jolt of the recoil, the tang of gunpowder. She witnessed Carlos collapse into a pool of his own blood, and poor Eddie's brains splattered across the blacktop.

She moved toward the bed and fingered the trigger. Having fired it once already, she knew with certainty she could do it again. Travis had taught her well.

It would be easy to pull the trigger right now, while he slept. Shoot him, take the money and leave. Only it wasn't enough. She wanted him to feel how much he hurt her. How his abandonment all those years ago had cost her the most cherished thing in her life.

She could no longer deal with the physical pain he so cruelly dealt out. And her emotional pain had grown roots. Long, unforgiving roots.

Though desperate for freedom, she'd learned she wouldn't get far without money. With each slap, punch, and unkind word, she'd earned every dollar bill inside that briefcase.

Holding the gun, she paced the small room. She stopped and studied her neck in the mirror. If all her marks and bruises failed to fade away, her body would look like a battlefield from a war she had fought and lost over and over again. It was time to even the ground.

CHAPTER 3

NICK

Nicholas D'Angelo, better known as Nicky D, drove his black S550 Mercedes Benz up to the wrought iron gates. He noted the intricate scrollwork surrounding either side of the initials R. S. in the center.

Ernesto Bario's tall, solid body cast a shadow on the hood of the car, the firearm at his side in full view. Nick slid the window down.

Ernesto stooped and peered in. "Ah, Nicky D. *Buenos dias, amigo.*" His lips curved into a smile, revealing a set of perfect white teeth. "It's good to see you again."

Nick returned the smile. "You too, Ernesto. Are you keeping that pretty wife of yours happy?"

Ernesto straightened and erupted into a belly laugh. "It's like they say, happy wife, happy life."

"So I've heard," Nick said. "But I wouldn't know about it firsthand."

"*Sí, amigo.* You are the lucky one. A bachelor."

Nick balked at the word bachelor. Single by choice, at times he wished for someone to warm his bed at night. "Don't fool yourself, it can get pretty lonely."

Ernesto winked, moved toward a panel by the gate, and pressed in a code. The gates parted, separating the R and S at the center. He stepped back and waved Nick through.

Nick cruised along the drive underneath the massive oak trees stationed on either side, cloaked in Spanish moss. Draped among the branches, the moss swayed gently in the warm breeze, their canopy a welcome respite from the hot sun.

A palatial home, with cream-colored stucco walls and red tile roof, came into view. The wheels of the Mercedes touched the circular drive and glided over the natural stone pavers.

Nick's green eyes scanned the manicured landscape. Ornate fountains graced the gardens. Exotic plants and flowers perfumed the air. Rows of bougainvillea already trained to tree-form stood fanned out along a path winding through the property. Weeping bottlebrush trees swayed in unison showing off fuzzy red blooms. Tall, narrow Italian Cypress pressed close to the exterior walls of the mansion. All these things were a demonstration of the wealth and power of the man who lived inside.

He emerged from the air-conditioned car and swore under his breath when the humid Miami air assaulted him. Nick hated Miami. He took no pleasure in the blistering heat or the rustle of palm trees. A New Yorker at heart, he loved how he could feel the charge in the air there. Give him concrete skyscrapers, the hustle and bustle, and the change of seasons. They could keep Miami. Hell, they could keep the whole state of Florida for that matter.

His body strained against the confines of the black tee shirt underneath the grey Hugo Boss suit. He stretched, loosening the muscles on his six-foot frame after the long drive. At thirty-six years old, Nick was in the best shape of his life. He didn't smoke, rarely drank, and took good care of himself. It wasn't vanity. In his line of work, he did it out of necessity.

Known as a ghost among his peers, Nick was at the top of his profession. Invisible, a sure bet to get the job done.

Nick hadn't come to Miami by choice. Ricardo Santiago requested he come. Ricardo, one of the world's wealthiest business owners and importers of goods, was also one of the most feared drug lords on the East Coast. Nick had done plenty of work for Ricardo. And today, Ricardo would give him all the details for his next kill. Nick didn't keep track of the body count. He did what Ricardo asked and was well compensated. A disgraced, former NYPD detective, who lost his way, Ricardo had saved him, and Nick would never forget it.

Nick strode to the massive, double oak doors. He swept a hand through his thick dark hair and adjusted his suit jacket. Before he could press the doorbell, Armando, Ricardo's butler opened the door. Fiftyish, short in stature with a receding hairline, his black and white butler's uniform was pressed to perfection. He dipped his head and bowed in Nick's direction.

"Ah, Mr. Nicky D, he is expecting you. Come in, please."

Nick crossed the entryway, and Armando closed the door behind him.

A grin flashed across Armando's face. "It has been awhile, *sí?*"

"Yes, it has, Armando," Nick agreed, glancing down and catching his reflection in the imported Italian marble floor lit by the cut-crystal chandelier suspended above.

"All is good with you, no?" Armando asked.

"Wouldn't do any good to complain," Nick said. He followed Armando down the long hall leading to Ricardo's study. Priceless art lined the walls. Nick glimpsed the latest additions to Ricardo's collection. Custom-installed lighting above two new works of art served to exhibit them in all their glorious detail.

Outside the study door, Chino, Ricardo's pure white Akita, lay stretched out on the floor. Chino rose and stood erect on all four paws, his massive one hundred, and thirty-pound body blocking the door. With a bite pressure of three hundred and fifty pounds, he could quickly dispatch any unwanted intruder. Gentle with those familiar to him, his tail beat against the tile floor as Nick approached.

"Hello, Chino." He bent and patted his enormous head. Nick could hardly believe Chino was the same dog he'd found chained to a tree in the backyard of one of his kills, the links on the chain digging welts into his neck, half-starved and scarcely able to move. Nick spared no expense nursing the beaten and abused dog he had rescued. Being on the road so much and knowing Chino would have a good home, he presented him to Ricardo as a gift.

"How are you, boy?" Chino wagged his tail faster while emitting a low growl of contentment, his dark eyes trained on Nick.

Armando tapped on the paneled pocket door and slid it open. Chino padded past him into the study. "You can go right in," Armando said. He moved away and disappeared down the hallway.

Nick entered the room and slid the door closed. He inhaled the scent of fine leather mixed with polished wood. Two walls held floor to ceiling bookcases filled with expensive custom bound books. The dark furniture, all imported and hand-made to specification anchored the room. An exquisite hand-woven rug from India partially concealed the rich Brazilian walnut floor underneath. The fireplace mantle held two bronze sculptures on opposite ends, one by Alberto Giacometti, and one by Henry Moore. Between them stood a single guilt-edged frame. Inside the frame was a picture of a striking young woman with long hair the color of caramel, full lips, and almond-shaped eyes.

No matter how many times he visited, Ricardo's study always impressed him. *He might be a drug dealer, but the guy sure had taste,* Nick mused.

Ricardo sat in a burgundy leather chair behind a large, mahogany desk and stared at a computer screen. Chino settled himself at the base, crossing his paws in front.

Nick took a moment to look at Ricardo before he glanced up. One would never consider this small man with skin the color of creamy mocha, to be anything other than a wealthy, cultured gentleman. Ricardo was certainly that. And much more.

Ricardo looked up. He smoothed his pencil-thin mustache and his silver-grey hair. Rising, he stepped from behind his desk.

"Hola mi compadre," he said, giving Nick a bear hug. "Welcome to Miami."

"It's good to see you, Ricardo, but you know how I feel about Miami," Nick teased.

Ricardo laughed. "Yes, you're, as they say, a die-hard New Yorker. Come, my friend, let's have a drink." He strode over to the burnished wood bar, raised a crystal decanter and poured two shots of AsomBroso Tequila. Handing a glass to Nick, he gestured for him to sit on the leather sofa opposite his desk.

Ricardo perched on the edge of his chair. "I know you hate Miami. Still, you should come to see me more often. If not here, then when I'm at my vineyards in California."

Nick relaxed into the soft leather. "Yes, you're right. I'll keep that in mind."

A slight smile appeared on Ricardo's lips. "I think you understand how important you are to me, my friend. There are not many people I can trust in this life." He raised his glass. *"Salud."*

The warmth of the tequila bathed Nick's throat with a smoothness only an eighteen-hundred dollar bottle of liquor could.

"Have you given any more thought to our earlier conversation regarding Carmela?" Ricardo asked.

Nick shifted his body, twirled the empty shot glass between his fingers. He cast a glance at the picture of Carmela on the mantle. He'd hoped to avoid the subject of marriage. Nick had known Carmela for a good number of years and watched her grow from a gangly girl into a captivating woman. As of now, she was away finishing her degree at Harvard. Her father's alma mater.

Carmela was pretty enough but way too young. Too young for a love interest, she was more like a little sister to him than a potential wife. None of that mattered to Ricardo. He wanted a marriage between them. Carmela was to marry someone Ricardo could count on to keep her safe after he was gone.

"Ricardo,' Nick began. "I care deeply for Carmela."

Ricardo's eyebrow shot up, his face questioning Nick's words. "But …"

"I don't think it's fair to her. She should marry someone who can make her happy. You know I'm not that guy, Ricardo."

Ricardo flashed a grin. "I think you are. Only you do not realize it yet. Carmela would be thrilled to marry you. We have already spoken of it."

Nick considered his next words carefully. "I'm honored you would entrust the future of your daughter to me. Any man would jump at the chance to marry her."

"Yes, but I won't accept just any man for my daughter, Nick. I think my reasons are well-founded."

Ricardo walked to the bar and picked up the decanter again. He gestured for Nick to hold out his glass and then poured each of them another shot.

Nick contemplated the amber liquid for a moment and said, "I'm good at the jobs I do for you, but running your business is not in my future plans."

Ricardo shook his head. "I would turn over my legitimate businesses for you to run. Neither you or my daughter would get involved on the other side." He tipped his glass and drained the tequila. "I won't press you any further today. Think about it." Amusement played at the corner of his eyes. "The idea may grow on you."

Nick nodded and finished his drink. He noticed the smile fade from Ricardo's face and predicted his mood was about to change.

Ricardo cleared his throat and set his shot glass aside. "Unfortunately, I have urgent business for you to take care of." Hands clenched at his side, he paced the room. "An incident occurred a day ago. Two of my men were murdered and a large sum of my money stolen."

A vein on the right side of Ricardo's forehead pulsed. Without warning, he scooped up the empty shot glass and flung it into the fireplace. Shards of glass exploded on the marble hearth. Chino, startled by the sound, lifted his head but made no attempt to rise.

Ricardo shook his fist. "This should never have happened. I must always keep a low profile."

Stunned, Nick cocked an eyebrow. "Who?" he asked. He was familiar with most of the people who worked for Ricardo.

"Carlos and Eddie." Ricardo observed the expression on Nick's face. He held up his hand. "I know what you're going to say."

"Well, they weren't two of the brightest guys," Nick said. "Only a matter of time before they did something dumb."

Nick sighed and leaned forward. The muscles in his chest tightened. The tequila lay heavy in his stomach as he processed the news. Carlos and Eddie didn't rank very high. They took care of the little jobs for Ricardo.

"As you know *amigo*, in this business you can't always hire the best." Ricardo pointed his finger at him. "Men like you are hard to come by."

"I appreciate the sentiment, Ricardo. Still, they didn't deserve to die. What the hell happened?"

"They were assigned to make a drop and pick up cash in Melbourne. Unfortunately, the feds were watching. I ordered them to abort the plan. Most likely, afraid to upset me, they decided to go ahead and make the drop using two locals."

Nick shook his head in disbelief. "Locals. What the hell! Even I can't imagine them stupid enough to trust outsiders."

"*Sí,* Carlos and Eddie made some bad decisions, but this by far was their worst. Now, I am paying the price for their screw up. It's costing me more than two million dollars. If anyone finds out how easy it is to steal from me, Ricardo Santiago—well—I have a reputation to uphold." He sat and folded his hands on the desk. "This situation must be handled quickly."

"Yes, of course," Nick said.

Ricardo's face turned dark. "When they didn't show up, I sent some of my men to look for them. They found them lying dead. Eddie shot in the head, Carlos in the throat. They removed the bodies and cleaned up the site. The police are not involved in this one."

"Lucky." Nick set his shot glass on top of the inlaid tile covering the mahogany end table.

"Yes, *lucky,* you say." Ricardo's hands gripped the armrests of the chair. "I want those thieves found, and I want my money. There can be no mistakes, Nick."

"Understood," Nick said. "I'll do whatever it takes to find them."

"I'm sure you will." Ricardo opened the desk drawer and took out a CD. "They shouldn't be hard to find. All my warehouses have hidden cameras, inside and outside." He crossed the room and slid the CD into the player.

"Only one problem, *amigo,*" Ricardo said. "The sound. The recorder never captured the voices. Still, you will see enough."

"I want you to find these people and recover the money." Ricardo's tone grew cold. His words sliced the air like a frigid north wind. "Once you have it, eliminate them. I won't tolerate anyone tampering with my business. I have to make an example out of anyone who steals from me. After you kill them, bring me their hands, and get rid of the rest."

The unusual request caught Nick off guard, but he didn't flinch. Ricardo had never requested body parts. He'd experienced Ricardo's anger before. This was something different. Nick recognized it wasn't about the money. Ricardo could well afford to lose two million dollars. This robbery dug deeper. Ricardo's pride was wounded.

The two men sat in silence and viewed the video, both of them fascinated by the scene playing out before them.

They watched as a tall, lean man, shot off a round at Eddie's feet. Pandemonium erupted after a dark-haired woman emerged from a car. A real beauty, Nick observed. Why was she hooked up with a creep like him? It made no sense.

He watched Carlos and Eddie dive toward the two of them. The woman raised what looked like a .45 caliber handgun and shot Carlos in the throat while the man shot Eddie with the same caliber gun. Nick could tell by the expression on her face and her stiff posture that she'd never fired a weapon before.

The video ended, and Ricardo strode over to his desk. He retrieved a large manila envelope and handed it to Nick. "Still photos along with two hundred and fifty thousand up front." He poured another shot of tequila and downed it.

"Find them, Nick. I want to put an end to this mess. This whole situation keeps me awake at night." His eyes met Nick's. "And remember the hands. I want their hands."

He'd do whatever Ricardo asked. To him, it was part of the job. "You can depend on me."

The two men walked to the door, with Chino following close behind. "That's all I wanted to hear," Ricardo said. "There is another two hundred and fifty thousand when you finish the job."

Ricardo placed his hand on Nick's shoulder. "Please, *amigo,* consider the honor I have presented to you." He motioned to the picture on the mantle. "While Carmela has a gentle heart, she is also brave and strong like you. You are a good match. It would mean everything to me to know my daughter is safe and well taken care of when I'm gone."

"I will think about it, Ricardo." Nick held out his hand. "I'll be in touch."

Chino trotted to the door alongside Nick. He hunched down, let Chino nuzzle his neck. "You stay on guard now. I'll see you again soon." He gave him a final rub on the head and continued toward the foyer.

Armando appeared out of nowhere and escorted him to the front door. "Take care, Mr. Nicky D, it is always a pleasure to have you here."

Outside, in the hot sun, with the air on full blast, Nick sped down the driveway. He decided to put his talk with Ricardo regarding Carmela to rest for now.

Over the years Nick had learned, when it came to business, patience was not on Ricardo's radar. Besides, he didn't savor dealing with the Florida heat. He'd complete this job and head north as soon as possible.

Nick grabbed the sunglasses clipped to the visor and slipped them on. For a few seconds, the video and the image of the woman played over again in his mind. His instincts told him her story ran much deeper than the robbery.

He reached the gates, and Ernesto punched in the code. Nick gave Ernesto a quick wave and cruised through. His assignment set, he would lay the groundwork for these next two kills.

CHAPTER 4

CARRIE

Night shadows gave way to slivers of early morning light. With Travis still asleep, Carrie finished getting dressed in the bathroom. Travis's flask of whiskey had done its job. Her suitcase stood packed by the foot of the bed.

She struggled to hold the tube of lipstick steady while she dabbed her lips in front of the small mirror above the sink. The marks on her neck had blossomed into shades of plum and blue overnight. Rifling through her purse, she removed a bottle and applied enough foundation to conceal them.

Unzipping the little black dress, she eased it up over her shapely legs and narrow hips then slipped her feet into her three-inch red stilettos. Every detail meant to placate his anger from the night before. Make Travis believe she wanted to please him. She picked up her brush and guided it through her long hair, letting it fall in loose waves down her back. Her heart thumped at his pounding on the door.

"Carrie, get out here *now!*"

"I'm almost ready," she answered. "I'll be out in a minute." She stepped back from the mirror, a look of satisfaction on her face. It was time. And she was ready alright. Ready to kill him.

"Hurry up. We need to leave," Travis called.

She gathered up her purse and opened the door. Travis, his back to her, tossed clothes into his suitcase.

"It's about time you came out." He turned and froze. As she expected, the dress worked its magic on him. He started to reach for her, but she managed to slip past him. His alcohol-infused sweat stung her senses, clearing her head.

"God, you sure are something else, girl. Getting yourself all pretty for me when we don't have time. I sure do like what I see. Save it for later. We gotta get the hell out of here," he barked. "They must have found the bodies by now."

Travis slammed his suitcase shut and then yanked the closet door open. "We'll be better off when we're hundreds of miles away."

Adrenaline surged through her body. Her muscles clenched while a chill skated down her spine. A torrent of emotions galloped inside her head. Memories of all the abuse she had suffered at his hands surfaced. She touched the bruised skin on her neck. Something erupted inside of her. Travis didn't sense it. Never saw what was coming.

Carrie reached into her purse. Her pulse spiked as she seized the .45 and dropped her bag on the floor. Holding the butt with both hands, she took aim. Her hand shook, but her finger rested firmly on the trigger.

Startled, Travis turned toward her, the briefcase in one hand, and his gun in the other. Riveted, he stared down the barrel of a .45 held by the woman he loved. Seconds ticked by. Neither one of them spoke. With the familiar click of his jaw audible in the silence, he took a step forward.

"Don't you take another step, Travis." She watched his face go dark, saw his posture stiffen. Her finger held steady as she gripped the butt of the gun. Her knuckles turned white. Beads of sweat clung to her brow.

"Well, well, just look at you, girl." He drew himself up and squared his shoulders, but his face blanched. "What do you think you're gonna do with that?"

"Whatever I have to do." Her voice remained calm against the terror raging inside her.

A sly smile crossed his lips. "Come on, put the gun down. This is no time for games." He advanced toward her again.

Carrie kept her aim steady, willing herself to stand firm. "Stop right there. Don't make this any harder. Give me the briefcase, Travis."

"Girl, you're out of your ever-loving mind." He nodded at the .45 in his hand. "I'd rather put a bullet in you before I'd let you walk out of here with all that money."

Her heart pounded against her rib cage. "You've given me no other choice. I want out."

Fire in his eyes, he moved toward her and raised his gun. "Never. I'll never let you go."

Carrie squeezed the trigger—twice. The sound exploded in the room, the recoil rocked her body and sent shock waves along her arm.

Travis collapsed, falling to his knees. The color drained from his face. He lowered his head and studied the red spot on the front of his white tee shirt. Within seconds, it fanned out and spread across his chest. He lifted his head, his weapon still clutched in his hand. "I can't believe you shot me," he croaked.

The air filled with the odor of gunpowder. Bile rose in Carrie's throat. The room swam before her, then righted itself. A shudder ran through her.

Travis tried to raise his gun, but it slipped from his hand. Knees buckling beneath him, he tumbled backward, his hand still gripping the handle of the briefcase.

Carrie lowered the .45. On impulse, she stepped toward him. Good or bad, Travis was the only man she'd known for the past sixteen years. Silence pierced the room, and she stopped. She broke out in a cold sweat and eyed the door. The sound of the gunfire had probably alarmed the other occupants. Someone was bound to call the police. She spotted her purse, picked it up, and put her gun inside. Setting it down again, she inched her way toward him.

She tried not to look at his face, but it was impossible. A gasp escaped his lips as he tried to suck air into his lungs. Blood oozed from underneath his hand as he pressed it against his chest. Carrie kicked his gun away and reached for the briefcase. Turning her head to avoid looking at him, she knelt and took hold of both sides of the briefcase pulling as hard as she could. Travis groaned, but his fingers remained clutched tight around the handle.

She tugged at it again, and he lost his grip. Her body jerked, causing her to reel backward. Travis, his hand latched onto the bottom of her dress, attempted to pull her to the floor. Her breath hitched. She reached down to push his hand away. His fingers continued to grip the hem of her dress. Finally, pointing her foot, she kicked at his wounded chest with the heel of her stiletto. He wailed, and his fingers slipped.

Carrie moved away. She set the briefcase on the bed. Frantic, she searched the floor and scooped up his gun.

Travis's breathing grew labored. "You bitch." His voice, a dying whisper, caught her by surprise. "I should never have given you a gun." Blood ran from the corner of his mouth. A low guttural sound passed his lips.

Blind fury filled her soul and mixed with all the torment she endured with him. "A gun? You think that's all you've given me?" She pointed to the bruises on her arm with the tip of the .45. "What about these? What about all the others that have faded away?"

He didn't answer. Instead, his eyes searched her face looking for any small measure of comfort.

The gun still in her hand, she stared down at him, her tears blurring his image. "You were supposed to save me from her. You broke your promise, and you abandoned us." The words she'd never dare speak out loud exposed the wounds hidden inside her. "Bobby's gone because of *you.*" She spat the words at him.

Mesmerized, she watched his blood seep into the dirty carpet. How much longer before he died? How long before his body grew cold and limp like her feelings for him? She hated him more than she thought possible, almost as much as her own mother.

Sucking in air, he struggled to speak. "I couldn't stay," he gasped. "I tried to explain it all to you. I needed to go."

Tears ravaged her face. She waved her fist at him. "You left me all alone, and she sold our son."

He began to shake from the loss of blood. "Now, lis … listen here, Carrie. I'm not the only one to blame. You left him with her."

His words hammered her ears. How many times had she berated herself for the same thing? Hardly a day passed when she didn't think of her child. Sixteen years had done little to ease her pain.

Travis stretched out his arms and pleaded. "Don't leave me. Please, don't leave me here to die. I love you."

Her insides raged. "Love? You don't love me. You're almost as bad as her." She moved away. "I feared you more than anyone, but not anymore, Travis. It's over. We're done. You're done." Someone else might have pitied him, but he'd lost her pity long ago. She heard him wheeze. His breath threaded, and he closed his eyes.

Carrie swung around, dropped his gun inside her purse, and snatched the car keys from underneath the pillow. Her legs wobbled beneath her. It would be too risky to stay any longer. Resting the briefcase on top of her suitcase, she wheeled it to the door. With one last glance at her past, she opened the door and disappeared into the blistering sunlight.

Carrie headed north toward the one place she might find solace. Travis couldn't hurt her anymore, but her instincts told her to keep moving. Other than stops for fuel, coffee, and restroom breaks, she drove the remainder of the day and into early the next morning. Driving through Melbourne, New Smyrna Beach, St. Augustine, and Jacksonville, she put much-needed distance between herself and the murders.

Travis was dead. It still didn't seem real. All those times she attempted to run, never getting far enough to stop him from dragging her once again into the horror she'd lived for most of her life.

In the past, fear and guilt had made her cave-in, give up hope. As the years passed, her bitterness grew and so did her resolve. She became determined to leave him, no matter how much the thought terrified her. The panic that ignited inside her each time Travis clicked his jaw had died along with him.

She had picked up a gun, and her world changed. Even when fear spiraled through her body, it never altered her decision to stand by him. She alone made a choice to pull the trigger and end a life. Pull it again and end another one. The price she'd paid to get out from under Travis was steep. Steep, but necessary. If she had stayed any longer, he might have killed her one day.

Carrie glanced at the briefcase lying on the seat. Sunlight pulsed through the window and skipped across the brown leather. She envisioned a different life, like the ones in the books she read. Images of the strong independent women played in her head—the women she read about, the ones she encountered over the years, cashiers, waitresses, and others were all heroes to her. Women like these reminded her of the kind of life she yearned for—and now maybe a life she could have.

In North Carolina, at dusk, she stopped in a wooded area and changed into jeans and a sweater. She opened the briefcase, lifted out a band of cash, and stuffed it inside her purse. Slamming the briefcase shut, she tossed it in the trunk and stole a few hours of restless sleep.

In the morning, still tired, she drove on, blending in with the surrounding traffic. Several hours later, she perked up at the 'Welcome to Virginia sign.' She exited the highway at a Holiday Inn. Still a bit on edge, she scrutinized the parking lot. Satisfied, she lifted her suitcase and the briefcase from the trunk.

After checking in, she raced into the bathroom, automatically locking the door behind her. She stripped off her clothes and then stepped into the shower. Hot water streamed down her tired and battered body. Free from harm, free of him, a sense of peacefulness engulfed her knowing Travis no longer lie in wait outside the door.

Carrie dried off and then slipped into her robe. She lit a cigarette and stared at the briefcase lying on the bed. After a few puffs, she stubbed her cigarette out and fiddled with the clasps until it snapped open. The crisp scent of the bills hung in the air.

Her hands shook as she counted the money and lay each stack neatly on the bed. Including the few bills she removed earlier, she was two million dollars richer. She hugged herself, rubbing her forearms. Her independence had arrived.

She placed the money back into the briefcase, snapped the locks, and shoved it under the bed. Travis had taken the cash from the plastic bag and stashed it in his suitcase, so she'd never know whether Carlos and Eddie had cheated them. Even so, they didn't deserve to die.

Exhausted, she searched through her suitcase for a nightgown. Her vision blurred for a moment when the pale blue material caught her eye. Hidden at the very bottom, she had carried it with her for the last sixteen years. The small blue blanket from her son's crib. The one thing from Breezy she couldn't let go.

Slowly, she held it to her breast and inhaled, wishing for a trace of his sweet baby scent. Her Bobby would be grown now, but in her mind, he was still her little boy. She laid it on the bed, careful to fold it just so and positioned it at the bottom of her suitcase.

Exhausted, she collapsed beneath the covers. Within minutes, she drifted off. Dreams of her little boy eluded her. Instead, her sleep filled with nightmare visions of guns, blood, and a briefcase full of money.

CHAPTER 5

NICK

Nick nosed into the parking lot of the warehouse in Melbourne. A second-grade detective at one time, his old instincts immediately kicked in. He replayed the video in his mind as he roamed the lot. Not a spot of blood on the ground to even hint at what had happened to Carlos and Eddie. He moved further along, and, except for a crushed cigarette butt, the lot appeared clean. A few more feet away, a set of tire marks stained the blacktop. Nick glanced up at one of the cameras. Too bad it hadn't captured the license plate on the getaway car. The angle wasn't right.

Everything about these two murderers screamed amateur. The shocked expression on the woman's face, her inability to move after she pulled the trigger, proved they had never committed a crime like this.

Satisfied, he left for his next stop. He'd go to the library and view copies of the local papers looking for any information that might lead him closer to finding the two thieves. Sometimes, news stories produced clues.

Inside the library, he clicked through the local papers on the computer screen, going back to the day of the robbery. Past experience had taught him a large part of detective work included digging into old files to connect the dots.

Browsing the papers conjured up the memory of the day he let go of the gold shield he worked so hard for. Undoubtedly, the worst day of his life. He lost his job, his reputation, and almost his sanity.

The bitter taste of defeat rose up and claimed him. His life spun out of control. A bottle of whiskey became his constant companion. Nights spent languishing in corner bars were his norm along with begging off desperate women looking for a man to put a ring on their finger.

His downward spiral continued until opportunity knocked, and Nick answered the door. He convinced himself, if the NYPD didn't want him on their side, he'd go to the opposite side of the law. Through no fault of his own, he was right where they wanted him to be.

He refocused on the computer screen. Within a few moments, a headline caught his attention. *'Man found shot in a local motel.'*   Nick scanned the article. There was no mention of a name except to say the victim, in critical condition, had been transported to Midway General Hospital. His hunch had paid off.

Nick smiled. Whenever you took lots of money and added more than one person to the mix, it always equaled greed. He left the library and headed for the motel. Afterward, he'd go on to the hospital to find out if the victim had pulled through. This would be the only way to get a positive identification and, at least rule, him in or out.

The motel's small lobby appeared deserted except for a woman who leaned against the far wall. Nick sized her up. The heavy makeup, teased hair, thigh-high boots, and fishnets gave her away. A working girl for sure. Only she was no pretty woman. She had plenty of mileage on her.

Eyeballing him like a starving alley cat ready to devour a meal, she strutted in his direction.

Nick held up his hand. "Don't waste your time, sister."

She stopped short and ran her hands up and down her body. Her smile revealed a broken front tooth. "If you knew what you were missing, you'd make time for this."

He gave her a wink. "There ain't enough time in the world."

"You don't have to be a dick about it," she mumbled. She flipped him her middle finger, wheeled around, and returned to her post by the wall.

Nick continued on across the lobby. Chipped, dull yellow paint peeled off most of the walls. A pungent odor, both sweet and sharp like overripe fruit, rose up from the faded blue carpet mottled with stains. The rips in floral upholstered sofa and chairs all told him the place was way past better days.

He approached a front desk, gouged and marred with scratches. The clerk eyed Nick's expensive suit, and Nick could tell this guy wasn't used to someone like him walking in the front door.

Nick gave him the once over and detected the aroma of cheap men's cologne. The guy's greasy hair, dirty fingernails, pot belly, and bug eyes told the story of someone who imagined himself to be a person of importance. Nick had come across his type before. Slipping a few bills his way would make him spill his guts.

The clerk perked up. He straightened his clip-on tie and smiled. "How are you today, sir? What can I do for you?"

"That depends," Nick said.

"Checking in?" He pushed the register and a pen toward Nick.

Nick spotted his nametag. "No, I don't think so, Marty." He frowned at the sight of the paper register and noted this dive didn't even use computers.

Marty snatched the register and slammed it closed. "Look, mister, I already told the cops everything."

"Cops," Nick said. "Do I look like a cop to you?" Marty's reaction said it all. The guy had information Nick needed.

"I thought …"

"You thought wrong. Look, I don't care what you did or didn't tell the cops. All I care about is what you can tell me."

He cleared his throat and squared his shoulders. "I beg your pardon. Who are you?"

Nick suppressed a smile. "Let's just say I'm an interested party. I'm interested in the guy who got shot here a while ago."

Marty flinched. His bug eyes protruded. "There ain't much to tell."

Nick pulled out the two still shots and held them up. "Either of these two look familiar?" He placed them on the desk.

Marty skimmed the photographs. He gave a half-shrug. "I don't think so."

He studied his body language. The guy was lying. "Look, buddy, I don't have all day," Nick said and reached into his suit pocket.

Marty threw up his hands and moved away from the counter. "Listen, mister, I don't remember too much of what happened that day."

"Easy, Marty." Nick brought the tone of his voice down a notch. "Just getting my wallet." He removed his wallet and held it up. "Maybe this will jog your memory?" He took out a hundred-dollar bill and slid it across the desk.

With a hand quick as a lizard's tongue, Marty snatched up the money and stuffed it into his pocket. He pointed at the picture of the man. "That guy's familiar."

"Familiar how?"

He squinted and inspected the photo again. "That's the guy who got shot. I didn't quite recognize him at first."

"What about the woman?"

He stroked his chin. "Her I'm not so sure about."

Nick slid another hundred across the desk. The little weasel was trying his patience.

Marty quickly palmed it. "I didn't mention this to the cops because I didn't think it was important. She looks like the woman I saw sitting outside while the guy in the photo registered."

Nick tried hard to restrain himself. "How is that not important?"

The clerk glanced around the lobby as if an entire audience was in attendance. "I don't like to talk to cops. I got into some trouble a few years ago. Don't want to be called as a witness either, if you know what I mean."

"Gotcha," Nick said. "But let me make myself clear. If I find out you lied to me about any of this, I'm coming back. And it won't be my wallet I pull out of my pocket. Understand?"

Marty's bug eyes grew larger. His face took on the look of a frightened bullfrog. "Understood."

"Tell me about the woman," Nick said.

"I had just arrived for my shift when I noticed the car pull in."

"What kind of car?'

"White. Maybe a Ford or a Chevy."

"Then what happened?"

"The man went inside. While he booked the room, she stayed in the car smoking a cigarette. I remember thinking to myself what a looker she was."

"Did she follow him to the room?"

"I guess so. As I said, I was about to start my shift, so it's not as if I hung around to watch."

"Show me the registration," Nick said.

Marty shook his head. "Look now, I'm not allowed to do that."

Nick peeled off another hundred and slid it across the desk. "That's all of it. Show me the registration."

Marty jammed the hundred in his pocket with the others. He opened the register and fingered the pages. "Here, I think this is him." He pushed it toward Nick.

"You think?" He wanted to give this guy a good pop on the head.

He glanced up. His right eye twitched. "No, I'm sure it's him. I'm positive."

Nick examined the signature. Travis Montgomery. "You're sure the woman in the photo was with him?"

"Like I said, she stayed in the car. I assumed they were together." He reached for the ledger and slammed it shut. "But the funny thing is, she was nowhere in sight when the cops arrived after the shooting."

Nick gathered up the photos and headed for the exit. The clerk had confirmed what his instincts told him. She shot the creep and took off with the money.

Almost to the door, he stopped and turned to the woman still stationed by the wall. He reached for his wallet again and strode toward her.

"Listen, I don't know how you ended up here," he said. "Take this and at least get a day's rest ... alone." He plucked three one-hundred-dollar bills from his wallet and handed them to her.

She reached for the money, but then dropped her hand. "Listen, mister, I can't take cash I didn't earn."

Nick took her hand, placed the money in her palm, and closed her fingers around it. "Believe me, you probably earned it and then some."

Her face flushed. "Thanks, mister. Sorry about before."

Nick crossed the lobby and exited the motel. He wanted to get straight to the hospital and see if this so-called Mr. Montgomery was still breathing. The article listed him in critical condition. If he had survived, he would luck out. Mr. Montgomery would lead him straight to the woman.

Reaching into his pocket, he studied the photo of the woman again. He had never killed a woman before let alone one as pretty as her, but his objective was clear. Her beauty could turn into a distraction and distractions proved fatal in his line of work. He placed the photo in his pocket, pumped up the air in the Mercedes, and set out for the hospital.

CHAPTER 6

CARRIE

Morning sunlight streaked across the hotel room. Carrie rubbed her eyes. Her mind filled with images of dead men, she managed to get little sleep. She scooted herself up and lay back against the pillows. Something gnawed at her. Reaching out her hand, she slid her palm over the sheet beside her. Cold greeted her palm. The tightness inside her slipped away.

For the past sixteen years, she had woken up with Travis lying beside her. How she used to dread every new morning not knowing what his temperament would be.

Carrie smiled and headed for the bathroom. She took another shower, basking in the sheer joy of being able to relax while the warm water coursed over her body. After toweling off, she dressed in jeans and a sweatshirt. And for the first time in years, she decided not to apply any make-up. Gathering up her hair, she swept it into a ponytail. She packed her things, and then pulled the briefcase out from under the bed.

Downstairs in the lobby, a young female hotel clerk called out, "Good morning, checking out?"

"Yes, I am." Anxious to hit the road, she set her keycard on the desk. "How far is it to the next rest-stop off of the Interstate going north?"

"About fifteen miles," the clerk replied, handing her a receipt. Smiling, she said, "May I help you with anything else?"

"No, I'm fine. Thank you." Carrie found herself smiling back. A simple thing, a smile. It made her realize how little she'd done it these past years.

Outside, cotton clouds were scattered across a deep blue sky. Carrie paused and sighed with pleasure at how beautiful it looked before putting her things in the trunk.

Out on the highway, she turned the radio on and settled on some country music. A short time later, she arrived at the rest stop. Automobiles, motor homes, buses, and semi-trailers filled the parking lot. Off to one side, stood fuel islands with lines of trucks and cars. Several people walked their dogs on a small green space.

Inside, a smattering of people sat at various tables. Several young couples, their children anchored in booster seats, ate mouthfuls of food in between feeding their little ones. Dozens of truckers, their plates piled high, devoured their meals. Relieved at no longer having to worry if some man looked at her, she seated herself at a small round table.

The waitress came, and she ordered a large helping of pancakes and coffee. Her appetite was ravenous, but she took her time, allowing the food to go down easy. She relished her simple, peaceful breakfast without the familiar knocking inside her stomach.

Almost finished, she couldn't help staring at a young couple with a small baby seated in a high chair. Without warning, tears welled up and clung to the corners of her eyes. No, she admonished herself. I won't cry.

The memories of her physical pain were not so bad for her to deal with. Those black and blue marks were not her greatest sorrow. Bruises fade over time. Not so the heartache inside her.

That first year they were together, Travis never laid a mean hand on her. Things started changing the day she delivered the news of her pregnancy.

They had gone for a drive and to get something to eat. Later, they set out for Breezy with Travis commanding the steering wheel with one hand, a cigarette in the other.

"Travis, I need to tell you something," she started. "I think..."

He glanced over at her. "What's up doll? You think what?"

"I think I'm pregnant."

Dragging deep on his cigarette, he'd let out a cloud of smoke and said, "You think, or you know?"

"I'm sure." Silent, she'd waited for his response.

"This is serious stuff. It means plenty of trouble for us if you are." He had lowered the window and flicked the stub of his cigarette out.

Nervous, she'd fidgeted with the hem of her skirt, trying to avoid his eyes. "I don't understand, Travis. What kind of trouble?"

"Of course, you don't understand," he said, his voice rising. "You're too young to understand. I can't believe this. I'm always so careful."

In her naivety, she searched for a solution. Her spirits lifted for a moment. "Let's get married," she said. "Raise the baby together. Be a real family."

He had pulled over and shut the engine. "Married? If anyone finds out, we'll be anything but married. I'll be in jail, and your Mama will damn near kill you. You can't have the baby."

"But I want the baby." She had looked down and rested her hands on her stomach. The thought of an abortion terrified her. No way would she kill her baby.

They drove to Breezy with Travis promising to take care of her. The months slipped by without any sign of him.

The day she told her mother the blows came at her one after the other. Slaps and punches anywhere her hands could reach, including her stomach.

"How could you let this happen? You stupid, selfish girl!" she had screamed.

Bruises marked the length of her body. Happily, for her, she hadn't miscarried. Her mother, on the other hand, wasn't happy at all.

"Are you okay, Miss?" The waitress glanced at her while refilling the coffee cup.

Carrie looked away from the young couple and wiped her eyes. "I'm fine. Can I have the check, please?" She berated herself for her immaturity all those years ago. Nothing could change the past. All she could do now was try to put all of it behind her and carve out a new life.

After paying her bill, she purchased a map. Determined to cover as many miles as possible, she drove with renewed energy. Leaving Virginia behind, she crossed over into Maryland and stopped to eat just over the Pennsylvania line before hitting the road again.

In the evening, she exited off the highway in Lancaster and settled in for the night. Spreading the map of Pennsylvania out over the bed, she lit a cigarette and studied it. If her memory served her correctly, the name of the town was Laurel. Her fingers trailed along the map until she found it. Tomorrow morning, she'd set out for Laurel in the Pocono Mountains, to the one person who she remembered had treated her with kindness, her mother's sister, May.

Thoughts of her aunt brought a rush of happy emotions. She had looked forward to her aunt's visits to Breezy each year. The few good memories she cherished from childhood she owed to her aunt.

But her visits abruptly stopped when Carrie turned twelve. She never found out why, but she couldn't forget her aunt and the way she talked about her home in the mountains of Pennsylvania. Growing up in the desert, she yearned to see the mountains and drive country roads lined with tall pine trees the way her aunt had described them. And, of course, snow in the wintertime. If her aunt still lived there, the chance to see her again gave Carrie hope.

Her life with Travis consisted of bland motel rooms, flat desert land, sweltering heat, cactuses, and palm trees. He had refused to go north, and he never did explain why.

She rose and stubbed out her cigarette. Pulling the window's heavy drape aside, she watched daylight retreat as the sun made its slow, steady descent.

Out of habit, she played with the gold band on her finger, the last physical reminder of Travis. He bought it for her, as a symbol of his love. Or, so he said. It didn't take much for her to figure out he wanted her to wear it as a deterrent to other men.

Carrie studied the circle of gold, luminous in the evening light. She twisted the band around one last time and then nudged it up her finger. The ring jammed at her knuckle, pinching so hard it threatened to stop the flow of blood. She yanked harder. Her throat closed, and she tried to swallow. She broke out in a sweat as she tugged at the ring, trying to push it up and off her finger. Her chest heaved, her breath coming in rapid spurts. She raced into the bathroom and grabbed the soap. Frantic, she rubbed it around her finger. Turning on the tap, she let the water spill over her hand. The ring shifted. With a final pull, it slipped off.

Carrie lifted the toilet lid, dropped the ring in, and flushed. The ring sank into the rushing water and disappeared. She examined her hand and the pale white skin encircling her ring finger. The knot in her stomach slowly unwound. Her heartbeat slowed, and her trembling settled.

She wandered over to the window again and stared out at the night sky. The last remnants of the day dipped below the tree line in the distance. Wrapping her arms around her body, she held herself tight. Here she was on her own, with plenty of money and ready to start over. All her life she had lived frightened of her mother and terrified of Travis.

Now finally, she was free.

CHAPTER 7

CARRIE

Carrie hit the road early the next morning. Her dark hair trailed behind her with the breeze rushing through the open window. The air, raw, crisp, and sweet, grew cool as the car climbed higher in altitude. She inhaled the fresh scent of pine and cedar. Tall evergreens stacked against an icy blue sky towered over both sides of the highway.

Sunlight filtered through the broad maples. The tips of their leaves were stained with hints of color in preparation for their yearly ritual. She smiled, knowing soon fall would introduce itself to the mountains. The trees would use the landscape as a canvas, and the hillsides would show off their vibrant hues of red, yellow, gold, and rust.

A veil lifted. The dull browns and greys of the desert she'd traveled for so long with Travis disappeared. She understood now how Travis had weighed her down, just as an anchor holds a ship securely in place. The ship bobs and weaves above the surface, struggling to break free. Like that ship, she remained anchored and afraid, until she gained the courage to cut the anchor away and sail free to her new beginning.

She sped past acres of apple orchards, their trees abundant with ripe fruit. Rows of meaty orange pumpkins dotted the surrounding farmlands. Her lips curled upward into a smile. A small herd of deer entered the road up ahead. She eased off the gas and watched them scamper into the woods before continuing on.

A lazy afternoon sun hung low in the sky as she drove into Laurel. Cute little shops with striped awnings above their windows lined the main thoroughfare. Rows of sapling trees adorned the sidewalks and baskets of flowers hung from old-fashioned light posts.

Signs announced the names of a series of local businesses. Sally's Cut and Dye Salon, Fred's Dry Cleaners, Chip's Hardware, Sprinkles Ice Cream Parlor, Brim's Accounting and Tax Service. Further along stood a post office, a firehouse, and a gas station. Pedestrians marched in and out of shops and scurried along the sidewalks.

Cottage style houses, positioned on manicured lawns branched off the main street. A sign in front of an old Victorian home, read, 'Bed & Breakfast.'

She parked and admired the wrap-around porch, stained glass windows, and clapboard siding. This would do until she found out where Aunt May lived. Right now, she just wanted to grab a bite.

While she booked her stay, the clerk recommended a diner. She placed her suitcase in her room and hurried back to the car. She decided to leave the briefcase in the car until she returned for the night.

She approached the diner, and glanced up at the blinking neon sign in the parking lot. '*Welcome to the Palisades Diner! Where Great Food Was Born!*' She parked in front where she could keep an eye on the car and her money.

The Palisades boasted the usual fare. A typical diner with a long counter down the center and red-topped swivel stools. Red leather booths hugged the walls along the sides. Several people perched on stools at the counter, the rest relaxed in the booths.

Of all the hundreds of diners she'd eaten in over the years, this one calmed her. Without Travis by her side, no repercussions awaited. Her hunger growing, Carrie planted herself in the first available booth facing the lot and studied the menu.

"Hey there." A woman's voice broke into her train of thought. "What can I get for you this evening?"

Bright brown eyes peeked out from a fringe of fiery red bangs and curly hair piled high on her head. Tall and slim, in her early thirties, she stood with a pen and pad poised in her hands. Her full lips wore a dark pink shade, and a faint dusting of freckles was scattered across her nose. Her nametag read Joann.

"Let's see," Carrie said. "I think I'll start with a cup of coffee. And how about the French Dip?"

The woman leaned closer. "You're sure?" She gave Carrie a wink. "Honey, you don't want the dip. Not today."

Carrie studied the menu again. "What do you recommend?"

"We have some delicious beef stew."

"Beef stew it is." She set the menu aside. Thankful for the warning, she gave Joann a quick smile.

"Good choice. I'll put the order in and get your coffee."

Carrie watched her walked to the pass-through window behind the counter and shout, "One bossy in a bowl." She always got a kick out of the diner lingo the waitresses and cooks used.

Thirty minutes later, when Joann brought the check, she decided to take a chance.

"Excuse me, could I ask you a question?" Carrie said.

Joann stuck her pen into her massive pile of curls. "Sure, honey, as long as it doesn't involve asking for money."

Carrie shook her head. "No, not at all. I was wondering if you know my Aunt May. I haven't seen her in years. I'm not from around here and, as far as I can remember, she's always lived here in Laurel."

"If it's May Overton you're talking about, she's the sweetest person God had the good sense to put on this earth."

Carrie's insides tingled. "Yes. Overton's her last name. Do you know where she lives?"

Joann glanced at her watch. "I get off in about fifteen minutes, so if you want to wait, I can take you by there."

"I don't want you to go out of your way. My car's outside if you'll give me directions."

"It's no trouble," she insisted. "Her house is an easy walk from here."

Carrie felt at ease, but she wasn't exactly sure why. "Okay, I'll wait for you then."

Twenty minutes later, she stepped outside with Joann. As they crossed the lot, she eyed her car. "Maybe we should drive."

Joann nodded toward Carrie's car. "Don't worry hon, nothing ever happens around here. Leaving your car is okay. Things are pretty safe here in Laurel."

Joann reached into her purse and pulled out a pack of cigarettes. "Do you mind, hon? I know it's a filthy habit, but I can't seem to quit."

Carrie rummaged in her purse for her own pack and a lighter. They looked at each other and laughed.

"I see we have something in common," Joann said.

"We sure do." Carrie lit both cigarettes.

"I'm Carrie, by the way." She grinned at Joann and let the smoke curl away from her lips. It drifted up into the chilly air and disappeared.

Joann laughed and pointed to the tag on her blouse. "And this is me."

They continued along Main Street, their steps lit by the old-fashioned lamp posts. They neared the end and made an abrupt turn to the left. They strolled up a tree-lined street, and Joann stopped and pointed ahead.

"May's house is the third one on the left with the green shutters. Sixteen Birch Street. I'm on the next block over, Waverly." She held out her hand. "Nice to meet you, Carrie. Give May my regards." She winked and strode away.

Carrie hesitated before calling out, "Hey, Joann."

"Yeah, hon?"

"Thanks so much."

"No problem. Maybe I'll see you around. That is if you plan to stay awhile."

"Definitely," Carrie said. She watched Joann walk up the block, and hoped Laurel might be her new home.

Street lamps behind her, moonlight lit her path the rest of the way. She delighted in the mountain air mixed with the tang of burning wood from rooftop chimneys. She passed the first two houses and spied lights on inside. The muffled sounds from television sets drifted through the air. It all screamed normal, but it was foreign to her.

She approached the tidy two-story house with white clapboard siding and green shutters. Out front, a bright white picket fence ran the length of the house. She strode over and unlatched the gate. She swung it wide open and stepped onto the red brick walkway, but her fingers rested on the open latch.

Her heart buffeted in her chest. She let the latch drop into the slot and followed the path toward the porch. Her footsteps tapped softly against the hard brick.

Light spilled out through the pale linen curtains framing the windows. She crossed the porch still uncertain, and then reached out and touched the doorbell.

Soon, she'd know if her instincts were right. Would the woman she remembered and loved from childhood embrace her? Or, would she turn her away?

CHAPTER 8
TRAVIS

Liquid fire shot through his body. He tried to raise his arm. Why was it so heavy? Travis touched the bandages on his chest and moaned when his fingers found their mark. Squinting, he pushed away the deep well of darkness surrounding him. His vision cleared and he focused on the monitors and intravenous lines by his bedside. He ran his tongue over his chapped, dry lips. He swallowed, and his saliva hit the back of his raw throat. Fuzzy images crept across his brain.

Fluorescent light streamed in from the hallway. A young woman dressed in blue scrubs walked in. She flipped on the light above his bed. Travis blinked and scowled.

"I see you're awake, Mr. Montgomery." Her voice was loud and cheery. "How are you feeling?" She adjusted his IV line and checked the monitors. "I'm Patti, your nurse for this shift."

"Thirsty," Travis whispered.

"Let's raise you up, and I'll get some water."

She pressed a button, and the bed rose beneath him. Filling a cup from the bedside pitcher, she dropped a straw in and held it to his lips. He sucked and immediately began to cough. Water ran from his mouth and down the front of his hospital gown. She held up the cup again. Embarrassed, he jerked his head away.

"It's okay," she said. "Your body needs to adjust. You've been out of it for a while."

"How long?" The rasps in his voice surprised him.

"Since the surgery six days ago. You were brought in with two bullet wounds in your chest. You're lucky to be alive. One of the bullets just missed your heart."

The fogginess in his head started to lift. He shuddered, remembering the last time he lay in a hospital.

Only eight years old, he'd come awake in a hospital with a cast on his arm. His parents told the doctor he had fallen climbing a tree. But the truth was a different story. He had dared to disrespect his father. As punishment, he had twisted Travis's arm so hard, it snapped in two.

He shook the memory away and motioned for more water. This time, he sipped, careful not to drink too fast. The last of his fuzziness lifted, and the missing pieces came together. His stomach clenched. That bitch! She shot him like a dog. Left him to die on that motel room floor.

Pattie reached over and adjusted his pillow. "If you're up to it, there's a detective outside who wants to speak with you."

"Detective?"

"Yes, he's been coming here every day and waiting for you to wake up."

Travis's chest heaved, worsening his pain. Of course, he'd want to speak with him. Cops had to investigate all shootings. Tempted to say no, his mind scrambled. He could end up cuffed to his bed rail. But excuses wouldn't make this cop go away. He'd have to speak to the guy. Might as well get it over with. This detective wasn't going away without some answers. Travis nodded.

"Good. I'll go tell him you're awake."

His head throbbed. Damn, did they have evidence? If they nailed him for the murders, he vowed to take Carrie down with him.

A tall gentleman dressed in a navy blue suit and maroon colored striped tie strode in. The fluorescent light appeared to brighten as the man towered over him. Travis made a quick assessment. The guy's sandy blond hair stood up in a typical buzz cut. He fit the mold. His looks screamed cop. He reached into his suit jacket and pulled out a badge.

"I'm Detective Morrison, Melbourne PD. I need to ask you a few questions if you're up to it."

Travis plastered a smile on his face. "Sure, detective."

Morrison dragged a chair from across the room. The legs screeched across the tile floor, rattling Travis's nerves even further.

"For starters, I would like to verify that your name is Travis Montgomery."

"Yes, it is," Travis answered. His voice still sounded odd. He cleared his throat, wishing to be done with the whole matter.

Morrison pulled out a small notepad and pen and scribbled. "Okay then, Mr. Montgomery. Do you remember what happened to you?"

"To be honest with you detective, no, I don't. The nurse told me I was shot."

Morrison shifted in the chair. "Do you have any idea who would try to kill you?"

Travis cocked his head to one side. "Let me see. I remember a knock on my motel room door. I opened it, and two men burst in. Something hit my chest, and I was out cold."

Morrison gave him a skeptical look and tapped out a few notes on his pad. "What did they say?"

"I'm not sure. It's all kinda hazy."

"Yeah, I bet," Morrison said, not trying to hide the sarcasm in his voice. "Had you ever seen these men before"?

"Not that I can recall. It all happened so fast."

"Could you identify them?" Morrison squinted at him. His brows formed an arch as he continued to write.

"Like I said, it all happened so fast. I didn't get a good look at them."

"Are you sure they didn't say anything?"

"I don't recall."

"What were they after?"

Travis hesitated. Did he know about Carlos and Eddie? The briefcase full of money? No matter what he wouldn't give anything away to this cop.

"I can't say. I remember so little of what happened."

Morrison eyed him. "All this seems strange, Mr. Montgomery. We found your motel room intact, and your personal items untouched. We couldn't identify any prints other than your own."

"Is that so?" Travis shrugged. "Well, detective, I'm just as bewildered as you."

"Can you think of anyone at all who might have some kind of beef with you? Someone mad enough to try and kill you."

He pretended to think. "No, can't say as I do."

Morrison stood up. "I'll leave you my card and if your memory should return, give me a call. Remember, Mr. Montgomery, they may come back. I'd advise you to come clean now."

"I swear, detective, I think it must have been a case of mistaken identity." He could tell Morrison didn't believe him, but he couldn't prove he was lying either.

His Carrie was smart. She must have taken his gun. This guy didn't have a clue regarding the murders.

After Morrison left, he replayed all the events in his head. The detective never mentioned the murders or the money. Relieved, his thoughts turned to Carrie.

He thought she was under his control. Good God, when did she get so confident? Liquid fire coursed through his chest. He cringed at the flashback of the bullets exploding inside him. Carrie shooting him like that was heartless. After all, he had rescued her from her beast of a mother and stopped her from living the rest of her life in Breezy. His fists clenched the stiff bedsheet.

Even though times were tough, he always managed to take care of her. He still loved her, even though she'd tried to kill him. Unable to get comfortable, he shifted. His craving for some whiskey and a cigarette boosted his anxiety.

Patti returned, wheeling a medication cart. "Any pain, Mr. Montgomery?"

He tilted his head to one side and scrunched up his face. "Yes, quite a lot in fact."

"Okay, the doctor has ordered more pain meds for you. His orders are as needed."

"I sure do need them," Travis admitted.

She dispensed two small yellow pills into a paper cup and handed them to him.

He put the cup to his lips, tilted his head back, and swallowed. She put a straw to his lips, and he took a long drink. The pills slid easily down his throat.

"Is there anything else I can do for you right now, Mr. Montgomery?"

"No, darling, that's fine. You're an angel." He gave her his best smile. "By the way, did the doc say when I could get out of this place?"

"That will depend on how fast you heal and when you're strong enough to be discharged."

He leaned back against the pillow. "Makes sense."

She wheeled the cart toward the door. "Buzz if you need anything, Mr. Montgomery."

"I sure will." He pressed the button and lowered the bed.

He'd find Carrie no matter how long it took. Thinking about her caused his physical pain to intensify. She'd pay the price for what she did, and he would take pleasure in teaching her a lesson she'd never forget.

"She will pay," he whispered.

Within a few minutes, the medication worked its magic. His pain diminished, and he drifted off into a restless sleep. Several hours later, he came awake, his heart pounding, the sheet beneath him damp with sweat. He took several deep, painful breaths. Was he afraid of Carrie? Hell no. Impossible. He wouldn't allow that to happen. He ignored the panic rising up inside of him in order to convince himself that as soon as he found her, he'd have Carrie under his thumb once again.

CHAPTER 9

CARRIE

Carrie eyed the two wooden rockers resting side by side and then glanced at the white lace curtains fanning each side of the windows as light from inside spilled out onto the porch. She pressed the doorbell. Soft chimes sounded and within a few seconds, the door opened.

An older version of the woman she remembered was framed in the doorway. Short, chin-length, gray hair cut in a bob brushed the bottom of both her cheeks. The slightest of fine lines traced her face and the corners of her hazel eyes. A soft, tan turtleneck sweater over black pants enhanced her slim figure.

She stared at Carrie for a moment. "Can I help you, young lady?"

A lump rose in Carrie's throat. "Aunt … Aunt May, it's me, Carrie, your niece."

Recognition flashed across her face. "Carrie!" she cried, placing a hand on her chest. "I can't believe it. What in the world? Oh, my lord, look at you. You're all grown up."

Tension slipped from Carrie's body. Tears welled up, threatening to spill over. She squeezed her eyes. "I'm so glad you remember me."

"Remember you! For goodness sake, child, how could I ever forget you? Your mother and I may not speak, but I've always missed seeing you." She stepped forward and held out her arms.

Carrie leaned away, hesitant to let her guard down. If her aunt knew the terrible things she'd done, she wouldn't be too quick to give her a hug.

"Carrie?" May said. "Honey, what's wrong?"

Carrie's cheeks heated. Trust was a luxury she couldn't afford. Look how her life had turned out with the two people she had trusted, her mother, and Travis. She stared into the warmth of her aunt's eyes. Maybe, with Aunt May, things could be different.

Giving in, she fell into the warmth of her embrace and let her feelings flow. After a few moments, they let go of each other and Carrie asked, "Did you?"

"Did I what?" May asked, frowning and raising her eyebrow.

"Miss me," she said, her words almost a whisper.

May continued to look perplexed. "What about the cards and packages I sent for your birthday and at Christmas time?" she asked. "Even though I never heard anything, it was my way of telling you I still cared."

"Cards … packages?" Carrie's heart sank. Her mother never even mentioned May's name.

She read the expression on Carrie's face. "It figures. Your mother didn't give them to you, did she?"

"No, she didn't."

May's eyes brightened. "Never mind, the important thing is you're here." She touched Carrie's arm. "You come on in. I want to hear what you've been up to till now." She pushed the door closed behind them and beckoned for her to follow.

The aroma of lemons from furniture polish permeated the air. A patterned sofa anchored the room, flanked by pine end tables. A matching coffee table in front of the sofa held a stack of magazines. Overstuffed chairs sat on opposite sides of the fireplace. A small TV set on a stand filled the corner of the room. A charming braided multi-color rug pulled the whole composition together. A few pictures of country scenes hung on the walls.

These surroundings were exact opposites of the long tin box in Breezy Meadows where she had spent her childhood. The trailer's small rectangle windows failed to let in enough sun. The few, worn, meager pieces of furniture offered no comfortable place to sit. The stench of stale booze and cigarettes clung to the walls. She used to wonder where the name Breezy Meadows came from. You couldn't find a cool breeze anywhere, and there weren't any meadows around for miles.

May clasped her hands together, joy spread across her face. "Come on into the kitchen where we can have a nice talk."

Carrie followed her into the dining room and stopped. On a sideboard up against the far wall, sat an array of photographs. She recognized one of them.

"I remember this," Carrie said. "I was seven years old." She picked up a gold frame. In it, she gripped the handlebars of a bicycle.

May walked over and placed an arm around her. "If I recall, you had just turned eight, the year I gave you your first bicycle. You rode that darned bike through the trailer park all day long. Your mother had to practically pry it out of your hands at supper time."

Carrie smiled. She didn't have too many good memories. Riding her bicycle, with its red and white streamers trailing from the handlebars, was one of her favorites. She had cherished the feeling of freedom as she sped past rows and rows of mobile homes, the wind blowing her long dark hair in plumes behind her.

"You didn't have that bike of yours for very long, did you?"

"What do you mean?" Pain filtered through Carrie's heart.

"Your mother told me how you left it out in the rain and it rusted so bad you couldn't ride it anymore."

Carrie bit her lower lip. What would her aunt think if she told her how her mother had taken a hammer to the bike and pounded it into a worthless heap of trash? Nothing remained of that bicycle except the red and white streamers which she kept hidden away in her room.

She patted Carrie's shoulder. "Oh dear, I'm sorry. I've upset you. It's alright. Children often don't take good care of their toys. When you're young, you don't always do what's right."

Carrie placed the photograph on the sideboard and studied the remaining ones. A small silver frame with a black and white photo of two young girls smiling into the camera grabbed her attention. Picking it up, she asked, "Who are they?"

"Why, that's your mother and me when we were little girls. Such happy times."

Carrie stared at the photograph, finding it hard to imagine her mother happy. The mother she knew seldom smiled unless she was high. Without drugs and alcohol, her eyes were dark wells of unhappiness.

"Believe it or not, we were inseparable at one time. Sisters and best friends," May said. A smile stretched across her face and color rose in her cheeks.

Carrie set the photograph down and faced her aunt. "What happened? Why did you part ways?"

May's face grew dim. "I don't like to bring up bad memories on a happy occasion. Follow me, and I'll put some coffee on."

Carrie trailed after her into a kitchen where bright white cabinets with glass fronts hung from the walls. Shiny copper pots and pans dangled from a rack above the center island and silver-grey granite countertops ran beneath the cabinets. Polished, honey wood floors gave the room a homey appeal. A round oak table and chairs sat in a nook at the far end of the room surrounded by windows on either side.

May prepared coffee in an old-fashioned stainless-steel percolator. Within minutes, the aroma of freshly brewed coffee filled the room. They settled in at the sturdy table, large powder blue coffee mugs in their hands.

"Your mother and I used to be close until she met your father," May said. "I don't like to speak ill of people, it's not the way we were raised."

"When she met him, she changed. I tried to tell her he wasn't good for her but she wouldn't listen. From the day they met, her life turned into one of misery. That man destroyed her." She reached out and patted Carrie's hand.

The warmth of her aunt's touch on her skin made her relax, and she imagined how different her childhood might have been if her aunt had raised her. The image of her own mother's face flashed across her mind, and she slid her hand away.

"You're the one precious thing to ever come from the two of them." May picked up a spoon and added more sugar to her cup.

Carrie sipped her coffee. Staring into her cup, she asked, "What happened to my father?"

May's brow creased. "He up and left not long after you were born. The way those two fought all the time, I think one of them would have ended up dead if he hadn't gone, but she loved that man." She sighed and tapped her spoon against her cup. "Almost too much."

"Her drinking started, and it never stopped. Alcohol stripped away the goodness inside of her." May's voice broke. "I couldn't … I couldn't stand to watch her disappear into a bottle. On my last visit, I tried to convince her to get help. She needed to stop. The alcohol was killing her."

Carrie set her cup on the table. "What did she say?"

"She screamed profanity at me and told me to get out. She said I better not come back again…or else."

May's shoulders sagged. "I didn't know what the 'or else' meant, but by the ugly glare in her eye and the violent way she—well, I never did go see her again, and for that, I'm sorry.

She leaned in, her eyes misted. "I want you to understand something, Carrie. I always loved you. As a matter of fact, I begged her to let me take you with me. She wouldn't hear of it."

Carrie raised her cup and sipped, letting the hot liquid push back the lump in her throat. Everything made more sense to her now. She began to understand her mother's hatred for her. She'd been a constant reminder of the man who had deserted them.

Nothing excused her mother from selling her own grandchild. Nor the abuse she inflicted. Not her father leaving, and not the fact her mother was an alcoholic and drug addict. Carrie understood, but she'd never forgive her. Not now. Not ever. Apparently, her aunt wasn't aware of the drugs. The drugs had started after the alcohol.

Carrie shuddered inside. She didn't dare tell her how much she suffered at the hands of her mother. The horrific things she had done. Her throat tightened. How could she tell her aunt what a horrible person her sister had become?

Wanting to change the subject, Carrie asked, "What about you? Did you ever marry?"

May's face brightened again. "Oh, I had my chances. Guess I like my independence too much. I've always had an independent spirit," May continued. "I can't complain. I love living here in this town. I've lots of friends." She chuckled softly. "No, they're more than friends, some of them are like family."

May rose and refilled their cups. "Okay, enough about me. What have you been doing all these years?"

Carrie laced her fingers together to stop them from shaking. Questions from her aunt about her life were inevitable. She hated to do it, but she had no choice other than to lie.

"There isn't much to tell," she said. "I left home a long time ago. Mother and I didn't get along." She chewed her lower lip and fidgeted uncomfortably in her chair.

"That's sad to hear," May said. "Mothers and daughters ought to be close."

The mention of the word close made Carrie cringe. When it came to her mother, a bitter bridge was the only thing linking them together.

"I've moved around a lot," she continued. "Different jobs here and there…" Her voice trailed off, and she stopped altogether. She focused on the steamy dark liquid in her cup.

"Carrie, child, look at me."

Heat rose in Carrie's cheeks. She raised her head. Her bottom lip trembled.

"Oh, sweetheart, what is it?" She got up and placed her arms around Carrie.

The image of her sweet little boy's face flashed before Carrie with such clarity the pain became unbearable. She fell into May's arms and sobbed.

May rocked her gently. She stroked Carrie's head and said, "Now, you let it all out. When you're ready, and you feel like talking, I'll be here. I'm not going anywhere."

The kind words and light scent of May's warm skin soothed her, and her crying ceased. She insisted Carrie go and get her belongings. She'd stay here with her for as long as she wanted.

Thirty minutes later, Carrie stepped out into the cool night air, confident that she'd made the right decision in coming here to Laurel. If only she could stop the guilt twisting inside her. She hadn't shed this many tears since the day she lost her son. But how could she confess? To come clean about her son, and Travis, how he forced her to commit murder would surely destroy her relationship with Aunt May.

She halted beneath a street lamp. What good would it do to pass on her pain and sorrow to this loving woman? It wouldn't change what had happened, and she'd lose the one person in the world who cared for her.

Feeling a little more at ease, she strolled over to the diner and retrieved her car. After checking out of the B & B, she popped open the trunk and set her suitcase inside. The brass locks on the briefcase shone in the moonlight, evidence of the life she wanted so desperately to leave behind. And yet, it had given her freedom and a fresh start. She took a cleansing breath.

For now, she'd stay at Aunt May's and figure out what to do next. She hoped somehow, living here in Laurel would help her forget some of her past.

"Take one day at a time," she said. "One day at a time."

CHAPTER 10

NICK

Nick crossed the hospital lobby, strode up to the reception desk, and smiled. Good looks and charm never hurt, he reminded himself. And, as luck would have it, he had both.

A middle-aged woman with short brown hair looked up from her computer screen. She removed the bifocals resting on the tip of her nose.

"Good afternoon. How can I help you, sir?"

He glanced at her nametag. "Good afternoon, Gladys. I'm here to visit a buddy of mine. I'm not sure what his room number is."

She beamed up at him. "Let's see what I can do to find him for you." She replaced her bifocals and planted her hands on the keyboard. "Now, let's see, what's the last name?"

"His full name is John Monteroy," he lied. As an ex-cop, he knew she'd be instructed to report if anyone asked for Travis. Shooting victims were always red flagged.

Her fingers tapped the keys. "I don't see a Monteroy, sir."

He leaned in closer. "Wow, that perfume you're wearing smells terrific. When it comes to perfume, some women tend to overdo it, but you've got it just right."

Her eyelids fluttered, and her cheeks flushed a pale rose. "Why, thank you. It's a light scent. I've never been partial to the heavier ones." Her pink-stained lips curved into a smile. "Let me try again and see if I can find that friend of yours. What's his admission date?"

"I'm not sure. I found out from a friend he was admitted to Midway General."

Her fingers moved swiftly across the keyboard again. "Sometimes when they input the data, there's an error if one name sounds like another. I see a Montgomery in room 637, but his first name isn't John. Maybe he's been discharged already."

She tapped a few more keys. "I could check the history for you."

He grinned and pulled out his cell phone. "No, that's okay. I'll call my friend and let him know John isn't here. Thanks for your help, Gladys." He pretended to make a call.

"Sorry, I couldn't be of more help, sir. You have a nice day now."

Nick winked. "You, too, Gladys."

He strode toward the main exit while holding the cell phone to his ear. He'd struck gold. Travis Montgomery was alive. Now all he needed to do was get a good look at this guy, make sure he matched the man in the video. Afterward, he'd call in a favor from one of the few friends he had left in the NYPD, have him run his name and see what came up. He slipped his phone into his pocket.

Most of his kills were people either in or related to the drug business. Not this job. These two individuals were definitely not connected. Any information regarding either one of them might help.

He canvassed the rear of the hospital looking for another entrance. On the far left end, he spotted a door tagged, 'Employees Only' with a keypad mounted outside the frame.

He left and drove to a shopping mall he passed by earlier. One of the shops inside probably sold scrubs. In a hospital that size, he could easily blend in as an employee.

Thirty minutes later, in full scrubs, he made his way to the hospital again. He parked and strolled toward the employee entrance. Within minutes, a young man in green scrubs crossed the lot, and Nick followed close behind.

The man swiped his badge across a reader and pulled the door open. Nick sped over as the young man held it open for him.

"Thanks," Nick said as he hurried past him and through the door. "Don't want to be late."

"I know the feeling," he agreed as the door swung closed.

He walked along a narrow corridor to a bank of elevators. The doors slid open, and a group of young nurses bailed out. He pressed six, impatient as the elevator made its ascent. He exited on six and followed the room signs toward 637.

The hallway bustled with activity. An orderly passed by pushing a gurney while two women dressed in blue scrubs walked in the other direction. He made his way past the nurse's station. A doctor dressed in a white coat, stethoscope in hand, conversed with a nurse behind the desk. He passed by unnoticed.

Two nurses rounded the corner at the far end of the hall. Nick ducked into the nearest room. An elderly gentleman laid propped up in a bed.

"Are you my new doctor?" he barked.

"Are you Mr. Peter Gaines?"

He tilted his head. "What did you say?"

"Mr. Peter Gaines?" Nick repeated.

"No, no, the names George. George Parker."

"Oh, sorry. Wrong patient," Nick said and slipped out.

He slowed his pace as he neared room 637. To his relief, the door was unguarded and halfway open. He'd expected to see a police officer stationed outside. Apparently, for whatever reason, this Montgomery character managed to put one over on the cops. He peeked around the doorjamb and recognized the guy sitting by the window from his profile. He began to stir, and Nick moved on to the end of the hallway and turned, deciding to make a second pass by the room.

Tempted to return and end things with a bullet to the guy's temple, he decided against it. The cameras in the hospital lobby and others in the building had captured him. He didn't take chances, and he didn't do sloppy work, one of the many reasons Ricardo trusted him. Besides, he needed this Montgomery guy to lead him to the woman. Without him, she'd be difficult to find.

As he passed by the room again, he observed the guy lying in bed. Proof he was ambulatory, from the chair to the bed unassisted. He'd go home soon.

Nick slowed and angled his head toward the door. For a split second, their eyes locked. He nodded and walked on past. This joker was definitely Travis Montgomery.

Inside the elevator alone, he relaxed. Now all he needed to do was wait. First, he would make a call to his buddy in New York and have him run the name, grab a quick bite to eat and set up surveillance. One by one, the pieces would fall into place, and he'd eliminate both of them.

More importantly, Ricardo would have their hands, and he would get a well-deserved paycheck. After, maybe he'd take a nice vacation. He flipped the air to full blast in the car. Yeah, a vacation sounded right. So long as it wasn't somewhere too warm.

CHAPTER 11
TRAVIS

Travis surveyed the open door as a tall man in scrubs breezed by. Maybe he'd be kind enough to sneak him a cigarette. He waved his hand, but the man kept on walking. Unable to tolerate his craving for a cigarette, he silently cursed. Damn hospital rules! There's hardly any place left to have a good smoke anymore.

Each movement of his body brought the searing pain. He ran his finger down the line of stitches on his chest and winced. Wanting to distance himself from his agony he focused on Carrie and the money.

He figured she wasn't smart enough to leave the country, and she'd never go home. Carrie hated Breezy. She didn't need convincing when it came time to leave that lousy trailer park. Her boy was gone, and she had nothing left worth staying for.

But she still believed he shared in the blame for her mother's ugly deed and told him he should have come back and taken care of her like he promised. That was when he almost confessed, and told her everything. Only it wasn't the right time. Her emotions were too raw.

Sixteen years later, he still hadn't come clean. But after what she did to him, Carrie needed to know the truth. This whole thing just wasn't right. Her acting so crazy, shooting him the way she did and running off with his money.

His stomach tensed and he balled his fists. Hell! Besides all that, he wasn't gonna drag around no kid. A baby didn't figure into his plans. No child was gonna get in between them. It's what children do. Children take the woman from the man. Before long, the woman loves the kid more than she loves you. After they left Breezy, he made sure she took her birth control, and he took precautions himself.

He believed all those things his father had instilled in him. 'The man is in charge. The woman doesn't run the show,' his father always said. A lesson he once forgot.

Before Carrie, there was only one other woman he had loved. He closed his eyes and pictured her all those years ago. Her body, a perfect ten, her long, dark red hair bordered on a rich burgundy falling in waves around her pretty face.

But when he met her, he grew weak. That weakness allowed him to make the mistake of letting her run the show and run him. And that was something he'd always come to regret. Later, he tried to reassert control, but she fought and kept the upper hand. Her constant need to challenge him had divided them.

They had shared some good times together up until she turned to booze. How he detested her drinking. She became a mean drunk, and Travis could not abide a mean drunk, making his decision to leave for good an easy one.

His jaw tightened at the memory of her hurling her empty vodka bottle at his head. That was when he marched the hell out and never looked back.

With Carrie, he made sure things were different. He kept his father's words front and center. His own mother hadn't run the show, and he wasn't gonna let Carrie run his show either.

Travis fidgeted with his hospital gown. Bile bubbled in his stomach as he recalled his mother and the blood in the snow.

Her blood leaving a long trail in the white powder the day his father beat his mother outside the house one winter. He made his boys watch so they would learn. Travis covered his eyes. His father, lit with fury, livid, had grabbed him and pushed his face into the bloody snow.

Travis touched his cheek. To this day, he could almost feel the cold, wet snow, on his face, still taste his mother's blood on his tongue. The love his family shared was always outweighed by the violence attached to it.

Those visions of his mother's blood kept him as far away from snow as possible. No amount of Carrie's begging and pleading could make him travel so she could see snow. He had never told her the real reason. He wanted her love, not her pity.

But in order to find Carrie, he'd have to revisit her past. Soon as he got discharged from this hellhole, it would be time to travel to Breezy to get the information he needed. Helen should be out of jail by now. She owned the old trailer free and clear. If she were still alive, she'd be at Breezy for sure.

Tired now, he rested his head on the pillow and slept while dreaming of Carrie. Hours later, as moonlight spilled across the sterile hospital room, his dreams receded, mere wisps of smoke. He stayed awake until the dark night gave way to sunrise, and an orderly brought him his breakfast.

"Good morning. How are we today?" She grinned at him and set the tray down. "Hope you have an appetite."

"Actually, I'm starving," he crowed. Travis pulled the tray table toward him. With a renewed sense of determination to find Carrie, he lifted the cover off his plate and dug into his meal.

CHAPTER 12
CARRIE

Carrie woke to sunlight and birds chirping their melodies in the tree outside her window. The aroma of bacon drifted up from the kitchen. She stretched her limbs underneath the comforter on the brass bed and sighed. Ugly dreams still haunted her sleep at night and sometimes, during the day, memories of Melbourne, Florida would surface. When they did, she could still feel the scalding heat and almost smell the coppery scent of blood.

Slipping out from under the covers, she grabbed her robe from the foot of the bed. She descended the stairs and peeked into the kitchen. Her aunt was scrambling eggs in a cast iron skillet. Hot maple-cured bacon lay piled high on a plate. Carrie fought the urge to wrap her arms around her. No one had ever treated her so kindly.

"Good morning," Carrie said, filling two cups with coffee. She held one out.

May smiled and reached for the cup. "It's a beauty of a day outside."

"You don't have to cook me breakfast. I'm a big girl. I can fend for myself."

"Rubbish. I love doing it. I've been living in this old house by myself for so long it feels good to do things for someone else."

Carrie lifted a small white pitcher and poured cream into her coffee. She paused. If her aunt knew the truth, she surely wouldn't be sitting down to this wonderful breakfast. Without warning, her hand trembled as she recalled the sight of Travis lying on the floor, gasping for air. She set her cup on the table and, in an effort to calm her mind, she grabbed two blue-flowered plates from the cupboard, along with napkins, and forks, and placed them on the table. She spooned scrambled eggs and bacon onto her plate. Unable to eat, she stared at the food before her.

May frowned. "Is something wrong, dear?"

She pushed away her memories of the murders. "No, no. It smells wonderful."

"Go on then, better eat before the food's cold." May stirred two heaping teaspoons of sugar into her coffee and sipped. "I have to get going soon."

"Where to?" Carrie took a bite of her toast.

"Oh, I didn't get a chance to tell you. I've taken a part-time job taking care of Jenny Hinson, a neighbor over on the next block. She suffered a stroke last year, and now she doesn't get around like she used to. Her son asked if I'd go over there a couple times a week to help her out."

"How sweet of you, Aunt May."

"It helps both of us. I get a little pocket money, and Jenny gets an extra pair of hands."

Carrie took a swallow of the hot coffee and stared at her aunt. What kind of income did she have? How did she manage to pay the bills and take care of the house? She could never repay her for all the kindness she'd shown. If her aunt needed money, she wouldn't hesitate to offer to help her.

"Aunt May, I don't mean to pry, but how are you able to get by? If you don't want to tell me, that's fine," she added. "I shouldn't have asked."

May waved her hand. "Oh no, it's quite alright." She set her fork down. "Remember when you asked me why I never married?"

"Yes."

"I did have a steady fella for quite some years. He was pretty well off, and when he passed away, he left money in a trust fund for me. I'm not rich, Carrie, just comfortable. There is enough to draw on to pay bills and buy groceries each month. Taking care of Jenny helps with the rest." She stood and began clearing the table.

"No, let me," Carrie insisted. She hopped up and shuffled their dishes to the sink. "You go get ready. I'll clean up. It's the least I can do."

"I appreciate it. I'll see you this evening."

"Do you need a ride?" she asked while loading the dishwasher.

"No, it's a nice day. I prefer to walk. You relax." May undid her apron and grabbed her purse off the hook by the door. She fished inside.

"Making sure I have my keys in case you go out. If you do, I left a spare key in the dish on the side table." She slipped into her sweater and then breezed out the kitchen door.

While she finished up, her mind drifted to the briefcase. Uneasy, she tossed the kitchen towel on the counter. Glancing out the window, she surveyed the yard. She spotted a small shed and headed outside.

Carrie yanked the door open. The tangy odor of oil, gasoline, and grass clippings hung heavy in the air. A lawnmower sat in the middle of the floor, and a narrow wooden worktable lined with tools sat against the far wall. Numerous paint cans stood on the shelf above it. Another corner held a variety of rakes, shovels, and hoes. She grabbed a shovel, a pair of work gloves and left both items by the back door.

In her room, she changed into jeans and a sweater and gathered her hair into a ponytail. She opened the briefcase and fished out a thick stack of bills, placing them underneath her clothes in the dresser drawer. She lifted the two guns from her suitcase, set them in the briefcase with the money, and slammed it shut.

Outside, shovel in hand, she searched for a spot to bury the briefcase. She stabbed at the hard ground and continued until she found a softer place shaded by sturdy oaks and pines. The surrounding fence rose high enough to hide her from view and the houses on either side were a reasonable distance away.

She started to dig. At times, the earth refused to give. It took her over half an hour to produce a hole wide and deep enough to accommodate the briefcase. Sweat clung to her body. Strands of her dark hair came undone from her ponytail and stuck to her neck.

She set the briefcase down and shoveled dirt on top of it. She scattered fallen pine straw over the fresh soil. As she turned to place the shovel in the shed, her foot faltered. Her body pitched forward, and she cried out.

"Are you okay?" A male voice called.

A teenage boy slouched against the back gate. Tall and thin with dark brown hair, a patch of which dipped above his right eye. He wore a long sleeve plaid shirt and jeans. His hands rested in his front pockets.

"Who the hell are you?" she demanded. "How long have you been watching me?"

He stepped toward her. "I didn't mean to scare you," he said.

She reeled back and raised the shovel.

He flinched and retreated a few steps. "Whoa, wait a minute. I'm not going to hurt you, lady."

"I asked you a question," Carrie said.

"Not long. My name is Will. I was looking for May. Is she here?" He pulled his hands out of his pockets and let them drop to his side.

She lowered the shovel. "She's gone out. Why?" She kept both hands gripped on the handle.

"I'm doing some work for her."

"What kind of work?"

He turned away. "I'll come back another time."

"No, it's okay. I didn't expect to see anyone standing there. You startled me."

Will shrugged. "Painting, caulking windows, stuff she can't do herself."

"Oh." Heat traveled up her neck and into her cheeks. *This kid must think I'm some kind of nut.* She held out her hand. "I'm Carrie, May's niece."

He gave her hand a gentle shake. "Are you from around here?"

"No, just visiting."

Nearer now, she studied his ice-blue eyes, angular cheekbones, and full lips.

An awkward silence fell between them. Will ran a hand through his hair, smoothing the patch of dark strands that drooped above his right eye. He glanced at the ground, and then up at her. "Well, I'll get started if it's alright with you?"

"No problem, I'm finished. I was checking for a place to plant some bulbs for next spring. Aunt May loves flowers. The grounds pretty hard. I think it might have to wait."

"I could dig for you if you want."

"No, I need to double check with May to see where she'd like them planted. Would you please return this to the shed for me?"

He reached out for the shovel. "Sure. Nice to meet you."

"Same here." She watched him head for the shed and then went inside.

Later in the afternoon, Carrie lounged in a rocker on the porch. She surveyed the maples trees. The leaves had begun releasing their brilliant hues. Smiling, she rested her head against the slats of the rocker. Cobalt blue filled the sky, not a single cloud swept across. The wind lifted, and a light breeze brushed her neck. She shivered and turned her attention to Will who was perched on a ladder painting window trim. Her son would be about his age now. It made her wonder again what kind of person he had grown up to be.

Will finished, hauled the ladder down, and returned it to the shed. Moments later, he reappeared from the rear of the house.

"All done?" she asked.

A smile broke through his lips. "For now. Tell May I'll come on Friday and finish up."

"Sure thing."

"So long now." He turned and ambled up the street.

She observed the way he carried himself. It seemed vaguely familiar. His tall, lanky frame reminded her of someone. He ran his hand through his hair and then glanced over his shoulder and waved.

Carrie returned the wave. He seemed like a sweet boy, but she'd sensed something. What was it? A certain sorrow. Yes, she recognized it all too well. Her own grief had taught her to see it in others. Her heartbeat quickened for a second, and she brushed it off. What did it matter anyway?

Later, as she sat with May at dinner and listened to her stories about Jenny Hinson, guilt surfaced again, making it hard to stay focused.

"She's a pip," May said. "Laurel's own gossip monger. Seems to be up on all the latest tidbits."

After helping May clear the table, she got a sudden urge to go outside. An unfamiliar feeling, the freedom to go where she wanted, when she chose, was scary and exciting, but liberating.

"Aunt May, I think I'll take a walk."

"Better grab a jacket. Do you want some company?"

Though she preferred to go alone, she didn't want to be rude. "Sure."

May hesitated. "Well, truth be told, I am a little tired."

"You stay here and relax. I won't be long."

Carrie strolled to the center of town and soon found herself outside the diner. A cup of coffee sounded good. She ducked inside and slid onto a stool at the counter. With the dinner hour over, she noticed only a handful of people still seated.

"Hey you," a familiar voice called. Joann grinned at her from the opposite side of the counter.

"Hey yourself. How are you?"

"Fine. Except I pulled a double shift. I see you decided to stick around. What for, beats me. I'd give anything to go someplace else right now."

"Really? I kind of like it here."

Joann laughed. "What about you? World traveler?"

"World no. Just some parts of the country," Carrie said.

Joann glanced around and lowered her voice. "Well, the town's okay. Maybe, I need something more. Born and raised here in Laurel, but I've always wanted to travel and experience other places."

"What's stopping you?"

She scratched her head and pretended to think. "Let me see now. Could it be money? Or is it this fabulous job I can't make myself part with? No, it's not that either." She slapped her forehead. "Oh, I know, it's those two kids I have at home. How could I have forgotten them?"

She let out a ripple of laughter, and Carrie found herself laughing too. She loved Joann's sarcasm.

"So, you're married?" Carrie asked.

"Heck no, we never married. Had two great kids, for all he cared. He ran out on us long ago. Someday, when the kids get older and can fend for themselves, I'll have more time for myself. Until then, Laurel is where I'll stay."

"I'm impressed. It must be tough. How old are your kids?"

"I've got a girl and a boy. Veronica's fifteen, but thinks she's eighteen and Justin's thirteen. I'm wading through those glorious teenage years. So far, they're nothing like I was at their age, thank goodness."

She watched Joann's face fill with pride, and she tried not to be envious. A familiar yearning tugged at her.

Joann grabbed a menu and handed it to her. "Before they fire me. What can I get for you?"

Carrie eyed the chocolate cake under a glass dome on the counter but decided against it. "Coffee, please," she said.

Joann poured her a cup and set it on the counter. "I'll be back in a bit. Have to check on my other customers."

Carrie dumped a spoon of sugar into the cup and sipped the sweet hot coffee. How ironic of Joann to believe she missed out by living in Laurel, while she longed for a home of her own in a quiet town like this one.

After the diner emptied, they parked themselves in a booth, coffee cups in hand and Carrie smiled inside, delighted to sit and have a normal conversation. A thing most people took for granted.

"What about you, mystery woman?" Joann winked at her. "I bet you have some tall tales to tell."

She hesitated and played with her napkin. If Joann knew she was having coffee with a murderer, she'd probably jump up from the table and run away.

"No, not me," Carrie said. "I left home at an early age. I've been drifting. Lately, I feel the need to settle down someplace."

"No special someone?"

Her stomach soured at the thought of Travis as her special someone. She gave a half shrug. "I guess I never stayed in one place long enough."

"An attractive woman like you should have no trouble finding a good man."

Carrie squirmed. For as long as she could remember, her beauty caused her nothing but trouble.

Joann sighed. "There I go, assuming you're looking for a man. I meant to say if that's what you want."

"No, for now, I think I'd rather be alone. Am I making any sense?"

"Sure, you are hon, sometimes we women have to be let alone. Find out who we are and what we want."

Carrie nodded in agreement.

Joann cleared their cups. "I need to ride on home. Have to check and see what my two teens are up to."

Carrie stood up. "I'm on foot. May I have a ride?"

"My chariot awaits." Joann placed her hands on her hips. "Well, honey, your facial expression right now, reminds me of the new kid on their first day of school looking for a friend." She giggled and said, "The feeling is mutual. Come on, let's blow this joint."

After Joann dropped her off, she lingered on the porch. Memories of the day she delivered her son surfaced. She lit a cigarette and slumped down onto the front steps.

She stared at her hands and remembered how the pain of labor had receded into some distant place while she stroked the soft curls falling around Bobby's face. Removing his blanket, she'd scanned his tiny body from head to toe, and inhaled the scent of his sweet baby skin. Tucking the blanket around him again, she'd kissed his forehead, and whispered 'I love you,' into his ear.

She longed to hold onto that memory, not the one of her mother stumbling in the door, high on drugs and without Bobby.

She glanced up at the ebony sky blanketed with stars. A nursery rhyme came to her mind.

"Star light, star bright," she began. "I wish I may, I wish I might, have this wish I wish tonight." Closing her eyes, she wished for the lingering images to go away. She wanted to believe one day she would see her son again. Most of all, she wished for forgiveness. If God did exist, somewhere, she hoped he'd forgive her. "Because I don't know how to forgive myself," she whispered.

CHAPTER 13

WILL

William Medlow perched on the edge of his bed, palms flush against his eyes, trying to rub the sleep out. He rose and switched the nightlight off, then let his pajamas fall in a heap on the floor. After hauling himself into the shower, his last bit of sleepiness disappeared. He dried himself off and pressed the play button on the CD player. Maroon 5 blared out at him.

He threw on jeans and a navy-blue hooded sweatshirt. He finished lacing up his red and white Nike sneakers just as his mom called out.

"William, breakfast is ready."

He cringed. "I'm coming, Mom." He hated when she called him William.

Backpack in hand, he took the stairs two at a time while his stepmother eyed him from below and shook her head. "One of these days, you're going to break your neck."

He executed a perfect landing right in front of her. At least a foot taller, he glanced down at the top of her head.

"Okay, shrimp," he crowed.

"You may be taller, but I'm still the queen of this castle," she teased.

Will pulled a chair up to a heaping pile of eggs and toast.

"Now, remember today is your father's birthday. Have you bought him a present yet?"

He looked up from his breakfast. A shadow crossed his face. "No"

"Don't wait until the last minute. You've earned enough extra money to go and pick out a gift on your own."

"I'll go today, after school," Will said. He wolfed down the remainder of his food and slung his backpack over one shoulder. "See ya later."

"Make sure you're home on time. I don't want your father getting all out of sorts."

Will stopped and turned around. "We wouldn't want that now, would we, mother?"

Her mouth drooped. "Will, I ..."

He studied her small, round face, the wisps of brown hair brushing the tops of her shoulders. Her hazel eyes met, his making him regret what he said.

"Okay, okay, I'm sorry. I didn't mean anything by what I said," he mumbled. "I gotta go."

Will bolted out the door, and started the mile-long trek to school. Having no driver's license, he preferred to walk rather than take the bus. He enjoyed having a little time to himself.

As he passed May Overton's place, he pictured the woman with the shovel. Why did she lie about burying the briefcase? He continued on, and his thoughts turned to Darcy.

"Darcy Grant," he said aloud. Darcy, with the stunning green eyes and long blonde hair that dipped below her waist, sat across from him in Chemistry. He was overjoyed when their teacher assigned him as her lab partner.

Sitting amid the test tubes forming a barrier between them, he hung on her every word. Just his luck he'd fallen for one of the most enviable girls at school. Darcy was out of his league, but Will didn't care.

Other than lab class, she didn't know he even existed. Her circle of friends was comprised of cheerleaders and football players, an exclusive group, who were very selective about who they allowed into their little world.

Will didn't go out for sports, deeply disappointing his father. The thought of having to live up to his dad's expectations overwhelmed him.

Besides, he liked watching sports better from the sidelines and watching Darcy cheer even more. She always attracted the most popular kids in school. All the girls wanted to be her, and all the guys wanted to date her.

Will, on the other hand, had few friends. Kenny and Bruce were the only two people he hung around with.

His mind drifted to home and how his mom tried so hard to make the three of them a family. She encouraged his relationship with his father and pushed them to do things together. Only Will didn't want to go fishing, or hunting, or anything with the old man. Not since the day, he turned eight years old.

An outing with his father, at his mom's insistence, it was supposed to be a birthday treat. Will wandered into the garage as his father readied his poles and fishing gear. Wanting to help, Will picked up the tackle box. The latch popped open, spilling all the contents out onto the floor. His father had raged at him and then drove off without him. Through tears, Will crawled across the cement floor and cleaned up the mess.

Like a drill sergeant who never intended to let his son out of boot camp, anything might set the old man off.

Will shivered, remembering his living nightmare, the dark, cold closet, nestled under the basement stairs. A nightmare coated in the smell of mothballs from the coats and sweaters towering over his head, morphing into ominous shapes—imaginary monsters and the pungent odor of urine whenever he had wet himself out of fear.

His confinements stopped at the age of ten, but the dark remained his enemy. At sixteen, he still slept with a nightlight on.

Will never complained. Complaints brought more heartache for him and his mom. Both of them victims of his father's abuse. No one on the outside was aware of what transpired in his house. And he was too ashamed to tell anyone, especially Kenny and Bruce.

His shoulders slumped, and he tried to envision a new life somewhere else, maybe in another city with Darcy Grant. A place of their own. He imagined waking up in the morning with Darcy next to him.

"Hey, lame brain, what's up?"

Bruce fell into step beside him. They always met up at the half-mile point. Bruce's spiked red hair and stocky frame reminded Will of a circus clown gone punk. All he needed were floppy shoes and a red nose. Bruce also walked instead of riding the school bus where, according to him, losers rode.

He nudged Bruce playfully on the shoulder. "Nothing much."

"Bro, I'm so bummed about the science test today. I haven't studied at all."

Will cracked a smile. "So, what else is new? When do you ever study for anything?"

"You got me there, bro. How about after school we go up to the quarry and hang out?"

Hanging out at the old rock quarry after they scored some weed had become a regular routine. Piling into Kenny's car, they'd ride out to the quarry, and smoke. Will liked to go there and kick back. The drug relaxed him as his troubles receded to some distant place.

Will frowned, remembering his stepmother's words. "I can't. It's my old man's birthday."

Bruce laughed and tapped Will's arm. "Boring."

"Maybe next time. You and Kenny go."

"Aw, come on. We won't stay long. You can still make the old man's party."

"It's hardly a party. Just some friends of my mom and dad's," Will lied. No relatives or friends ever came to visit.

He increased the length of his stride. "Come on, pick up the pace. I don't want to have to get a late pass."

They reached the high school and spotted Kenny lounging on the steps leading to the entrance. His dirty blond hair tucked behind his ears, hung almost to his shoulders.

"What's up, guys?"

Bruce pointed his finger at Will. "I'm trying to talk dick head here into going to the quarry later."

"Sounds good to me. I can score. What's the problem?"

"It's my dad's birthday. We got people coming over to the house."

Kenny laughed and elbowed Will on his side. "All the more reason to get messed up."

"Maybe," Will said.

They mounted the steps of the school together. Will debated going to the quarry and then quickly made up his mind.

He'd cave into his friends, go to the quarry, smoke some weed, and get messed up. He also knew, without a doubt, he would pay the price.

Will gazed at the smoke curling up toward the late afternoon sky and relaxed into the buzz. Kenny had scored some good weed. He took another hit, and the tightness in his body eased.

"Hey, don't hog it. Pass the blunt over here," Bruce said. He nabbed it from Will and inhaled.

"Bro, did you see what Darcy was wearing today?" Will asked. "When she leaned over the lab table, I could see clear down her blouse."

"Bet you had fun," Kenny said. "Yeah, Darcy is one bad kitty."

Bruce passed the blunt to Will again. "You do know you'll never tap that, right?"

"Anything's possible, bro." Will took another hit and passed it over to Kenny.

"Naw, Darcy hangs with all the jocks. No way she's coming over to our side," Bruce said. "Besides, why bother with someone who looks down their nose at you?"

"She's actually pretty chill," Will said. "We talk in class."

Bruce ran a hand through his spiked red hair. "Yeah, and it's the only time she'll talk to you."

Will felt too mellow to argue. He wanted to stay in the moment and let the weed work its magic. "Whatever you say, Brucie." He punched him lightly on the shoulder. "Let's see how you make out with Jillian Chambers."

"That's different."

"A fantasy is a fantasy, bro," Will said.

Kenny lit another blunt and passed it between them. They continued taking hits until the blunt burned to a nub.

Will's brows drew together while he watched the sun dip below the pines. He checked his cell phone. Nighttime seeped in drawing a curtain over the quarry. The black shapes of the surrounding hills loomed around them. The last thing Will wanted to do was be out after dark.

"Hey guys, I gotta bounce," Will said. He scooped up his backpack and scurried up to the main road. Kenny and Bruce followed close behind. They jumped into Kenny's beat-up black Camaro. Windows down, music blasting, they sped toward Laurel.

Kenny rolled to a stop in front of Will's house. "See you later, bro."

Will high-fived them both and jumped out. Kenny hit the gas and careened away from the curb. Will laughed as the back-end of the Camaro fishtailed, and they disappeared around the corner.

He strolled to the gate and pushed it open. His father's car wasn't in the driveway. Maybe he'd lucked out. The fear mounting inside him calmed until he spied his mom waiting for him on the porch.

"William Medlow, where have you been? Your father is out looking for you."

Will's stomach curled. He'd arrived too late. His relaxing buzz slipped away.

CHAPTER 14

CARRIE

Carrie rested the newspaper on the counter of the Palisades Diner. The latest want ads spread out before her. 'Administrative Assistant,' she read. 'Must be proficient in Excel.'

Excel? She hadn't touched a computer a day in her life nor worked any kind of job. Travis had never allowed her to get a job. They moved around so much she couldn't have gotten one, anyway. Besides, she didn't have a clue as to what kind of work she qualified for. She chewed her lower lip and stared at the paper, hoping to at least try to find something before her aunt became suspicious.

Tracing along a column with her index finger, she became more and more discouraged to find each ad wanted someone experienced. Folding the newspaper, she set it on the empty stool beside her.

"Hey, girlie," Joann came toward her. They had fallen into an easy friendship in a short amount of time. "What's new?"

"Same old thing," she answered.

Joann stepped out from behind the counter. She grabbed Carrie's hand.

"Come, I want you to meet the loves of my life." She pulled her toward a booth in the corner. Two children, a girl, and a boy sipped milkshakes. They smiled up at Joann.

"Veronica, Justin, I want you to meet a good friend of mine, Carrie."

Both said hello to her in unison.

Carrie smiled. "It's so nice to meet you. Your mom talks about you all the time."

She half listened to Joann's playful banter with them. The old feeling welled up and made her think of what might have been. What kind of personality did her son have? Hopefully nothing like his father's. She liked to picture him a gentle and kind person, living in a good home with parents who loved him. Nothing like her own childhood.

Joann waved a hand at her. "Earth to Carrie."

She shook off her thoughts and anchored herself in the present, afraid if she kept thinking about him she might fall apart. "Oh, I'm sorry," Carrie said. "They're adorable.

They strolled back to the counter. "So, what can I get for you?" Joann asked.

Carrie examined the menu. "I think I'll go with a western omelet and a cup of coffee."

"You got it." Joann scribbled on her pad and tore off the top sheet. She clipped the chit on the carousel, leaned into the pass-through window, and shouted, "One cowboy with spurs!"

Carrie lifted the paper and returned to the want ads. The corners of her mouth edged down.

"Hey, why the somber face?" Joann poured a cup of coffee, and set it in front of Carrie.

Avoiding Joann's gaze, she poured some creamer into her cup.

"Just a little discouraged about the job hunt," she said. "They all want computer experience, which I, unfortunately, don't have."

Joann leaned both her elbows on the counter, chin in her hands.

"If you're not too picky, I know of an opening. Nothing glamorous, but it pays the bills." Straightening up, she pointed to a handwritten sign posted on the wall behind the counter. It read, 'Waitress Wanted.' She turned to Carrie. "Besides, I have an in with the boss."

She shook her head. "I don't know how to waitress."

"Nothing to it. I'll be glad to teach you if the boss hires you. With a little inside influence, I think it can be arranged." Joann gave her a quick wink.

Her jaw dropped. She placed her hand over her heart. "You'd do that for me?"

"I can't make any promises. Let me see what I can do." Joann disappeared through the double swinging doors into the kitchen.

A few minutes later, Carrie met with Rick, the owner of the diner. A tall, heavyset man with a bushy mustache, he perched on the edge of his chair behind a metal desk and waited for her to finish filling out the job application.

She worked her way through the questions. Name and address were easy. Past experience, she left blank. Her heart thudded when she read the question, 'Have you ever been convicted of a felony?'

No. Not yet, Carrie thought. She finished and handed the application to Rick.

"I ... I know I don't have any experience, sir. I appreciate your taking the time to speak with me."

He gave her a half-smile. "When Joann vouches for you, it means something."

His statement made her cringe. Joann wouldn't vouch for a murderer. Carrie steadied the guilt rumbling inside her. She wanted this job.

"So, what's kept you out of the job market? Stay at home mom?" Rick asked.

"Um ... no." She chose her next words carefully. "I have no children. My husband preferred I stay home."

"Why the sudden change of heart? If I give you this job, I don't want him coming around and hassling you. It's happened in the past."

"You don't need to worry about him. We're not together anymore, and he doesn't live in the area.

"I see you haven't been in Laurel long. Where did you live before?"

She blurted out the first thing that came to her mind. "Texas. We lived in Texas."

Rick's face relaxed. "I'll tell you what. I'm going to give you a chance."

She gripped the edge of her chair to stop herself from jumping up and down.

"Thank you. Thank you so much."

Rick's face grew serious again.

"It pays minimum wage, and you'll be on probation for thirty days. Starting tomorrow, you'll train beside Joann. Don't make me regret giving you this chance."

"You won't regret it. I promise," Carrie said.

She could have skipped all the way home from the diner. To her, this wasn't just a waitressing job. Her desire to be normal, to be one of those women she fantasized about had come true.

She drove over to a used car lot she passed coming into town. The Impala held too many reminders of Travis and what happened in Florida. With the title stashed in the glovebox and a little handy forgery, she traded it in for a used cream-colored Toyota Camry with the dealer helping with tags and insurance. Her mood lifted the minute she drove off the lot. New car, new job, new life.

At supper, she let May know about the job, but she lied about the reason she traded the car in.

"That car gave me trouble off and on. I managed to get good money on a trade-in," she told her aunt.

"Wonderful," May said. "I guess this means you'll be staying awhile."

"If it's okay with you?" She smiled as she wiped a blue flowered dish, and placed it in the cupboard above.

"It's more than okay. You're welcome to stay as long as you like. I love having you here. It can get a little lonely at times." She tapped Carrie's arm. "Why don't you put the coffee on while I start a fire? It's chilly enough tonight to enjoy it."

Carrie put the last of the dishes away and prepared the coffee. She took two cups into the living room and settled next to her aunt by the fire. Bright orange flames licked the wood. The pop and hiss of the sap burning off comforted her.

May settled in with a book while Carrie flipped through a magazine. Her body relaxed, and her mind turned away from dead bodies, the blood pooling underneath them, and Travis, his hand holding tight to the hem of her dress. That night, for the first time in weeks, she slept without nightmares.

CHAPTER 15

WILL

William hustled up the front steps, anxious to get inside. His mother leaned toward him and sniffed as he slipped past her.

She drew back. Her face paled. "I can smell the marijuana on your clothes. Hurry up and change before your father finds out you've been smoking out at the quarry again."

"Mom, chill, please. I'm okay."

"You ruined your father's birthday. He's furious."

Will started up the steps, but he hadn't gone far before the front door flew open with such force it smacked the wall knocking a glass picture frame loose. The picture crashed to the floor, sending shards of glass across the hallway.

His father glared up at him, a storm building in his eyes. "So, screwing up as usual. Where the hell were you?" He stationed himself at the bottom of the stairs, his bulky frame blocking the last step. "Hanging out at that damned quarry, right? Don't stand there like an idiot, get down here now, and answer me!"

Will's adrenaline pumped. He took several steps down the staircase. Fear mixed with rage coursed through his body. He didn't have to take this anymore. He'd fight the old man with each drop of hatred inside him. When Will reached the bottom step, his father lunged and clutched the front of his shirt, shoving him up against the wall.

"I asked you a question."

His skin pinched tight beneath his father's meaty hands, Will winced. Hatred surged inside, and he balled his hands into fists. He stared at his mom.

"Russ, please," she pleaded, placing her hand on his arm. "Let him go."

Deep red flushed his face, and he shook her hand away. "I'd stay out of this if I were you, Claudia."

Her bottom lip quivered, and she fell silent.

Will stared at her face. She was always the reason he'd never retaliate. He unclenched his fists and flattened his palms against the wall behind him.

Russ tightened his grip. He leaned in closer, inches from Will's face.

"Listen, mister, I will not tolerate a junkie in my house. Don't you have any respect for your mother or me?"

Will's palms ached from pressing so hard. His chest throbbed with each probe of his father's fingers.

Finally, he released Will and pointed to Claudia. "She's the reason I don't throw you out onto the street. You better thank your lucky stars you have her."

Will pushed away the raw fury inside of him and relaxed his hands, knowing if he lashed out, she would suffer, too.

Russ continued to hover over him. "Raise your hands to me, and it will be the last thing you ever do. And if I catch you using drugs one more time or if I find out you were anywhere near that quarry, I'll break both your legs."

Every fiber of Will's being, twisted inside him. He didn't care about his father's threat of broken bones.

"Look at me." Russ held out his hand. "Give me your cell phone."

Will reached into his pocket and handed him the phone.

In one swift movement, he threw it down and crushed it beneath his shoe. "No television, no music," he continued. "Right home from school except when you have work over at May's place. Am I making myself clear?"

"Yes, sir," Will said.

Russ spun around and stalked off into the living room.

"I told you this morning to buy the birthday gift and come right home," Claudia said. "Why didn't you listen to me?"

"It's okay," Will said, his voice tinged with sorrow. "You're right, it's my fault." He ran up the stairs to his room.

Full of thwarted rage, Will threw himself on his bed and punched his fists into the pillows. So many times he'd promised himself he'd stand up to his old man. The crucial moment had come, and once again he failed to follow through.

His bitterness boiled to the surface, and he brooded, remembering how he had tried to get her to admit the truth, instead of putting up and shutting up. When he turned thirteen, he told her what he thought.

They were sitting side by side on the porch swing. His mom held a ball of yarn in her lap. Her knitting needles clicked softly as she pulled strands of dark green wool up and over them.

"Mom, were you ever happy?" he asked.

"Silly, what are you talking about?"

"I mean with, Dad."

Her needles tapped faster. "It's complicated. I don't think you're old enough to understand."

She had brushed him off, and it made him mad. "He hits you!" Will fumed. "I swear, one day I'm gonna—"

"Will, hush." She stopped working the yarn. "Your father is a troubled man, but he wasn't always the way he is now."

Will's pent-up bitterness spilled out all at once. "He hates me."

"Please, Will, that's just not true." She picked up her knitting, the needles moved quickly again. "Please, can we not talk about this anymore?"

Will never broached the subject again. She'd never give him the answers he was looking for. Letting out a sigh, he stretched his legs. With no cell phone, music, or television, he had little in the way of entertainment, and homework was the furthest thing from his mind.

He heaved himself up off the bed and wandered to the window. His surly mood lifted as the image of Carrie burying the briefcase scurried across his mind. Why would someone bury a briefcase in their yard? Only one reason, they have something to hide. Was the old lady aware of what Carrie had done?

But what if … what if he took a look? He could dig it up and then return it before anyone found out. No harm in that. Will continued to stare out into the darkness as curiosity overtook him. It wasn't going to let go until he found out what Carrie had buried in May Overton's backyard.

CHAPTER 16
TRAVIS

Travis bummed a cigarette from an orderly outside the main entrance. Elated at his discharge, he took a drag and savored the sweet taste of the tobacco. He patted the pocket of his hospital donated clothes, checking for the bottle of prescription pain pills. He signaled the cab turning up the drive and leaned his head in the window.

"You familiar with the Marque off the main highway?" he asked.

"That dive? You sure you want to go there, Mister?"

"Yeah, I'm sure." He ducked inside.

"Hey, buddy, no smokes in the cab."

"Yeah, don't get your balls twisted." Travis curled his lip and lowered the window. He tossed his cigarette into the gutter.

The driver tried making small talk during the ride. Travis promptly made him aware that he preferred silence, while he focused his mind on his next moves.

"Wait here," he said to the cabbie when they pulled up in front.

"Listen, buddy, I have to keep moving to make a living."

Travis flashed him a grin. "I'll make it worth your while."

"How much?"

"A cool hundred." He caught the cabbie's eyes in the rearview mirror.

"That'll do it."

Except for the clerk behind the counter, the motel lobby appeared vacant. The clerk glanced up and let out a low whistle. "Oh, man, I thought you were dead."

Travis slapped his hands on the front desk and leaned in.

"Surprise, surprise. Here I am." He took stock of the clerk's frog-like eyes, the way they jutted out of his head like two shiny marbles. "Listen, fella, I hope you still have my suitcase."

"Sure do, Mr. Montgomery. They ever catch the person who shot you?"

Heat traveled up Travis's neck. "That's none of your business. Hurry up and get my suitcase, then I'll settle things up with you."

"I'll go get it right now, Mr. Montgomery."

"Hurry, I got a cab waiting out front."

The clerk zipped through a side door and, seconds later, returned with the suitcase.

"I'll need you to sign for this," he said.

He shot the clerk a look. "I'll sign, but everything better be intact."

The clerk placed two forms and a pen in front of him. "We have policies around here. We're not allowed to disturb people's things. If anything is missing, it's the police who are to blame, not anybody who's employed here."

Travis glanced at the forms. "What's this here miscellaneous?" he asked.

"It includes clean-up. There was quite a bit of blood. And—"

Travis held up his hand. "I get it." He signed the forms and shoved them across the counter. "Now, give me my suitcase."

The clerk hesitated. "Normally, the motel policy says you have to pay me first."

"This ain't normally, fella." Travis raised his fist. "Now, I ain't gonna ask you again."

The clerk picked up the suitcase and slid it across the desk.

Travis rushed over to one of the worn-out sofas in the lobby. He unzipped it, tossed his clothes aside, and lifted the lining of the false bottom. His mouth curved into a smile. Those stupid cops had messed up.

His hands traveled over the bands of cash and the spare gun he always kept there. He shoved a wad of cash into his pocket and stuffed his clothes back inside. He returned to the front desk and set two crisp hundreds down.

"Here, this ought to settle things. There's even a little extra in there for you."

"Why, how generous of you, Mr. Montgomery."

"Don't mention it." He grabbed his suitcase and stepped toward the exit.

"Mr. Montgomery," the clerk called after him. "There is something else you should be aware of."

"Oh yeah, what?" Travis glared at him. "You better not waste my time."

"I think I have information that might be worth something to you."

Travis stalked back to the desk and tossed another bill on top. "Spill it."

The clerk eyed the bill and quickly palmed it. "A guy came in here a while ago asking about you."

"Who? What did he look like?"

"He looked like a cop to me, but he denied it. Expensive suit, tall, dark hair. Wanted to know if I've seen you before. Showed me some pictures."

"Pictures?"

"Yeah, of you. Oh, and your pretty lady."

The lines around Travis's mouth creased. "What did you tell him?"

The clerk fidgeted with the penholder. "Nothing. Nothing at all. What's there for me to tell?"

"Thanks, fella," Travis said. He nodded and exited the motel. How could someone have pictures of him and Carrie? Like a thunderbolt, it hit him. Cameras!

The driver's face lit up when Travis handed him the hundred.

"I need you to do one more thing for me. Take me to the closest used car dealer." He needed to get his own set of wheels fast.

"Sure thing." The cabbie executed a U-turn and headed toward town.

If he believed what the clerk told him, it meant Carrie was in serious trouble, too. He must find her and soon. That guy, whoever he was, sure wasn't looking to make new friends.

Within the hour, he purchased a car with a good set of tags. Money did amazing things. It could make people work magic. He drove off the lot in a used black Honda Accord. Nothing flashy. Later, when he retrieved his money, he'd get a more expensive ride.

After gassing up, he purchased a pack of cigarettes and some water. He pulled a cigarette from the pack, tapped the end against his palm, and lit up. Inhaling, he let the vapor fill his lungs. A sigh of pleasure escaped his lips as he blew smoke out. The rush from the nicotine buzzed inside his head.

He collapsed into the vinyl seat and took another drag. Fumbling around for a radio station, he found some country music and flipped the volume. He smirked. Another song about some woman doing a man wrong. Yup, that's always the case.

He flipped the radio off. His mind drifted, and he recalled counting all the money while Carrie showered. Two million dollars lay in that damn briefcase. It infuriated him all over again that Carlos and Eddie had tried to pawn off forty thousand dollars instead of the fifty they promised. His jaw tensed and clicked.

He slid the window down and flicked his cigarette butt out. A slow grin appeared on his face. He never thought he'd see so much money in his lifetime. It made him giddy. A large sum of money opened up a whole new world of possibilities. Freedom to go wherever, buy whatever, and do almost anything he wanted to do.

Without warning, the image of Carrie aiming the gun at him flashed across his mind. His chest muscles tightened, and he brushed his fingers over his scar tissue, unable to erase her venomous words from his memory.

He studied his hands. The same ones that slapped her, pushed her, and left bruises on her, were also the same hands that loved her and refused to live without her. It wasn't his fault she made him lose his temper. Even so, he'd never stoop to shooting her.

Besides, the murders must have caused her to act crazy. She got shook, that's all. Deep inside, she loved him. He was sure of it.

Travis drove all afternoon. When he reached the Louisiana border, he bought a bottle of whiskey and checked into a cheap motel. Tucking his cash underneath the pillow, he collapsed onto the bed. He pressed the remote until an old black and white movie flickered on the television.

He needed rest, but his mind kept wandering to the last time he saw her. How amazing she looked in her little black dress. After they were together again, he'd buy her a hundred dresses. He ached to touch her, hold her close. His desire climbed to new heights, and he jumped up and headed for the shower.

He stripped, stepped into the tub, and faced the showerhead. He turned the tap and let the cold water hit his body full force. Shivering, he leaned in and pressed his palms against the light blue colored tile. The frigid water poured over him until his need subsided.

With a towel snug at his waist, he twisted the cap off the container of pain pills. He popped one into his mouth and took two long draws of whiskey. The familiar tingle coursed through his body.

Later, his whiskey bottle three-quarters empty, he reached over and shut the light. Sometime during the night, the need for her returned to him again. Just as he knew it would.

CHAPTER 17

NICK

An ebony sky gave way to an overcast cloud-filled one while Nick sipped black coffee in the parking lot of Travis's motel. His buddy at the precinct had pulled up the stats on the thief. Only small, petty misdemeanor crimes showed on his rap sheet. He was amateur all the way.

Another hour passed before Travis sauntered across the motel parking lot. He stopped, lit a cigarette, and made small talk with another guest. Nick laughed to himself. This Montgomery guy was too preoccupied to notice anything else around him.

Nick tailed him to a gas station about ten miles further along the highway and followed him inside. He watched Travis meander up and down the isles pocketing candy before pulling a cold beer from the refrigerated case. Nick shook his head. Once a thief, always a thief.

He hurried to his car while Travis paid for his beer and a map, making it easy for Nick to come to a conclusion. He figured they were lovers. The woman, unhappy with the situation, shot him, grabbed the cash, and split town in a hot mess. It all made sense.

He did admire her guts. The way she shot Carlos in the neck and then this Montgomery guy. What a shame he would have to kill her.

Outside, Travis spread the map out across the trunk of the car and ate his pilfered candy. A disheveled looking man came out of nowhere. He approached Travis, mumbled something, and held out a shaky hand.

Nick slid his window down, sure this would be quite entertaining. He observed Travis glance around before pushing the poor man to the ground and yelling, "Get a job, you bum." When the man attempted to get up, he kicked him in his side.

Nick seethed, wished he could grab the creep and end things right there. Guys like him showed no sympathy for the less fortunate.

Travis folded the map and strutted to the men's room. Nick waited until he stepped inside and then rushed over. He pulled the man to his feet and stuffed a hundred into his pocket.

Dazed, the man pulled out the bill and stared, first at the money and then at Nick. "Gee, thanks."

"No problem," Nick said. "Go get yourself a hot meal before you buy any more whiskey." He returned to the Mercedes before Travis emerged from the bathroom.

Keeping a safe distance behind Travis, he noted they were headed west. Curiosity made him wonder what had brought Travis and the woman together. The guy looked a lot older than her. Probably made it easier for him to take control.

He guessed she got fed up with not having a say in things. If that was the way it happened, he didn't blame her. From the short time he had tailed him, this guy proved to be a total asshole.

Tailing Travis brought to mind his own first kill. The first should have been his hardest, but it turned out to be his easiest.

Crazy Rudy from the South Bronx. A real piece of work, he mused. A small-time hustler, like Travis, who tried to muscle in on Ricardo's action.

He'd taken his time and followed Rudy to familiarize himself with his routine. Found he had his meetings in an abandoned building. The sucker didn't even have office space somewhere.

With two weeks' worth of beard on his face, he posed as a homeless man and cased the building, getting Rudy's routine down pat. Then he paid a couple of vagrants to distract Rudy's bodyguards. As the bums ran outside, he slinked inside.

Rudy's bodyguards broke rule number one. Never leave the side of the person you're supposed to protect. A good bodyguard knows the importance of staying with his client.

He took aim and pumped two clean shots into Rudy's skull. It was the first time he experienced the now familiar adrenaline rush, like an electrical charge, rocketing through each muscle and nerve in his body. It soared through his veins, made his surroundings crystal-clear. It became his natural high.

After killing Rudy, he never looked back. Soon, he made the leap to Ricardo's personal hit man. As time passed, he honed his skills, becoming a first-rate killer. In his newfound profession, his survival depended on it. Not long after that, he earned the title of ghost.

It almost amused him at times to think that losing his shield over drug money had landed him a job as a hired killer for a drug lord.

He had a new life. A life given to him by Ricardo Santiago. Nobody else understood. Nobody cared. They all turned their backs on him except for Ricardo.

With a nice sum of money stashed away in the Caymans and Europe, his investments guaranteed he'd have a great retirement one day. Maybe he should make these two his last and then talk to Ricardo about retiring.

If somehow, Ricardo agreed, Nick knew it would mean his marrying Carmela. He didn't care to spend his life married to someone he wasn't in love with. Most of all, he didn't want to spend it running drugs.

Ricardo claimed he would let him run his legitimate businesses. Nick didn't believe him. The drug business remained much a part of all of it. Each aspect intertwined out of necessity. Drug money needed to be laundered.

It also afforded Ricardo a particular lifestyle. One that came with a hefty price. Nobody who ran drugs remained safe from either side. The law watched and waited for that one mistake while your enemies did the same. While the law tried to put you away, your enemies waited to put you down.

Nick owed Ricardo his gratitude and loyalty, but he had also paid a steep price for it. The bodies were piling up. Bad people or not, each time he took a shot, he played God. There wasn't any way to vindicate himself. No absolution hung on the horizon. No amount of prayers was enough for an act of contrition.

For now, he would concentrate on getting this job done. He kept Travis in sight, more determined than ever to finish this kill.

CHAPTER 18

CARRIE

Carrie clipped a chit to the wheel stationed at the pass-through window and called out, "One Adam and Eve on a raft and wreck 'em." She grabbed a fresh pot of coffee and headed for the end of the counter.

"Here you go, Marvin. Fresh and hot."

The large man in bib overalls winked. "Thanks, Carrie. Can't start my day without the Palisades morning Joe."

She loved her job at the Palisades. A quick learner, she fell into step with the daily routine. Her diner vocabulary grew under Joann's tutelage, and she became confident calling out orders. She left the diner at night with her feet aching and a sense of pride.

The first time she dressed for work, she laughed to herself. The uniform was far from anything she might have worn around Travis. He would have detested the plain white shirt, black skirt, and shoes with thick skid-proof rubber soles.

The regulars, who frequented the diner, grew accustomed to her and some asked for her by name. A few of the male customers flirted with her, but she never took it seriously. At this point in her life, she had no desire to get involved with another man.

One evening, after work, Carrie drove with Joann to the mall in Allentown to do some shopping. She needed to purchase a heavy coat for the coming winter, and a cell phone seemed like a good idea. Owning one would be another milestone for her.

Later, their shopping finished, they stopped for coffee at the food court.

"Wow, I can call you like a normal person instead of ringing May's house phone." Joann teased.

Carrie stirred cream and sugar into her cup and took several sips. She glanced around and giggled.

"What?" Joann asked.

She shook her head. Here she was having coffee with a friend for the first time in her life.

Come on, Carrie. What's up?"

"It's silly," she answered, the grin still planted on her face.

"Not for nothing, but I could count on one hand the number of times I've seen you smile."

"Oh, I was thinking how lucky I am that I met you the first night I drove into Laurel."

Joann's cheeks flushed. "That's one of the sweetest things anybody ever said to me."

"Oh, Joann. You must have tons of friends who think of you the way I do."

"Tons …no, I don't think so. Two or three maybe, including you. Believe it or not, I was once considered a loose woman around Laurel." Joann erupted into the hearty laughter Carrie loved so much.

"You? Loose?"

Joann set her cup down. "Things were different back then. If you got pregnant in high school and in a town as little as Laurel, it became somewhat of a scandal. I had the nerve not to marry the baby's father and to make matters even more scandalous, have another kid with him."

"If it made you happy, I don't see anything wrong with it," Carrie said. She would be the last one to judge her, or anyone else.

Joann arched her brow. "Yeah, I guess it did. I didn't think twice about having those kids. It never occurred to me to get rid of a pregnancy."

"And their father? Does he ever come around to see them?"

"Nah." Joann shrugged and picked up her cup. "I can't blame him much. We were young and stupid. The second one scared him. He up and split one day. His family moved away, and I have no idea where he is." She frowned and sipped her coffee. "I guess if I wanted to find him, I could, but what's the point? Child support? I'm not going to chase after money I have to force out of somebody. Maybe it's dumb, but that's how I feel."

"No, it's not dumb. I admire you for raising your children all by yourself."

"My parents help out sometimes. They're good to the kids. You'll see, Carrie, one day you'll have kids of your own. It turns your life inside out. Your priorities change. You realize some of the things you believed were so important before, aren't important at all. I couldn't picture my life without them."

"Yeah, someday," She gave her a half-smile. The empty place inside her wanted to scream. She would give anything to see her son again.

Joann's face grew curious. "I don't like to pry, hon, but what about you? Any major loves in your life?"

Carrie gripped her cup tighter. "One.   I ran away with him when I was real young." She hung her head and felt a hot flush creep across her cheeks. "I was an easy target so to speak. I had nothing, and he knew it. He treated me okay in the beginning, but then he changed."

"Changed how?" Joann leaned in and rested her chin in her hands.

"He started getting mad all the time." Memories of Travis circled Carrie's brain. All the ugliness of her past threatened to spill out, but Joann had become a dear friend, and she felt she owed her at least part of the truth.

Joann frowned. "Do you mean he started hitting you?"

"Growing up, no one gave a damn," she continued. "So, he came along, and I thought someone actually cared."

"What about your folks?"

Carrie's heart filled with shame as she forced the words out. "My mother is an alcoholic and a drug addict who used to beat me. I never knew my father. I was an infant when he cut out on us. My mother never got over him. I'm not making excuses, but I think that's what led her to drink. The drugs came later."

Joann's mouth fell open. Her hands flew to her chest. "Oh, Carrie, I'm so sorry. I shouldn't have started this conversation." Her eyes watered.

Carrie looked up. "No, please don't get upset. It's okay. You told me about your life, it's only fair I tell you a little about mine." Underneath her uniform, cold sweat trickled down her sides. How could she explain the sheer terror of having to live with someone like Travis? Pushing her angst aside, she continued.

"Outside of my mother, he became the meanest person I ever knew."

Joann's face sagged. "Carrie, honey, when a man hits you, it's not love. If he loves you, he will never put his hands on you."

"I know that, now," Carrie said. She lit with shame thinking how she used to feel she deserved those beatings. Just punishment for leaving her son with her mother. It took Travis almost choking her to death for her to realize she didn't. Her punishment lay deep inside. One that repeated itself virtually on a daily basis, always waiting to remind her of the loss.

"Hon, no one should be mistreated, especially not someone as sweet as you," Joann said. She reached out and patted Carrie's hand.

Carrie averted her eyes and looked out over the food court. Sweet wasn't a word she would use to describe herself.

"So, you left him?" Joann asked.

"No. I mean yes. I mean … I came to Laurel to start over." She slipped her shaking hands onto her lap. It was natural for people to be curious, but it didn't make it any easier to keep telling lies.

"Carrie, what are you saying? Does he know where you are? How did you leave things with him?"

She met Joann's eyes. "No, I don't need to worry about him. I made myself very clear before I left. He won't come looking for me."

Joann fell silent and studied Carrie's face.

"Really, it's all good. He won't bother me," Carrie quickly said. She sensed her friend doubted she had told the whole truth.

Joann drained the last of her coffee. "We better head out. I got hungry kids to feed."

On the drive back to Laurel, Carrie felt some relief. It helped to convince her things might continue to work out in her favor.

They drove with the radio blasting, singing aloud whenever a song played they both knew. Carrie wanted to hold on to what she was feeling right now, here, with Joann. Only deep inside, a voice shouted out a warning to her, unleashing a torrent of self-doubt, telling her she didn't deserve this happiness. Not after what she had done.

But she pushed the thoughts away, refusing to listen as Roy Orbison's "Pretty Woman" blared from the radio. She glanced over at Joann and laughed. They belted out the song together while the car wound its way toward Laurel.

CHAPTER 19

WILL

Will trekked up the street to May Overton's, his hands stuck into the front pockets of his black jeans, the tail of his blue denim shirt hanging out. The bottoms of his oversized work boots scraped along the sidewalk. Still under house arrest at home, except for school and doing work at May's place, he cherished this little bit of freedom.

He approached the house just as Carrie came through the gate. She waved and then strolled toward Main Street. Kenny and Bruce had told him she worked at the diner. They talked about how pretty she was and how they planned to become regular customers. Will thought they were ridiculous. As if a grown woman like her would bother with teenage boys.

Will opened the gate and jogged up the porch steps just as May strolled out the front door. Her eyes lit up when she saw Will.

"Why, hello, young man. How are you today?"

"Fine, thanks. I thought I'd finish painting the rest of the trim on the front windows."

"Good. It needs to be finished before the cold weather settles in and it's too cool for painting. All the supplies are in the shed. I'm headed to Jenny Hinson's place."

Will gave her a slight smile. Guilt brimmed up inside. May Overton was one of the sweetest old ladies in the neighborhood.

"Okay, thanks," Will said.

After she rounded the corner, Will sprinted to the shed, grabbed a shovel, and made a bee-line to the spot where Carrie buried the briefcase.

He bent and brushed away the pile of leaves and pine straw. Shovel in hand, he dug into the rich dark earth. The earth gave way, and he smiled to himself. He'd hit the right spot.

Intent on digging, he ignored the blast of wind racing across the yard. The front gate banged. Startled, Will dropped the shovel. Sweat traced across his brow and ran down his forehead. Had May Overton come home? Or Carrie?

He crept toward the front of the house, his heart pumping fast against his chest. If either one of them returned, he'd never be able to explain his digging. He glanced out at the street. It was empty. He eyed the gate and realized he must have forgotten to latch it. The wind probably slammed it shut.

Will resumed his digging. From time to time, he glanced up, worried either one might reappear. A few minutes later, the shovel struck something. Heaving the last two shovels of dirt onto the mound, a glint caught his eye. The briefcase poked up from the ground. He crouched and lifted it up with both hands. More cumbersome than he expected, he quickly set the briefcase down on a pile of leaves a few feet away.

Will refilled the hole, covering the area again with leaves and pine straw. After he finished, he placed the briefcase inside the shed behind a large sack of birdseed.

In case May checked, he'd do a little painting. He spent the next hour painting some trim on the front windows, the briefcase sitting in the shed making it hard for him to concentrate.

After cleaning the brush, he put the paint in the shed. He snatched up the briefcase, carrying it in his arms rather than by the handle. Before going out the gate, he scanned the block and then raced up the street to his house. He placed the briefcase under the wooden steps by the rear door of the house and stepped inside.

"Mom, I'm home," he yelled.

"I'm in the living room, Will."

Will peeked in the doorway. Claudia sat in the recliner with her head down, knitting needles fast at work.

She looked up and frowned at him. "Oh, my goodness, look at your clothes. What did May have you doing? You're covered with dirt." She placed her knitting aside and grabbed the armrests to push herself up.

Will checked his clothes. His shirt and pants were filthy from all the digging. He held up his hand. "No, it's alright. I'll hop in the shower and leave my dirty clothes in the laundry when I'm done."

"Ok. Dinner will be in an hour."

"Sure thing," he said. Will bolted through the kitchen. He brought the briefcase up to his room and stashed it under the bed. He removed his clothes and stepped into the shower. A mark, the color of red wine and the size of a silver dollar, stamped his forearm. He studied it, running his fingers over the red star-shaped patch of skin. He frowned as he recalled his mother telling him it was a birthmark, his lucky star. As far as he could tell the darn thing never brought him any luck.

Will dressed and locked the door. He grabbed a towel from the bathroom and laid it on the bed. He hoisted the briefcase up onto the bed and toweled the dirt off. He pressed the two gold locks, and the cover flew open. Will jumped back.

"Holy shit," he said, drawing a deep breath. He swiped a hand through his hair. He crept toward the bed and picked up one of the two guns. He turned it over in his hands several times and then lifted the other one out.

Will laid them both on the bed and then stared at the stacks of bills. Did Carrie rob a bank? The weapons, the money, all pointed to something illegal. He plopped onto the bed next to the open briefcase.

Will picked up a stack of bills and fingered it. Returning it to the briefcase, he popped up to his feet and paced the room. What if he kept the money, or at least part of it? This might be his shot to get far away from his father.

Grabbing the guns, he placed them on top of the money and slammed the briefcase shut. He rested his ear against the door. The sound of a pot banging reassured him his mother was busy cooking dinner. He searched the room and then opened his closet, shoved the briefcase into the far corner, and placed a pile of clothes on top of it.

Anxious, he wished he could tell someone, anyone. He gathered his dirty clothes and dropped them off in the laundry room downstairs. In the kitchen, he sank into his seat at the table set for two.

"Is Dad eating with us?" Will asked.

"No, your father called, and he has to work late."

His body relaxed. He preferred it be just the two of them.

Claudia set down two full plates of food and seated herself across from him.

Hungry, Will wolfed down several mouthfuls before asking, "Mom, if you had a choice, would you stay here?" He swiped at the patch of hair hanging over his eye.

She looked up from her plate. "What are you talking about?"

"I mean if you could leave here without Dad, just you and me." Will stopped eating and stared at her.

"Leave here with you, without your father?" She blinked several times and pushed her plate back.

"Please, don't get upset," Will pleaded. "We both know we're not happy here with Dad. He's always so angry."

She jerked her chair back and stood. "Stop it, stop talking nonsense, William." She snatched up her plate and crossed to the sink.

Will followed her, tension building inside him. His hands clenched into fists. "You have to hear me out. I can't take much more." Will's nostrils flared. "I never fight him," he declared. "But I swear to God, he makes me so mad I want to—"

"William, don't do anything foolish. I saw you ball up your fists. I was terrified." The fragile skin around the corners of her eyes creased. A pained expression planted itself on her face. "He'll hurt you if you come at him."

Will puffed up his chest and waved his fist. "I'm not afraid of him. You're the reason I don't defend myself."

She began to cry, and Will's body sagged.

"Mom, please stop crying. None of it's your fault. I know you're scared."

"No, it's okay." She leaned in and patted Will's cheek. "As your mother, I'm ashamed. I'm supposed to protect you. I haven't done a very good job, have I?" She slumped into a chair and wiped her tears with a napkin.

Will pulled up a chair next to her. "Listen, if there was a way, would you go?"

"Where?" she asked.

Will smiled. "Anywhere we wanted to go. I can't explain right now. I'm working on getting enough money to leave here and start over somewhere else. We'd never have to worry again."

She gave him a worried look, "I don't want you getting into trouble."

"I won't." He'd need to figure out a way to explain the money. For her sake, Will flashed her a smile. "Please, Mom, at least think about it."

She hesitated, her expression doubtful. "Okay, I will."

Later in the evening, Will propped himself up in bed, nightlight on, eyes locked on the closet door. Determined to get out of Laurel, he decided to keep the money. When the time was right, he'd take his mom and go where they never had to be afraid again. He turned on his side, and for the first time in months, his sleep was undisturbed.

CHAPTER 20

TRAVIS

Bone tired, Travis ignored the speed limit and drove west. As he rolled into Louisiana a blinking liquor store sign in a strip mall beckoned to him. After purchasing whiskey, he booked a motel room for the night. He settled in and twisted the cap off the whiskey bottle. Taking two long swallows, he mentally traced the burning sensation as the alcohol tumbled passed his throat, but the whiskey failed to numb the melancholy inside him. It grew in intensity each day while thoughts of Carrie consumed him.

He brushed the window curtain aside and peered out. The last bit of sun slipped behind the horizon casting long shadows on the walls. Like those shadows, she had slipped away from him.

Still, he forgave her for what she had done to him. She had committed murder to protect him from Carlos and Eddie, surely that meant something. Turning from the window, he finished half of the whiskey bottle before crawling into bed and drifting off to sleep.

The next morning, his eyelids heavy, he drove through Texas and on to Colorado. The beauty of the mountains filled with rusts and vibrant shades of bronze evaded him. Sweet, clear air and brilliant rays of sun moved through the trees, but none of it able to lift his sour mood. By his calculation, he'd arrive in Arizona by late afternoon.

The blacktop sizzled in the heat by the time he arrived at Breezy Meadows. Travis cruised along the endless rows of trailers baking in the blistering heat. Propane tanks stood at attention alongside each one, while power lines hummed above. Most of the homes were devoid of decoration except for the occasional scattering of plastic lawn chairs in front. The scorched earth held a few patches of green grass struggling to stay alive. He passed by several people who dared to venture out in the excruciating heat, most stayed indoors this time of day.

Gravel crunched beneath his tires as he drove to the end of the last row. Relief washed over him when he came upon the old faded blue and white 1972 Shasta trailer in all its glory. Rusty metal trim ran around the windows and along the length of the trailer. A string of colored lights hung haphazardly at angles from the roof beside a satellite dish. Garbage peeked out from underneath the lid of a grey metal trash can. A red Ford pickup with multiple gashes and dings across its fenders sat in the front yard.

He stepped out of his car and trusted that Helen still lived in this dump. The scent of sage and rabbit brush filled his nostrils. He jumped as a banded gecko scurried across his boots. Scowling, he kicked desert sand toward it. It blinked its eyes and ducked beneath the wheels of the trailer.

Full of apprehension, he climbed the wooden steps and tapped on the metal door. Seconds ticked by before muffled footsteps from inside grew louder. He jumped at the sharp snap of the latch springing free. The door flew open.

Travis cocked an eyebrow in surprise. He scarcely recognized the woman in the doorway. Ghastly yellow skin masked her face. A mosaic of red and blue skinny veins traveled along her nose. Her once lovely, thick, dark red hair had thinned and turned burnt silver. It hung in loose strands around her head. She glared at him through hollow eyes.

"Helen?" he asked. It's me, Travis."

A flicker of recognition flashed across her face. "Travis?" She staggered backward. "I … I can't believe it."

"Yeah, it's me."

Her icy glare drilled into him. Travis grew uncomfortable. No way could he let her have the upper hand like before. He forced a smile and wiped beads of sweat from his forehead. "Sure is hot out here."

She motioned for him to come in. The air reeked of stale booze mixed with cooking grease and cigarette smoke. Inside the sparsely furnished living room sat a small plaid sofa, chair, and TV set. Faded floral curtains dotted with dark brown stains hung from the dirty windows. The carpet below his feet lay threadbare and so old he couldn't distinguish its true color. A ceiling fan whirred, its blades wobbling dangerously above.

He took stock of the figure before him. Helen's thin body and bloated belly were all out of proportion. She looked as though someone had played a cruel joke and sewn her flesh together in mismatched pieces.

She scowled at him, arms folded across her shrunken breasts. "What are you doing here after all these years?"

Treading carefully, he gave her a broad grin, "Well, I was passing through and I—

"Passing through!" Her middle finger shot up, and she hissed. "Don't make me laugh. I haven't seen or heard anything from you in over fifteen years." Her voice cut like a whip across his thoughts.

"Now, Helen. I realize I'm the one in the wrong here. Can we talk calmly for a few minutes?" He crossed the room and sat on the sofa, relaxing into the cushion. "There's no reason we can't be friendly toward one another after all this time." He frowned, then leaned forward and away from the rough plaid fabric scratching through the back of his shirt.

"Friendly?" She narrowed her eyes. "Do you have any idea how you ruined my life? You walked out and left me here with a brat to raise all by myself." She planted her hands on her hips. "And then the little bitch pushed out one of her own."

He rose and moved in close. "I'm sure it wasn't easy on you." He rested his hand on her shoulder. "I'm glad to see you're doing okay."

She yanked her shoulder back. "All you ever cared about was yourself. I loved you, Travis. I would have done anything for you. Didn't you know that?"

Her voice wielded that savage edge he remembered so well.

"Sure," he agreed. "Face it, Helen. You and I weren't getting along so good anymore. Your drinking and mean spirit drove me from you."

"Do you think I'm stupid?" she said, her hands on her hips. "My drinking didn't drive you away. You wanted to leave. It's what started me drinking in the first place."

"Look, I don't want to argue. What's done is done." He pulled out his cigarettes, lit two, and held one out to her.

Defiant, she hesitated. "I can't believe you have the nerve to show up here."

"Come on, Helen. Don't be difficult."

She gave him a dirty look before taking the lit cigarette. Shuffling to the open kitchen, she swiped two glasses from the drain board and then smacked them down on the table.

Holding up a vodka bottle, she asked, "Drink?"

Travis shrugged. "Why not." Impatient, he puffed on his cigarette. This whole thing was taking too long. He couldn't wait to leave this miserable dump.

She handed him a glass, and they drained their vodka together.

Travis cleared his throat and set his glass on the table. "By the way, whatever happened to that sister of yours?"

Her scant eyebrows formed an arch. "Who, May? Why do you care about, May? You never liked her, and she for sure didn't like you."

"Just curious, I guess." Anxious to leave, he stubbed his cigarette out in the ashtray. There was no point in prolonging things. "Is she alive?"

Stiffening at the curt tone in his voice, she said, "How would I know? We stopped speaking years ago." She waved a dismissive hand at him.

Darting to the side, she attempted to slip past him, but he grabbed her arm. "I need to know where your sister is. We can do this the easy way, Helen, or the hard way. It's up to you." He took the lit cigarette from her and placed it in the ashtray.

She jerked back and tried to pull away. "Let go of me."

Travis held on, his fingers digging into the thin flesh on her upper arm. "All I need is your sister's last address." He squeezed tighter.

"Stop, you're hurting me." She whipped her arm in a circle, in an attempt to free herself. "What do you want with my sister?"

His jaw tightened, the familiar click escaping his lips. "I have to find Carrie. It's the one place she might go."

Helen's expression turned to one of shock. "Carrie? What does May have to do with Carrie?" Her lip trembled. "Does she know? I never told that little bitch anything."

"Never mind what I did or didn't tell her. You need to tell me where May lives or I swear to God, I'll make you sorry." He snatched her other arm and pushed her up against the wall.

She let out a howl. Her eyes drilled into him. "You're an animal. A no-good, rotten animal!" she screamed and railed against him. "You're worse than I ever thought."

He pressed his fingers into her flesh. "No more than you. You think I don't know how you used to beat on that girl?"

"And you're so much better than me?" she hissed. "Does Carrie know you helped me sell her precious boy to that no-good half-brother of yours?"

"You got no reason to complain, Helen. You gladly snagged your drug money out of the deal. It was a fair exchange between the two of you."

"Fair? That boy was probably worth triple what he paid me." She scanned his face. Struggling harder now, her body shook. "I did the right thing, selling her boy. Even though it landed me in jail, I got clean of them drugs, and he got a better life." She lifted her leg and kicked him in the shin. "You bastard. Get off of me!"

"You bitch!" he cried and slammed his body against hers. "The right thing," he scoffed. "You wouldn't know the right thing to do if you tripped over it. They should have locked you up for good, but none of your foolishness matters now because I'm gonna make it right, Helen. I'm gonna find Carrie." He pressed his fingers deeper, enjoying her pained expression.

"I still don't understand what you want with her."

"I took her with me after you sold the baby." He smiled with satisfaction at the surprised look on her face. "She's been with me all these years."

Helen's face curled into a tight sneer. "Oh, so she ran out on you, huh? How about that. My precious girl did herself a favor. You disgust me. You're nothing but scum! *Scum!*" She tried again in vain to free her arms. "Carrie should only know who you really are and what you've done. Now, let me go, Travis!"

"Enough, you obnoxious drunk. Now give me the address." He reached with one hand for a knife lying on the counter and held it up to her throat.

Terror in her eyes, she stopped struggling. "Okay, okay. Please don't hurt me. Like I said, I haven't talked to her in years. The last I know of she still lives in Pennsylvania in a town called Laurel. It's up in the mountains.

"You better be telling me the truth."

"I swear—Laurel is the last place she lived."

Travis stared into her eyes. In them swam all the hate, all the beatings, and harsh words Carrie had confided in him. In one swift movement, he brought the knife down and plunged it into her chest.

She cried out and drew in a sharp breath. Her chest heaved, and she labored to take in air. Hands flailing, she tried to reach for him.

Travis released his grip and watched her crumple to the floor. Blood seeped through the front of her blouse. Her half-dead eyes searched his face. "Why, Travis?" she gasped. Her breathing slowed and then stopped.

"That's for Carrie," he said.

He left the blade in her chest and wiped the handle. Turning away, he rinsed the glasses in the sink and dried them with a dish towel. He put the cigarette butts in his pocket and wiped the door handle with the same cloth on his way out.

Travis rolled out of Breezy Meadows, leaving the murdered Helen behind him. His new destination focused and fine-tuned. He needed to get to Laurel. He needed Carrie.

CHAPTER 21

NICK

B right rays of sunshine glared off the hood of the Mercedes forcing Nick to squint through his sunglasses. He chugged on a bottle of water and cursed the heat.

Parked a couple hundred feet from the entrance to Breezy Meadows, he waited for Travis to reappear. Surrounded by the beige tones of the desert sand, he longed for green trees and a stroll in Central Park in the crisp autumn air. If he got lucky, the trail would lead north away from this inferno.

Nick had abandoned his Hugo Boss suits several states ago for jeans and polo shirts. He never carried out his kills in a suit. They cost too much to end up spattered with blood if he stood close to his mark.

He eased out of the car and stretched just as a cloud of dust swirled up in front of his vehicle. A baseball bounced off the hood. In one quick movement, Nick caught the ball. He turned it over in his palm. The stitches were unraveling, and a piece of leather had gone missing from it. He slid his sunglasses down and peered over the top. Two scruffy young boys scampered toward him. He grinned at them and held up the ball.

"Looking for this?"

They stood silent and stared at him. The taller one wore a baseball glove on his hand. He whispered something in the little one's ear. Placing his hand on the smaller boy's shoulder, he gave him a gentle push. "Go on," he said.

The boy took a few cautious steps and held out his hand. His baggy pants dipped above his ankles, and his torn shirt appeared two sizes too large. Badly in need of a haircut, his dark hair hung well below his ears.

Nick removed his sunglasses and crouched to meet him eye to eye. He tossed the ball up and then palmed it. "You can come closer, I won't bite."

The younger boy turned his head looking for approval from the other boy. After an okay nod, he moved closer.

"Looks like this ball has been put to good use," Nick said. "I think it might be the only one you have?"

The boy nodded and pointed, a slight stutter tripped his tongue. "Y…yes, it belongs to m…m my brother."

"What's your name?" he asked.

"M…m Michael, b…b but they call m…m me MJ."

The name woke the pain sleeping inside Nick as he met the boy's eyes again.

"Well, MJ, it looks like you and your brother could use a new ball and maybe another mitt for you." He tossed the ball back to the boy, stood, and slid a hundred out of his wallet.

"Now, this is for you and your brother to buy a new ball and mitt, okay?"

Eyes wide in disbelief, the boy reached up his tiny hand and grabbed the money. "Th… thank you," he said.

"You're welcome, MJ. Make sure you use it for a ball and mitt."

The boy turned and ran toward his brother waving the hundred-dollar bill. Nick watched the two boys disappear into the entrance of the trailer park. He climbed back into the Mercedes and leaned against the soft leather seat.

"Michael," he whispered. Words failed to express how much he missed his brother. Michael had always steered him in the right direction. Never let him run the streets with the other bad boys in the neighborhood and taught him how to defend himself when the older kids tried to gang up on him. Those bullies earned his respect after that first beating Nick gave them. They never bothered him again. Michael was so proud of him for standing up, telling him he was the best little brother anybody could have.

The entire neighborhood knew the D'Angelo brothers. Raised right, they never disrespected their elders. His mother and father would never have tolerated it. But both were unaware of how much their boys were feared out on the streets.

They protected their younger sister, Marie. He smiled at the memory of his sister. So pretty, all the boys wanted to date her. He and Michael kept them at bay. They needed to ask them for permission to take her out on a date.

Nick's senior year of high school was turning out to be his best year—until Michael died. Losing Michael was like losing a limb. His brother's death ripped a hole in his family that nothing could ever fill.

Life had dealt him and Marie a cruel hand. Only Marie handled the loss better than he could. She never wavered in her resolve to push through her grief, but while Marie's bitterness lessened, his grew.

After Michael's brutal murder, Nick made it his mission to become a cop where he quickly climbed the ranks to detective. He wanted to put the criminals where they belonged, behind bars. As a cop, he wanted to try and make things right for his brother and their family.

But the eventual loss of his career delivered the final blow. His bitterness overtook him, a bitterness that allowed him to turn a blind eye each time he pulled the trigger as a hired killer.

Nick set his sunglasses on the dash. A dull ache formed behind his forehead. His past was edging closer. At the same time, he didn't want to think about the future. Restlessness overtook him, but he needed to stay focused, not allow his thoughts to get in the way of his kill.

He picked up his sunglasses and frowned as his eyes locked on Travis leaving the trailer park. Thankful he hadn't stayed too long, he pulled out and followed at a discreet distance. A couple of hours later, the trail led north. If Nick believed in God, he'd have thanked him for small favors.

Finally, he could feel himself edging closer to finding the woman. Soon, this kill would be finished.

CHAPTER 22
CARRIE

Carrie flung the front door wide open to begin her morning stroll to work. Autumn in the mountains was in full swing. The brisk air exhilarated her, made her feel alive. She took a breath and let it fill her lungs. Pausing at the top of the steps, she smiled. Her aunt had dressed the front porch with clay pots full of Mums in rose-red, yellow and coral. A homemade wreath adorned with miniature gourds hung from the front door and on either side sat two hefty orange pumpkins. The surrounding trees proudly wore their vivid autumn colors.

She relished each day in Laurel. All those ordinary things so long out of reach had finally arrived. Last night, she'd plucked a book from among the many on the living room shelf and then snuggled underneath her comforter content to read without interruption. A small pleasure Travis had always made difficult for her.

Along Main Street, she delighted in the rich jewel tones of the falling leaves. She loved the feel of this small town and its people. One day, she hoped to have a place of her own here in Laurel.

Her job at the Palisades had given her the opportunity to view herself in a different light. The job and a steady paycheck helped to hide her lies. Still, she didn't dare get too comfortable around people. One slip of her tongue and her new life would end for sure. Buried in her aunt's yard lay proof of the crime she had committed.

With her nerves settling, for the most part, she slept undisturbed until the memory of her baby boy sprung to life. It never failed to surface when young mothers strolled into the diner with their little ones in tow. She'd make small talk as she set up a highchair or booster seat, but inside, she longed for her son.

She reached the front steps of the diner. Joann called from across the parking lot.

"Hey, girlie!" Red curls piled high, her cheeks flushed from the cool air, she strolled toward Carrie. "How are you this morning?"

Grinning, she replied, "Just fine."

Inside, the night shift rolled silverware, stacked jelly, and sugar packets, and refilled ketchup and mustard bottles. Early bird customers sat scattered at the counter and in booths drinking coffee and waiting for their breakfast. Carrie and Joann moved through the swinging kitchen doors arm in arm. They punched their time sheets and then hung up their coats.

Joe, the short order cook, flipped pancakes on the large commercial stove. The aroma of fresh batter and bacon hung in the air.

"Good morning, ladies," Joe called out.

"Good morning!" They both shouted in unison.

Stocky, in his mid-forties, with dark hair and a broad face, he liked to tease Carrie. He called her a heartbreaker when she refused to go out on a date with him, but Joe never overstepped his bounds. She appreciated it and the way he always took things in stride. Joe never griped if an order was sent back to the kitchen.

Pete, the busboy, whirled through the kitchen doors, a pan full of dirty dishes in his hands. The doors swung back and forth and then slapped shut behind him. Tall, and bone thin, with messy blond hair the color of apple cider, he loved telling silly jokes.

He nodded in their direction. "Hey Carrie, why are televisions attracted to people?"

She spun around, hands on her hips. She smirked and said, "I give up, Pete. Why are televisions attracted to people?"

"Because they turn them on." Pete chuckled, then got busy rinsing dishes and loading the dishwasher. "Get it, Carrie?"

Joe groaned. "How many more of your stupid jokes do I have to listen to today?"

"It wasn't a joke, Joe," Pete said. "It's a riddle. There is a difference."

"Joke, riddle, whatever it is, I don't care. It sounded stupid."

Pete grinned. "That's the whole point. Riddles are supposed to be silly and stupid. Right Carrie?"

"Oh, no," Carrie said. "You're not putting me in the middle of this, Pete. I have work to do. You two battle it out." She tied her apron, stuffed it with mints and straws, and pushed the swinging doors open. She ran the counter and register today while Joann and one of the other girls worked the floor.

Dressed in dark blue coveralls and a navy baseball cap, Byron Johnson slid onto a stool. The town's one mechanic, he arrived most mornings and ordered breakfast. The word around town was when you had car trouble, you took it to Byron. Also known around town, Byron had developed a crush on her.

Carrie handed him a menu. "Hey, Byron. What can I get you today?"

"Good morning, Carrie. Something sure smells good." He fingered the menu but his eyes focused on her.

She grinned. "Probably Joe's pancakes. They're always a good choice."

"Okay, pancakes it is and a side of bacon. No butter, please. The doctor has me watching my diet." He winked. "We won't tell him about the bacon."

"I can keep a secret if you can," she said. She tore the order from her pad, clipped the chit on the carousel, and called through the pick-up window. "One dry stack and a side of pigs!"

Carrie set a cup and saucer in front of Byron then placed a napkin and spoon beside it. "Got a fresh pot brewing, Byron. It will be ready in a minute."

He leaned in toward the counter. "Hey, my brother's coming for a visit soon. Driving up from Texas."

"How nice," she quipped. Carrie lifted the fresh pot of coffee off the burner and began pouring him a cup.

"Pete tells me you used to live in Texas while you were married. What part of Texas?"

Her insides froze. She rummaged through her mind trying to remember if she'd told Pete anything about being married or living in Texas.

"Whoa!' Byron jumped up from his stool. Coffee flowed over the rim of the cup and raced across the counter toward him.

Carrie quickly righted the pot and removed the cup. "Oh, I'm so sorry. Hold on a minute." She turned and grabbed a towel and mopped up the spill.

Byron smiled. "No harm done."

After tossing the towel, she placed clean cutlery and napkins on the counter. She poured him a fresh cup and set it down.

"So, if you don't mind my asking," Byron said. "Whatever happened to that husband of yours?"

"I think you're mistaken. I've never been married."

His cheeks flushed a bright red. "Oh, I'm sorry. Pete said you were married and lived in Texas at one time."

She couldn't let on any further how much his question upset her. "I did live in Texas for a bit, just west of Austin. A tiny town called Sonora."

He rubbed the stubble on his chin. "Never heard of it."

"Like I said, it's quite small, a blip on a map. If you blink, you'll miss it. Don't listen to Pete. He has a habit of mixing stuff up sometimes."

Carrie pretended not to notice Byron's confused expression. She wasn't used to people asking so many damned questions. Apparently, she'd slipped with Pete. She eyed two new customers seated at the end of the counter. "Excuse me, Byron."

The rest of the morning flew by, but the uneasiness of her conversation with Byron stayed with her. She needed to think first before answering people's questions, or she might get tangled up in her own lies making people all the more curious. Having to explain about a husband no longer in the picture, could prove difficult. She needed to keep her story straight. Besides, she was never legally married in the first place.

Later, during a lull, she plucked a cigarette from her pack. "Pete! Taking a smoke break," she called out. "Holler if someone comes in." She motioned to Joann to join her.

They slipped out the back door, and Joann held out her lighter. "Boy, hon, you sure caught on fast. You're doing great, and the customers love you."

Carrie lit her cigarette, took a drag, and handed her the lighter. "Thanks. Most of the customers are really nice."

"They can't help themselves. Just look at you."

"What do you mean?"

"Sweetheart, don't you realize how gorgeous you are? There's a good-looking fella sitting in my station. He can't keep his eyes off you."

Carrie puffed on her cigarette and looked away. "I didn't notice. The counter's been pretty busy this morning." How men and sometimes women reacted to her failed to boost her ego. Travis used to tell her she was pretty. It meant nothing. Especially, when he beat her.

Joann folded her arms across her chest. "Hon, I meant that in a good way. Sure, you're more than pretty on the outside, but your heart is what makes you beautiful, too. I hope I haven't upset you."

"No, it's quite alright." She touched Joann lightly on her arm. "Thank you for the compliment." But inside Carrie's guilt rumbled to the surface. Beautiful heart. Not after what she'd done. Her head dropped, and she rubbed her ring finger. An old habit she hadn't grown out of even though she no longer wore Travis's ring. The white line where it used to rest had faded.

She examined her hands, her palms were rougher now from honest work, but these same hands had killed two people. It was her truth, a truth hard to hide from herself, no matter how many lies she told to replace it. Her vision blurred, and she swiped at her eyes.

"Well, anyway, that guy sure ain't from around here," Joann continued. "Not very talkative either. The one bit of information I could pry out of him was what he wanted to eat. Take a look. Nice eye candy that one."

"Honey, are you alright?" Joann moved closer and took her hand. "Listen, you know you can tell me anything. I'd never judge."

Afraid to lose her friendship, she'd managed to dodge the questions Joann asked about her past. "I'm okay," she said. "There are certain things I'm not ready to talk about. I hope that it won't affect our friendship."

Joann nodded. "Of course not. Whenever you're ready to talk, I'll be here to listen." She jerked her thumb toward the door. "We better hurry. Lord knows, what the heck Pete's up to."

They laughed in unison at the image of Pete running the diner. They stubbed their cigarettes out and went inside.

Joann nodded in the direction of a man sitting in her station. Carrie turned to take a look. Their eyes met, and they both looked away at the same time. He certainly was handsome, but a man was the furthest thing from her mind.

She finished ringing up a customer as he approached the register. His broad shoulders and easy swagger stirred something inside her. Carrie brushed it aside.

"How was everything?' She caught a glimpse of his green eyes and found he was even more handsome close-up.

"Fine, Carrie." He dipped his head to fall within her line of site. "The food's not bad for a diner," he said smiling.

Her cheeks heated as she handed him his change. "Glad you enjoyed it. I hope you'll come back and see us again."

"I might," he answered and winked.

She ignored the funny feeling creeping across the pit of her stomach as she watched him leave and concentrated on helping another customer.

The rest of the day sped by. During the lunch rush, Pete cut himself on a broken glass, leaving Joann and her clearing and rinsing the dishes piling up in the kitchen. Carrie was more than ready for her shift to end. She finished closing her register and punched out. Calling out goodnight to Joe she followed Pete out the rear door.

"Pete, we need to talk."

Pete stopped in midstride and turned. A muscle twitched above his lip. "Oh, no. Whatever I did, I'm sorry."

"Look, Pete, a customer repeated some things to me I might have said in confidence. They said you gave them the information."

Pete's cheeks flushed red. "Like what?"

"That I was married." She pointed her finger at him. "I never told you anything of the sort."

Pete ran a hand through his scraggly hair and fished out his cigarettes. "I could swear Rick told me you were married and lived in Texas at one time."

Her insides tightened, and she fingered the collar of her blouse. She remembered now. During her interview with Rick, she had mentioned a husband. "But why would you repeat that to one of our customers?"

"I'm sorry, Carrie. I guess I wasn't thinking." He pulled a cigarette from his pack, lit it, and held it out to her. "Peace offering?"

His sad expression eased her irritation. She couldn't stay mad at him knowing she had told Rick precisely what Pete repeated to Byron. "I'll skip on the cigarette, Pete. Please remember I like to keep my personal business private."

Pete's shoulders slumped. He shuffled uneasily on his feet. "I know. I suck at keeping secrets."

She gave him a pat on his shoulder. "It's okay. All is forgiven."

"There you are." Joann stepped out the door. "I was waiting out front. Ready?" She placed her arm around Carrie's shoulders then glanced at Pete. "Pete, are you flirting with my friend? She's not interested, sweetie. You have to grow some peach fuzz first." She winked, a grin spreading across her face.

"Walking my way?" Carrie asked, joking around, wanting to forget about her talk with Pete.

"You lead, and I'll follow, Miss Beautiful."

Carrie cringed and recalled the day her mother caught her staring into a mirror. She had ripped it from the wall, smashing it to pieces, telling her beauty would never get her far in life. Ultimately, she came to believe her mother.

With Travis, her beauty became a possession. He used her beauty against her as a weapon, always accusing her of flirting with other men. In truth, she'd used her beauty to try and free herself. It taught her under the right circumstances, she might be able to escape, like at the truck stop. In the end, Travis always caught up with her, and she'd pay the price, time and time again.

Joann waved her hand in front of Carrie's face. "Hey, you, ready to blow this joint?"

She forced a smile. "Sure thing, I'm more than ready." She gave Pete a quick hug. "See ya later, Pete."

"No hard feelings?" Pete asked.

She shook her head and smiled. "None."

Joann raised her eyebrows.

"Don't ask," Pete said. He turned and sauntered away.

The two women strolled toward the front of the building. Joann opened her purse and frowned. "Damn, I forgot my cigarettes. I'll be right back."

"Meet you out front," Carrie called after her. She took out her own pack, slid one out, and placed it between her lips. Pulling out her lighter, she glanced at the passing traffic on Main Street. Her breath caught, and the cigarette fell from her hand to the ground unlit.

She ducked, scurrying sideways against the wall of the diner, her eyes planted on the man behind the wheel of a black car traveling slowly down Main Street. He reminded her of Travis and even had his peculiar way of driving, leaning against the door, his free arm thrown over the top of the seat. She pressed her body against the cement wall. Her legs trembled, almost crumbling beneath her. She failed to notice Joann approach.

"Sorry, I gave a cigarette to Joe earlier and left the pack on the counter in the kitchen…" Joann dropped her purse and put both hands on Carrie's shoulders. "Are you alright, hon? Your whole body is shaking. Come on, sit for a minute." She eased Carrie down into a sitting position.

"I'll go get help."

"Joann, please, no." she pleaded. "I'm okay. I felt a little faint, that's all. I haven't eaten much today."

Joann squatted in front of her. "Can I get you something? Tell me what I can do, hon. You're so pale. You look like something gave you an awful fright."

"No, I'm starting to feel a little better." With Joann's help, she managed to rise to her feet. Her legs wobbled a bit, and her insides refused to calm.

"Let's get you home to May's," Joann said.

They walked up Main Street together. They reached May's house, and she thanked Joann and reassured her she was okay.

Slipping inside, she closed the door behind her and locked it. The aroma of chicken broth and fresh vegetables wafted through the house. Dishes rattled in the kitchen, and she found her aunt setting the table while a steaming pot of homemade soup bubbled on the stove.

May looked up. "Hey, darling, I hope you're in the mood for some chicken noodle soup. The perfect thing on a cool autumn night."

"It smells delicious," Carrie said. "I'm going to go and get out of this uniform."

Upstairs, she shed her clothes and put on a sweatshirt and jeans. All the muscles in her body were wound tight, her nerves on edge. She thought about the car again. This person might have resembled Travis, played a trick on her mind. She hadn't gotten a good look at the man behind the wheel of the car. Maybe he just shared Travis's mannerisms.

She washed her hands, catching her reflection in the mirror. She tried to reassure herself. "Travis can't hurt you anymore. He's dead." Her nerves began to settle. Now, the whole thing appeared silly to her. Of course, Travis was dead. She killed him.

Downstairs, she crept up to the front window. Pulling the lace curtain aside, she peaked out. Dusk settled in while, one by one, the street lamps lit in unison. A black and white cat scampered across the road. A red automobile zipped past, its horn wailing at the cat. Startled, she drew away from the window. Her pulse raced again.

"No need to panic. It's just your guilt conjuring up ghosts," she whispered.

"Carrie, supper is ready," May called out.

A plate with slices of fresh baked crusty bread sat on the table. May ladled hot soup into two oversized white porcelain bowls. She placed them down and smiled. "Nice and hot."

Carrie managed a sparse grin and settled into her chair without saying a word.

"Cat got your tongue?"

"Oh, sorry. Thanks. It looks delicious." She ate her soup while May chatted away. Carrie tried her best to smile and respond.

"Lord that Jenny is a hoot sometimes. It takes a heap of patience to deal with her. Thank the Lord, I'm a patient woman. Anything new at the Palisades?"

"No, just the usual," she replied, hardly able to stand the sound of her aunt's voice. Each word seemed amplified. The whirring in her mind refused to calm itself. "Mostly the regular customers," she said. "Once in a while, someone from out of town passes through."

"Have you managed to learn the routine?"

"Little by little. Joann's a tremendous help, and the people are so nice to me. I like working there. I hope I pass probation."

"Why, of course, you will. I'm sure they're happy to have you." She reached out and squeezed Carrie's hand. "Are you okay, dear? You're awfully quiet tonight?"

Carrie gave her a weak smile. "I'm a little tired."

They continued light conversation, with her aunt doing most of the talking. She finished up her chat about Jenny Hinson and moved on to Will Medlow and his work around the house.

"I think it might be nice to create a garden pond for the wildlife in the corner of the yard near those tall pines. Maybe Will can dig one for us. What do you think, Carrie? The wildlife will have a safe haven to come and drink, and we get to watch them from the kitchen window."

"What?" Carrie asked. Her head throbbed. That's all she needed. Thoughts of Will digging and finding the briefcase swirled in her head.

"I said, I thought Will might dig a small pond in the yard."

"Maybe it's not such a good idea right now, the grounds' pretty hard this time of year."

May sighed. "I guess you're right. Spring would be a better time."

Carrie rose to clear the table. The telephone rang, startling them both.

"Who could that be?" May said. "No one calls me this late."

She picked up the receiver from the wireless phone on the counter. "Hello. Yes, this is she. Yes, I know her."

Carrie stood still and watched as the color drained from her aunt's face.

"What did you say, Detective?" May asked, her voice a tight shrill. "Murder!

The dishes slipped out of Carrie's hands and splintered across the floor. Startled, May looked in her direction.

Carrie held her breath. She couldn't move. Murder. Was this it? Had the police found out? Every nerve in her body wound tighter.

May continued her phone conversation, without taking her eyes off Carrie. "I don't understand, Detective. How? How is this possible? Oh, my God, I can't believe it. Yes, Detective. No, I haven't spoken to her in many years. Yes, of course. Thank you."

May hung up, and Carrie braced herself for the inevitable. "Aunt May, what is it?" she asked.

May's knees buckled, and she grabbed the counter. Carrie ran over and helped her to a chair. Her shoulders slumped, and she said, "Carrie, you better sit down too."

She eased into a chair opposite her aunt. May's whole body shook, making her own anxiety rise to a fever pitch. First, the incident with Pete, followed by the driver who held an uncanny, if not downright spooky, resemblance to Travis, and now what she feared most. Would her aunt hate her? Turn her in? Carrie prayed the detective wasn't calling looking for Travis's or Carlos's murderer, looking for her.

"Carrie—"

"Don't say it." She placed her head in her hands and slumped over in the chair. "I love you, Aunt May. I never meant…I don't, it's just that I—"

"Aww, darling, I love you, too," May said. "But I'm afraid I have some bad news. That was a detective calling from Arizona."

Carrie lifted her head. "Arizona?"

"Yes, dear. Your mother was found dead in her trailer."

"Dead?" She gripped the edge of the table with both hands. Her jaw went slack. She pressed a hand to her throat. Her aunt's words tore through her, traveling to the core of her soul.

"I'm afraid so. The detective said someone stabbed her to death. A neighbor called them when your mother didn't answer the door. They think she died several days ago. He said it's an ongoing investigation. They discovered one of the last letters I wrote her, still sealed, with my name and address on the return.

She reached for Carrie's hand. "Who would do such a thing? It's just awful. We need to go to Arizona."

"Arizona?" The thought of going to Breezy made Carrie's stomach clench as if gripped in a vise. Her pulse threaded. She broke out in a cold sweat.

"I'll make all the arrangements. We'll fly out together. After all, she is—was—my sister and I want to make sure she has a proper burial."

Without a word, Carrie bolted from the room and ran up the stairs. She closed the door and leaned against it in a futile attempt at keeping out all the bad memories. Her nostrils flared. She squeezed her eyes shut, as her mind and body relived the torment her mother had put her through. Her heart reared against her chest, and she gulped to take in air.

There was a soft tap on the door. "Carrie, honey, I know all this comes as a shock. Please let me in."

Defeated, she collapsed onto the bed. Nails digging into her palms, she attempted to come to grips with her mother's death. No way would she return to Breezy Meadows. And the time had come to tell her aunt why.

"It's okay. Come in," she said.

The door opened, and May came and sat next to her. "I'm so—"

"Stop," Carrie interrupted. "Please stop saying you're sorry because I'm not."

May's eyes widened. "What do you mean?"

"You've been so good to me since I came here to Laurel." Carrie shifted and faced her.

"Of course," May said. "You're family. How else would I be?"

"You deserve to know the truth about my mother."

Confusion settled on May's face. "I don't understand."

"The truth is my mother never loved me."

May frowned. "How could you say such a thing? Of course, she did. Every mother loves her child."

She didn't want to hurt her aunt, but she continued. "What mother who loves her child beats them so hard they have black and blue marks on their body? Slaps them with such force across the face that it knocks their tooth out."

May reeled back in horror. "What are you saying? She—she did those things to you?"

"Yes, and more," Carrie said. "When I started school, she'd hit me where the bruises wouldn't show. She wanted to make sure no one saw any marks on me. And that beautiful bicycle you gave me was never left out in the rain. After you left, she took a hammer to it and smashed it to pieces."

May's shoulders drooped. "Oh, my God! Carrie, why didn't you ever tell me?"

"I couldn't. She threatened me."

"I'm so sorry I failed you. I should have known something was wrong." Tears slid down her cheeks, and she shook her head in disbelief.

Carrie reached over and took hold of her aunt's hands. "You couldn't have known. No one did. This is why I haven't told you. I don't want you blaming yourself for any of it. The visits from you were so meaningful. Those memories are so special. I never forgot your kindness toward me."

The lines around May's eyes appeared deeper now. "Tell me. Did it stop? Did the beatings stop?"

"One night, she came at me, and I fought her. I didn't win, but I think it made her wary of me. The beatings became far and few between, but her drinking got worse. Only her precious Vodka and drugs mattered. I was glad to leave her. Leave Breezy."

"Drugs?" May's face drew into a hard line. "I thought—"

"No, drugs, too."

Carrie let go of May's hands and raked her fingers through her scalp, tugging hard at her hair with a need to feel something, anything, besides this emotional pain surging inside of her. Keeping the rest from her aunt served no purpose. Unable to look at May, she directed her focus on the braided rug. "I left when I turned sixteen."

"Sixteen? Carrie, how could you take care of yourself at that age?"

"I wasn't alone. I met someone before that and I ended up pregnant. He promised to help me." Her eyes misted over. "He never kept his promise." She met May's eyes. "I loved my little boy more than anything. I wouldn't treat a child of my own the way she treated me. I swear."

"Of course, you wouldn't, dear. I know you wouldn't hurt anyone, let alone a child." May wiped the remainder of her tears with her apron. She studied Carrie's face. "What happened to the baby? You had a boy?"

Her insides knotted, and a wave of nausea swept over her. "Yes, I named him Bobby. My mother, that monster, sold him for drug money."

Aunt May covered her face with her hands and sobbed.

Carrie rose from the bed, wandered over to the window, and peered out into the darkness. "The police never found him, and she was sentenced to ten years in prison. I guess she ended up at Breezy after her release from jail."

May came and stood beside her. She placed her hand on Carrie's shoulder. "I hardly know what to say."

"I wonder about him all the time," Carrie said. "Where he is, what he's doing? Does he have a good life? I want to know he's okay." She gripped the windowpane, touched her forehead to the cold glass, and wept.

"Oh, sweetheart, I'm sure he's in a home with nice people. Most people desperate for a child can't have children of their own. They want a child to love and care for. Under all those dire circumstances, you couldn't have continued to raise him yourself."

"I swear I would have found a way, Aunt May. I would have done anything to keep him with me." She stumbled to the bed and reached underneath for her suitcase. The familiar blue blanket gripped in her hands, she showed it to May.

"This is the only thing I have of his." She clutched it to her chest and dropped down onto the floral comforter, her long black hair splayed out across the pillow. Her body heaved, and her tears fell hard and fast.

May reached out with a trembling hand and stroked her hair. "I wish I knew how to make things better for you."

Carrie turned to face her, the blanket still near. She propped her hand on the side of her head, while she brushed at her tears with the other. "I'm afraid nothing will make losing him better."

May hesitated and then said. "What about the baby's father?"

"He eventually showed up, and I left with him. There was no reason for me to stay in Breezy all alone. I hated the sight of that place."

"How long did you stay together?"

"Too long. He started to mistreat me. I was afraid one day he'd kill me." She started to cry again.

"Ok, we won't talk about him," May soothed. "That's your past, and it's over and done. Only you do understand I must go to Arizona and take care of things. If you don't want to go, it's okay. But I'm worried you won't have closure."

Carrie's bitterness overwhelmed her. She looked directly at May and said, "When it comes to my mother, I had closure a long time ago. Arizona would open up old wounds."

"It's settled then. You'll stay here in Laurel. I'm going to go downstairs and finish cleaning up. You rest."

After May left, she put the blanket away and sat on the edge of the bed. She hadn't told the whole story, but for now, it was enough. As for her mother's death, she couldn't allow herself to grieve. If she did, she would shatter into a million pieces just like her aunt's dishes. Her mother never loved her. She had chosen her addiction over her child.

Her mind drifted again to the scene outside the diner. Travis couldn't have survived the shooting. Not the way she left him. She wouldn't let what she thought she'd seen ruin everything.

In Laurel, she had found an aunt who loved her and the beginnings of a new friendship. The simple life she once dreamed of was now within her reach. Her safety and sanity lay here in this mountain town, and she wasn't going to let anything convince her otherwise.

CHAPTER 23

NICK

Nick breezed into Laurel right behind Travis. His gut told him he was close to ending this kill. After Travis checked into a small motel right outside Laurel, Nick drove to the nearest real estate office. He wanted a rental outside of Laurel, up the mountain where he could take care of business without interruptions.

"I need a nice quiet place to get some rest and enjoy nature," Nick told the agent.

They drove to a small, furnished cabin, surrounded by ten acres of woods about seven miles outside of town. He signed a two-week lease, and after the agent left, he surveyed the woods around the property and found it secluded enough for what he needed to do.

He left the cabin and drove to Laurel. On Main Street, he purchased bottled water, coffee, creamer, sugar, paper goods, and two bags of ice. Next, he stopped at a hardware store where he bought a large roll of 20-MIL plastic, duct tape, and a small cooler. He tossed everything into the trunk of his car beside an ax and a handsaw.

He unzipped a small black leather case. Inside were assorted pairs of handcuffs, syringes, and gloves. A cooler held vials of morphine and sodium pentothal. Working for Ricardo had taught him to keep certain things handy.

He drove up to the cabin and deposited the roll of plastic, the ax, and handsaw inside one of the bedroom closets, put the groceries away and the ice in the freezer.

Nick unpacked his suitcase, hanging several pairs of jeans, and four polo shirts in the small closet. Not knowing where he might end up, he always kept two long sleeve pullovers, a light jacket, and one heavy jacket with him.

Folding the pullovers, he placed them in a dresser drawer. He laid a pair of hiking boots on the closet floor beside a pair of sneakers. He liked to keep things in order. Messy surroundings led to a messy job. And messy didn't apply to him.

It was still early afternoon, so he decided to head to town, grab something to eat, and have another look around. He grabbed his 9 mm and checked the magazine. He flipped open the glove compartment, attached the silencer, and set it inside.

Nick slid the window down and inhaled the fresh air. The tension drained from his body. It wasn't New York, but it sure beat Florida. Autumn remained his favorite time of year. The mountains elated him. Visions of bland desert sand and the feel of the hot sun faded as he eyed the trees, their leaves filled with a tapestry of colors.

He eased into the diner parking lot and, within minutes, settled into a booth. A tall, smiling redhead took his order of roast beef and mash potatoes. She tried to make small talk, but Nick knew the less said, the better. He would keep to himself in case anything should go wrong. He didn't want this waitress to be his downfall.

A few moments later, she placed his order on the table. "Can I get you anything else?"

Nick glanced up. "No, thanks. This is fine."

Ready to take his first mouthful of food he picked up his fork. His hand stopped in midair. She came through the swinging doors of the kitchen. He almost dropped the fork from his hand. The black and white photo didn't do her justice. In person, she was stunning.

Her long dark hair pulled into a ponytail showed off her high cheekbones. She tilted her head to the side and laughed at something a male customer sitting at the counter said. Her eyes bordered on astonishing, so blue, they teetered on the edge of violet.

He witnessed the same woman, who pumped a bullet into Carlos and tried to murder her partner, carry on a casual conversation in a local diner. It all seemed surreal.

Gorgeous women were never a distraction for him. Once he got familiar with them, their looks proved to be superficial, without substance, but this woman intrigued him. And he had proof of her substance.

His curiosity started to get the better of him. He wondered what made her hook up with this Travis Montgomery. Was money the driving force or did other things factor into what she did? He sensed himself moving down a precarious path. He never cared about his kills. Never gave them a second thought.

Nick tried not to stare as she refilled the man's coffee cup. Something told him she was different, the kind of woman who brought your feelings to the surface. The ones you wanted to keep hidden. The ones you were afraid to feel. If you weren't careful, she'd make you lose control. With so much at stake, he couldn't afford to lose control.

For a second, his eyes met hers. Other than that brief moment, she didn't seem to notice him at all. Nick didn't mind. Keeping a safe distance remained a good thing in his line of work. He looked down at his plate and forced himself to finish eating.

She stood behind the register when he paid the bill. Standing so close to her unnerved him. Her full lips caught his attention, and he was surprised to find other than a soft rose-colored lipstick, she didn't have a stitch of makeup on. Not many women could pull that off and still look good. He glanced at her nametag.

"How was everything?" she asked, reaching for the check.

"Fine, Carrie. The food's not bad for a diner."

He handed her cash. Her lips curved up into a smile, and he noticed a small crease dance across the corner of her mouth.

"Glad you enjoyed it. I hope you'll pay us a visit again soon."

He gave her a quick wink. "I might."

Nick stepped away and turned for one last look as she disappeared through the doors to the kitchen. On his way out, he observed the shift change as two new waitresses arrived. He sat in his car and waited for her to appear. He'd take this opportunity to follow her and find out where she lived.

He watched Carrie come around the building with Joann. Halfway to the front, they stopped. Joann said something, turned and walked toward the rear of the building. Carrie continued on, pulled out a cigarette, and then glanced at the passing traffic. He followed her gaze. Travis Montgomery cruised along Main Street, slowing as he passed. Nick looked back at Carrie. The color drained from her face. She slumped against the building and almost slid to the ground.

What were the odds? Nick mused. She had just seen a ghost. He could imagine how she thought she left this guy for dead and now he turns up here, alive and well.

But did she believe what she saw? He surmised one of two scenarios would play out. Carrie would either take the money and run again or stay and refuse to accept seeing Travis.

Nick watched Joann help her to her feet and guide her up the street. He cruised out of the lot and followed at a discreet distance. The two women turned down a side street, and Nick pulled over. After Joann left, Carrie stepped through the front gate of a white house with green shutters.

Nick rode past making a mental note of the house number and parked further up the block. A few hours later, with no sign of her splitting town, Nick sped over to Travis's motel to check on him. He'd take the chance that Carrie would remain in Laurel.

Travis's car sat in the motel parking lot. He would wait to see what Mr. Montgomery had up his sleeve next. Having them in the same town made his job easier.

It wasn't long before Travis emerged, and Nick followed him into Laurel. He watched Travis cruise into the diner parking lot. Either Travis knew she worked there, or he'd get lucky and discover she did.

Either way, it spelled trouble for her. Nick decided the sensible thing would be to grab him first, then deal with her. He'd figure out for sure who had the money and finish the job.

CHAPTER 24
TRAVIS

Travis fought to stay awake as he drove into Laurel. Total exhaustion set in. His muscles ached from the long drive. He checked into a motel outside of town and crashed.

By the time he woke, an array of orange and vivid pinks washed the sky on either side of the setting sun, and the air turned brisk. He threw on his jacket and tried to shake off the chill. Hungry, he climbed into his car and headed for the main drag. He cruised past a couple of restaurants before he settled on a local diner.

Darkness had descended when he nosed into the diner parking lot. A sliver of pale moon, along with a spattering of stars planted themselves across an ebony sky. The crisp mountain air skimmed the back of his neck. He righted his collar and zipped his thin jacket.

Inside, the diner was relatively empty except for a few couples in booths and another customer at the far end of the counter. The place felt familiar, like one of many dozens of diners he and Carrie visited over the years.

Rows of generic white coffee mugs stood at attention on a shelf by the far wall. Glass domes holding various pies and cakes with slices missing lined the counter. The tangy scent of cooking grease graced the air.

Travis parked himself on one of the red swivel stools, removed his jacket, and hung it on the seat next to him. He rested his palms on the smooth countertop and glanced around.

A young, trim waitress approached him. Her short brown hair brushed the sides of each cheek, and her lips, painted a bright red, revealed a set of perfect white teeth when she smiled.

"Hi, there. What can I get you?" Brown eyes, the color of bittersweet chocolate, sized him up.

Travis dabbed at some spilled sugar granules, then picked up a laminated menu. He gave her a quick wink and glanced at her name tag. "Well, Elizabeth, maybe you could tell me what might satisfy a hungry man on a chilly autumn night like this?'

"Our special tonight is an eight-ounce ribeye with mashed potatoes. It's very good."

He rubbed his chin as if deep in thought. "Steak and mashed potatoes sound about right."

"How would you like that cooked, sir?"

"Make it well done, please, Elizabeth. I can't stand the sight of blood." He chuckled to himself at the irony of his words.

She jotted down his order, walked to the pass-through window, her hips swaying and called out, "Saddle it well, in a fog." She strolled back to the counter. "Anything to drink?"

"Coffee, black, darling. Thanks." He studied her face while she poured the coffee and placed it in front of him. Early twenties, he guessed. "If you don't mind my asking, are you from Laurel?"

She tilted her head and smiled. "Born and raised."

"Are all the gals around here as pretty as you?"

Her cheeks flushed pale rose, and she giggled. "I guess so. I mean…." She tucked a strand of her hair behind her ear.

Travis needed information, and he knew how to get it from this girl. He began reeling her in. "I'm here on a visit. Seems not much has changed since I was here last."

She studied his face. "Who are you visiting?"

He swiped his palms along the front of his jeans. "It's sort of a surprise. Someone I haven't seen in twenty years. I'm not even sure she still lives in Laurel."

Elizabeth perked up. "If you don't mind telling me her name, I might know her."

"Why, that's so nice of you. It's my sister, you see. We had a falling out many years ago."

She touched her hand to her heart. "Oh, brothers and sisters should always be close."

"Do you have any brothers or sisters?"

Her face brightened. "Yes, two sisters, and two brothers."

"Wow, what a handful. You all get along?"

"Mostly," Elizabeth admitted. "I couldn't dream of not seeing them for twenty years."

"Then you can imagine how I feel after all this time." He inspected the cuff of his shirt and pretended to pick lint from his sleeve. "I want to make things right between us. It'd be awful if something happened and we never spoke again."

"What's your sister's name?"

"It's May, May Overton.

Elizabeth leaned toward him. The corner of her mouth quirked up. "I know May. Most everyone around here knows her."

Relieved, Travis said, "I worried she might have moved away."

"I've known her all my life. She's a sweet lady, and I'm sure she'll be thrilled to see you after all these years. Her house is right off of Main. Sixteen Birch Street. It's the white house with green shutters."

"That's just how I remember it," Travis said. "A white house with green shutters." He gave her a lopsided grin. "Listen, my coming here is a surprise. I wouldn't want it to get out before I have a chance to see her."

"Sure thing. Most people love surprises," she said.

The cook shouted from behind the pass-through window and Elizabeth grabbed the hot plate and set it down in front of him.

"Looks great. Thanks." He devoured his food with gusto. He'd done it. May was alive and well and living in Laurel.

She leaned in again, hovering over the counter. "That means you must know her niece, Carrie. Ever since she came to town, she's been staying at May's place."

Travis's throat tightened around the piece of steak in his mouth. He tried to swallow. His throat closed and he choked, coughing uncontrollably. Grabbing a napkin, he spit the steak into it.

Alarmed, Elizabeth poured him a glass of water. "Here, quick, drink this." She blinked and chewed on her lower lip. "Are you okay? Should I get someone to help you?"

He shook his head and gulped the water. After clearing his throat, he said, "Thanks, sorry I scared you." Just the mention of Carrie's name had produced a physical reaction in him.

"That's okay. Sure you're all right?"

Travis smiled and shrugged his shoulders. "I'm fine. Eating too fast. I need to slow it down a bit." He rested both hands on the counter. "So, tell me, how well do you know Carrie?"

"Oh, Carrie's a sweetheart. Works the day shift with Joann, one of the other waitresses."

His chest burned, and a gnawing set in where the bullets had ripped through almost killing him. Yeah, she's a real sweetheart alright. He forced himself to remain calm and carry on the conversation.

"You said she works here?"

"Yes. Carrie started a little while ago. She caught on real quick." Elizabeth glanced at the other end of the counter. A customer eased onto one of the stools. "Excuse me a moment."

"Sure thing."

A sour taste clung to his mouth as he made an effort to finish his food. Defeated, he pushed his plate away. His jaw tightened. He found it hard to comprehend Carrie wielded such power over him. He signaled Elizabeth for the check.

Grinning, she said, "It's been a pleasure talking to you, Mister …''

"Overton. Let's just keep my being here quiet for now. I'd appreciate it if you didn't say anything to Carrie. I'm the uncle she never met, so I'd like to surprise her, too. I'm sure May would want to handle things in her own way. You understand, Elizabeth."

She smiled and fiddled with her hair again. "Oh, you don't have to worry about me. I understand. Your secret is safe."

"Great." Travis winked and handed her the money for his check. He added a nice tip. She was well worth the extra cash. "Thanks, again."

Outside, he climbed into his Honda and drove out onto Main Street. He reached Birch but didn't make the turn. If Carrie caught sight of him, she might run or might even do something stupid like trying to shoot him again.

Besides, he'd have to deal with that meddling aunt of hers. How he detested that woman. May had always stuck her nose in his and Helen's business. Since Carrie lived in her house, he considered her a threat, too.

He wondered about his two million. Carrie must have taken the job at the diner as a cover. She could never explain all that cash to May. Damn! That girl is pretty smart.

Disgusted by his reaction to hearing her name, he pounded his fist on the steering wheel. He executed a U-turn and drove toward the motel. His jaw ached, his face heated red-hot with rage.

He needed to think. The last thing he wanted was for Carrie to run from him. Having to forgive her for shooting him would prove difficult. And trying to convince her they could share a life together, even harder. And if she did agree, could he trust her?

Grabbing his cigarettes from the console, he lit one as he pulled up to the motel. His head throbbed, ready to explode. Carrie dared to start a new life here on her own. He'd put a stop to that.

Travis ambled toward his room, unlocked the door, and stuck the key card in his pocket. Something stung his neck, and he dropped his cigarette.

He swayed as his legs collapsed beneath him. The hazy image of a man towered above. He swung his arms at the fading figure.

Unable to hold on, his body gave way, his arms fell limp at his sides. Powerless, he drifted toward unconsciousness. Travis let go and slipped into the darkness around him.

CHAPTER 25

NICK

Nick secured Travis in one of the bedrooms. Unconscious since the shot of Pentothal and morphine, he was easy to transport and would sleep through the night. He found the combination of the two drugs worked well together. A doctor in Argentina had taught him mixtures and dosages on one of his many trips for Ricardo.

The next day, Nick stood in the bedroom doorway, sipping coffee from a large Styrofoam cup. It was almost noon, time to bring Mr. Montgomery around and have a little talk with him.

Travis lay on his side, handcuffs on his wrists and duct tape around his legs. Nick set his coffee on the nightstand and then pulled Travis up into a sitting position against the headboard.

"Ok, Mr. Montgomery, wake up." He slapped him hard across the face several times. "Come on now." He pulled a chair next to the bed and retrieved his cup.

Travis's eyelids fluttered, then flew open.

"What the hell—where am I?" He struggled, attempting to free himself.

"Don't waste your time, asshole. You're not going anywhere."

He stopped moving and directed his attention to Nick. "Who the hell are you?"

"Never mind who I am." Nick scowled at him. 'The important thing is why you're here."

"I have no idea," Travis said. "Do I know you?" He squinted, trying to focus as the drugs lost their effect.

"No, you don't. But I know you. And I know what you did."

Fully awake now, Travis glared at him. "I ain't got any idea what the hell you're talking about. This is some kind of mistake."

"Oh, it's a mistake all right," Nick said. A huge mistake and you made it." He pulled his chair closer. "You see, Mr. Montgomery, you made the mistake of killing two people and stealing a briefcase full of someone else's money."

Travis shook his head. "I didn't kill anyone, and I don't have a briefcase full of money."

"I stand corrected," Nick said. "You and your lady friend killed two people. Afterward, she shot you and ran off with the money. Am I about right?" He swallowed the last of his coffee. Let what he said sink in. "Or maybe, she shot you, panicked, and left. You could still have the money, and you want revenge."

Travis's face blanched as white as the sheet beneath him. "The whole thing was all her idea. She shot them both. I didn't shoot anybody. For Christ's sake, she shot me! She has the money."

Nick couldn't believe this creep. Without blinking an eye, he put all the blame on her, thinking he could save himself. He tried hard to restrain himself from putting a bullet in Travis's head. "Lying isn't going to save you," he said.

Travis grew silent. He stared at the far wall. "Believe me, she's dangerous, and I have the scars on my chest to prove it." He lowered his eyes to his chest. "Go on, look. Just look at what she did to me."

"I don't need to see anything, Mr. Montgomery. That's not quite the whole story. Shall I solve the mystery? It's like the old children's game of Clue." His tone hardened. He stood, dragged the chair away from the bed, and crushed the empty Styrofoam cup in his hands.

"First question. Where did the crime take place? Answer. In a warehouse parking lot. Next question, how? You shot two people to death. Third and last question, why? To steal a briefcase containing two million dollars." He picked up the syringe he had prepared earlier from the nightstand.

"What the hell are you doing?" Travis shifted his body and tried to squirm away.

"Making certain you don't try something stupid." He grabbed the shoulder of Travis's shirt and ripped open the seam exposing his skin and then stuck the needle into his arm.

"This will hold you for a while."

"Wait! You can't leave me like this. What's gonna happen to me?"

"For now, you'll go to sleep."

Travis mumbled a few more words before losing consciousness. Nick closed the bedroom door and grabbed his keys. Hungry, he headed for Laurel.

Later, inside the diner, he settled into a booth and studied the menu.

"Hi there. It's nice to see you again."

Her voice, low and warm, washed over him. He looked up and gave her a half-smile.

"It's nice to see you, too, Carrie."

Her ink black hair hung past her shoulders in a ponytail. Again, she wore a touch of lipstick and no other makeup. Long dark lashes glistened against the violet-blue of her eyes. Her crisp white blouse stood out against the pale rose of her cheeks. The short black skirt exposed her shapely legs.

"What will it be today?"

He ordered the pot roast special, but he didn't care what she brought him as long as he got another chance to look at her up close. He drew in a breath and reminded himself she was part of the job. It was important he stay in control.

She returned and set his plate down. "Will there be anything else?" she asked.

"No. Thanks." He detected a light floral scent. Within minutes, his appetite diminished and he pushed the plate away. At the sound of a commotion, he turned his head. Some goon in a rumpled business suit leaned on the register. He mumbled something and shook his finger at Carrie.

Nick hurried over. "Are you okay?" he asked.

"I'm fine," Carrie said. "Fred was just leaving. Isn't that right, Fred?"

Nick focused on the man. He smelled like a brewery.

"You heard the lady, Fred. I think it's time you left."

He glared up at Nick. "Listen, buddy, I ain't finished."

"Oh, you're finished all right." He gripped the man's arm, steered him outside, and planted him at the bottom of the steps.

Carrie stationed herself at the top of the diner steps. "Look, Fred, we both know you've had one too many. Go home and sleep it off," she admonished.

He hesitated and then swung wildly at Nick, losing his balance and falling onto the pavement.

Carrie bolted down the steps and held her hand out to Fred. "Come on, listen to him, Fred. I know you didn't mean to cause a scene." She helped him struggle to his feet.

He shook his fist at Nick and stumbled across the parking lot.

"I hope he's not driving," Nick said.

"No, his wife took his keys away a long time ago." They both burst out laughing and walked inside.

Nick slid into the booth and stared at his food again.

"Is something wrong with your order?" Carrie asked.

He glanced up. No, it's fine, thanks. Guess I'm not as hungry as I thought."

"I can put it in a to-go box for you."

"That would be great," he said.

She removed his plate and left the check. A few moments later, she returned with his food.

"Thank you for helping out with Fred, but it wasn't necessary. He's harmless. I've handled him before."

Nick grinned. "I'm sure you have." He paid the check and left. He was half-way to his car when she called out.

"Excuse me, sir. You forgot your food."

As she came toward him, Nick scanned every inch of her. Bewildered by his strong reaction to her and how it threw him off his game, he tried to get a handle on his next move.

She smiled, handed him his food, and turned to go.

"Hey, Carrie, wait a minute." He cleared his throat and adjusted his collar. He was turning into an utter fool.

"By the way, my name is Nick. I'd like to buy you a cup of coffee when you get off your shift."

Her expression looked doubtful. "Well, I...."

"Just coffee," he said, grinning. "I'd appreciate coffee and conversation. Unless I overstepped, but I didn't see a ring on your finger."

Her face relaxed. "Okay, Nick, but I prefer not to do it here. I don't want my co-workers reading anything into it."

"Well, there's a coffee house not far from here off the highway," he said.

"Yes, I'm familiar with the place. I get off at four. I'll meet you there at five."

"I could pick you up."

"No, let's meet there. I prefer to take my own car."

"Sure, no problem." He drank in the view from behind as she strutted across the lot. Her ponytail swayed from side to side in time with her hips. At the door, she gave a quick wave before disappearing inside.

A smile on his face, he drove toward the cabin to check on Travis. Halfway there, his cell phone rang. He glanced at the number and frowned. It was Ricardo.

"Hello, *compadre*. I was thinking how strange it is that you have not communicated with me." Ricardo's voice never lost its power, even over the phone.

Over the years, he had gained Ricardo's confidence, and in return, he counted on Nick's loyalty. Their relationship was one of mutual respect. Their reliance on one another had created a bond between the two men.

"I guess I owe you an update," Nick said.

"*Sí*. Have you made any progress?"

"This job has taken a little longer than usual. The trail led me up north."

A low chuckle drifted through the line. "North. I'm betting that you're happy."

"I'll be happy when I get the job done," Nick said. "I have the man, his name's Travis Montgomery. A small-time petty thief."

"And the woman?"

"I'm about to take care of her, too."

"Please keep me informed, Nick. I have no doubt I can rely on you."

Nick ended the call as he pulled up the gravel drive. He paused before getting out of the car. In an hour, he'd sit down and drink coffee with someone he planned to kill.

It was crucial he get his head on straight and fast. Focus on the facts. The facts were plain and simple. She had shot a man in cold blood and almost killed another. It proved she wasn't the person she portrayed to the outside world. She was a killer. Besides, if he didn't produce results soon, Ricardo would be very unhappy.

He retrieved his 9mm from the glove compartment and his black bag. Travis looked up at him, awake but drowsy. Nick removed a hunting knife out of the bag. As he approached, Travis's face filled with fear.

"Please mister, let me help you get the money. I can handle her. Where is she? Is she here?"

Nick slid the knife along the duct tape on Travis's legs, freeing them. "You have two minutes." He placed the barrel of the gun against the small of Travis's back. He steered him to the bathroom and stood by the door.

"Do your business. I can't afford to have you mess up my rental."

When Travis finished, he brought him to the bedroom, shoved him onto the bed, and bound his legs again.

"To answer your question asshole, she's not here but she will be soon, and I'll find out where the money is." He prepared another injection and increased the dosage to make sure Travis stayed out for a good while.

"Hey, that's not necessary, I ain't going anywhere." Travis squirmed in an attempt to move away.

"I know you're not." Nick grabbed him and then plunged the needle into his arm. He waited until Travis fell asleep and then changed into a dark grey, long sleeve polo shirt. He tucked his 9mm behind him underneath his shirt and threw on a light jacket. He checked his Rolex. Time for coffee with Carrie. Afterward, she wouldn't be returning to number Sixteen Birch Street.

CHAPTER 26

CARRIE

Carrie finished waiting on a customer then took a break. Lighting a cigarette, she plopped onto an empty crate by the kitchen door. Unease filtered through her, and she berated her naivety in agreeing to coffee with a total stranger. She wasn't ready for coffee with a man or anything with a man for that matter.

Since she started working at the diner, several guys had asked her out. Her response was always a flat no. She couldn't figure out what made Nick different.

"Why did I say yes?" she blurted out.

No, she couldn't do it. She'd tell him sorry and call it off. Besides, if this guy knew about her past, the last thing he'd do is ask her out for coffee.

She replayed his dark good looks and his easy tone. Letting another man into her life was the furthest thing from her mind. She needed time to figure out her future. After Travis, she'd never allow another man to control her. No thanks.

Taking a final drag on her cigarette, she stubbed it out and returned to her station. No need to mention the coffee date to Joann. It wasn't going to happen.

Her shift ended, and she begged off her usual walk home with Joann, telling her she needed to run some errands. She arrived home to an empty house. Earlier in the day, May had boarded a flight to Arizona to claim her mother's body. She didn't like her aunt going alone, but Breezy was off limits. Like Melbourne, Florida, it brought a ton of bad memories to mind.

She showered, dried her hair, and let it hang loose. Jeans and a heavy black turtleneck would do to call off a date. Out of habit, she applied fresh lipstick and decided against any makeup. The past few weeks, she'd worn little or none. She dabbed some perfume behind her ears and at the pulse points on her wrists. Slipping into her black ballet flats, she jumped in the car and drove in the direction of the coffee house.

Preferring silence as she drove, Carrie kept the radio off. She honed her mind on Nick, unable to shake her uneasiness. Even though he had helped take care of her situation with Fred, she shouldn't have said yes to having coffee with him.

Sliding the window down she gulped in the fresh air and attempted to quiet her mind. Minutes later, she sailed into the parking lot and parked amid several other cars. Upon entering, she inhaled the aroma of various coffees and freshly baked pastries.

Café tables and chairs were scattered throughout the room. A long counter ran across the rear and, above it, shelves with chrome espresso machines and bean grinders. The thick whir of a frothing machine erupted above soft music playing from various speakers placed strategically in the room. A few customers chatted at various tables. Others sat alone, their fingers tapping on cell phones. The rest stared at laptops and tablets.

She glanced around. With no sign of Nick, she seated herself at a small round table in the corner, her eye on the door.

Nick sauntered in a few minutes later. He grinned sheepishly. "Sorry, bad first impression, I guess."

"No worries," she said, smiling.

An awkward silence descended between them. Carrie glanced around the room.

"I'm sorry. I haven't been out lately—with anyone," she said. "I don't think I should have agreed to have coffee with you."

He clasped his hands together and rested them on the table. "Look, I don't normally make it a habit of asking out women I hardly know. My business keeps me on the road quite a bit. You're making a lonely traveler happy." An easy grin spread across his face. "One cup of coffee, okay?"

She studied him a moment and felt silly making such a fuss. One cup and she'd head home to Laurel. "I guess you're right."

They ordered their coffee, his black, and hers hazelnut with extra sweetener. A slight chill marched up her spine reminding her she had never sat this close to another man other than Travis. Determined not to let her thoughts spoil things, she refocused on the present. She cupped her hands around the steaming mug and took several sips. The hot liquid slid down her throat spreading its warmth through her.

She wondered what he was doing in Laurel. He didn't fit in against the backdrop of a small town. Planting a smile on her face, she said, "So, what brought you to Laurel?"

His face grew serious at her question. "I needed to take some time off. I wanted to get away and regroup, so to speak."

"Away from where?"

He took a swig before answering. "New York. New York City is home base."

She set her mug down and leaned a little closer. "I've always wanted to see New York. I haven't gone, yet, but I hope to."

"It's quite different from your little town," he said. It's a fast-paced, tough city."

"I just want to visit, not live there," she said and smirked. "You know, do the tourist thing."

He smiled. "I guess it gets pretty boring in the mountains after a while."

"Are you staying in town?" she asked.

"No, a little cabin. Several miles out. And you? How long have you lived in Laurel?"

"Not too long. I'm fairly new. I'm staying with my aunt. She's lived here most of her life."

"Where are you originally from?"

She fidgeted with the wooden stirrer, and said, "Arizona."

"This must be a real change," Nick said. "Weather-wise, I mean."

"Yes. I love it. The desert is too flat and too hot compared to the mountains."

"I won't argue with that. What's your favorite thing about the mountains?"

She paused, thinking. "All the trees, the colors of the leaves, the air. I'm looking forward to the first snowfall. I've never seen snow up close."

A sense of weightlessness engulfed her. She relaxed and admired the angles on his face, finding it hard not to be attracted to him.

He laughed. "I guess you have more than a few reasons why you like it so much. As for snow, some people hate it, although, it's pretty when it first falls."

Carrie rested her chin in both hands as he spoke about his work as a salesman. She examined his features and took notice of how his green eyes held tiny flecks of gold within them. His chiseled features underneath dark brows, the dimples etched on either side of his face appearing whenever he smiled added to his strong jawline and richly tanned skin. Like a magnet, he was pulling all sorts of feelings out of her, making her imagine doing things with him. She sipped her coffee and forced herself to concentrate.

"It must be tough traveling so much."

"Yeah, it is sometimes. I make a good living, so I guess it's worth it" He leaned back in the chair. "You mentioned Arizona. Where in Arizona?"

The question caught her off guard. "Phoenix." Her lies were piling up.

"Sure hot enough there," Nick said.

They were almost finished drinking their coffee when she said, "You're aware I'm single, any special person in your life?"

"Not anymore," he said. "Not for a long time."

He tugged at his collar and shifted uncomfortably in his chair. For some reason, her question bothered him. "I didn't mean to pry."

He gave a half-shrug and stood up. "It's all good. Ready to go?"

Immediately, she regretted asking him the last question. Disappointed he cut things short, she took one last sip and stood. "Sure. I'm ready if you are." She had enjoyed his company and the conversation.

Outside, black clouds gathered while twilight touched the fringes of the sky. Reluctantly, she headed for her car with Nick walking beside her. He opened and held her door while she slipped inside.

"Thanks, Carrie. I appreciate your spending time with me after being on your feet all day at the diner."

She grinned up at him. "Thanks for asking me. I enjoyed it."

Carrie headed toward Laurel eager to reach May's house. A mile up the road, her car bucked and then faltered. The engine light came on, and she cursed. Turning the wheel toward the side of the road, she placed the gear in park. She hit the ignition. The starter clicked, but the engine failed to turn over.

"Damn it," she hissed. She glanced in her rearview. Nick pulled up behind her, and she lowered the window.

"Car trouble?" he asked.

"Yeah. I hope it's nothing serious. I just bought the darned thing."

"Pop the hood." He had her try the ignition and hit the gas. "Sounds like a bad starter, but I'm no expert." He glanced up. "The sky's not looking too friendly, and it'll be dark soon. Let me give you a lift into town. You can send a tow truck out later."

Hesitant, she viewed the gathering clouds and then followed him to his car. Again, he held the door open for her. Such a small gesture on his part and one she wasn't used to experiencing. Travis had never opened doors for her.

He pulled out onto the main road, while she settled into the soft leather seat. Within a few minutes, she became alarmed when he made an abrupt turn up a side road. A dull rumbling inside told her something was wrong. She peered out the window. Icy panic crept in.

She looked over at Nick. "This isn't the way to town."

"It's okay. I want to show you something."

Her palms broke out in a sweat. The muscles in her stomach coiled together like springs.

"No, Nick. Take me back to Laurel."

Without a word, he killed the engine. The door locks thumped closed. He leaned toward her, his face inches from hers. The sharp scent of his cologne bit at her nostrils and she drew back.

"We're not going to Laurel, Carrie. Don't give me a reason to hurt you. The choice is yours."

She grabbed the door handle. "Please, please let me out."

Adrenaline rushed through her veins and soared to her head. She'd made a fatal mistake in trusting this man. Nick's plans for her included more than coffee.

A sudden realization hit her. "You—you did something to my car." she blurted out.

Nick's hand gripped her arm, pulling her toward him. Carrie tried to pry his fingers away, but he pressed harder. She looked down and gasped at the gun in his other hand. Her heart whirled faster as she held back a scream and pleaded with him.

"Please, what do you want from me? Where are we going?"

"Settle down, Carrie." He let go of her arm. "Now, I'm going to start the car. If you give me a hard time, I will have to hurt you." He motioned with the gun. "I don't want to, but I will."

She squeezed her eyes shut and held back her tears. It would be futile to try to escape. The look on his face told her he wouldn't hesitate to shoot her. She opened her eyes and nodded.

He started the car, and they drove a few more miles, her eyes glued to the gun. Gravel crunched beneath the wheels as they pulled up to a small log cabin surrounded by thick woods and shielded by shrubs below the windows. The door locks released, and he ordered her out of the car.

"Don't try to run because I'm not in the mood to go chasing you through the woods," Nick said.

She trembled, barely able to stand, her legs buckled beneath her. Clutching at the doorframe, she tried to steady herself. The wind gusted through the trees hitting her full force, knocking her to the ground. Her head dipped into a pile of leaves. The odor of pine needles and rich soil skimmed the air. Fear spiraled inside her. High above, thick, heady clouds advanced across the sky while thunder bellowed, the sound echoing through the surrounding woods.

She scrambled to her feet. Dead leaves clung to her hair. Frantic, she tore them away and scanned the area in the fading light. The isolation doubled her fear.

In three strides, he was by her side. His face set, stone cold, devoid of any lightness it held an hour ago at the coffee house. He took her by the arm and led her inside. The deadbolt slammed closed behind her, and she flinched.

Nick pointed to the sofa. "Sit, please." He tossed her purse beside her.

Retreating into the worn cushions, she surveyed her surroundings. Early evening shadows formed across the wood-paneled room. A dank odor wafted up from the pine floorboards. Cold ashes filled the fireplace. A small open kitchen with a table and chairs ran along the opposite wall.

With only one door leading out, if she dared to try, her chances for escape were not good. She shivered while her heart battered against her ribcage.

He produced a pair of handcuffs from an end table drawer and tossed them to her. His features turned dark.

"Put them on, Carrie."

"I don't understand. Why are you doing this to me?"

When he didn't answer, she picked up the cuffs and clamped them shut around her wrists. The cold metal sent sharp chills up her arms. She eyed him warily as he sank into an overstuffed armchair opposite the sofa.

"I'm sorry, Carrie. You brought all this on yourself. You can't kill someone and not expect consequences."

Her mouth went dry. Stunned, she sat silent and waited.

"Tell me why you took a man's life by shooting him square in the throat."

She stared at him and bit her bottom lip to keep it from trembling. Cold sweat clamped to her skin making her fear more palpable. She'd driven the memory of the bullet ripping Carlos's throat apart into the deep recesses of her mind. How could she make him believe she never wanted to kill Carlos?

"I— I can't explain it," she said. "I was a different person then. I'm not that person anymore."

Carrie wanted to believe the words she spoke were true. She tried to convince herself that she had become a better person, but she'd never be able to right the terrible things she did or make sense of them. In the end, all she had wanted was the chance to change her life.

"Is that your excuse for murdering someone in cold blood?" Nick spat.

Carrie turned her head away. If she hadn't defended Travis, there was a good chance she'd be dead, but telling Nick probably wouldn't save her life.

Tears of defeat filled her eyes and tumbled down her cheeks. She could never explain what she'd gone through with Travis. The fear inside driving her to do things she'd never choose to do on her own. The numerous threats, the abuse, the beatings, trapped like an animal with no hope of escape.

Carrie's vision blurred from the force of her tears. Her nostrils flared as indignation mixed with fear surged up inside her. She was furious at this stranger who painted so broad a picture of her. Things weren't that simple, at least not for her.

She looked into Nick's eyes. "I didn't have a choice."

"Come on, you can do better. At least, tell me something that makes sense," he snapped. "Was it greed? Two million dollars is a lot of money. Money makes people do things they wouldn't ordinarily do. Was it the money?"

Angry now, she said, "You don't know me or anything I've been through."

His brow arched. "Enlighten me then."

"Like I said, I didn't have a choice. The man I was with—

"Yeah," he interrupted. "Tell me about him."

Her head swam. Things were getting more and more complicated as she made an attempt to explain. She forced out the words. "He's dead now."

"Dead?"

"Yes. I shot him."

He leaned back, his eyebrows rose. "This is getting even more interesting. So, you shot him, too? Seems I got a genuine, cold-hearted killer here."

"No, you don't understand. I needed to get away from him before he killed me."

"So, it was self-defense?"

"Not exactly."

"You could have just left."

His statement almost made her laugh. "Leave him? Oh, I tried to leave him all right, too many times to count. I was scared to death of him, but I tried anyway." She shook her head. "There was no way he would ever let me go."

"There's always another way," he said vehemently.

"No, not with him," she said, her voice almost a whisper.

Her wrists strained against the cuffs, the metal digging into her skin. Not wanting to answer any more of his questions, she focused on the braided rug beneath her feet. Nick couldn't understand how she had suffered. He was going to kill her. Payback for the crimes she had committed.

"I think it comes down to the money," Nick said. "You decided you wanted it all for yourself so at the first opportunity you got rid of him, grabbed the money and left. Then again, I could be wrong. Maybe you left without the money. Working as a waitress when you have two million dollars doesn't add up to me."

She raised her head. "Yes, the money played into it, but not for the reasons you think. Whether you want to believe me or not."

The sound of pelting rain stung the roof. Lightning flared as a loud crack of thunder rocked the small cabin, making her jump. Heavy sheets of rain channeled along the panes of the curtainless windows.

"I deserved that money," she said.

"It doesn't belong to you," Nick shot back. "It belongs to the man I work for, and he wants his money." He moved to the edge of the chair and pointed his finger at her.

"You have no idea what you've done. It isn't about his money, Carrie. This runs much deeper than you could ever imagine. He wants you dead. And he needs to send a message to others as foolish as you. That message is your hands in a box."

She tried to grapple with Nick's words. Her hands in a *box!* The wind shrieked as the storm continued its assault outside. Terror sank in, and she rose from the sofa.

He stood and pushed her back down. Her muscles pinched, compressing her body and she gripped her stomach with her cuffed hands.

"Nick, please, I never wanted to kill anyone. I only…"

Someone was calling out her name. She jerked her head, trying to distinguish where it was coming from. The rain pounded harder making her uncertain as to what she heard until it settled in her veins like a cruel strike of ice-cold venom.

A voice she could never mistake for any other called out again. It tore through her body, her heart, and her soul. Invisible fingers raked her spine. She shook uncontrollably.

"Carrie, is that you? Carrie, are you here? It's me, Travis."

CHAPTER 27

WILL

Will fiddled with his pen while the teacher's voice droned on. Complex numbers and systems of equations were the furthest things from his mind. Thankful this was his last class of the day, he found algebra torture with the briefcase in his closet waiting.

Last night before going to bed, he removed the briefcase from the closet, opened it, and gazed at the stacks of cash. He'd picked up one of the guns, tightening his hand around the grip. He aimed at the far wall, his finger resting on the trigger. Then he pictured his father's face.

Will slouched in his chair, going over countless scenarios in his head trying to come up with an explanation he could tell his mom. Nothing made sense. If he told her he found it, she'd make him report it to the police.

He jumped at the sound of the period bell ringing. A hand slapped his shoulder as he gathered up his books and stuffed them into his backpack.

"Hey bro, what's going on?" Bruce asked. He fell into step next to Will. Bruce's red hair was chock-full of gel as always. Rows of stiff red spikes stood at attention across the top of his head.

"Nothing much."

"Still grounded?"

"Yeah," Will answered. His lips set in a firm line. His hands curled into fists at his side as they walked to their lockers.

"Hey, no big deal. You'll handle it. You always do."

They released their locks and traded out books as numerous students around them did the same. Metal clashed against metal and echoed along the hallway.

"Me and Kenny are going over to the diner to grab a burger and look at the new chick working there." His face broke out into a grin. "She is blazing, man."

Will laughed. "She's way outta your league, man. A little too old, too."

If they knew how much of a mystery Carrie was, what would they think of her then?

Bruce shrugged. "Still, it can't hurt to look."

They met up with Kenny in the parking lot. He leaned out of the open window of his Camaro, his long hair gathered in a ponytail at the nape of his neck. OneRepublic boomed from the radio. "Hey, what's up?"

"I told dufus here we're going to grab a burger at the diner so we can stare at the diva," Bruce said. He whistled, brought his hands up, and made a downward gesture tracing an hour-glass shape of a woman's body in the air.

"Yeah, she sure is something," Kenny said. "Man, her eyes are sick. Have you seen them? They're almost purple, man. I've never seen anybody with purple eyes."

"Idiot," Bruce said. Her eyes are violet. It's a rare color."

Will laughed. "Purple eyes. You're nuts, Kenny."

"Violet, purple whatever, I sure never saw anyone else with eyes like hers."

"Elizabeth Taylor had eyes like that," Will said.

Kenny lowered the volume on the radio. "Who?"

Will blew out an exasperated breath. "Never mind." He tossed his backpack onto the rear seat of the car. They piled into the Camaro, laughing and ribbing each other. Kenny gunned the engine, burning rubber as they sped away. They reached Will's street, and he flew past.

"Hey, turn around bro. Drop me home!" Will slapped Kenny's seat. "Come on, man, turn around."

"Bro, a quick burger won't hurt."

Will's stomach cramped. "I mean it, Kenny. Drop me home."

Kenny punched the gas pedal and continued driving in the direction of the diner. He zipped into the parking lot, tires squealing.

They hauled themselves out of the Camaro. Will slammed the door closed. "I told you to drop me off."

Kenny sprinted to the door. "Don't be mad. We'll have a burger, and I'll drive you right home after. It won't take long."

Will turned to Bruce and curled his lips. "One of these days I'm gonna get him good."

Bruce tapped Will's shoulder. "We won't stay long."

Will slid into a booth across from Kenny and Bruce as Joann approached.

"Hey, boys, what's new?"

Kenny looked past her. "Where's the new chick, Joann?"

Joann's eyebrows formed an arch. "I beg your pardon."

Kenny's face blushed crimson. "Oh, sorry. I mean the new lady."

"If you mean Carrie, she's gone for the day. I'm stuck working a double, so you'll just have to make do with me."

Bruce sighed. "Oh, man."

"Gee whiz," Joann said. "I didn't realize my waiting on you instead of Carrie would be such a hardship for you boys."

Will spoke up. "It's fine, Joann. Ignore these two jerks."

They ordered shakes and hamburgers. After shoving down the last mouthful of food, their conversation turned to some of the girls at school.

"Oh man, Jillian Chambers. Is she hot or what?" Bruce said. "I would love to tap that."

"In your dreams, freako," Kenny said. "She wouldn't give you the time of day."

Bruce ran his fingers through his spiked hair, laying it flat. Within seconds, it sprung up, standing erect again. "How do you know, dip shit?"

"I know what I know," Kenny smirked. "How about you Will? Darcy Grant giving you any action?"

So preoccupied with the briefcase, he'd all but forgotten Darcy these last few days. "She's okay," he said.

"I'd say she's more than okay," Kenny said. "Why don't you take a chance and ask her out, bro?"

Will fidgeted with his napkin. "Maybe I will." He slid out of the booth. "Listen, I need to get home. I'm still grounded."

"Okay, okay," Bruce said. "Let's bounce."

A few minutes later, they pulled up to Will's house. His father's car sat in the driveway.

"Sorry bro, Kenny said. "It's all my fault."

Will tried to make light of it. "No worries. See you tomorrow."

"Yeah later," Bruce called as the car careened away from the curb.

Will's palms grew damp, his heart drummed inside his chest. He crept inside. The living room was vacant. He continued into the kitchen. The table was set for dinner. The chairs were empty, and pots containing food sat idle on the stove.

Will jumped when his father's voice thundered down from the second floor. "Will, come upstairs, *now!*"

A sour taste formed in Will's mouth. The burger he ate earlier rose up into his throat, and he swallowed hard. He eased up the steps one at a time. When he reached the top, he came face to face with his father standing outside his bedroom door.

Arms folded across his chest, legs planted firmly in front, he nodded his head at Will. "It's about time you came home."

"Dad, look I know I'm grounded, and I should have come right home—"

"Grounded? That's the least of your problems. Let's see how you explain this." He jerked a thumb toward Will's room.

Will slunk past him and stopped. His heart pulsed. Beads of sweat gathered on his forehead. The briefcase lay wide open on his bed, the money, and guns in full view. His panic grew at the sight of his father's discovery. How stupid he'd been. He should have found a better hiding place.

Claudia perched on the edge of his bed, her eyes red and puffy from crying. "What is all this? What in the world did you do?"

"Mom, please don't be upset. I didn't do anything bad."

Russ crossed the room and grabbed Will's arm. "What in the hell do you mean you didn't do anything bad. I found a briefcase full of money and guns hidden in your closet."

Will wrestled his arm away and then retreated a few steps. Pain shot through his gut. "I can explain."

"You better start *now.*" Russ boomed. His face filled with rage.

Will told them how he had dug up the briefcase in May's yard. He left out his meeting Carrie and said he came upon it by accident while digging flower beds for May. "My shovel hit something, and there it was," he finished.

Russ pointed his beefy finger at Will. "What would an old woman be doing with all that money?"

"I ... I" Will's voice faltered. No explanation would be good enough.

"What about these?" He pointed to the guns.

"They were in the briefcase when I found it."

"Who else knows about this?"

He shook his head. "No one."

"Not even any of those nitwit friends of yours?"

"No, no one else knows. I swear."

"Yeah, sure, you swear."

Russ balled his fist and lunged at Will. Will ducked too late, and the edge of his father's fist caught his mouth. Will hit the wall and tumbled onto the carpet, the taste of blood on his tongue. His lip throbbed and soon swelled. He put up a defensive hand when Russ leaned in close and raised his fist to strike him again.

Claudia jumped up. "Russ, *stop!* Please, leave him alone."

He ignored her and came at Will again. "Get up. Get up on your feet."

Will pressed his body against the wall and eased himself up on shaky legs. Blood dripped from his chin forming beads of red on the grey carpet. His eyes welled up, but he refused to cry.

"I'm … I'm sorry, Dad."

"Yeah, I bet you are now. When did you plan on telling us about this?"

He hung his head and stared at the floor. "I…"

"Exactly what I thought. You didn't, did you?" He snatched Will by his shoulders and shook him. "Making some kind of plans of your own?"

His father's grip tightened. Stinging pain traveled down Will's arms.

"There were no plans. I didn't make any plans. I was going to tell you."

Russ released his grip. He snapped the briefcase closed and lifted it off the bed. "You think I'm an idiot? I don't believe a single word coming out of your mouth. If you intended to tell us, you wouldn't have hidden it." He brushed past him.

Will's eyes fixed on the briefcase. "What are you going to do with it, Dad?"

"That's none of your business. You have gotten us into a whole world of trouble. You're grounded indefinitely."

His father tore from the bedroom with the briefcase, taking his new life, taking his freedom and his mother's with him. Will placed his arm around his mom. "Believe me, I never meant for—"

"Please, don't say another word. I never dreamed you would keep something so serious from us." She disappeared into the bathroom and returned with a cold cloth. She wiped the blood from his lip. "Just look at what you made him do."

Will pushed her hand away. "What I made him do? Look at what he did to *me*." He touched his bruised lip. "Don't you see? This was our chance to get away from him."

"Oh, Will, honey. You saw the guns. Whether May is aware or not, someone did a terrible thing to get it. It's the reason why they hid it in the first place. Nothing positive can come out of it."

After she left, he collapsed onto his bed. With all his plans destroyed, he was unable to stop his tears. He berated himself for not being more careful in hiding the briefcase. He made no mention of Carrie to his parents, and he wasn't sure why.

His mom was right. The guns and the money said it all. Carrie didn't want anyone to find them. He sat straight up. A slight smile formed on his lips. What if he helped her get the briefcase back? Tell her he took it. Of course, she'd be mad, but grateful. He'd tell Carrie and then convince her to help him.

Will wiped his eyes. Exhausted, he rolled onto his side, his lip still pulsing. Within minutes, he fell asleep, his dreams of a safe place maybe possible once again.

CHAPTER 28

RICARDO

Ricardo relaxed into the chair cushions inside the screened patio at the rear of the house. Chino sprawled on the floor next to him.

His face lit up with anticipation as Armando lifted a steaming bowl of *Ajiaco* off a silver tray and placed it before him. The definitive Colombian dish was one of his favorites. The aroma of potatoes, chicken, and corn permeated the air. It mingled with crema, guascas, capers, and avocado.

"*Gracias,* Armando." He dipped his spoon and delighted in the savory broth as it slid over his tongue.

"*Con gusto, Señor.* Will there be anything else?"

"Set another bowl and please tell Carmela to come and join me for lunch."

Armando nodded. "*Sí, Señor.*"

Moments later, a soft hand grazed his shoulder. Carmela sat down opposite him.

"*Buenas tardas, Papá.*"

"*Buenas tardas, mi amor.*" His smile slipped away as he frowned at her tight white jeans, the lemon-colored sleeveless blouse, the hem, barely brushing her narrow waist.

"Carmela, why do you dress this way? A little less skin showing would be nice."

"Papá, I'm in America, no? This is how American women dress," she said, her eyes sparkled with laughter.

He hated to admit how Americanized she had become. He wondered if her native Columbia held the same place in her heart as America. At the same time, he understood her desire to adapt and fit in.

After his dear Natalia passed away from complications giving birth to Carmela, he had no desire to marry again. He was content to raise his daughter, his one heir, alone.

She lifted her spoon and tasted the *Ajiaco.* A sigh escaped her lips. "Oh, this is so good. It's nice to be home eating real food for a change."

"You don't eat real food at that expensive college?" Ricardo teased.

Ricardo removed a small loaf of freshly baked bread from a blue flowered porcelain plate. He broke off a piece and dipped it into his soup.

"Oh *Papá,* you know what I mean."

She smoothed a curtain of hair the color of brown sugar away from her face, bent over the bowl of soup, and spooned another mouthful. "Studying leaves little time for gourmet meals. You fly by the seat of your pants most of the time."

"How are your studies coming? Am I to expect to see my daughter graduate soon?"

"I accelerated my studies. I finish this coming winter."

"Excellent, *mi amor.* Stay focused." He took a sip of cool water and cleared his throat. "By the way, Nick came by not too long ago."

"That's nice," she said. She finished her last bit of soup. Turning sideways, she crossed her legs and folded her arms. "What brought him here?" She drew in her bottom lip and tossed her napkin on the table.

"It's true he doesn't come around often," Ricardo said. "Nick hates the heat."

"That's not what I asked you, *Papá.* What was he doing here? Nick shows up when you need him, not for family visits." Her expression turned somber.

He let out a sigh. "Of course, he comes here on business, but I like to think he also comes to see us."

"Us?" She gave him a skeptical look. "Really, *Papá?*" She fiddled with one of the gold hoops dangling from her earlobe.

"Carmela, please. He cares very much for you."

Her lips formed an angry pout. "Not in the way you want him to."

Ricardo bristled. "Okay, enough. It's no secret I want the two of you to marry someday. Nothing could make me happier than to know my daughter is safe, loved, and well taken care of."

"Loved? *Papá,* Nick doesn't love me. He still sees me as a little girl. A sister maybe, not a wife."

"Don't speak of things you know nothing about. I have had several talks with him about your future."

"Talks!" Carmela flew up from the table, hands on her hips. "I don't need you talking to Nick about me behind my back."

He pushed his bowl away. "Sit *down.*"

Carmela stood, defiant, eyes fixed on her father.

Heat flashed through his body. He loved her, but he would not tolerate any form of disrespect from her. Nor would he give in to her bad temper.

"I said, sit down, Carmela." Irritated, he gestured toward her chair.

She collapsed into the chair and stared off into the distance.

"Look at me," he said, his voice, low and demanding. "Lose the attitude, *now.* You will not disrespect me in my house."

She hesitated and then turned to look at her father with defeat written across her face.

"I know what is needed for you long term. Right now, you're still young, still in school, but that's not going to last. I'm not going to last either," he said.

Her face grew fearful, and his sorrow rose. He wished he hadn't said those last words.

"Don't talk like that, *Papá,* " she said.

"It's a fact of life, *mi amor*. One day I will no longer be on this earth. I will take comfort knowing you will be okay. I'd never do anything to cause you unhappiness." His voice softened. "You must understand, as your father, I want what's best for you. Nick is the one person I trust to take care of you." Her eyes misted and he crumbled inside.

"No *Papá,* you want what's best for *you*." She rose, kissed him on top of his head and left.

Ricardo sighed. How could he make her see marrying Nick was paramount to her safety? She knew nothing of his drug business, and he'd never discuss it with her. Some risks came with his choices, and she, like it or not, needed Nick's protection.

He retreated to his study with Chino trotting behind. A feeling of unease washed over him. By now, the job should be finished. He should have two sets of hands and two million dollars.

He poured some tequila and sat on the leather sofa while Chino settled in at his feet. After downing the tequila, he set the shot glass on the end table. Reaching down, he patted Chino on the head.

"Good boy. Yes, you're such a good boy, Chino. Such a loyal protector."

The word loyal hung in the air. Was it possible Nick had deviated from the job he sent him to do? Should he be questioning Nick's loyalty?

He couldn't bear to think the man whom he loved almost like a son could be disloyal to him in any way. He shook the bad feelings off and stroked Chino's soft fur again.

"No, Chino it's not possible. Nick will finish the job soon. He will finish, and he will say yes to marrying Carmela."

Ricardo leaned against the soft leather. He wanted to believe these things were true, but in the pit of his stomach, an unfamiliar dread took hold and refused to let go.

CHAPTER 29

NICK

Nick had never witnessed anything like the scene playing out before him. Carrie's body shook so hard she was on the verge of convulsing. She appeared to be in a full-blown panic attack, her fear much greater than what he had witnessed earlier. Her hands fought against the cuffs as she tried to free herself.

He rose from his chair and kneeled in front of her. Her chest heaved in and out. Taking hold of her wrists, he tried to steady her hands. He felt the jolt of her pulse beneath his fingers. Her eyes filled with angst.

"Carrie, look at me!" He pressed his hands down against hers. "Look at me." He cupped her chin. If he didn't calm her soon, her terrified state would lead to her collapse.

"Carrie, listen to me, he can't hurt you." He pulled her face toward him and then raised her cuffed hands to his chest.

She blinked rapidly at him. "Yes—yes he can. He will hurt me after what I did to him," she said. "You don't know him like I do." Her bottom lip trembled uncontrollably.

"No, Carrie," he said. "I won't allow that to happen." As soon as those words slipped out of his mouth, they became true. He'd never let that bum hurt her. Her reaction was enough to make anyone feel for her. He saw and heard all he needed to with regard to Travis Montgomery.

From the first time he caught sight of her at the diner, he didn't want to admit to himself, something changed. It wasn't only her beauty that drew him. Something made him want to know more about her as a person. What led her to robbery and murder?

Sitting across from her in the coffee shop earlier, he had to remind himself over and over to finish the job and move on. Still, as she spoke, he followed each small movement of her body. The way she tilted her head to one side while listening to him talk. The small crease at the corner of her mouth he first noticed at the diner. The perfectly sculpted lips. The hollow of her neck drawing him in until he cut things short so he could refocus.

Now, he recognized the frailty beneath her sturdy exterior. A fragility born out of fear, if not horror. His eyes fixed on hers. Their deep wells of violet filled with tears, and with them came the knowledge his life would never be the same. His last bit of resolve crumbled. He would protect her, not kill her.

"Carrie, slow down. Breathe, just breathe." He released her hands and stood up.

She grabbed at him, her eyes wild. "No, don't leave. He's here."

Nick couldn't believe, she clung to him, the man sent to kill her, rather than face the one tied up in the bedroom. He knelt and placed his hands on top of hers again. "I promise he won't hurt you. Okay?"

She stared at him and shook her head.

He went to the bedroom and closed the door. Travis lay on his back, his face lit up when he saw Nick.

"Hey, you found her, didn't you? Did she tell you where the money is? She has the money, I told you, man. I can get her to talk. Untie me, and I'll make her tell you."

"Yeah, I bet you will. You're not going anywhere near her. I want you to listen closely. I am not going to repeat myself. You are not to say another word. Not one single word, because if you do, it will be the last word you ever speak."

Travis eyed him, the blackness in his eyes challenging. His lips parted, but he quickly snapped his mouth shut.

Nick smirked. "Now, you lie there like a good boy and stay quiet. If I hear any sound, any sound at all coming from this room, you're done. Nod your head yes."

Travis nodded his head.

Nick left the room and shut the door behind him. He rested his hand on the doorknob for a second, thinking and then walked over to her. "Can I trust you not to run away from me?"

She nodded and studied his face. "What are you going to do?"

"Nothing yet. I have questions. Those questions need answers so I can make some kind of sense of this whole thing and figure out what to do." He took a key from his pocket and removed the cuffs.

Carrie rubbed at her wrists. "But you said the man you work for wants me dead."

"Yes, and I'm afraid that won't change unless I can convince him to spare you."

She started to speak when he put up his hand. "Not here." He motioned toward the bedroom door. "Not with him around."

"Now what?" she asked.

"I'll give him something to keep him quiet."

He returned to the bedroom and prepared another shot. Travis tried to roll away.

"Hold still," he ordered. He grabbed Travis's arm and plunged the needle in.

When he came out of the bedroom, she was over by the front window peering out, her reflection distorted by the heavy rain beating outside. She spun around when he approached.

"Nick, I don't—

"Let me ask the questions first, please. It's important. Where is the money?"

"It's safe. I took a little bit and buried the rest in my aunt's yard along with the guns."

"Who else knows about it?"

She eyed the bedroom door. "No one except Travis."

"Good."

"Nick, if your boss gets his money, will he reconsider?"

He wanted to answer yes, only that wasn't the truth. Ricardo Santiago would never allow anyone to get away with murder and robbery. The odds of him granting clemency were close to impossible.

"I'm afraid it's a bit more complicated. You need to let me handle this, Carrie. I'll try to make this right somehow with him."

"Why, Nick. Why are you doing this for me?" she asked, her face full of questions.

He couldn't explain why when he didn't know the answer himself. He reached out and took both her hands in his. She flinched and pulled her hands back.

"I get the impression no one has done anything for you in a very long time. So, give me a chance to do this." It made no sense for her to trust him, and he couldn't blame her. How badly had she been abused by that prick?

"We'll drive to your aunt's house, and tomorrow, we'll dig up the money," he said. "Is your aunt at home?"

"No, she's out of town. I'm not sure when she'll be home."

"Perfect." He handed Carrie her purse and ushered her out the door. She hesitated and glanced over her shoulder, and then up at him.

"You don't have to worry about him."

They drove to Laurel through a series of torrential downpours. By the time they reached May's house, night had closed in. The rain pelted them as they ran up the steps and slipped inside the house. She pushed the door closed behind them.

"I'll get some towels," she said.

They dried off, and she led him into the kitchen. Shivering in her wet clothes, she filled the teapot, and set it on the stove.

She looked hard at Nick, questioning. "All right?" she asked.

He nodded. "Sure."

She lit the burner and set two cups with tea bags on the counter. Things were awkward between them while they sat in silence at the kitchen table waiting for the kettle to boil.

He studied those eyes holding in all her secrets. She'd built a wall to keep others out. A wall he could almost physically feel. It was essential he penetrate that wall. If he had a chance at freeing her from Ricardo's wrath, he wanted all the details.

He leaned in and clasped his hands on the table. "I need you to tell me what happened, before and after the robbery."

"I still don't understand why you want to help me. You don't know anything about me except that I'm a thief and a murderer."

He reflected for a minute. She was right. Why should she trust him?

"I know all of this is strange," he said. "If I can, I would like to try to figure out a way to help you. But I can't unless you're honest with me."

The kettle's whistle broke the silence. Carrie poured the water, and then set the cups down between them.

Still hesitant, she lifted a spoon and stirred sugar into the hot liquid. She cleared her throat and began.

"I've been with Travis for a long, long time. Things didn't start out as bad as they ended." She stopped, and, with a trembling hand, took a sip of her tea.

Nick could tell how painful it was for her to get the words out. "Go on," he said softly. He listened quietly as she poured out her life story. How she left home with Travis to escaper her alcohol and drug-addicted mother in Arizona. And she mentioned the father she never knew. How, as a child, she prayed he would come and rescue her. Every so often she'd look away as a tear slid down her cheek.

She spoke of Travis before he turned mean, as she put it. How he had changed over the years. His threats and the many beatings she suffered at his hands. Shadows crossed her face, her eyes grew vacant. He waited, letting her form each word when she was ready.

Last, she told him about the violence the day of the robbery. How he forced her to kill for her own survival. She continued with the night he almost strangled her, compelling her to take action against him and ended with the recent murder of her mother.

As she talked, Nick's anger intensified. On the outside, he remained calm. Inside, his rage churned, building up like storm clouds. It took all of his willpower not to get up, go to the cabin, and put a bullet in Travis's head. Her visceral reaction to Travis's voice made sense to him now.

As for her mother's murder, after the things she had done to Carrie she deserved whatever fate dished out. He figured Travis must have killed her when he stopped at the trailer park. He decided to keep that bit of information to himself.

"I'm so sorry," he said. No one should have to live in fear the way you did."

She lifted her head, and he wished he could erase the pain etched on her face. He wanted her to believe she was worth so much more than somebody's punching bag.

She drew her arms to her body. Her shoulders slumped, making her appear child-like in the chair.

"I'm so ashamed, Nick. I will never be able to make things right. I murdered one man and tried to kill another. How am I supposed to live with that?" Tears spilled from her eyes. She lowered her head and looked away. Her dark hair fell in waves around her face.

Nick's heart softened, and he ached to comfort her. "You have nothing to be ashamed of, Carrie. You're a victim. Your survival instincts kicked in when you needed them. And your history of abuse allowed you to let Travis abuse you just like your mother had.

Nick stood up. He took both her hands and lifted her from the chair. Pulling her close, he wrapped his arms around her. She struggled to free herself. He sensed her fear and her lack of trust.

"Stop! Let me *go.*" Her tears fell hard and fast. She pushed against him, trying to escape.

"Carrie, I'm not going to hurt you." He held on until she collapsed into him.

Nick bent his head close to hers, and the light scent of jasmine tinged his nose. He waited for her crying to subside. When her body continued to tremble, he guided her toward the living room. He steered her to the sofa and eased her down. After opening the fireplace flue, he set the logs and then grabbed some newspaper. Within minutes, bright orange flames lit the room.

He lowered himself beside her. The sharp aroma of the burning wood engulfed them. Sap popped and hissed. He reached over and put his arm around her. She arched her neck and then rested her head on his shoulder. He drew her closer. This time she didn't pull away. They sat in silence, staring at the fire until the embers faded and the rain stopped.

CHAPTER 30

TRAVIS

Travis rolled and pushed up into a sitting position. The rain stopped. He cocked his head and listened to the sudden stillness. There hadn't been any sound coming from the other room since he woke up from a drugged sleep. He ran his tongue over his dry lips and tried to ease his throbbing throat by swallowing hard.

Still groggy, his head feeling like it was filled with handfuls of sand, he shook it back and forth. Travis guessed the guy who grabbed him must be the one the motel clerk had mentioned. The son of a bitch would pay for what he did.

Inching his way to the edge of the bed, he swung his bound legs over the side. He heaved himself up. His legs shook beneath him, and he lurched forward. He hopped to the door, leaned against it, and listened. Nothing, not a sound on the other side.

Grasping the doorknob with both hands, he forced it open and peeked out. Travis hopped from the bedroom into the kitchen. He bent and tugged on a cabinet drawer. It flew open, came off the track, and crashed to the floor. Silverware clattered around him, and he spied a steak knife. He worked the blade across the tape on his legs.

Careful, his legs unsteady, he grabbed the edge of the counter and stood. He searched for a flat piece of metal. Among the silverware scattered across the floor, he spotted a pen. He picked it up and managed to pry the clip away. It was thin and narrow enough to use as a shim in the locking mechanism on the cuffs.

He inserted it between the locking mechanism and the teeth. With the clip in place, he tightened the cuff a notch and then pushed on the clip.

The cuffs sprang open, and he removed them. He shook his hands and rubbed at the red marks on his wrists.

Thirsty, he grabbed a bottle of water from the refrigerator and chugged it down. He crept to the front window. Seeing nothing but pitch black, he slipped outside. The clean smell of fresh rain and rich dark earth sailed past him.

Following the moonlight, he bolted toward the woods. The drugs were wearing off. The fresh air helped clear his mind. Startled by a deer as it ran from underneath the tall pines, he retreated a few steps and stopped. The deer glared at him before dashing into the brush and disappearing into the night.

He sprinted through spongy layers of leaves. The crunch of dead pine needles underneath his feet filled the night air. Weak, he pushed on determined to make it to Laurel. The driving force inside him always focused on Carrie. If she were in Laurel, he'd find her.

Darkness closed in as he darted among the trees, making it difficult to see. His limbs grew lighter. A sense of happiness engulfed him. Hearing Carrie's voice had given him strength. The one thing standing in his way was the jerk who threatened to kill him, but he wasn't gonna let that stop him. He'd do whatever was necessary to get to her, take his money, and leave Laurel behind them.

Cautiously, he approached the main road. He stayed close to the tree line beside it and made his way down the mountain, following the lights in the distance until he reached Laurel. To get to his motel, he would have to go through town.

He faded in and out of the shadows past rows of houses filled with unsuspecting residents. The rain had done him a favor by keeping folks inside. He reached the end of Main Street and continued on the road toward the motel.

His bruised muscles ached as he sprinted across the parking lot. Relief washed over him when he saw his car. The remainder of his money lay inside. He fished the motel key card out of his pants pocket.

Travis peeled off his damp clothes, caked with mud from his journey through the woods. He showered and then put on fresh clothes. Grabbing his things, he hurried outside. He removed his revolver from the suitcase and stuck it in his waistband. Reaching underneath the seat, he felt around for the bands of cash. His fingers slid over them, and he grinned.

He drove straight to May's house and cruised past. Soft light streamed from the windows. A black Mercedes Benz sat out front.

"Probably his fancy car," he hissed. Well, he'd have his own fancy car once he got his money. He parked further down the block where he could watch the house. His insides burned at the thought of Carrie with another man.

He lit a cigarette and fidgeted with the lighter. His patience wearing thin, he tossed the lighter onto the console. He flipped open the glove box and rummaged through it. His eyes lit up when he found a screwdriver. He crammed it into his jacket pocket. No more waiting. Time to take a peek for himself.

Travis ditched his cigarette and crept up the porch steps. He pressed himself up against the clapboards by the window, leaned over, and looked in.

His stomach did a slow burn as he watched the two of them sitting together by the fire. His jaw clicked. How easy it had been for her to shoot him, leave him for dead, and then be with another man. After all, he'd done for her. Rescuing her from Helen and Breezy obviously meant nothing to her. From the moment he first saw her, all those years ago, he knew what he would do.

Tired of drifting, he had returned to Breezy, foolish enough to believe he could rekindle his relationship with Helen until he got a glimpse of her hauling out the trash. Any hope of patching things up with her disappeared. Alcohol had lay claim to what was left of her beauty.

Before he turned to leave, Carrie stepped out of the trailer. All thoughts of Helen fled his mind. Carrie had grown-up into a dazzling young woman at just fourteen years old.

An infant at the time he left, Carrie had no memory of him, and he made damn sure Helen didn't know when the two of them started sneaking around. He never carried any guilt about the choice he made. The emotions Carrie stirred in him couldn't be ignored.

When he learned of her pregnancy, he stayed away until after the baby was born. When he came back to Arizona, he heard from a friend that Helen had added drugs to her list of vices. He knew then, Helen could play right into his hands.

Helen didn't like babies. Carrie's upbringing was proof enough of how she felt about them. Babies were expensive. Babies got in the way of her booze and drugs. So, they made a deal. His half-brother bought the baby, and unfortunately for her, Helen ended up in jail.

The end of little Bobby was the beginning of his life with Carrie.

Now, standing here on May's porch, he wanted that life with her again. And he wanted his money. Before this night was over, he'd have both, and then he'd get back at her good. His physical pain wouldn't measure up to hers when he told her the truth about her little boy, and about himself. He'd put a hurting on her that she'd never forget.

Drawing away from the window, he trotted to the rear of the yard. A small shed stood in the corner of the property. Sprinting across the yard, he lifted the latch and slipped inside.

In the darkness, he tried to quiet his fury. He wanted to erase the image of Carrie sitting there, her head resting on another man's shoulder. How could she? She'd pay dearly one way or the other.

All he needed to do now was wait for this jerk to head back to the cabin. The purr of the Mercedes engine would tell him she was alone. Then he'd make his way inside.

CHAPTER 31

CARRIE

Carrie touched her puffy lids. She hadn't shed that many tears in a long time. The retelling of her abusive childhood and her life with Travis had drained her.

Nick stood up and fished his key out of his pocket. "I need to go. Will you be okay?"

"I think so. And Travis? What's going to happen to him?" Muscles tingled in the pit of her stomach at her words.

"Let me worry about him. You get some rest, and I'll be back in the morning."

She grappled with the mixed emotions inside of her. Even after all he'd done, Travis's fate weighed on her mind.

"Don't hurt him, Nick," she said. "Please, just make him go away. He wasn't always a bad person, he changed … we both changed after…"

"After what?"

She couldn't speak the words. Afraid of what he'd think of her if she told him. She clutched a hand to her heart. "I don't want you to hurt him."

A flicker of irritation shone in Nick's eyes. "Why are you trying to protect him after all the terrible things he's done to you?"

'I don't know how to explain it." Her skin grew hot. She raked her fingers through her hair and paced. "Because I understand him," she said.

"Carrie, it's not that simple."

"You can't—you have to figure another way out for him. You have to, Nick."

She knew it was crazy to bargain for the life of the man she tried to kill. No matter how awful Travis had treated her, she didn't want to be responsible for his death. His having survived the shooting meant she could forgive herself. The guilt from one murder was enough.

"Listen," Nick said. "I'm not going to make any promises. It's impossible for me to do that. Right now, I need you to trust me."

She wanted to trust him, but her trust had been broken so many times before. Anxiety churned inside her. Still reluctant she said, "Okay, I'll try."

"Do you have a cell phone?" he asked.

"Yes." She rummaged through her purse and handed it to him.

"I'll put my number on speed dial. Press 2 if you need me. Make sure you lock all the doors. Try not to worry."

After Nick left, too tired to change, she slipped underneath the comforter fully clothed. She switched off the bedside lamp. Memories of Travis exploded inside her brain like flares in a dark night sky. Hearing his voice again had ruptured her soul. The knowledge of him having survived the shooting and what he was capable of unnerved her.

Restless, she flung the covers away and sat up. Here she was in Laurel, living with her aunt, and working her first job. All of it accomplished by building up the courage lying inside her. She couldn't let Travis or Nick take it away.

There was no reason to trust the man sent to kill her. His boss wanted her dead. Why should she believe him? He killed people for a living. Then again, if Nick wanted to kill her, would he have brought her home? She shook her head. Too many unanswered questions flashed through her mind.

Beyond exhausted now, she collapsed onto her pillow and drew the covers up around her again. Although she didn't trust Nick completely, she had exposed herself to him, told him almost all the dirty secrets of her life. Except for the one secret she held inside. She couldn't muster up the courage to speak about Bobby.

Before long, her eyes grew heavy, and she made an effort to quiet her mind along with the dread hovering below the surface. She began to drift off. A rustling from across the room jerked her awake.

Blinking into the darkness to adjust her eyes, she glimpsed slivers of pale moonlight filtering through the linen curtains as shadows played on the walls. She sat up and scanned the room, able to make out the shapes of her dresser, the tall antique mahogany wardrobe on the far wall, and the overstuffed chair in the corner.

Her skin prickled sending gooseflesh down her arms as a figure rose and advanced toward her. She held back a scream and clutched at the comforter pulling it closer.

"Who's there?" she called out.

Nearer now, his face lit by moonlight, she recoiled in horror. She inched her way to the opposite side of the bed. Her monster was alive.

"Please, please don't hurt me. What do you want? The money? I'll give you all of it. I don't want it."

"What do I want?" he hissed. His mouth twisted and he moved closer. "Surely, you must know, girl." His words rough as sandpaper scraped across bare wood. He reached out, flipped on the bedside lamp, and eased himself onto the bed.

"What were you thinking trying to get away from me? I told you from the beginning, I would never let you go. You and me, we belong to each other in more ways than you could imagine." He glanced around the room. "First things first, where is May?"

"Arizona. She left to go and bury my mother."

"Your mother?"

"Yes, the police called. My mother was murdered."

"You don't say. What a shame, a real shame. Bet you're all broken up about it."

Her limbs shook. She eyed the open doorway. In one swift movement, she threw the covers and bolted from the bed. Pain shot up her arm as he took hold of her wrist, turning it and forcing her back down onto the bed.

"Please, stop. You're hurting me." She twisted her body and tried to wrestle her arm away. Her pain intensified as he gripped harder. He pulled her across the bed, flinging himself on top of her, pinning both her arms up over her head, his hands encircling her wrists. The full weight of his body pressed against her as his temper spiraled out of control.

"After what you did to me, I should do much more than hurt you a little. Giving you a gun proved to be the worst mistake I ever made."

He hovered over her, and she took in the deep wells of blackness in his eyes as she fought against him, trying desperately to push him away. "Let me up. I can't catch my breath."

His grip slackened, and he released her. He lifted himself up and off the bed. He stood glaring down at her.

"I love you, Carrie. I ain't never loved a woman the way I love you. How could you do that to me? Haven't I always taken care of you all these years? Sure, I've made mistakes, but I tried hard to make a life for us. And what do I get in return?"

She inched up into a sitting position and rubbed her wrists, her fingers almost numb from the pain. Her head buzzed. Nothing in her life had changed. Travis was here, dragging all the agony and torment of her past with him. The new life she worked for, fought for, killed for, was slipping away. The thought of returning to her old life crushed her inside. How could she make him understand?

"I can't live that life anymore, Travis. A life full of your schemes. The constant moving from place to place and you lashing out at me all the time." Her tears welled up, blurring his face. "Those men … those men we shot. I never thought I'd be capable of doing something so horrible." She covered her face with her hands and sobbed.

He reached out, pulled her hands away, and with two fingers lifted her chin. "Look at me, girl. You never thought you could kill someone?

How am I supposed to believe you when you tried to kill me, too?" He pulled his shirt up and traced his finger along the scar on his chest.

Mesmerized, she stared, the jagged scar proof of her awful deed. Did her hatred justify murder? If so, it made her as evil as him. She could have taken the briefcase while he slept. Spent a lifetime looking over her shoulder rather than try to kill him.

"I'm sorry. What I did was so wrong," she said.

"Then why, Carrie, why? You're my whole life. I won't live without you by my side." He sat on the bed and faced her. "And you need me, too."

She saw desperation and a flicker of vulnerability written all over his face. Maybe she could get him to listen. "Can't you see, it's not good for us to stay together? I don't feel anything for you anymore."

He thrust out his chin. "What are you saying? I'm not good enough for you?"

"No," she said quickly, determined to finish. "I don't love you, Travis. I'm not sure if I ever loved you. I was barely sixteen years old. After losing Bobby, I didn't know what to do, and I couldn't stand to stay in Breezy any longer and think about him."

Eyes flashing, he said, "You did love me. I felt it. You loved me once before that boy came into this world." He pointed his finger at her. "That's it, isn't it?"

The familiar ache inside her returned. "You changed, Travis."

He shook his head. "No, no you're wrong, I didn't change. I never stopped loving you."

Indignation mixed with fear filled her. How did he not see what he'd done to her? He made her think she deserved those beatings. Guilt-ridden for so long, she believed him to be her punishment for the loss of her son.

But not anymore. She proved she could learn to live with her decision to leave her son that day. She'd never forget the past but she was willing to accept it and the part she played. All she wanted now was to put her life back together without him.

"Please listen to me. I'll give you the briefcase. You can take the money and go far away before he finds you. I won't say anything, I promise. I just want to stay here in Laurel and live my life."

His hands balled into fists causing her to retreat into the bed pillows. He edged toward her. Fury lit his face, and he hissed at her. "You're dreaming if you think I'm gonna leave you here with him! You think I don't know what you got up your sleeve, girl. I saw the two of you all snuggled up by the fire."

Fear clawed through her. He must have spied on them. "It's not what you think. I was upset and he—"

"He what? C'mon Carrie, tell me. You think you're gonna have a fancy new man and throw me away like a piece of garbage?" His teeth clenched around the words.

Within seconds, he pounced, dragging her off the bed by her hair. She swung her arms at him, pain stinging her scalp. She lifted her leg, kicked him hard on his shin.

"You *bitch!*" He pinned her up against the wall and placed his fingers at the hollow of her throat and then increased the pressure against her windpipe. Sheer panic engulfed her, and her muscles grew slack. She dropped her hands.

Travis pressed harder. "You're coming with me. I'm keeping the money, and you and me are leaving Laurel together."

He let go, and Carrie gasped. She tried to draw air into her lungs. Her legs gave way, and she slid down the wall. She looked up, and her mind registered the gun sticking out of his waistband.

"Okay, whatever you say." Carrie held up her hands in surrender and then eased up. She reached for his gun with one hand while her other formed a fist. She swung, but Travis ducked, avoiding her punch, but he couldn't stop her from grabbing his gun.

Carrie's heart hammered. She planted her feet. Hands shaking, she aimed the gun.

"Hands up, Travis. Walk to the door," she ordered.

Travis's glared at her. "Now, listen here, girl. You had better give me the gun. I ain't gonna do this dance with you again." The corner of his mouth twitched.

Carrie's stomach dropped at the thought of pulling the trigger again. No matter what, she wouldn't shoot him, but she needed him to think she would. She gripped the gun tighter.

"If you don't do as I say, we'll be doing more than dancing, Travis. Now, get over by the door, hands in the air."

Scowling, he raised his hands and moved to the door.

"Step out into the hall." Carrie scooped up her cell phone and jammed it into the front pocket of her jeans. "Downstairs, now," she ordered.

She kept the gun aimed at him as they descended the stairs. When they reached the foot of the steps, she motioned toward the sofa.

"Sit down, Travis."

"You're making a helluva mistake," he said. "That creeps coming here as soon as he finds out I'm gone. Guess you're just gonna let him kill me. He has some hell of a nerve getting cozy with you."

"Shut up, Travis. No matter what you think, nothing happened between us." She eased into the chair opposite the sofa.

"Yeah, but I bet you want it to," he snapped. "Now, I wonder, where is that briefcase, Carrie?"

"I buried it in May's yard."

"Why the hell did you do that? We don't have time to go digging before he gets here."

"That money is staying right where it is. It doesn't belong to either one of us."

He swiped his hand through his hair in frustration. "Does he know where the money is?"

"Yes. I told him."

He waved his fist in the air. "Stupid bitch. You could have lied."

"You're not hearing me, Travis. The money stays right where it is. We are giving it back to the person it belongs to."

"I can't believe you would give up the money. Choose him over me."

"If I thought for a moment you'd take the briefcase and go away, I'd let you dig it up," she said. "The thing is, I know you would never do that. Not without me." She pulled her cell phone out and pressed two with her free hand.

"Yes, he's here," she said. "No, I'm fine. Hurry."

Travis leaned toward her. "I will kill you for this."

Before she could respond, he charged at her. She gripped the gun tighter as he grabbed for it. He forced her hand up, and the gun fired. The bullet shot straight up into the ceiling before Travis tore the revolver away from her.

His temper sure and swift, he slapped her hard across the face. Carrie screeched and rocked back in the chair. Fear found its familiar place inside her once again.

He motioned for her to get up. He pointed to the window. "Sit over there on the floor where I can see you."

She slid to the floor beneath the window. Her anxiety rose. Nick was walking right into Travis's trap, and she had no way to warn him. Her fear continued to mount as she pleaded with him.

"If we give him the money, he'll go away," she said. "It belongs to the man he works for. A real bad man. We have to give it to him."

His eyes bore into her. "Give the money to *him?* No way I'm gonna give it up … or you. I'm tired of having nothing, and you should be, too. No, we'll wait right here for him to come and once I get rid of him, we'll dig it up."

Travis cast a glance out the window, squinting into the darkness.

"Yeah, he'll be dead, and you and me are taking the money and leaving Laurel, together again like always, only this time we'll be rich.

CHAPTER 32

NICK

Nick leaned on the gas, the knot in the pit of his stomach telling him he'd screwed up. A true professional left no room for mistakes. One mistake could jeopardize everything. He had never deviated from a job for any reason, and especially not for a woman.

The Mercedes roared up the mountain toward the cabin. He never should have left Travis alone for so long. The sedative would have worn off by now. His head throbbed. He'd made his decision. Now, he would need to figure out a way to keep Carrie alive. Ricardo wasn't going to be an easy fix. Not for her—and not for him.

The time had come for him to get out of the business, but getting out from under a drug cartel was nearly impossible. You didn't just quit.

Until today, his loyalty to Ricardo had remained concrete. That loyalty should count for something. He hoped Ricardo could see his way clear and let him go. It was a slim hope at best.

He thought about Carmela and Ricardo's expectations. His refusal to marry Carmela would be a direct insult, lessening his chances of convincing Ricardo to let Carrie live.

Hard pavement stopped, and gravel churned beneath the wheels as he pulled up the drive. The Mercedes' headlights beamed across the door. It leaned half-open. On instinct, he grabbed his gun from the glove compartment. He crept to the door and kicked it open. His heart hammered and he gripped his 9mm tighter. Silverware littered the kitchen floor. The handcuffs lay open, the bedroom empty.

He balled his fist. His insides did a slow burn. If the son of a bitch did anything to Carrie, he'd put an end to him right there. He removed his cell phone from his pocket and tapped the tracking app he had downloaded into Carrie's phone earlier. She was still in Laurel. He tore out of the cabin and sped toward town. Halfway there, his cell phone rang.

"Carrie, is Travis there with you?" he asked. "Did he hurt you?"

Her voice sounded steady, but Nick knew better after what he witnessed earlier. He could only imagine her terror.

"I'm on my way."

He eased the Mercedes through town in the darkness. Careful not to arouse suspicion, he slowed to a crawl along the main thoroughfare. He spotted Travis's empty car parked a block from Carrie's home, drew in behind it and parked. The streets were deserted. Most people were asleep at this time of night.

He had no intention of approaching the front door. Travis might have the upper hand, forcing her to say she was okay to get the jump on him. He made his way over to the next street and scaled the fence at the rear of the house.

Except for a barking dog a few houses away, all was quiet. He drew out his 9mm, edged to the door, and tried it. Not surprised to find it open, he slipped inside.

Nick crept into the kitchen. Voices drifted toward him from the other room. First, a man's, and then a woman's. He raised his gun, advanced, and peeked into the living room. His body jerked alert, responding to his rush of adrenaline.

Carrie, her head down, sat at Travis's feet, while he stared out the front window.

He waited, his eyes trained on the two of them as the seconds ticked by. If Travis saw him first, he'd grab Carrie and use her as a hostage.

Come on Carrie, look at me, look at me, Nick willed.

Finally, she lifted her head, sheer terror planted on her face. She caught sight of him, and he put a finger to his lips. He held up a count of three and motioned for her to move away from him.

She shook her head, silently pleading with him.

He mouthed okay, lowered the gun, and motioned again for her to move on his count.

On three, Carrie sprang to her feet. Nick bolted across the room. Travis spun around. Nick drew his fist and landed it square on Travis's jaw.

Eyes wide, he crumpled to the floor, his gun landing a few feet away. Nick hit him again on the head with the butt of his gun, knocking him unconscious. He turned to Carrie. "Are you all right?"

"I'm okay. A little shook up, that's all. I thought I could control him until you arrived."

He rested a hand on her arm. "The main thing is you're not hurt. You did well, Carrie."

She glanced down at Travis. "What now?"

" I'm taking him to the cabin."

"Please, don't do anything tonight. I need time to think," she said.

"I'm afraid this decision isn't yours to make." Nick picked up Travis's gun. He thrust a hand through his dark hair and studied her face.

"For tonight. For you," he said. That's all I can agree to right now." He handed her the gun. "Watch him. I'll only be gone for a few minutes."

"Nick...."

"Carrie, please, watch him."

Carrie took the gun and pointed it at Travis. "Nick, you need to be aware that even when I had the gun, I wasn't going to use it."

"I believe you, Carrie. I promise I'll be back before he comes around."

Nick took off, and, within minutes, he pulled his car up the driveway. He fished out a set of handcuffs from the trunk and rushed inside.

Travis lay moaning on the floor, a purple bruise marked his jawline. Carrie stood across the room, the gun in her hand. He dragged Travis to his feet and cuffed his hands behind him.

"You're coming with me."

Travis's swayed, almost losing his balance. "Hey, what the hell…."

Nick grabbed his arm, his face inches from his. "I said you're coming with me."

Travis eyed Carrie. "Are you just gonna stand there and do nothing? Shoot *him!"*

"Don't listen to him. Empty the gun and give it to me," Nick said.

She removed the bullets from the cylinder and handed Nick the gun.

"No, Travis. I'm not going to shoot anybody ever again. You're lucky he didn't shoot you when he had the chance. Go with him, Travis. You created this mess, maybe he can get you out of it. Do whatever he says."

"I can't believe you would turn your back on me. I'm in your blood. You must have figured it out by now. Please, listen to me, Carrie. You know deep inside who I am, don't you?"

Carrie froze. Her eyes blazed into his. "Did you say please? How many times have I said that word to you? How many times, Travis?"

Her hands curled into fists at her side. She moved closer, and shouted, "Please don't hit me, Travis. Please stop, Travis. I know who the hell you are. You're the man who broke me. The man who made me feel worthless and afraid. I don't want your sick, twisted love. Let me go. That's all I want. Let go, Travis."

"Carrie, don't do this." A flash of temper lit his face. "You'll regret it."

"I regret ever having met you." She turned away and disappeared up the stairs.

"Don't walk away from me. Carrie, I'm—"

Nick snatched Travis's collar and spun him around. "Not another word. Shut up and move." He shoved him outside and then forced him into the trunk of the car.

"If I hear any more noise out of you, I'll pull over and pump a couple of bullets right into that fat head of yours," Nick said, slamming the trunk shut.

By the time Nick reached the cabin, his mind was set. He flipped open the center console and put on his black leather gloves, and then hauled Travis out of the trunk. The 9mm snug against Travis's spine, he nudged him forward and inside. He grabbed one of the kitchen chairs. "Sit down."

Travis glared at him. The muscles and veins in his neck strained against his skin. He clenched his teeth. His jaw clicked in the silence. "I don't think so."

Nick jammed the barrel into the side of Travis's head. "I said, sit down."

"Look, fella, this here is all wrong." Travis eyed him and then dropped down onto the chair. "I ain't got the money. You already know Carrie has it."

"It makes no difference to my boss who has the money." He watched as the light came on in Travis's head. "I see you finally get it."

"Wait," Travis said "There must be some way we can make this right. With your boss, I mean."

Nick smirked. How stupid, how naive this jerk was. "I'm afraid not. He's not a forgiving man. You killed two of his men and made off with a couple million dollars."

"Look here, it wasn't just me involved in all of this. I suffered, too. Carrie killed Carlos, shot me, and ran off with the money."

Nick locked eyes with him, simmering inside. "Save your story. I'm well aware of who did what. From the day she met you, that poor woman never stood a chance. First, her own mother abused her. Then you came along … the devil who wanted to control her through fear. Congratulations on your accomplishment."

Travis looked away. "You don't know nothin'. I love that girl more than life itself, and she loves me. Carrie is my whole world."

"You love *her!*" Nick spat." Carrie is scared to death of you. Is that your definition of love?"

Travis whirled his head around, his voice filled with rage. "Carrie's tied to me. She's my blood. Do you hear me? My *blood!*"

The muscles in Nick's chest tightened. At a loss for words, he fell silent, sick to his stomach, not wanting to believe what he heard.

"Are you telling me Carrie's … Carrie is your daughter?" Nick stammered in disbelief.

Travis leaned back in the chair. He puffed out his chest. "That's right, fella, my own flesh, and blood. I told you she's tied to me. I'm the reason that girl is in this world."

Nick inhaled, trying to control the rage building inside him. He recalled Carrie's face, the sparkle in her eyes reduced to ash when she confessed that as a child, she used to pray her father would come to her rescue. He eyed Travis. Hot bolts of rage shot through him. "Does she know?"

Travis stayed silent. He curled his lips, his face a mask of defiance, but his trembling limbs told a different story. Nick could see right through it all. He was terrified.

He moved closer, raised the gun, and aimed at Travis's forehead. "I said, does she know?"

Travis's indignation retreated, the color drained from his face. Beads of sweat formed on his brow and upper lip. "No, no. I never told her."

Knowing this monster was her father would break Carrie completely. Travis had planned on telling her. Nick was sure of it. "But you meant to. You started to tell her at the house, didn't you?"

"Maybe," Travis muttered. "I wanted to tell her the truth after all these years. How much I love her. How much we belong to each other."

Nick erupted into full-blown fury. "You sick bastard. You abused and slept with your own daughter!"

Only one thought came to Nick's mind. Carrie must never find out who her father is. She'd never come to grips with it. He grabbed the back of Travis's shirt and pulled him up to his feet. "Outside, *now!*"

Nick marched Travis into the woods behind the house. Mist rose up and dissolved in the cool air as daylight began to filter in. Beds of crisp fallen leaves and twigs popped and snapped beneath the weight of their feet. In a small clearing under towering pines mingled with the scent of bark and fertile earth, Travis begged for his life.

"Please, please, there's gotta be a way to fix things."

Nick pushed him forward. "Nothing could ever fix what you've done. Keep moving."

They reached a thick bed of green moss. Nick pushed him onto his knees and held the barrel of the gun to the back of his head.

Travis shook, the cuffs on his wrists rattled. "Wait, wait. Listen. Let me talk to your boss. I can explain what happened."

Nick pushed harder and planted the barrel firmly against Travis's head. "Not good enough."

"Okay, okay. Please tell me what I can do. Surely, there's something. I don't want to die!"

Nick remained silent, rocked by what Travis had revealed to him.

"I know what you want!" Travis cried. "It's Carrie. If you let me go, you can have her."

Nick tightened his grip on the gun, disgusted by this creature, this thing he was about to kill. Travis Montgomery wasn't worth the cost of the bullet about to rip through his brain.

"Carrie isn't a possession you can give away," Nick said. "If you had one ounce of decency inside, you would know that." He wrestled with his promise to her and glanced up at the sky. Dawn began to break above the treetops.

Nick stared down at Travis. "You think I'll strike some kind of bargain with you? Problem is, I can't trust anything you say."

"You can— you can trust me," Travis said, his pleas coming faster. "I'll go away. She'll never see me again. I won't bother her anymore."

Nick stepped back. "And I'm going to make sure you don't."

Adrenaline surged through his body. His senses heightened. He squeezed the trigger twice. The soft sound of two short bursts from the silencer on his gun hit the air as the bullets shattered Travis's skull.

Their nest disturbed, a band of black crows, high up in the trees, squawked, scattered, and took flight overhead as Travis slumped into the wet bed of moss. He watched Travis's body twitch and then go still.

Rays of sunlight swept across the dead man lying in the woods. A new day had arrived. Nick turned away. His promise to Carrie fulfilled.

CHAPTER 33

CARRIE

D awn breached her bedroom and Carrie opened her eyes. A quiet dread swirled in the pit of her stomach. Her heart galloped, and she took several long breaths to steady it.

She tiptoed to the window and peered out. A car sped by dusting up a pile of leaves. They danced and swirled like acrobats across the pavement. An old grey Ford pick-up cruised past and then backfired, making her jump. She moved away and surveyed her surroundings. The sun's golden rays seeped into her room. So menacing in the dark, now the soft blue walls comforted her. Her unease lessened. The pounding in her chest ceased, and she began to relax.

Later, after showering, she stood in front of the mirror blanketed with steam. She cleared the mirror with her towel. Ugly purple bruises lined the sides of her throat. Brushing them with her fingertips, she prayed that this would be the last time he marked her body. Eager for Nick's arrival, she pushed away thoughts of Travis and the events of the night before.

She tugged on a pair of jeans and a heavy maroon colored sweater. The telephone rang, interrupting her thoughts. She raced downstairs to grab the phone.

Aunt May's voice sailed through the line. "The authorities are still holding the body due to the investigation. I'm not sure when I'll return to Laurel."

"Oh, Aunt May. I'm sorry you're there all by yourself."

"Don't apologize, I understand why you couldn't come."

"Is there anything you need me to do from this end?"

"No, dear. No worries. I'll catch the first available flight when everything is settled."

Carrie thanked her again for taking care of things in Arizona. Luckily, her aunt hadn't witnessed what happened here in her own home last night.

She was pouring her first cup of coffee when a tap on the kitchen door made her spin around. Nick strolled in. Still a bit on edge from last night, her tension eased. His broad shoulders stooped, a look of exhaustion covered his face.

"I think you could use some of this." Her hand trembled as she held out the cup.

He smiled, his green eyes full of gratitude. "Yes, thanks."

She motioned for him to sit. "About last night, I…" Carrie said.

He took several sips of the coffee. "We don't have to talk about it."

Carrie's muscles grew taut. Afraid to ask, she waited.

Nick set his cup down. "Travis is gone. He won't bother you again."

At the mention of his name, her body grew rigid, knowing it was impossible to make Travis do anything. She studied Nick's face, convinced he hadn't told her all of what happened. The truth lay hidden behind his eyes. And the truth was also the knot in her stomach when she woke. Its meaning clear. Right now, she didn't want to hear it, wouldn't know how to deal with it. For now, she'd push the truth away, knowing one day she'd have to face it. Instead, her focus needed to be on getting the money to Nick's boss.

"What do we do after we dig up the money?" she asked.

He looked puzzled. "We? Carrie, there is no *we*. I have to take the money to my boss and try to fix things."

"Maybe if I go with you—"

"That's not a good idea. No way you're going with me. I'll handle this. I told you, I can't make any promises. I'm not sure what's going to happen. If things don't go well, I will come back for you."

Carrie shot up from the chair. She looked down at her hands. Spreading her arms out, she stepped toward him. Tears stung her eyes.

"Do what you need to do now. If you have to kill me, just do it!"

Nick rose and faced her. "Carrie, no matter what happens I'm not going to kill you. If I intended to kill you, don't you think you'd be dead by now?"

She shook her head and stared at the floor. Should she believe him? He could change his mind at any time and kill her. She didn't know how much power his boss held over him.

Nick reached out, and his warmth engulfed her. He drew her close and held on. She didn't try to fight him. After a few moments, he let go, cupped her face with one hand, and swept her tears away with his other.

"Carrie, I meant what I said. I won't hurt you. I know that's hard for you to believe. You haven't trusted anyone in a long time. With all that you've told me, how much you suffered, I could never contribute to that."

Nick brushed a strand of hair from her cheek. His eyes searched her face as he cradled it in his hands. "I could never hurt you."

A strange flutter traveled across her stomach. Excitement mixed with longing. All of it foreign to her, but she still wasn't sure what to believe.

His hands fell away from her face, and she arched her neck. His compassion showed itself when he caught sight of her bruises. He bent his head, and his lips left a trail of soft kisses on her delicate skin, and then his mouth took hers, gentle but urgent and she leaned into him. He finished the kiss, and her arms came up. She let her fingertips skate across the back of his neck.

But then, her wounds still raw, she drew back. "Nick, I can't."

He let his arms drop. "It's okay, I understand. This is all too fast for you. The last thing I would ever do is force you."

She fidgeted, unsure what to do next. She hadn't wanted to admit she'd been attracted to him from the start. It meant opening herself up to the possibility of another man taking over her life. Only Nick wasn't just any man. She sensed he understood her … Travis, the murder, everything.

Carrie dropped down into the chair. She studied the dark depths of the coffee mug. "I'm not used to—"

He sat opposite her. "I know. I'm a patient man, Carrie. I can wait."

She peered up at him. "What did you mean then, when you said you'd come back for me?" Her long tear stained lashes glistened like silk thread.

"I said I'd be honest with you and I meant it. If my boss doesn't agree to let you go, I'm going to protect you from him, but I want you to understand it means leaving Laurel."

Stunned, she sat up straight. "Leave Laurel? I don't want to leave Laurel." Thoughts of Aunt May and the town she had grown to love lay heavy inside.

"You might have no choice. Staying here puts your life and those around you in jeopardy. My boss will send someone else to take my place. As a matter of fact, we'd both be in danger."

She placed a hand on her chest, her heart skipped beneath her fingers. *Danger.* The word coming from his lips held a deeper meaning.

How could she leave with a man she hardly knew? She did that once before, sixteen years ago. It hadn't ended well.

"How do I know I can trust you, Nick?"

He leaned forward and rested his hands on the table. "Look, if my not taking your life isn't proof enough, there isn't anything else I can do."

Still doubtful, she chewed her bottom lip. "I want to believe you, but it's hard."

"It's the only way, Carrie. If you stay, you'll die. I can protect you, but you must be prepared to leave here."

She shuddered inside at his words. "And go where? For how long?' she asked.

"Let's not get that far ahead." He nodded in the direction of the kitchen door. "I guess you better show me where the briefcase is buried."

Carrie hesitated, letting Nick's words sink in. She refilled their cups. "For now, I won't ask you anymore questions, but before we dig up the briefcase, we should eat. I'll fix some eggs and toast, and then we'll go out to the yard."

Nick glanced around impatiently. "We need to get started."

A smile tugged at her lips. "No arguments. It's the least I can do."

Nick's stomach rumbled. He threw up his hands. "Okay, sounds good." He settled into a chair at the table.

As she prepared the eggs, she realized that she wasn't used to speaking her mind. It was almost exhilarating to be able to say what she wanted and not worry about repercussions.

They finished eating and went out to the yard. She grabbed a shovel from the shed and led him to the corner of the yard. He took the shovel and stomped on the blade, driving it into the dirt.

The slight morning breeze carried the scent of the dark, rich soil through the air. She plopped down and sat among the cinnamon-colored pine needles. Hopefully, Nick would return the money, and all would be well. Maybe she wouldn't have to leave Laurel after all.

Ten minutes later, a sleek band of sweat across his forehead, he stopped digging and leaned against the shovel. "Are you sure this is the spot?"

Carrie jumped up. "Positive." She pointed to the hole next to the mound of dirt. "It should be right here. This is the spot." Her mind reeled. She replayed the day, step by step. Blood drained from her face, and her heart lurched.

"Oh my God, it can't be," she said.

"What is it? What's going on?" Nick tossed the shovel down. "You either lied to me about where the money is or—"

"I didn't lie to you." She gestured toward the mound of dirt. I buried it right where I said I did. But…"

"Carrie, this is serious. Did anybody see you bury it?'

Her mouth went dry. "Only one person could have." She told him about Will Medlow standing across the yard.

"Where does this kid live?"

"Nick, you can't go there, he's just a young boy. He doesn't realize how much trouble he's caused. Let me handle this, please."

"You can't handle this, Carrie. This boy has a whole shit load of money and guns. His life is at risk now, too. We don't know who else he might have told." He shook his head. "No, leave this to me."

Carrie was adamant. "Not this time. I messed up, and I want to take care of this, Nick. I think I can get him to trust me. I can't explain it. There was something about him."

"What do you mean?"

"It sounds silly. He had this look on his face. And his eyes...I can't explain it. They were sad. Please give me a little time to see what I can find out."

"Time is one thing we don't have. I'm already in deep with my boss. All this should have been settled by now." He tossed the shovel aside and strode toward the house. "Let's go inside, I need to wash up."

Nick finished at the sink, and Carrie grabbed two cold beers from the fridge. She handed one to him.

"Thanks." He took several sips, and then set the bottle on the counter. "Look, I'll give you a chance. But in the meantime, I'm going to go and see my boss."

"Without the money?"

"No."

"But we haven't got it."

"I do. I have more than enough of my own money. It may buy us some time," he said.

"No, Nick. I can't let you do that. This is my fault. I should have been more careful."

"At this point, we don't have a choice." He grabbed the bottle and drained the rest of the beer. "Meantime, you go and talk to this kid. Make him understand how important that briefcase is." He studied her face for a moment. "If you're unsuccessful, I'm afraid I'll have to handle things."

"I know what I have to do. I can take care of this." She grabbed his hand and squeezed.

His eyes held hers, and he brought her hand to his lips and kissed it. He led her to the door. "I'll come back as soon as I can." He leaned down, kissed her softly on the lips, and left.

The silence of the small kitchen closed in, and she wished Nick hadn't gone. Somehow, he eased the turmoil inside her. Nick understood her. He didn't judge her, and she wasn't one to judge anybody's life.

She started to go upstairs when the front doorbell rang, interrupting her thoughts. Even though Nick had assured her Travis was gone, her insides shook as she walked to the front window. She clutched at the curtain and pushed it back. It was Will Medlow.

CHAPTER 34

NICK

Nick drove toward the heat of Miami and his fate. Beside him on the front seat lay a briefcase containing two million dollars of his own money. He could well afford to lose the cash after ten years in Ricardo's employ. Between the money he made and investments, he was set for the rest of his life. The two million made but a small dent in his savings.

A cooler rested in the trunk. Inside the cooler, lay a pair of hands requested by Ricardo Santiago. After he killed Travis, he buried what was left in the woods. And although Carrie brewed coffee and cooked breakfast as if it were a normal day, he sensed she knew the truth, felt her turning from it. The homemaker routine was her way of dealing. However, it sure did feel nice for those brief moments.

He reflected on the soft curves of Carrie's body up against his, the scent of her hair beneath his chin. Echoes of her stayed with him. She was the type of woman who led you even when you didn't want to follow.

Carrie deserved to have a good life. She'd suffered horrific abuse, fractured, crippled with a fear fed to her by one of the most disgusting human beings Nick had ever come across. He could never erase the scars life left on her. Only time could help do that.

Nick longed to give her all that she desired and more. Though he imagined she'd ask for very little. Working as a waitress in a small town with two million dollars in her possession was testament to that.

No other woman had ever affected him the way Carrie did. Murder had formed a common thread between the two of them. Pulling them closer to one another. He'd make it his mission to help her heal. Help her learn to trust again, to trust him. Although they'd gotten closer before he left, he could tell her skepticism still remained.

His own healing was another matter. There wasn't any justification for all the murders he committed for Ricardo over the years. The majority of them were criminals in their own right, but killing them had brought him down to their level.

Today, he knew with certainty that Travis was his last kill. He'd commit murder again only if Carrie's or his own life were at stake.

Nick pulled up to the wrought iron gates, knowing the man who lived behind them would decide his future. A man who depended on his loyalty and had saved him from himself all those years ago. His debt to Ricardo stole away his freedom bit by bit the longer he stayed a killer.

The damage was done. His course set. Ricardo could never understand how Carrie changed his life. How a marriage between him and Carmela would be even more futile now.

He lowered the window. Ernesto stooped, peered in at him. "Nicky D, this is a surprise, *amigo.*"

Nick had decided not to call ahead. "It's important I see him."

Ernesto's brows drew together. "*Espera un momento.*" He walked several feet, cell phone up to his ear, he nodded his head. "*Si señor. Si hombre jefe.*" Ernesto turned, punched in the gate code, and waved Nick through.

Armando waited at the front door. "Mr. Nicky D. It is good to see you again."

"Thanks," Nick said. He followed Armando to Ricardo's study. True to form, Armando tapped on the door, opened it, and disappeared.

Nick set the cooler down and closed the door behind him. Ricardo leaned against his desk. Ever faithful, Chino sat erect on the floor next to him. He whimpered a soft greeting as Nick approached.

"I was beginning to worry, *compadre,*" Ricardo said.

Nick didn't respond but handed him the briefcase instead.

Small lines of confusion and doubt formed on Ricardo's face.

"Come, sit." He gestured toward the leather sofa. "You look tired from the drive." Ricardo placed the briefcase on his desk.

Chino's cold, wet nose nudged Nick's hand. He gave him a pat on his head while Ricardo poured two shots of tequila and handed one to him. Both men raised their glasses.

"Salud," Ricardo said.

Nick took a sip of the tequila. For the first time, the amber liquid didn't go down easy. He set the glass on the end table ignoring what was left.

Ricardo glanced at the shot glass and then eyed Nick.

"Ricardo, we need to talk about this last job."

Ricardo opened the briefcase. "First, let me see what you have brought." He nodded with approval at the neat stacks of cash. "Nice work, Nick." Ricardo retrieved the cooler. He lifted the lid, and surveyed its contents.

"Did you forget something, *amigo?*" Ricardo slammed the lid shut and dropped into his chair behind the desk.

Chino, curious, started toward the cooler.

Ricardo pointed his finger at the dog. *"Sentarse, Chino!"*

At the command, Chino's hind legs dropped, and he sat, his enormous head angled, eyes questioning his master.

Nick rubbed his palms together. "Please, allow me to speak before I answer that question."

"Go on. You have my attention. What is this all about?"

"I've always done what you've asked me to do. This time, the circumstances were different. Complicated."

"Circumstances? Complicated?" Ricardo looked puzzled. "What are you trying to say? The job was simple. Find the people who killed Carlos and Eddie, get the money, and deliver their hands."

Nick's spine stiffened at his words. "No, it wasn't simple. At least, not for me."

Ricardo's face tensed. "You are not being clear, Nick. Start making sense. I'm losing patience."

"I found the man and the woman. I killed the man, Travis Montgomery, brought you his hands and the money. The woman is still alive."

Ricardo's expression soured. "What do you mean, she is alive? Those were not your orders."

"I'm more than aware of that." Nick kept his voice steady. "She was forced to do what she did. The blame lies solely with this Travis Montgomery."

Nick was no fool, Ricardo wanted Carrie dead. It was a matter of pride and respect in the drug business, but he wanted out, and he wanted Carrie with him even though the consequences could prove deadly.

Ricardo rose and came around from behind his desk. His eyes blazed.

"When did I ever care about whose fault it was?" he said, his voice a cold bar of steel. "I cannot believe what you are telling me. All these years, you have never given me a reason to question your loyalty. And now, a woman— a woman has caused you to disgrace your profession and destroy our relationship. We were soon to be relatives, *mi yerno.*" Grabbing the decanter from the bar, he poured another shot and downed it.

Nick wasn't surprised at Ricardo's reaction, but how could he explain he needed Carrie in his life? For the past ten years, he had never let anyone in. Never let his guard down. He'd lost too much. With Carrie, he was willing to take a chance, extend a bridge, if she would cross it. If she wouldn't cross that bridge, he'd build one to her heart. No one, not even Ricardo, was going to stop him.

Ricardo paced the length of the room. He scowled at Nick. "How could you let her live even though I gave you orders to the contrary? She is out there now, free, and two of my men are dead."

He had expected Ricardo's reaction. Bracing himself for worse, he forged ahead. "I know how unhappy this makes you—"

"Unhappy! No *compadre,* this makes me much more than unhappy. You have taken my trust in you and thrown it in my face."

"I have always been loyal to you but just this once I need you to cut me some slack," Nick shot back. "Yes, I let the woman live. I took pity on her, whether you like it or not. She has no knowledge of you or your business. It won't harm anyone if she lives."

"No, no, *compadre.*" Ricardo shook his head. "I sense there is something you are not telling me. This woman, just how much does she mean to you? I think she has more than your pity."

Nick let out a breath of frustration. "Since you asked the question, I won't lie to you. Yes, she does have more than my pity. I have strong feelings for her. I can't explain how it happened. It just did."

Ricardo banged his fist on the desk. "You are like a son to me, Nick. I knew things were not going well. But out of loyalty to you, and respect for all we have been through together, I chose to ignore it. What you have done insults the kindness I have shown toward you. It interferes with my business and my reputation as well."

He scrutinized Ricardo's face and the anger boiling just below the surface, but he needed to finish. "There is one other thing I need to say. This was my last job. I'm done. If my loyalty to you has counted for anything over the years, then you'll understand I've had enough. No more kills for me."

Ricardo locked eyes with him. "Things do not work that way. You know this, Nick. No one walks away from me, not unless I let them go. I'm afraid that is something I cannot do. You have dishonored me. And you have dishonored my daughter."

A sudden tap at the door made both men turn.

"*Papá,* it's me." Carmela's voice rang from the other side.

Ricardo grabbed the cooler and stashed it underneath his desk along with the briefcase. "Come in, *mi amor.*"

The door opened, and Carmela crossed the room, a warm pool of light filling the chasm between the two men. Her white ruffled blouse set off her brown eyes and caramel skin. Dark jeans hugged her slim body above white leather sandals. Her hair, swept up and knotted neatly on top of her head exposed her gold hoop earrings swaying gently. She smiled and held out her arms toward Nick.

"Hello, stranger." She took his hands, pulled him close, and planted a kiss on each of his cheeks. The earthy scent of sandalwood drifted in the air.

"It's good to see you, Carmela," Nick said.

Her mouth edged up at the corners, and she wagged a finger at him. "I hope you weren't going to leave without saying hello."

"Never. You're too special for me to do that."

Carmela glanced at her father.

Ricardo's face, relaxed, showing no outward sign of his anger.

"I was hoping to show Nick the Arabian you gave me."

Ricardo smiled. "Of course, you must. He's the most impressive horse to complement our stable."

Going to see Carmela's horse was the last thing he wanted to do. Out of politeness, he said, "I would love to see him."

"Good, I'll leave the two of you to finish your business. Come to the patio when you're done." She smiled at Ricardo. "Maybe you can convince him to stay for dinner, *Papá*. Armando is preparing *Sudado de Pollo*." She turned, and her eyes settled on Nick. "If I remember, it's one of your favorites."

"Yes, it is," Nick confessed. "But I'm not sure if I have time to stay for dinner." He watched her glide past him to the door.

"See if you can persuade him, *Papá.,*" she called over her shoulder. Carmela focused her attention on the dog. "Come, Chino, you need some exercise."

Chino hesitated, eyes focused on his master, waiting. Ricardo snapped his fingers and then pointed toward Carmela. *"Seguir, Chino."*

Chino padded over to her.

"See you later, Nick," she called out.

It struck Nick how Carmela took the light with her. The one lit candle in the room had gone out, leaving blackness around the two men as they stared at each other.

Ricardo spoke first. "Tell me, Nick. How is it you have no feelings for Carmela? You've known her almost all of her life. Yet, you tell me, this woman, a person who you never knew existed before the robbery means something to you, knowing that she murdered Carlos in cold blood. Help me to understand."

"I didn't plan on this happening." Nick swiped a hand through his hair in frustration and sat on the sofa. "But I can't disregard my feelings either."

"I see." Ricardo collapsed into his chair. He leaned forward, his hands clasped so tight his knuckles turned white.

"You disappoint me, Nick." A shadow clouded his face. "Most of all, Carmela will be disappointed. She may not admit it, but she is in love with you. This will break her heart."

"I'm sorry, Ricardo. Carmela is wonderful. She will make someone very happy one day. Even if this woman was not in the picture, I told you before, that man is not me."

"So then, you have chosen your path. You refuse to put an end to this woman, and you bestow this great insult on me concerning my daughter."

He stood up. Nick rose from the sofa. They faced each other.

"I won't ask your forgiveness," Nick said. "But I want to thank you for saving me when I thought I was beyond saving. It will always mean a lot to me." He held out his hand.

Ricardo didn't reciprocate. "Your words have meaning, but they will not change anything."

Nick saw the thunder behind the man's eyes. Ricardo's hatred lashed him like a whip across his back.

"Remember, Nick, there is no walking away. Not from a betrayal like this. I can't let you do that."

Nick dropped his hand. "I understand." He walked to the study door. "I'll go see Carmela before I leave. But I'm warning you, Ricardo. When you come after us, and I know you will, I'm going to fight like hell to keep this woman safe."

"I would expect nothing less," Ricardo said. "And I will fight like hell to destroy you both."

Nick slid the door closed for the last time. This CHAPTER of his life was over. He'd gambled and turned the page onto a new more treacherous one.

He found Carmela on the patio playing tug of war. Chino growled and held onto the opposite end of the stick in her hand. She turned when she heard him walk in. Her face lit up.

"There you are. All done with business?"

He grinned and shrugged. "All done."

"Come, let's go over to the stables." She hooked her arm through his, and they strolled toward the barn. Chino ran ahead.

"He's a different dog from when you found him, Nick. It's good you have a soft spot in your heart. It suits you."

"Any decent person would have done for him what I did."

They stopped at the barn door, and Carmela called out, "Mateo, bring Allegra out to the pasture, please."

A short, stocky, dark-skinned man wearing a white Cattleman's hat poked his head out.

"*Si señorita*, right away."

Carmela grabbed Nick's hand and led him to the pasture. "Wait until you see him. He's magnificent."

They reached the white rail fence with Mateo leading Allegra. Nick released Carmela's hand and rested his own on the fence. Mateo opened the gate and slipped the lead rope from around the horse's neck.

The Arabian pranced around the pasture. His coal black coat, his long, lean neck, the impeccably formed white crest on his forehead brought one word to mind. Majestic. Nick could only imagine what Ricardo had paid for the horse.

Carmela called to Allegra. Allegra's ears pricked up, and he ambled over. She hoisted herself onto the top rail to meet the horse face to face. Allegra lowered his head and nuzzled her. Carmela laughed with delight.

"See, he knows me already. Such a smart horse you are, Allegra." She cocked her head. "What do you think?"

"He's something else, Carmela, a real beauty, like his owner." Nick gave her a wink.

Allegra trotted around the pasture and then bent his head to nip at the grass. Carmela jumped down from the fence and faced Nick.

"So, what secrets are you hiding behind those green eyes of yours?"

"Secrets? I don't have any secrets." He hated lying to her. "Especially not from you."

She stepped closer to him. "Yes, and it's no secret my father wants us to marry."

"Carmela, I…."

Carmela pressed a finger to his lips. "It's all right, Nick. You don't have to say anything." She trailed her finger along his cheek. "I know you're not in love with me. You wouldn't be the man I admire and love if you married me because my father wanted you to."

Relieved, he took her hand. "Carmela, you're a wonderful girl, and the right man will come along."

She laughed and said, "See, you still think of me as a little girl."

Nick laughed, too. "No, the little girl I remember with the scrawny legs, braces on her teeth, and bad attitude is long gone. Standing here now is a smart, well-educated, gorgeous, wild young woman. The kind of woman men chase in hopes of taming."

He examined her face, locked his eyes on hers. If she knew the type of work he had done for her father, would she still accept him? With her privileged upbringing, murder, lies, deception, and the drug business had never touched her. Ricardo made sure of that.

"Promise me something, Carmela," Nick said.

"Anything for you." She squeezed his hand.

"Don't ever let anyone tame you, put out the fire inside of you. The world is a tough place. It will serve you well when you need it."

"I promise." She held onto his hand as they walked toward the house.

He said goodbye and kissed her on each cheek and then whistled and motioned to Chino. Chino padded over, and Nick rubbed his neck. "Be a good boy now, Chino," he said.

As he drove away, he watched Carmela grow smaller in the rearview mirror. A tiny figure, she receded into his past, unaware he would never return to this place. Unaware of the impending battle about to begin.

CHAPTER 35
WILL

Will Medlow, hands pressed deep in the front pockets of his jeans, waited for Carrie to answer the doorbell. If she agreed to give him some of the money, he could go ahead with his plan to find a safe place for him and his mom to live. He just needed to convince her.

Carrie peered out from behind the front window curtain. The lock gave a loud snap, and the door opened.

Will hesitated and then forced a smile. "Hi, I'm Will Medlow. I don't know if you remember me."

Carrie pulled the door all the way open. "Of course. I remember you. Come inside."

Will followed her. She pointed to a chair at the kitchen table.

"Sit down, please."

She grabbed two cans of soda from the refrigerator and placed one in front of him.

Nervous, his throat dry, he popped the top and gulped the soda. He hoped Carrie would give him the chance to explain things.

"It's okay, Will." A slight smile creased her face. "I think I know why you're here."

Seconds ticked by. A clutch of panic hit the pit of Will's stomach. He laced his fingers together to keep them from trembling. "Well—then you know I stole the briefcase you buried."

"Yes, I do." She folded her arms. "I also know you had no business doing that."

Will's shoulders slumped. "You're right, I didn't." He shifted his body, feeling even more uncomfortable in the hard-wooden chair. "Can I tell you why I took it?"

"Go on," Carrie said. She swallowed a small sip of her soda.

"I watched you bury it, and I came back to the house and dug it up." He waited. Carrie's silence made him uneasy. Should he have come here and confessed?

"What you did was wrong, Will. You put people's lives at risk."

Will swiped a hand through his hair, brushing it away from his eye. "Listen, I never meant to cause any trouble, but when I opened it and saw all that money." He stopped. How could he explain things to a virtual stranger?

"It's okay Will, you can tell me."

Will clasped his hands tighter. He'd never trusted anyone enough to tell them his dark secret. His shame rose to the surface, but he needed her help. He forced himself to continue.

"I thought I could use the money to help me and my mom."

"Is she in some kind of trouble?"

He avoided her eyes. His chin dropped to his chest, and he stared at the floor. The right words wouldn't come.

"Will, trust me, I'm not one to judge. I'd like to help if I can."

He lifted his head, still avoiding eye contact. "You see, my dad's not a nice person. He does things when he gets mad."

Carrie sat up straight. "Will, look at me."

Slowly, he met her eyes, his shame almost too much to handle.

"What things does your Dad do?" she asked.

Will's hands balled into fists. "He hits."

"Hits how?" She reached and laid a gentle hand on top of his.

Will pulled his hand away. His eyes abandoned hers once again. "Hard. He hits hard."

"Is that what happened to your lip?" she asked.

"My father," Will said. His chin trembled.

Carrie slipped around the table and sat on the chair next to him. Will flinched and held up his hands warning her not to draw closer.

"Oh, I'm so sorry," she said. "I…''

"Don't." I don't want you to feel sorry for me. I can take it when he hits me. It's my mom who needs help."

"He hits her too?"

"Yes, sometimes." He looked down at his balled fists, uncurled his fingers.

"Does anyone else know about this? Family, relatives, friends?"

"No. No one. I never told anybody. You're the first person I've told the truth to."

"But, Will, why the briefcase?"

The desperation inside boiled over. Tears shone in his eyes, collecting in large pools beneath his lids. "I came here today to ask you if I get the briefcase back, will you give me part of the money?"

Her expression changed from shock to one of disbelief. "What do you mean? You don't have it?"

"N—no." Will's heart thumped. "My dad found it. He took it and locked it in his study. He said he is going to decide what to do with it."

"I bet," Carrie said. She pushed her chair away from the table and popped up. She paced around the small kitchen.

"Listen, this is a bad situation, Will. I would be more than glad to give you some of it, but the money doesn't belong to me."

"It doesn't?" He sucked in his bottom lip, despair washing over him. "Who does it belong to then? And the guns, what about the guns?"

She shook her head. "I'm not going to discuss who the money belongs to or the guns with you. For your own safety, the less you know, the better. I'll help you any way I can. First, where is your Dad now?"

"At work, but my mom's home."

Carrie stood up. "Okay. Let's go."

Will's stomach cinched. "I'm not so sure that's a good idea."

"Don't worry. Let me handle this."

A few minutes later, they arrived at Will's house. They stepped into the front foyer as Claudia emerged from the living room.

"Oh, you're home." Her eyebrow raised in surprise at the sight of Carrie. She looked to Will for an explanation.

"Mom, this is Carrie. She's May Overton's niece."

She offered her hand. "It's nice to meet you, I'm Claudia."

"Nice to meet you, too." Carrie shook her hand. "Mrs. Medlow, we need to talk."

"Please, call me Claudia. Come, sit down."

Will's body tensed. The room grew smaller. His mother was about to find out he'd revealed to Carrie what no one outside of these walls knew.

"It's about the briefcase," Carrie said.

Claudia fidgeted and then cleared her throat. "I can't discuss this with you. You'll have to speak with my husband about it. He'll be home any minute."

Carrie perched on the edge of the sofa. "Look, I'm not upset with Will. He didn't realize all the trouble this caused, but it's extremely important I get the briefcase back."

Claudia stood up, her body started to shake. "I can't do that. My husband would be very upset."

Carrie took note of her shaking. Her heart faltered for a moment. She saw so much of her past self in the woman standing before her. She rose and faced her. "I understand your fear. I was abused by a man for a long time."

Claudia's face flushed. The skin beneath her left eye twitched. "I have no idea what you're talking about." She whirled around to Will. "What have you been saying to her?"

"Please, don't get mad. I had to tell her."

Claudia chewed her bottom lip and looked from Will to Carrie. The color drained from her cheeks. "I don't want you to think—"

"The thing is," Carrie said. "If I don't get that briefcase back, there is going to be a whole lot of trouble, for you and your husband. And Will, too."

"I knew it the moment I saw those guns," Claudia said. Her hand flew to her heart. "I told Will someone did something bad." She dropped onto the sofa, shrunk into the cushions, and looked up at Will.

"Please, listen to her. Do what she says. She'll help us," Will implored.

Claudia, I understand what you're feeling. Honestly, I do," Carrie said. "That's why I'm sure, without a doubt, you already know what the right thing to do is, and I'm going to help you do it."

Her body shaking, she pushed up from the sofa. "Follow me." She led them to Russ's study and pointed. "It's locked in the closet, and I don't have the key."

"Will, get a screwdriver," Carrie ordered. Will bolted from the room, returning seconds later, and handed her a screwdriver. She played with the lock until the door popped open. Carrie reached for the briefcase.

"What the hell is going on here?"

Russ Medlow's voice echoed through the room like thunder across a canyon.

CHAPTER 36

CARRIE

Carrie wheeled around and came face to face with a hulking figure. His arms folded across his chest, his massive body blocking the doorway. "I'll ask one more time. What the hell is going on here?"

Carrie stepped toward him. Her spine stiffened while her leg muscles flexed tight. "Mr. Medlow, I'm Carrie, May Overton's niece." She pointed toward the closet. "That briefcase belongs to me, and I'm taking it."

He drew his shoulders back, his brows creased above steel grey eyes. "I don't think so. The police might take a real interest in what's inside, especially the two guns."

Carrie stood her ground. A sour taste clung to her tongue. She recognized his type. A note of contempt crept into her voice. "And I bet the police might take a real interest in how you beat your wife and son."

He pointed his beefy finger at her. "Who the hell do you think you are? Leave my house *now!*"

"She's not leaving without the briefcase," Will said. "Get out of the way, Dad."

Carrie turned, and her jaw dropped. The briefcase lay open on the closet floor. Will stood, a gun aimed at his father. "Will, no. Put the gun down."

His face twisted with fury, and he looked past her. "Dad, you let her take the briefcase, or I swear—"

"Or you'll what? Shoot me!" Russ pushed past Carrie and lunged at Will. They crashed into one another, wrestling for control of the gun. The crack of a gunshot erupted in the room.

"No!" Claudia screamed.

Gasping, Russ gripped his chest. His eyes bulged, and he slumped to the floor. Will stood over him, the gun still in his hand, aiming, ready to shoot again.

"Will, look at me, look at me," Carrie said. "Give me the gun, Will."

The color had drained from his face. He looked over at Carrie. "I didn't mean to do it. I didn't want him to hurt anyone."

"I know, sweetheart. It's okay," she said. "Give me the gun." She eased toward him. Relief flooded through her when Will let her take the gun from his hand. Fighting to remain calm, she looked at Russ Medlow. He lay still. She knelt and felt for a pulse. "He's gone," she said.

Claudia rushed toward Will. Without tears or recriminations, she held out her arms. "It's over," she said. Will fell into them and wept. "It's all right, Will." She placed her hands on his shoulders. "You need to be strong now."

Will wiped his eyes, and stared at the body lying on the floor. "I'll try," he said.

Claudia turned and faced Carrie, her motherly instincts restored with her husband's death. "Can I trust you with my son?" she asked.

"What do you mean?"

"I want you to leave and take Will with you. I'll call the police, tell them someone broke in," Claudia said.

Carrie hesitated, not sure what to do. If Nick were unsuccessful, she'd be leaving Laurel. "Claudia, I—"

"I know it's a lot to ask, but if he stays, the police are going to question him. He'll fall apart. I don't want my son to end up in jail. Please, take him with you," she pleaded.

Carrie recognized the suffering behind her eyes. A mother's eyes. Claudia was right. It was a real possibility that Will might go to jail. She dropped the gun into the briefcase and slammed it shut. She turned to Will. "Go get some clothes and hurry." Will glanced at his mother.

Claudia nodded her head. "Go on, Will, now."

Will ran from the room and returned a few minutes later, carrying an oversized backpack. His face filled with angst. He hugged Claudia again.

"I love you, Will. You're going to be okay." Claudia's eyes watered. "Honey, don't worry about me. I have nothing to fear anymore." She patted his cheek and stroked his head. "Here, take my cell phone. I have the land line. You go with Carrie. Do this for me. This is the one time I can protect you, so let me do it."

Will leaned down and hugged her neck. "I love you. I promise I'll come back."

"Don't worry, now go."

Claudia placed a hand on Carrie's shoulder. "It's better if you go out the rear."

The two women hugged. "Don't worry, I'll take good care of him. He'll contact you when it's safe." Carrie said. She gripped the handle of the briefcase and slipped out the door with Will.

When they reached May's house, she settled him in one of the upstairs bedrooms. He hadn't spoken a word. It broke her heart to see this young boy withdraw into himself. She wondered about the thoughts running through his head. What happened today would leave scars.

"Will, if you're ready to talk, I'm here."

"No, I don't want to talk about it."

She decided not to pressure him. Sooner or later he'd have to face his father's death. "You try and rest. If you need anything, I'm right downstairs." She closed the bedroom door, whipped out her cell phone and punched in Nick's number. He answered as she headed down the stairs.

"Are you alright?" he asked.

"Yes and no. There was a problem. She continued and explained what happened.

"You handled it just like you said you would."

Carrie broke off and took a breath. "Nick, Will's with me."

"What do you mean, he's with you?"

"I had to bring him with me. I couldn't leave him there and have the police question him. If he got scared, he'd break down and tell them everything. I didn't know what else to do." Unsure, she waited through the silence on the other end. "Nick, are you there?"

"Yes. I'm here. You did the right thing."

She was thankful for the strength in his voice, his reassuring tone.

"I'm on my way to Laurel. I need you to pack. We're leaving as soon as I get there."

"It didn't go well, did it?" she asked.

"No, it didn't. I expected as much. But I made things clear to him. I'm not going to do anything to hurt you."

The weight of his words sunk in. "Oh, Nick, this is all my fault." The decisions she had made these last few months all led to this moment. "I could have tried to do things differently, tried to—"

"Carrie," Nick interrupted. "I told you before, you don't have to feel guilty. Travis gave you no other choice. Now, listen, please. I'll be there before dawn. Promise me, you'll be ready to go."

"We'll be ready by the time you get here."

While she packed, her mind raced. She'd no idea where Nick would take them, but her instincts were telling her leaving was the right thing to do. She remembered Nick's words. If she stayed, she'd die.

Carrie finished packing then spent the next hour writing a letter to May. Just days before, she'd have never fathomed writing such a letter. Laurel had become her home. At the kitchen table, pen, and paper before her, she began the emotional, heart-wrenching letter, all the while trying to ignore the police sirens wailing outside. They were on their way to Will's house for sure.

Without too much detail, she explained her sudden departure as going to help a friend who needed her. Sorry to have to leave without saying goodbye, she promised she'd be in touch soon. She thanked her aunt for her kindness and the invitation to live in her home. Saying goodbye became almost unbearable.

Carrie finished the letter then checked on Will. She leaned against the doorway and stared at the young boy asleep in the bed. Claudia had entrusted her with her child, and she was determined to keep him safe. She retreated to her room to grab a few hours' sleep, not knowing what lie ahead of them.

It was still dark when she decided to wake Will. Nick would be arriving soon, and she wanted them to be ready.

"Will," Carrie said softly. She tapped him awake. "We need to get ready to leave."

Will sat up, sleep in his eyes, he asked, "Where are we going?"

"I'm not sure where, but we must leave Laurel. A friend is coming to help us."

"You're not sure where, or you don't want to tell me."

"Look, Will, I'm being honest with you. There is no time to argue. Get your things together and meet me downstairs."

Nick arrived before dawn. Gone was the black Mercedes and in its place, a white Range Rover. Following a quick introduction, Will helped Nick and Carrie load up the SUV.

Afterward, Nick ushered them inside. "One more thing," he said. "I need a headshot of you and one of Will. He raised his cell, took a picture of Will, and then one of Carrie. "We may need these later on for passports."

Will's head snapped from Nick to Carrie. "Passports?"

"Right now, you have to trust him," Carrie said.

Nick had Carrie delete his cell phone number and gave her and Will his new one. He asked Will not to use his cell until he told him it was safe.

Will sighed. "Like I have a choice."

Outside, she motioned for Will to take a seat in the rear. She wanted a minute to talk to Nick alone. They finished locking up and stood together on the front porch.

"Nick, I hope you understand I couldn't say no."

He took both her hands in his. "I promised you I'd protect you. That goes for Will, too. If he's important to you, then he's important to me."

She met his eyes and beheld the calm below the surface. It soothed her, making her more at ease about agreeing to go with him.

Carrie settled next to him in the Range Rover. A lump formed in her throat and she blinked back tears as they journeyed away from Laurel, the first place she started to call home. She glanced at Aunt May's house, watched it recede into the distance and disappear as they rounded the corner. The shops on Main Street zipped by. Her heart fell when they passed the Palisades Diner. She promised herself, one day she'd make sure to tell Joann how much her friendship meant.

They left the mountains of Pennsylvania behind and six hours later, as night fell, crossed over into Ohio, and continued on, stopping only to eat and refuel. Carrie wondered where they'd end up.

Carrie noted the fatigue on Nick's face, and when they stopped in Illinois, she offered to drive. He agreed and gave her instructions to crossover into Iowa, then South Dakota. Nick reclined in the passenger seat and within minutes, his eyes closed, and he fell asleep.

Carrie glanced over at him. Even fast asleep, his presence was magnetic. His solid muscular body reclined against the tan leather seat, long legs stretched out in front, and his hands resting comfortably in his lap. A killer's hands, she reminded herself.

Not long ago those same hands pointed a gun at her, but the very same hands held her close, soothed her, and made her feel safe again.

Nick was an enigma, a puzzle she didn't quite have all the pieces to. Hopefully, she'd made the right decision to leave Laurel with him. Her gut told her that she did, but she trusted someone once, a long time ago and regretted her decision ever since. And now, she had entrusted her life, and Will's life, to a man she hardly knew. She didn't even know his last name.

Carrie thought about Travis, convinced he was dead. She sensed it the morning she woke up, with her heart pounding. Still, she couldn't bear to hear the words from Nick. If only Travis had been willing to let her go, things might have ended differently for him. For her own sanity, she'd have to put her past with Travis to rest. She had left Laurel behind. Little by little, she needed to distance herself from her memories of Travis.

Carrie looked up at the rearview mirror. Will slept, his body draped across the seat. Leaving his mother under such awful circumstances was tough. She hoped he'd be able to come to terms with what happened between him and his father.

As daylight crept in, Nick took the wheel again. They entered into the Black Hills of South Dakota, their final destination. Nick stopped in front of a pair of wrought iron gates built into the custom stonework. He lowered the window and pressed in a code. The gates parted, and they drove up the paved driveway surrounded by thick green ponderosa pines and umbrellas of aspens, their thin white spotted trunks rooted on either side. A mile later, they pulled up to a massive stone and timber home. A big open porch ran along the front of the house.

"Holy shit," Will exclaimed. The first words he'd spoken since leaving Laurel.

Carrie's jaw dropped. "Nick, where are we? Whose house is this?"

"It belongs to a good friend of mine. You'll meet him soon enough. He offered to let us stay here awhile." Nick plucked a key from the ledge above the door. He inserted it into the heavy oak door and pushed it open.

In the entryway to the left was a mudroom with two closets on either side of a cedar chest. Above the chest sat a long shelf with coat hooks.

They continued down a long hall to a huge great room. Will's mouth dropped open, and he gaped at Carrie. "This is awesome."

Dark wood beams crisscrossed the ceiling above polished wood floors. In the center of the room stood an immense stone fireplace flanked by brown leather sofas strewn with thick throws and fluffy pillows.

A wall of glass let in the magnificent views of the surrounding forest. Oak and ash trees, their leaves orange, yellow, and candy apple red mixed with the deep green of the ponderosa pines. Rugged mountain-tops strained toward the sky in the distance.

Carrie stepped into the open kitchen, ran her fingers across the black granite countertop embedded with flecks of gold. She sized up the large island anchored in the middle of the kitchen and delighted in the warmth of a long line of maple cabinets. There was an unobstructed view of the dining room and a long wooden table and chairs. A large hutch hugged one wall. She rushed to the sliders and slid one open. A natural stone patio with a huge outdoor fireplace complemented the backdrop of the mountain sky.

Nick called out, and she hurried into the great room. "I can't believe people actually live like this," she said.

Nick laughed and reached for Carrie's hand. "Come, let me show you the rest of it."

Will traipsed behind as Nick ushered them into another great room. Mounted above the fireplace was a second large flat screen television. A burgundy sectional rested in front of it. The opposite end held a pool table and a polished wood bar. Another room contained a fully equipped gym.

Upstairs, they trailed through seven bedrooms each with its own on suite. Nick paused in the doorway of the largest one. The master suite.

A king-sized bed faced floor-to-ceiling windows. A sitting area with a fireplace was at the far end. Carrie surveyed the huge master closet.

She sighed with pleasure when she spotted the Carrera marble that graced the floor of the master bath and the tops of the dark mahogany vanity. Twin gilt-framed mirrors hung above each of the double sinks. There was a jetted tub, a spacious walk-in shower, lined from floor to ceiling with honed Travertine tile. Custom shelving held an abundance of fluffy white bath towels and scented soaps.

She could hardly speak. "This is too much."

Amusement played at the corners of Nick's eyes. "Don't get too excited. Like I said, it belongs to a friend. He owns the house and all one hundred and twenty acres surrounding it."

"Wish I had friends like that," Will said.

"Comes in handy," Nick said. "Carrie, this one is yours. Will and I can each use one of the other bedrooms."

Carrie shook her head. "No, I'll take a different one."

Without another word, Will bounded down the hall to stake his claim.

Nick's mouth set in a firm line. "I insist. You get settled." He handed her his cell phone. "I need you to enter your full name and date of birth for me."

"Sure." Carrie typed the information into his phone and handed it to him. She figured he would need it for the passports he mentioned earlier. Leaving the country was something she couldn't even think about right now.

"Good. I'll get Will's information, and then I'll drive into Rapid City to get some supplies." He turned to her and grinned. "I'm going to assume you can cook more than scrambled eggs."

She put her hands on her hips. "You'd be surprised at what I can cook. Bring me a roast, potatoes, carrots, fresh rosemary, and a can of beef stock, and I'll make your head spin."

Nick's face lit up. "You got it. Get comfortable. You're safe here. I have to go out for a while and check on a few things."

They walked downstairs together, and before he left, he kissed her cheek. "Relax. I'll be back in a few hours."

Inside the enormous house, without Nick, she felt small and vacant. It left her unsettled. When Nick was close, he filled a room. She couldn't explain it. Didn't dare to question it. Her world wouldn't feel right until he returned. Any doubts she had earlier about leaving Laurel with Nick receded.

Carrie unpacked her things. Before closing her suitcase, she ran her fingers across the blue baby blanket. She hung everything in the master closet where a variety of men's clothing hung in a neat row on the opposite glider. No women's toiletries or perfume stood on top of the vanity, just several bottles of men's cologne. There was no trace of a woman anywhere.

Her familiar urge to light up was gone. She grabbed her pack of cigarettes and marched into the bathroom. Standing over the toilet, she broke the remaining cigarettes into pieces and tossed them in. They were the last thing that bound her to Travis. She didn't need them anymore.

Dying for a shower, she snatched up her robe, closed the bathroom door, and, for the next fifteen minutes, enjoyed the hot steamy water. She lathered herself and rejoiced in the lavender scent. The rich foamy bubbles raced along her skin. She was almost as happy as the day Aunt May gave her that bicycle, and she soared through the trailer park.

Slowly, the feeling dissipated as reality crept in. With their lives at risk, in all probability, moments like this would be rare.

She toweled off and dressed. Downstairs, the television blasted. She sat beside Will on the leather sofa and didn't let her disappointment show when he inched away.

"Will, don't you think we should talk?"

He leaped up from the couch and frowned at her. "I told you before, I don't want to. Why can't you leave me alone? I killed my father. There is nothing else to say. It's over and done."

Carrie rose and stood toe to toe with him. "Will, you may think it's over and done, but I know better."

Will's brow furrowed, and he glared at her. "How would you know? You never killed anyone." He stepped back., his eyes grew large. "Or, maybe you did," he added. "I wondered about those guns."

The truth in Will's words stung her, but she pressed on. "Listen, Will, this isn't about me. You have to talk this out. Otherwise, it will eat you up inside. You'll never get over it."

His cheeks flushed red. "Get over it? You tell me how I get over all the times he hit me. Hit my mom." His hands balled into fists at his side. "All the times he locked me in the closet. Left me in the dark. You don't understand anything. I'm glad I killed him. I'm glad he's dead. How do I get over feeling that?"

Shocked, Carrie groped to find the right words as he bolted up the stairs. She flinched at the slam of his bedroom door. His anger had taken root deep inside. It was all too familiar. When memories of her mother and Travis reared up unexpectedly, she'd pushed them away, just as Will did now.

Talking with her aunt about some of the terrible things from her past, helped to wash away a little of the darkness inside her. Telling Nick also made the light grow brighter. Today, she almost believed she could begin to heal.

Carrie climbed the stairs and paused outside of Will's bedroom door. She pressed her hand to the polished wood and sighed. Time, she told herself. He needs time. Their futures still so uncertain, she hoped Will had enough of it to help him heal.

CHAPTER 37

NICK

Nick sped toward Rapid City to see Brody Gibson, an hour's drive away, secure in the knowledge that Carrie and Will were safe at the house. Brody, if that was even his real name, kept things on the down low. Nick sent him a text to let him know he was on his way.

He reflected on his conversation with Ricardo. It was unfortunate it had not gone in his favor. He didn't like Ricardo's position, but he understood it. All he could do now was devise a plan to keep the three of them safe.

He arrived downtown and parked the Range Rover across from Avery Hardware and went inside. The store in Rapid City sold more than it advertised to its regular customers.

Rick, the owner, looked up from the register while he rang up a customer. He smiled at Nick and said, "Those items you wanted came in. They're in aisle six."

Nick proceeded down a long aisle filled with plastic pull-out bins full of nails and screws. At the rear of the store, the sign on the read 'Private.' Nick glanced around before slipping inside. He maneuvered around stacks of boxes full of inventory and past another door which led to the basement.

Downstairs, Brody's scrawny frame hunched over a work table. With a magnifying glass in hand, Brody scrutinized a piece of paper. The hanging fluorescent ceiling light reflected off his shaved head. He popped up and spun around on the swivel stool. Setting his magnifying glass on the table, he flashed Nick a huge grin.

"My man, Nicky D. How the hell are you? It's been ages."

The two men shook hands. Brody motioned for him to pull up a chair.

"How about a cold one, man?" Brody grabbed two beers from a mini fridge. His plaid flannel shirt, cowboy boots, and large brass belt buckle screamed cowboy. But Brody's looks were deceptive. Brody was one of the best forgers in the country.

"Thanks, Brody." He swiped the bottle of beer from Brody's hand and settled into the chair.

Brody sat down opposite him, his long legs stretched out in front. He rapped the neck of his bottle on an end table, and the cap flew off. "So where are you off to, you lucky son of a bitch? Spain, Paris, Morocco maybe?"

Nick twisted the cap and took a long draw on his beer. "It's different this time, Brody. I need three books."

Brody looked confused, shook his head, and let out a slow whistle. "It's gonna cost you." He rubbed the pale stubble on his chin. "At least a hundred grand each."

"Money's not a problem Brody, but time is."

Brody ran a palm across his slick head. "How soon do you need them?"

"Like yesterday," Nick said.

"The best I can do is a week. You know my books are prime. They're undetectable by Border Patrol and TSA."

"Without question, you're the best, Brody. It's why I always come to you."

Brody tipped his beer and swallowed. "Something tells me this may be the last time I see you. Am I right?"

"The less I tell you, the better."

He scanned Nick's face. "Aw *no!*" Brody slammed his bottle down. "You screwed with Ricardo Santiago. Are you out of your mind?"

He met Brody's eyes. "Let's just say, Ricardo and I have had a parting of the ways."

Brody arched his brow. "No one has a parting of the ways with Ricardo. At least, not to live to tell about it."

"Brody, I'm trusting you. I need a head start."

"Relax, partner. I don't work for Ricardo, and I've moved locations three times in the last six months. Matter of fact, I'm doing it again. Soon as I'm done with your job, I'm gone. If you need anything else, you know how to find me. Ricardo knows nothing about my connections."

"Thanks, Brody." He finished his beer and pulled out his cell phone.

"Here's the information for the books."

Brody studied the screen. "Hmm. You're Michael Warren, now?"

"Yep."

"And the other two?"

"Names are real. Ricardo doesn't know anything about them."

"Pictures on your cell, too?"

Nick nodded, and Brody connected it to his computer. He downloaded the headshots of Will, Carrie, and Nick.

"Wow! Bet I know the cause of the falling out. She's one gorgeous woman."

"Part true," Nick said. "There's a little bit more to it."

Brody studied him. "Are you positive about this, Nick? There's still might be a chance to make things right with Ricardo."

"Not this time. Ricardo and I are history, for sure. I didn't want it to end this way. Ricardo insisted."

Brody took another pull from his beer. "Yeah, I bet he did." He stood up and held out his hand. "Okay, bro. I'll hit you up when the books are ready."

After Nick left Brody, he picked up the items Carrie asked for and additional staples they would need and headed back to the house. He pulled up to the garage and punched a code in. The door lifted and he drove inside. His arms full of groceries, he brought the bags inside and set them on the kitchen island.

Carrie pranced in and rummaged through the grocery bags. She nodded her head in approval. "You did well. I'll get started. You go relax. You've done enough for one day."

"Thanks," Nick said. He started to leave the kitchen and then stopped. "Where's Will?"

She sighed. "Upstairs. We had a little discussion. I'm worried, Nick. He refuses to talk about what happened. Plus, he mentioned being locked in a closet. I think he suffered much more than we realize at the hands of that animal."

"Give him space. Don't push. When he's ready, he'll come around."

"You're right. It's best to leave him alone for now." She unpacked the groceries and removed the roast from the bag. "Wow, this is a beauty."

Nick chuckled. "Yeah. Now, let's see those cooking skills of yours. I'll be back after I wash up."

Nick showered and changed into jeans and a grey tee shirt. He passed by the closed door of Will's room and decided to let him be. The boy didn't know him. Barely knew Carrie either. They both needed to build his trust.

At the bottom of the landing, the tantalizing aroma of meat roasting in the oven greeted him. He crossed the great room and was almost to the kitchen when he stopped to savor the scene in front of him.

Carrie stood at the stove stirring a pot. Her jet-black ponytail dipped below her shoulders. She picked up a spice jar and added a dash to the pan. She leaned over and lifted the wooden spoon to her lips. She blew air, tasted, and smiled.

It came out of nowhere. The feeling consumed him, pulsed through his body. The air around him changed whenever he looked at her. He could breathe again for the first time in years. Carrie took the clouds away from his eyes, made things hidden visible again. The sweetness in her permeated a room. If he had any doubts before now, they disappeared. He'd made the right decision.

It pained him to think how Travis had treated her and he remained puzzled by her efforts to protect him. He wouldn't judge her for it. He was not one to judge anybody. His demons had moved in long ago, made a permanent home. Vampires, each one, they couldn't be brought out into the light, and there weren't enough wooden stakes to destroy them all. As long as they stayed hidden in their dark place, he'd be okay.

He watched those remarkable eyes of hers light up when she turned toward him. In that split second, he saw his future.

"You're in for a treat," she boasted. Her mouth curved into a smile.

"Smells like it," he said. "I'm no expert, but I know my way around a kitchen pretty well."

She giggled and looked at him in disbelief. "You?"

"Yes, me. D'Angelo's my last name. I'm full-blooded Italian. My mother taught her daughter and both her sons to cook. With my lineage, it would be a sin not to know how to prepare a good meal."

"Well, excuse me," she teased. "In that case, the next dinner's on you."

"If I survive this one," he said.

They burst out laughing as Will walked in. He stomped past them without saying a word and plunked down on a stool by the island.

"Hope you're hungry. Dinner's almost ready," Carrie said.

Still sullen, Will rested his elbows on the counter, chin in his hands. "Sure, I could eat."

Nick peeked over Will's head and winked at Carrie. "How about a quick game of pool before dinner, Will?'

Will lifted his head. "I never learned how to play."

"No problem. I can show you."

Will slid off the stool. "Okay, I guess so."

While Carrie finished preparing dinner, he taught Will eight ball. Will caught on quick, surprising Nick at how adept he was at pocketing balls. During the game, Nick took note of the haunted look on Will's face.

Carrie's assumption was correct. There was something not quite right with him.

"Come and get it while it's hot!" Carrie called out.

They dropped their sticks into the cue rack. Will turned toward the kitchen as Nick reached out and touched his shoulder.

"Will, I—"

Will reared back, his hands balled into fists. He raised his arms in a defensive mode. Stone-faced, his eyes full of hatred, he spit the words out. "Don't touch me. Don't you touch me."

Surprised, Nick moved away. Someone hurt this kid bad. "Whoa— I'm sorry. I just wanted to say if you need to talk, I'll be more than glad to listen."

Will glared at him. "You and Carrie. Both of you want me to talk. I already told her I don't want to talk." Will dropped his arms but his fists remained clenched.

"We're only trying to help."

"You can't help me. Neither one of you knows what kind of hell I lived through in Laurel."

"You're only half-right about that," Nick said.

"What do you mean?"

"Carrie suffered through some nasty stuff. As terrible as things were, she made it through. She's trying her best to move forward. Talking helped."

Nick sensed Will needed a whole lot of healing. "If you hold all the bad stuff in, Will, you'll never be able to live a decent life."

"What *bad* stuff did you and Carrie do?"

Nick raised his brow. "What are you talking about?"

"You know. The guns, the money. Carrie said none of it belonged to her. Who does it belong to?"

Nick folded his arms across his chest. This kid was no dummy, but telling him the truth right now, served no purpose. It would, in fact, make matters worse.

"Don't let your imagination run wild. The money and the guns belong to me. I earned that money, and I put it in an offshore account for tax purposes. I don't use American banks. The guns were for protection. Two million dollars is a lot of money."

Will stood silent, seeming to digest what Nick said. His fists opened, and he relaxed his hands. "So, you left Laurel because of me?"

"No. We were leaving anyway. Carrie told me what happened, and we both agreed it was best to take you with us until things settle down at home."

Will shoved his hands into the pockets of his jeans and looked up at Nick. "Thanks."

"No problem. Look, Will, it doesn't have to be today. When you're ready, you can talk to us." He motioned to the kitchen. "Sure smells good, and I'm starving. How about you?"

"I guess so."

"Good, let's not disappoint Carrie."

The three of them ate at the dining room table. Carrie and Nick kept the conversation light. He thought Will's mood had lifted but was disappointed when at the end of the meal, Will abandon them for his room.

Nick helped Carrie clean up the kitchen. After they finished, he faced her and performed a slight bow. "I concede. Dinner was great. You can cook more than eggs."

She laughed and pointed her finger at him "It's your turn next. You can show me just how good a cook you are."

He removed a bottle from the wine cooler and collected two glasses from the dining room hutch. "How about a glass of wine on the patio?"

"It's a little cool outside isn't it?"

"I'll make a fire. There's plenty of wood," Nick said.

Carrie hesitated. "Okay, give me a minute. I want to check on Will first."

"I'll go with you," Nick said.

Carrie tapped on Will's door and turned the knob. She padded over to the bed while Nick leaned against the doorframe. The bedside lamp cast a soft glow across his face. His eyes were closed. Carrie resisted the urge to smooth the wave of brown hair that fell across his right eye. She reached out to turn off the lamp.

Will's eyes flew open. "No, leave it on."

"Oh, I'm sorry. I thought you were asleep."

"Please, go away and leave the light alone."

Carrie moved away. "Okay, Will. No problem." She closed the door and retreated to the patio with Nick.

"Poor kid, he's afraid of the dark," Nick said.

Carrie shook her head. "I'm sure he is after what he said earlier."

Nick uncorked the bottle and poured two glasses of wine. He collected some logs from a sizeable wrought iron hoop next to the fireplace as Carrie settled herself onto the plush cushions of the wrought iron sofa.

Minutes later, after the fire roared to life, he gathered up one of the throws from inside and draped it across their laps.

They sipped their wine and watched the sky turn an array of pastel pinks, burnt orange, and golds. The sun inched its way down the sky and dipped below the pines. In the distance, a great horned owl hooted in the trees. A slight breeze jetted across the patio and nipped at the flames making them glow brighter.

"Where did you learn to cook?" Nick asked.

"We rented a house in Texas once," Carrie said. "The longest we ever stayed anywhere. I started to believe my life could change. Travis treated me better. No more motel rooms, no more beatings. It was the closest thing to a real home."

Carrie's face softened. "I tried different recipes. Got pretty good at it. I enjoyed cooking. It took my mind off my unhappiness."

"What happened?"

"After about six months, Travis grew restless." Carrie hesitated and stared into the fire. She had watched that restlessness grow inside him, sprouting up like a bad seed until its ugly vines wrapped around him destroying what might have been.

"I remember the day he loaded up the Chevy. I begged and pleaded, but it made no difference to him." She remembered how the fear inside returned, sunk its teeth in, and held on.

"He put his hands on me again. Mean hands that hadn't touched my body in a good while. I ended up with another swollen lip to match the ones that came before it. I had resigned myself to living in fear."

Memories flooded back. Her eyes glazed over. "Until he tried to choke me and I thought, this time he'll kill me for sure." She brushed a tear from her cheek.

Alarmed, Nick said," Carrie, you don't have to continue. I didn't' mean to spoil things by having you bring up your past."

She blinked and brushed the tear away. "No, no. It's quite all right." Her eyes strayed beyond the patio and out toward the mountains. "I've never experienced peacefulness like this. With Travis, I mean. A simple thing like sipping wine and watching the sunset wasn't in his wheelhouse."

Her chin dropped, she tugged at the throw. "Nothing was easy with him. Everything had hard edges to it. Do you know what I mean?"

He reached for her hand, locked his fingers with hers. "I think I do. This is new for me, too."

"Impossible," Carrie said. I think you're quite good at the easy things. Which means you must have had a lot of practice."

She smiled, and there it was, the small crease at the corner of her mouth he loved so much. "Not at all," Nick said. "The business I was in left no room for easy."

"Was?"

"Absolutely. We wouldn't be sitting here together if I still worked for him." He detected her body stiffen beneath the throw. "Listen, Carrie, I'm not going to sugar coat anything. From this point on, I won't lie to you, but if you feel you can't handle my past, I'll understand."

Something inside him had shifted. Here was the release he'd been looking for. Carrie had committed murder, but he'd done much worse over the years. He meant what he said about not lying to her. Nick didn't want lies to ever come between them.

"I can't judge you, Nick. I'm not walking around with a clean slate either. You know most of my story." She took another sip of wine. "Tell me a little about you before—before your old boss."

"Fair enough," he said. "Both my parents were children of immigrants who came here from Italy. I grew up in New York. Little Italy to be exact. Still a New Yorker at heart to this day. I have no complaints with regards to my childhood."

Carrie sipped her wine. "You mentioned a brother and sister."

Nick let go of her hand. He drained what remained of his wine, and rolled the wine glass back and forth between his palms. He wished he'd never mentioned his siblings to her. No lies, he told himself.

"It's okay if you don't want to finish, Nick."

"No. I want to tell you. I used to be an NYPD Detective. I joined the force after my older brother was mugged and shot to death."

"Oh, I'm so sorry," Carrie said. "I—"

He held up his hand. "It's all right. It happened a long time ago."

"Please, go on," Carrie said.

"I excelled at what I did. I worked hard for my gold shield. I knew it could never erase what happened to my brother, but I put away scores of bad people. I think in a way, it helped me cope with his death."

"You were close then?" Carrie asked.

"As close as brothers could be. It nearly killed my parents when he died. I think my being a cop helped them get over his death to a certain degree."

"What happened? Did you quit the force?"

Nick sat upright. "Quit? Hell no. I would've never quit. I loved it. I was driven out." He stopped talking for a moment and stared at the fire.

"I'm thankful my folks didn't live to see it. They died in a car crash two years prior." An awkward silence fell between them.

Carrie touched his arm. "That's awful," she said.

He let out a sigh and continued. "We did a major drug bust. I was lead detective on the team. When you recover drug money, the protocol is, you do a count at the scene, walk it all the way in and do a final count before it goes into evidence."

"That day, I did something I'd never done. I left early to go to my sister's wedding. I promised her I'd stand in for my father, give her away. I left it to my fellow officers to finish the count and do the right thing."

He set his empty wine glass on the small end table. He pushed the throw off his knees and threw more logs on the fire. Bright yellow flames licked the wood. Sap sizzled and popped. The scent of burning wood filled the night air. He turned to Carrie, wanting to finish it all and put it to bed.

"By the time I arrived the next day, I was called into the captain's office and told there was money missing. Next thing I know they already have search warrants. Claimed they found the missing money in my storage locker. I tried fighting them, but the corruption ran too deep."

"People I thought were my friends closed ranks against me. Politics and powerful people were behind all of it. They looked at me as a threat. I did the job the right way. I had no choice but to cut a deal with the brass instead of going to jail."

All the ugliness from long ago surfaced once again. Nick paced the stone patio while observing the mix of emotions on Carrie's face. He stopped and eased down next to her.

"What did you do?" she asked.

"I drifted for a bit. Drank too much. The woman I was engaged to marry left me. Then one night, fate stepped in, and I started working for him. At first, I worked as his bodyguard. He trusted me. I gained a certain respect for him and things escalated. The people I killed for him were all criminals."

Nick wanted her to know he'd chosen his path in life. He took full responsibility for all the things he did for Ricardo. Only now he felt the need to release it, put it out there for someone else to digest, so maybe he might feel a little free. Free from all the fear he remembered in the eyes of some of his kills. Free from the heavy weight of falling from grace and his transformation into a lone, dark figure in the shadows, waiting to complete his next kill.

She glanced away. He could tell she was at a loss for words.

"Look, I'm not trying to justify anything I did for him. I'll live with it, but I want you to understand one thing. He saved me when no one else would. I owed him my loyalty."

"And you broke it for me?"

"Yes, but it couldn't have come soon enough. I was ready to quit."

She continued to stare at him. "And your sister?"

"Marie married a guy with roots in Italy and moved there with him. They have three kids. She's the one person who believes I was innocent, but there wasn't anything she could've done.

"Nick, that's so sad."

"Marie understands how it is with me. She's not aware of what I did for a living, she thinks I travel a lot for business. I've seen her five, maybe six times in the past ten years."

They sat in silence and gazed at the dancing flames. He draped his arm around her. "So, now you know about me. Let there be no more secrets between us."

"No, none," Carrie said.

Nick reached around with his other arm and brushed his hand across her cheek. Then he fell into those incredible eyes and claimed her lips. First, gently, and then more forceful as she began to respond. Her arms came up, and she pulled him closer, made the kiss go deeper, both of them exploring new territory.

Their lips parted, and she buried her head in his neck, and he took in her scent, made it his own. Her warm breath fanned his skin.

Carrie raised her head and slowly traced her fingers over his features. She stood and reached for his hand.

"Are you sure, Carrie?"

"I've never been surer of anything in my life."

Nick stood, and she led him inside. For the second time in his life, Nicholas D'Angelo was saved.

CHAPTER 38

CARRIE

Carrie marveled at Nick's lean, powerful body. Her hands traveled over the sculpted muscles on his chest and arms and then through his dark hair. She soaked in the deep pools of green in his eyes. The need inside her immediate, aching to be satisfied, her lips met his again, and again. Her heat matched his as their naked bodies tangled together.

His hands, fingertips like lit matches, traveled over her breasts. Carrie arched her back, swallowed air, and moaned at the rush of pleasure. She hung on, nails digging in as his tongue licked and teased. He pressed his body against hers. Her hips joined his, and they fell into a perfect rhythm. Nick spoke her name over and over as they climbed higher and rode the wave together. Uncontrollable pleasure rocked her body, and she cried out as they climaxed.

Their bodies relaxed. Nick slipped beside her and held her close. She nuzzled his neck, her desire for him not yet spent. He was her haven, a safe place where she could abandon herself. She reveled in this new-found freedom, a gift she'd given herself.

Before dawn pushed the darkness over the horizon, their bodies joined together once more. This time, they banked the fire inside of them. Let it build gradually into a roaring flame until satisfied, they fell into restful sleep.

In the morning light, Carrie leaned on her elbow and studied Nick's face as he slept. All of this scared her. He scared her. The desire inside her so unfamiliar and, yet, she gave herself to him without reservation. He'd awakened long forgotten feelings. In all her years with Travis, she'd never experienced what she had with Nick. She needed time to digest it. Examine its meaning.

Nick stirred awake and opened his eyes. "Good morning, gorgeous."

She chewed her lower lip and studied him. "You're not so bad looking yourself."

He reached out and pulled her close. She snuggled against him and rested her head in the crook of his arm. He kissed the top of her head. "Last night meant a lot to me."

She held back, searching for the right words. Things were moving fast, and her old fears threatened to return. Would he end up trying to control her like Travis?

Nick gently lifted her chin. "Silence is not what I was expecting to hear."

She moved away and sat up against the pillows, the blanket snug across her breasts. Nick told her he wouldn't lie to her anymore. If she trusted him, she should do the same and tell him what she was feeling at this moment.

"Nick, I have to be honest with you."

"I hope you'll always be honest with me. Is there something wrong?"

She breathed in and began. "I can't even find the words to express how I felt with you last night."

"But…."

"When I lived with Travis, he controlled me. He controlled everything. That's why I loved living in Laurel. No one controlled me anymore. I made my own choices. I left Laurel with you because I had to. You said my life is in jeopardy, and I believed you, but I want you to know, I will never let another man control me again."

Nick sat up. "You think I want to control you?"

She shrugged. "Right now, today, no. But that could change."

"Carrie, I only want you to be happy. Any plans I make for us, including Will, are to keep you safe. Controlling a woman is not my thing. And I don't have any respect for men who treat women that way."

Nick's expression clouded over. "Outside of safety's sake, I 'd never force you to do anything. You make your own decisions."

She witnessed the irritation on his face, caught it in his voice. "Okay, I just wanted to be clear," she said.

Nick got up and searched for his clothes. "This was a mistake. It's my fault. I should've known you're not ready." He tugged on his jeans and faced her.

"Mistake?" she said, her confusion spreading. "What do you mean? Please, don't call last night a mistake."

He grabbed his shirt. "This isn't some kind of power game for me, Carrie. I'm falling in love with you. I want more than last night, but if you don't, please let me know before we go any further."

His words caught her totally off guard. She started to get up. "Nick, I..."

He put up his hand. "I don't think we should talk anymore right now. I'm going for a run. I'll see if Will's up. Maybe I can get him to go with me."

"Wait, Nick. Don't go."

He turned away. "Sorry, I'm not in the mood to talk. Like I said, last night was a mistake." He strode away without looking back.

After he left, she slipped underneath the covers, utterly bewildered by his reaction. If he wanted her honesty, why did he get so upset? She wasn't comparing him to Travis, but she wanted him to understand her fears. Their bodies were in sync last night. Today, their minds were apart.

He said he was falling in love with her. She wasn't sure how she felt regarding that.

Travis said he loved her, but she couldn't recall ever telling Travis she loved him. Not even in the beginning. What did that say about her?

Carrie left the warm bed and grabbed her robe. She walked up to the immense span of glass. An amber sky prepared to greet the sun rising over the mountain. She spotted a lone figure running in the distance. Should she push her fears aside and believe him when he said he didn't want to control her? Moving closer, she touched her forehead to the cold glass and watched her breath lay claim to it.

She remembered his words. "No more secrets," she whispered. She still kept the secret of the child she lost, and Nick kept his about Travis. Someday, they'd have to deal with all of it.

A heaviness settled in her chest. Bad dreams still invaded her sleep. In them, her mother and Travis reached out to her from the dark depths below, trying to drag her under with them.

What dreams did Nick and Will have? What monsters from their pasts haunted them during the night? She was positive memories of the people Nick killed lay sealed deep within him, and Will's memory of shooting his father tortured his mind.

It was hard to admit her feelings for Nick grew stronger each day. It was becoming hard to imagine her life without him now. Each time he left, emptiness welled up inside her as she waited for him to return and fill it.

By the time she showered and changed into jeans and a black turtleneck, she found Will downstairs on the sofa, watching television.

"Didn't go for a run with Nick?" she asked.

"No, it's too cold. Weather forecast says snow is coming."

Her eyes lit up. She clapped her hands. "Snow!"

Will cocked his eyebrow. "You act like you've never seen snow."

"I haven't, smarty," she said. Her heart lifted at the prospect.

"How about that. You've never seen snow?" A man's voice boomed through the room.

Carrie whirled around. Will jumped up from the sofa.

A man, well over six feet tall, stationed himself before them. He wore a beige Stetson, rugged jeans, a heavy coat, and black cowboy boots polished to a high shine. A bushy speckled grey mustache played on his upper lip. He tipped his hat. "Sorry for the intrusion."

Will frowned. "Who the hell are you? You'd better leave, mister, before Nick comes back."

He let out a belly laugh. "Yeah, I better run right out the door before Nick gets here."

Carrie eyed him. "How did you get in here?"

"Patio slider." He raised an eyebrow and wagged his finger. "Someone left it unlocked. Mighty careless."

She started to answer when the front door opened and Nick burst in. Winded from his run, he paused and then looked over at them. His face lit up.

"Dalton, you son of a bitch! You didn't tell me you were coming." The two men shook hands and then bear hugged.

"I needed to make a trip out this way, and I couldn't pass up the chance to see you."

Obvious the two were old friends, she relaxed.

Nick turned to Carrie and Will. "I'd like you both to meet Dalton Burgess. He's the owner of this house. Dalton, this is Carrie and Will."

Dalton stretched out his hand to Will who, hesitant at first, shook it.

He looked at Carrie. "It's good to meet you."

She smiled. "You have a lovely home. Thank you for allowing us to stay here."

"You're quite welcome, little lady." He glanced at Nick. "After meeting her, you don't have to explain a thing."

"I was about to cook some breakfast," Carrie said. "Will you join us?"

Dalton removed his hat and tossed it onto one of the leather sofas. "Don't mind if I do."

"I'll wash up and join you in a few minutes, Nick said. "I'm a little raw from running."

Dalton pretended to pinch his nose in disgust. "Yeah, good idea."

Nick laughed. "Tell me again why I miss seeing you?"

An hour later, they lingered at the long dining room table after eating a breakfast of eggs, bacon, toast, and coffee. Dalton kept them amused with stories of his other home, a cattle ranch sitting on over three hundred acres.

Carrie studied Nick's face as the two men bantered back and forth. Dalton spoke about the first time Nick came to his ranch and learned to ride and rope cattle.

"Carrie, I lost track of how many times he fell off that darn horse." Dalton's laughter filled the room while Will and Carrie joined in.

Nick's ears turned red. "Oh, come on, Dalton. I didn't do so bad for a city boy. I got the hang of it after a while."

"Yeah, after the poor horse almost gave up and offered to rope the cow himself."

Glad to see Nick so relaxed, she reached over and poured the last of the coffee into Dalton's cup. "Will said there's snow coming."

"An early winter storm," Dalton said. "The trees haven't even shed all their leaves. Sure to be a whole heap. Two feet, maybe more. As a matter of fact, I have to get going soon. They're predicting a whiteout. A plow will come by sometime after the storm passes and clear the drive. Feel free to use the snowmobiles parked outside the garage." Dalton winked at Will.

"There's plenty of trails to ride, and there are ski clothes and gear in the mudroom. Helmets in the garage. I keep a variety on hand for guests. I'm sure something will fit."

Will grew excited. "Snowmobiles?"

Nick gave him a wink. "Contrary to popular belief." He nodded his head in Dalton's direction. "I do know how to operate a snowmobile. Quite well, I might add."

Carrie cleared the table while the men retreated into the great room. Will started to follow when Carrie said," Will, stay and help me finish. I think the men need to talk."

As swiftly as it had gone, his sullen mood returned. "I know. I'm not stupid."

Later, after Dalton bid them goodbye, Will disappeared to his room once again. Nick built a fire in the great room. Outside, the sky turned a battleship grey and filled with low hanging clouds. The wind picked up and howled among the eaves.

"How do you know Dalton?" Carrie asked.

Nick took the iron poker and jabbed at the logs. "Dalton and I go way back. Did each other many favors over the years. He's a good guy."

"I'm not questioning his character. I like him a lot," she said. "How did you first meet?"

He put the poker aside and faced her. "Carrie, there are some things you're better off not knowing." His expression guarded, he continued. "I will say Dalton is ... in the same business, but he doesn't work for my ex-boss. He's sort of an independent contractor, so to speak."

Carrie realized he was right. There were things she'd rather not know and some she didn't want to tell. She wandered toward the wall of windows. Plump flakes streamed from the sky dressing the green Ponderosa pines in the valley below. The wind whipped, causing them to swirl and dance across the porch. The snow fell hard and fast until all Carrie could see was a sheet of pure white.

Nick sidled up behind her. "So, what do you think?"

She stared at the dazzling display pouring down. "It's amazing."

His arms encircled her. Her skin tingled at his touch. Glad his anger had receded, she leaned against him, feeling the warmth of his body. She reached up and held onto his arms.

He lowered his head. "I'm sorry, Carrie. I mean it." His voice was gentle and sweet.

She freed his arms and faced him. "I know you do. Saying you're sorry is all I need to hear. Nobody other than my Aunt May has ever said that to me."

"I hope I never have to say it to you again. I shouldn't have lost my temper earlier. You were only trying to express how you feel. I don't want you to be afraid to speak to me about anything."

She studied his eyes, and the reflection of the snow cascading within them. A sudden calm entered her heart. "What you said earlier today. I do, too." Her arms encircled his neck. "Want more."

He bent, his lips found hers, and he kissed her hard and long. She held on tight, afraid to let go, wanting only to be here, locked in his arms with the thick white flakes falling furiously outside.

The sun rose over a landscape buried in two feet of snow. With Nick fast asleep, Carrie eased out of bed. She put on a pair of jeans and a heavy cable knit sweater and slipped out of the bedroom.

Downstairs in the mudroom, she found heavy quilted ski coats, bibbed ski pants, gloves, and boots. She tugged on a ski jacket and tried on several pairs of lace-up boots until she found ones that fit. Standing on her tiptoes, she fished out some gloves from a pile on a shelf above. A dark green knit hat hung from a hook, and she grabbed it, too. Her excitement welled up, and she giggled.

Struggling against the snow piled outside the door, she forced it open. A hazy sun broke from behind the clouds. Its rays cast a shimmer across the white powder making it sparkle in the light. The surrounding pine trees dipped their branches beneath the weight of the snow. A row of icicles hung from the roof, like spikes of glass shot through with rainbow colors, they glistened in the sun.

Carrie absorbed the stillness amid the thick blankets of white. Ankle deep in fresh layers she bent, scooped up a handful, and examined it. Frosty wind sailed past and her lungs filled with cold air. She puffed out. Her breath became mist and disappeared.

Stepping off the porch, she plunged up to her knees into the heavy snow. She forged ahead, lost her balance, and fell backward. Laughing, she struggled to her feet. Snow covered her coat and jeans. Ice crystals clung to the ends of her long hair streaming out from under her wool hat.

She reached and scooped up another handful, and rolled it between her palms. Her first snowball. Carrie flexed her arm letting the snowball fly out overhead where it smacked into the base of an aspen tree.

Three others sailed through the air before she retreated to the porch. Satisfied at her first foray out into the snow, she slipped back into the mudroom. She tossed her coat on the rack and dusted off her jeans. She sat on the wooden chest and peeled off the hat, gloves, and boots.

A wave of melancholy washed over her. She remembered how Travis refused to travel far enough north or west. She had begged him once. Told him she wanted to see snow close up, not on mountains in the distance, but he insisted those places were too cold for his taste. She never believed him and always detected an underlying sadness.

Carrie sighed and forced herself to perk up. Today was no day for sadness, she admonished herself. She left the mudroom and put on a fresh pot of coffee. The house remained quiet. She sat at the center island and delighted in drinking the first mug alone, safe in the knowledge that the man she cared for slept soundly upstairs.

Carrie reflected on what Nick told her regarding Dalton. It made her a little uneasy. Another killer for hire. Meeting him, no one would ever guess. She couldn't imagine how many there were out in the world. At least there was one less now.

Nick said he gave up killing. She was thankful for having a hand in it even though it put them all at risk. Going forward, she wouldn't ask any further questions regarding his past. The pain on his face was evident whenever he talked about it. She'd trust him and believe a future waited for them out there, a future without running, a future without fear.

Footsteps sounded, and she looked up as Will came bounding into the kitchen. "Hey, did you see all the snow? It's a lot like the mountains of Pennsylvania."

Happy to see his enthusiasm, she said, "I was already outside. Fell right on my butt."

"Oh no, you're kidding me." Will laughed and hopped up on the stool next to her.

Carrie wished he'd smile more often. "As soon as Nick gets up and we eat breakfast, we'll try out those snowmobiles."

"Did somebody say breakfast?" Nick stood in the doorway. Sleep still visible in his eyes, he stretched and yawned.

"You look like you could use some coffee," Carrie said. "Your T-shirt's on inside out." She giggled and poured him some.

Nick looked down and laughed. He pulled it off and flipped it right side out.

She handed him the cup. As he sipped, steam rose up around his handsome face, and it made her heart fill.

The three of them settled themselves at the island. She listened while Nick and Will discussed the storm and the snowmobiles. A strange feeling engulfed her, something unfamiliar.

Slowly, it dawned on her, and she drew it all in. She gazed at the two of them. This is what family looks like. This is how a home should feel.

CHAPTER 39

NICK

Nick and Will dug out snow and lifted the covers off two Polaris snowmobiles. Their shiny black paint gleamed against the white snow.

"Before we head out, I want to show you a couple of things," Nick said.

Will's expression soured. "I've ridden before back home. My friend has one."

"That may be the case, but safety comes first," Nick insisted.

He instructed them on the operation of the snowmobile, cautioning about body positions when riding uphill and downhill.

"Remember the deeper the snow, the more speed you'll need. Since it's her first time, Carrie will ride with me."

They donned their helmets and climbed on, Carrie seated behind Nick who took the lead. Will brought up the rear. They sped off, white powder kicking up around them. The hum of the engines split the quiet morning air.

Reassured by the way Will handled the snowmobile, Nick was thankful he didn't have to keep an eye on him.

Over the next several hours, they rode the marked trails on the property. He loved the sensation of sailing over the snow with Carrie's arms holding tight around his waist, so different from all the times he rode alone. He wished they could stay longer, and enjoy Dalton's house and the magnificent land surrounding it.

Nick recognized the hazard in getting too comfortable. Inside their small circle, news traveled fast. Dalton assured him that so far it didn't look like Ricardo knew their whereabouts, but a rumor was circulating that Nicky D had gone underground. He urged Nick to secure the books and leave the country as soon as possible … before Ricardo found out their location.

Dalton was a good friend. One who owed Nick his life. He first met Dalton when both their bosses had set up the same kill.

Eight years ago, while perched on a rooftop, Nick had peered through the scope of his M2010 rifle as he waited for his mark to exit the building across the street. He sighted his rifle when without warning Dalton appeared in his scope in a kill position on the rooftop across the way. Creeping up behind him was Cantino Quartez, a known bodyguard for Nick's kill. A split second later, Cantino slumped to the rooftop dead. Dalton, a look of confusion on his face, searched for the trajectory of the bullet, while Nick disappeared like a ghost was supposed to do. Later, Dalton found Nick through his connections.

From that day on, they became friends, Dalton more than grateful to him for saving his life. And now, Dalton just might be saving his. Once Brody called to let him know the books were ready, they'd head across the border, to Canada, until he assessed the situation and planned for a permanent destination.

It was afternoon when despite Will's protests, they turned off the trail and headed toward the house. They parked the snowmobiles and covered them. Will, helmet in hand, left for the house, leaving the two of them alone.

Inside the garage, Nick waited as Carrie removed her helmet and shook out her jet-black hair. It spilled down in waves, framing her face. He hadn't told her how he spied from the window while she made her foray into the snow.

When she fell backward laughing and struggled to her feet, he fought the urge to get dressed and accompany her outside. Instead, he trusted his instincts and stayed inside. That moment belonged to her. He remembered the ride to the coffeehouse. How excited she was about seeing snow. Nick delighted in the fact he'd given her the gift of her first snowfall.

"That was so much fun," she said, breaking into his thoughts.

He took their helmets and put them on a shelf. "Come on, admit you were at least a little bit scared. You squeezed me so hard I thought my insides were going to burst."

Hands on her hips, she stared him down. "That was my signal for you to go faster. You just have to get used to my signals."

Nick grabbed her and pulled her close. He kissed her lips, warming them with his own. "How do you like *my* signals?" he asked.

Standing on tiptoes, she reached up, put her arms around his neck. "I love your signals. They're much better than mine."

Her kiss, deep, hot, unexpected, rocketed through his body. He almost couldn't stand it when she let go.

"I have one hungry man and a teenager to feed," she said and turned toward the door.

He caught her hand. Her cheeks flushed pink from the cold, her lips parted waiting for another kiss. His desire for her gripped him like a vise. Overwhelmed by his feelings, he needed to feel her warmth beneath the heavy clothes. With Carrie, everything felt new.

"Can't you tell this man isn't hungry for food?" His voice softened. "He's hungry for you." He let her go and punched in a code. The garage door slid closed.

Carrie smiled. "We better be quick, before Will wonders where we are."

Within minutes, their heavy clothes lay strewn across the cement floor. Nick pulled a wool blanket from a shelf in the corner and spread it beneath them. He beckoned with his finger, and they knelt face to face. He held her close and then swept her hair toward her back and kissed the length of her neck. He eased her down onto the blanket. His craving for her white-hot inside, he pressed against her, amazed by the depth of his emotion.

Her desire for him evident, she responded. Warm breath escaped their lips and vaporized against the chilly air.

They didn't feel the hard floor underneath the blanket. Didn't hear the icy wind pick up and blow outside. They slipped into a world of their own. A world of gasps, moans, and gentle pleading. Their bodies rose and fell in unison until neither one could stand anymore.

They collapsed, gratified, content with one another and let the world around them seep back in, its sounds alive and real once more.

Carrie shivered while Nick collected their clothes. Without a word between them, they dressed, stepped out into the biting cold, and went up to the house.

They dropped their ski clothes in the mudroom alongside Will's. In the great room, Will sat, sandwich in hand, watching television.

Nick retreated to the kitchen with Carrie. She fixed a fresh pot of coffee, and they drank coffee and ate sandwiches at the island. They were finishing up when Will came in.

"Can I take the snowmobile out again?"

"I think it's enough for now. Tomorrow's another day," Nick said.

Will pinched his lips and looked at Carrie. "Aw, come on, please."

"You're not as familiar with the trails as Nick," she said.

"I can follow the tracks we left. I won't go far."

Nick caught Carrie's pleading look. "Listen, you can go," he said. "It's two now, so I want you here by four o'clock. No later. It gets dark early, and it's easy to get lost out there. Stay on the marked trails and take your cell phone with you."

Will's face brightened. He raised his arm and pumped his fist. "Yes!" Before either one of them could say another word, he was gone.

She loaded their cups into the dishwasher. "Do you think he'll be all right by himself?"

"It wasn't me who wanted him to go out," Nick said. "I saw the look you gave me."

She sat and laced her fingers together on the countertop. "I know. It's just that he's so sad all the time. Today was the first day he seemed happy."

"Neither one of us has raised any kids," Nick said. We're both new at this. I always put safety first. It's just the way I'm built. If he doesn't do anything crazy and stays on the trails, he should be okay."

Nick stood and put out his hand. "I'm going to take a shower. I'd love some company."

Her eyes flashed a darker violet as she took his hand. "Only if you promise to share the soap."

CHAPTER 40

WILL

Will gunned the snowmobile and tore out onto the first trail. Racing along the trails allowed him to forget what happened back in Laurel. Carrie and Nick wanted him to talk about it but he couldn't, not to them. Pouring his heart out to two people he hardly knew wasn't at the top of his list.

He liked Carrie, and he knew she meant well. She didn't have to take him with her. It did show she cared.

Nick was nice enough. Treated him, okay, but Will still didn't trust him. He sensed an undercurrent of danger, and he was convinced there were reasons, other than his father's death, which made Nick take them away from Laurel and bring them here to South Dakota. The money and the guns in the briefcase all pointed to something illegal.

He didn't believe the story Nick told him regarding offshore accounts. His thoughts kept returning to the same nagging question. Did Carrie and Nick commit a crime together?

Carrie said they were friends. He wasn't stupid, they were hooking up for sure. Not that it mattered to him. Adults always did whatever they wanted, anyway. There were so many unanswered questions rattling around in his mind. Sooner or later, he'd find out the truth.

Will zipped along the trail. The freedom of riding through the frigid air exhilarated him. The snow reminded him of Laurel and the mountains back home. He missed his mom and his friends. Although Nick warned him about using his cell phone, he hadn't listened. He'd used it twice, once to call his mom and another time to text Bruce and Kenny.

Finding no evidence to the contrary, the police believed his mom's story about an intruder breaking into the house. As long as she was doing okay, he could stand to be away. With his father dead, there was nothing left for her to fear.

He told Kenny and Bruce, he would be staying with a relative for a while. The last thing he wanted was them asking his mom any questions.

Will meant what he said to Carrie. He didn't feel bad about his father's death. Alive or dead, he hated the man. With him gone, it made Will even more curious about his mother. His father never spoke of her other than to say his biological mother died after giving birth to him.

He wondered if his life would be any different if she hadn't died. He promised himself that when he returned to Laurel, he'd try to find out as much as he could.

Will grew bored riding up and down the same trails. He veered off in a different direction away from the marked trails. The drifts grew higher. He stood and shifted his weight to balance the machine. Increasing the throttle to maintain speed, he got into a kneeling position to navigate up a steep embankment. Thrilled when he made it to the top, he punched the throttle and charged toward the next hill ahead of him. Using the same kneeling tactic, he flew up the hill.

At the top, Will swung the vehicle around. Snow shot out in thick plumes behind the machine. He leaned back as far as possible and aimed at the bottom of the hill. With the vehicle in low gear, he tapped the brake to avoid sliding sideways while he steered down the hill. When he reached the bottom, he drove further away from the trail. He approached the second set of ridges much larger than the rest. After three successive climbs, he reached the highest point and shut off the engine.

Will jumped off into snow up to his knees. He lumbered over to the edge and surveyed the vast valley. In the distance, the sky turned pale gold as the sun slid inch by inch behind the mountains. He hadn't kept track of the time. Darkness would descend soon.

Will settled himself on the snowmobile again. He needed to find the marked trails and return to the house before dark. He rode down the first hill. Angling too much to one side, the snowmobile tipped and slid.

Leaning in the opposite direction, Will struggled to keep the snowmobile upright. It pulled to the left, down a steep embankment and then lurched to the right almost causing him to eject into a pile of snow, finally coming to a stop inches away from a tall aspen tree.

Will hit reverse, revved the engine, and tried to back up. The vehicle dug in, its engine whined, straining against the heavy snow beneath it, but failed to move. He hit the auxiliary shut off switch to kill the engine. He swore and climbed off the snowmobile.

Will removed his helmet to get a full view of his dilemma. Digging with gloved hands, he tried to remove the snow piled against the vehicle. The bitter wind stung his cheeks as he dug. Twenty minutes later, he still couldn't free it. He examined his surroundings. Fear knotted his stomach.

Excited when Nick said yes, he hadn't stopped to get his cell phone. With no ability to communicate with anyone, Will put his helmet on and grabbed the emergency flashlight from the storage pack along with two flares. He stuffed the flares in his ski pant pockets and made the slow descent downhill on foot.

By the time he managed to reach the bottom, panic set in. He couldn't decide which way to go. His tracks crisscrossed, leaving a pattern in all different directions.

Confused, he picked a trail and plodded ahead, flashlight in hand. Twilight descended across the woods as the temperature dipped. Not long after, moonbeams lit up the vast expanse of snow. Prisms of color sparkled across its surface. Thick forests loomed all around him. He followed the yellow beam of light cast out in front.

Will shivered. Keep moving, he told himself. Don't stop and you'll be okay. He advanced farther and wished for the warmth of Dalton's house and the sound of Carrie and Nick's voices. It was getting harder to see through the helmet's tinted visor.

Huge ponderosa pines cast long shadows on either side of the trail. Will forced himself to keep moving, thankful at least for the full moon's extra light. He'd driven pretty far from the house and worried that he could be miles away.

Inside his boots, his feet tingled from the cold. He thought about his mom at home in Laurel and her reaction when they relayed his death out in the woods of South Dakota. He'd never see her or his friends again. He grew tearful with all the thoughts running through his head. This could be the end of his life, his punishment for shooting his father to death. They'd find his body lying out here, frozen solid.

He concentrated on the circle of light in front of him, afraid to look behind and acknowledge the dark. There were no comforting nightlights here in the woods.

Up ahead the trail opened up into a small clearing. Will made his way to the center and glanced around in the stillness. Rows of thick bushes outlined the clearing. A rustling shook the bushes to his right. Will froze. His scalp prickled. Terror shot through his body while a mournful howl invaded his ears.

The rustling grew louder. He spun in a circle, aiming the flashlight into the bushes. Amber eyes caught the light. Lips, curled back in a snarl, exposed pointed white teeth. Their paws silent on the packed snow, they slunk into the clearing. Will gasped. Within minutes he was surrounded by a pack of wild coyotes.

CHAPTER 41

CARRIE

Carrie finished blow drying her hair. Twilight invaded the room, and she switched on the bedroom lamp. She glanced at the clock on the nightstand. It was four-thirty. Will should be back from snowmobiling.

Nick came out of the bathroom, a towel snug at his waist. He advanced toward her, but she slipped past him.

"Listen, mister," she said. "You're about to wear me out."

Nick raised an eyebrow and smiled. "Who, me?" He grabbed her and spun her around to face him. He leaned in and kissed the tip of her nose.

She wiggled herself out from under his grasp and tightened the sash on her robe. "First, it's the nose, then the lips, and then you know what."

Nick laughed. "No, you tell me what."

"Okay, wise guy. I'm going to check on Will and figure out what we're having for dinner."

She scooted out the door to Will's room. His door hung open. There was no sign of Will, but his cell phone lay on the dresser. She called out his name. An odd sensation crawled up from the pit of her stomach.

"Don't get ahead of yourself," she warned. Trying to ignore her rising panic, she rummaged through the kitchen and decided there was enough leftover roast and vegetables for dinner. Still, she couldn't calm the nervous knots traveling through her body.

She rushed from room to room switching on lights. Outside the great room windows, grey clouds hung low in the sky. A sure sign of more snow on the way. Unable to ease her worry, she ran upstairs. Nick, towel still wrapped around his waist, lay sprawled out on the bed fast asleep.

Carrie threw on jeans, and a heavy sweater. She grabbed her cell phone and tore downstairs to the mudroom where she donned her ski pants, jacket, hat, and a heavy pair of wool gloves.

A cold wind blasted her head on as she waded through the snow toward the garage. She pulled on the door intending to get a helmet. The door wouldn't budge. She eyed the keypad and cursed. If Will were hurt, it would be her fault. Nick hadn't wanted him to go out alone.

Flinging the cover off one of the snowmobiles, she jumped on and turned the key. The engine whined but failed to catch. She tried again. "Damn it! Come on start," she swore at the machine.

After several more attempts with no luck, she was about to try another snowmobile when she remembered what Nick had taught them earlier. She found the kill switch, released it, and stepped off. Reaching down, she opened the choke and pulled the manual start. The engine sputtered, almost catching. She pulled again. The engine roared to life.

Carrie leaped onto the seat. She pulled her wool hat snug around her head and sped off toward the first trail.

Sharp, bitter wind stung her face. With no helmet, she would have to fight the bone-chilling cold blasting at her head on. Hunched down against the wind, she gripped the handles and accelerated again.

She tore along the trail leading past the woods, looking for any sign of him. Thoughts of the promise she made to Claudia clawed at her. If anything happened to Will, she'd be the one responsible.

With no sign of him at the end of the trail, she turned the snowmobile around. Darkness closed in making the path even harder to navigate. Carrie flipped on the headlight and entered the second trail. She ducked and veered to the left to avoid a hanging tree limb. The end snagged her hair as it brushed the top of her head.

Things, once friendly in the daylight, became her enemy as she tried to avoid fallen branches and blowing drifts.

Halfway along the trail, she saw tracks stretching up and off to the right. She slowed, let the engine idle, and studied them. They led up a steep set of hills, and she forged ahead with moonlight helping to guide her across the packed snow.

Carrie transferred her weight from side to side to keep herself balanced in the deep drifts. Thankful for another lesson learned with Nick, she knelt on the machine and charged up the steep embankment.

Ice crystals clung to the ends of her wool hat and stuck to her eyebrows. Her nose and lips grew numb. Her eyes watered from the force of the wind. As the temperature dropped, her fear increased. On the crest of the second hill, a couple yards away she noticed a separate set of tracks and followed those.

Carrie sped along until she spied still another set of hills and tracks rising off to the left. More tracks zigzagged back down. Confused, she stopped. Will must have ridden several different trails. If he hadn't made it down this one, he could be stuck at the top.

Carrie gunned the engine, but the packed snow proved to be much heavier than she first thought and she struggled to keep the machine upright. After making it up the first hill, she advanced to the second. With one more hill to go, determined to find him, she rode on.

She reached the bottom of the third hill and gasped. Will's snowmobile lay on its side by a tall aspen tree. She let her engine idle and grabbed the emergency flashlight. Sprinting across the snow, she called Will's name.

Carrie reached the vacant machine. She fanned the light along the ground and spotted what looked like footprints. She cringed. Will had made the worst possible choice. To leave the snowmobile and set out on foot in the freezing cold could end in disaster. Nick instructed him to stay with the machine if anything happened. There were too many miles of trails and woods for a person to get lost in.

She climbed onto the snowmobile, her headlight pointed at Will's tracks. Chunky white flakes tumbled from the sky. She hoped it wouldn't turn into a white-out and cover Will's tracks before she found him. Slow and deliberate she cruised along. More tracks took her through a set of woods. Despair washed over her. She stopped, turned the engine off, and called his name.

In the stillness of the woods, a lone howl made the hairs on her neck stand up. Another lone cry answered the first one. A burst of orange light shot up in the sky. She switched the engine on, and then headed toward the light.

She emerged from the woods into a clearing. Shielding her eyes, she peered through the swirling snow. Her heart pumped up. There was Will, a lit flare in one hand, while he swung his helmet with the other at a pack of coyotes.

Carrie revved the engine, charging ahead, straight at the pack. At her onslaught, they turned and snarled, white teeth flashed in the moonlight. Without hesitation, she descended on them again. Snarling at her, they scattered and disappeared into the woods.

She pulled the snowmobile beside Will, hopped off, and shut off the engine.

"Are you alright?"

"I—I thin—think so."

Carrie grabbed his arm and led him to the snowmobile. He shook uncontrollably. His face turned chalky, and his movements were slow and stiff.

"We have to get to the house. Can you ride?"

Will nodded. "Yes."

She helped him climb onto the snowmobile. "Put your helmet on."

Carrie flipped the engine on and gunned it. She tore through the woods and found the trail leading to the house. Barreling ahead, she squinted, trying to focus, while the snow fell harder and faster now. A single light came into view, and she drove toward it. She rounded the drive just as Nick appeared from inside the house.

"Carrie, what the hell—?" He leaped down the front steps.

"Help me get him inside!"

He removed Will's helmet and tossed it into the snow. Struggling to stand, Will got off the snowmobile and put an arm around Nick's shoulder as Nick grabbed Will's waist. They held onto each other as they struggled up the steps.

Inside, Nick settled him on the couch in front of the fire.

Will looked up, frightened and pale. He started to speak. "I'm s—sorry, I…

Carrie shrugged off her ski clothes letting them fall in a heap to the floor by the fireplace. She threw her wet gloves and hat on top.

"Don't try to talk," Nick said. He glanced at Carrie. "He's got hypothermia, I'll get some blankets." He ran from the room and brought blankets from the hall closet. He bent and removed Will's gloves, jacket, boots, and ski pants. Unbuttoning Will's shirt, he said, "This needs to come off too."

"I'll get a fresh shirt," Carrie said. She ran up the stairs and returned with one of Will's shirts and noticed his shaking had grown worse.

Nick fumbled with Will's shirt sleeve.

Carrie knelt beside him. "Here, let me help."

Nick managed to get the left arm free while Carrie worked on the right. She gave one final tug, and the shirt came off.

"After his shirt is on, wrap those blankets around him. I'll throw some more logs on the fire," Nick said.

Carrie grabbed the clean shirt. Without warning, the air in the room thinned. Her heartbeat accelerated. Will's shirt slipped from her hands. Her eyes locked on his right arm. She brought her hand up to her chest and stepped away.

Nick picked up the blankets and put them around Will. He massaged Will's shoulders, and arms while Will's trembling lessened. Color seeped into his cheeks. Nick eased him into a prone position. He looked at Carrie, mistaking her angst for worry.

"Babe, it's all good, he's okay."

Carrie tried to move, but her legs stayed rooted. Her bottom lip quivered while she stared at the young boy lying on the couch. Her pulse throbbed.

"Didn't you hear me? He's okay now. I wish you hadn't gone out there without me. It took a lot of courage to do that. If he'd been stranded out in the cold any longer, things might have ended a lot different. How did you find him?"

Half-listening to Nick, she said, "Flares."

"What?"

"I found him in the woods, surrounded by a pack of coyotes. He lit a flare. It kept them at bay and led me straight to him. They took off when I came at them with the snowmobile."

"All things considered, he's a brave kid," Nick said.

Impatient, Carrie needed confirmation. Maybe the firelight had played a trick. She pushed Nick away, her focus on Will. Only a cruel God would deliver her son to her after all these years, broken and abused. Guilt roared inside her, tripling in intensity. She was to blame for all his suffering.

Nick took a step toward her. "Carrie, what's the matter with you?"

An ache rose in her chest. She wanted to grab hold of Will and tell him how sorry she was. Tell him she'd give anything to make things better for him.

She looked away from Will and then up at Nick. "I can't do this."

"Tell me what's wrong. Otherwise, I can't help." Nick said. "Will is fine."

Carrie pushed past him. "I need to be alone."

She bolted up the stairs, closed the bedroom door, and locked it. Collapsing onto the bed, she held her head in her hands and wept. Why had she made the horrible decision to leave her son with her mother? The memory of her mother's face invaded her thoughts. Carrie rose up and shook her fist. "Damn you, damn you. I hope you rot in hell!" she cried.

All the years she wondered about her boy, tried to convince herself, he had a better life without her. A life with parents who took good care of him and loved him. She thought about Claudia, the woman who, together with her dead husband, bought her son. How could the woman she met live with that? Claudia loved Will, but not enough to protect him from his animal of a father.

A chill skated down her spine. The parallel between her and Will struck. Just like Will, she shot her abuser, too.

"Like mother, like son," she whispered. Carrie threaded her hands through her hair. Her stomach twisted thinking how she could never make things right.

She recalled Will mentioning the dark closet. That was the reason he didn't want her to turn the light out. Tonight, lost in the woods, he must have been terrified when night fell, and he couldn't find his way back.

She jumped at Nick's tap on the door. "Carrie, honey, please open the door and talk to me."

She knotted her hands. Talk to him? And say what? I gave birth at fifteen, and my mother sold my baby for drug money. No, she wasn't ready to tell him or Will.

She imagined Will's reaction. His hatred for her. Inevitably he'd ask about his father. How could she tell him his father had abandoned them both when he found out about her pregnancy? That later, he turned into a monster who abused her. And what about her mother, his grandmother who sold him in exchange for crack cocaine?

Will hadn't even begun to deal with the shooting back in Laurel. She, more than anyone, knew that sooner or later, guilt would rear its ugly head.

Nick's voice, urgent, full of worry, came at her from the other side. "Carrie, are you okay? Please answer me."

Although reluctant, she unlocked the door. She turned away, and his arms came around her from behind. He held on. Several minutes passed before he spoke.

"What can I do? Tell me, how can I help?"

She released herself and faced him. "It's all right. I'm all right. Will—out there in the freezing cold—if something had happened to him…"

"But you found him. Other than the beginning of hypothermia, he's fine. You got to him in time. I'm sure he's learned his lesson. He'll never pull another stunt like that again."

Carrie didn't answer. She walked past him, and he followed her to the great room. Will lay bundled underneath the blankets, a pained expression on his face, his eyes filled with regret. She bent and stroked his head. His soft curls slipped through her fingers while she soothed him, her memory of doing the same thing all those years ago tangible, yet almost unbearable.

He looked up, his blue eyes liquid, about to spill over. "I'm sorry. I should have stayed on the trail. Please don't be mad."

"It's okay, Will. You scared me half to death."

The lump in Carrie's throat eased, and she steadied herself. "Mad," she said. "No, we're just glad you're all right."

"I was so scared. Those coyotes surrounded me. If you hadn't come when you did, I'm not sure what would've happened."

Carrie retrieved the fresh shirt from the floor. "Put this on. You need to stay warm."

She slid the covers back, and Will sat up. He dipped his left arm in first. Carrie brought the shirt around his shoulders and held it. He lifted his right arm, and she took his hand before he could finish.

Will followed her eyes. "Oh, that," he said. "It's a birthmark. Mom called it my lucky star." He scowled a bit. "Some lucky star."

Carrie let go of his hand and finished helping him with his shirt. "Sometimes luck takes a little longer to show itself than we like," she said. "If you keep believing, it will come."

Will eased down. His eyelids closed and he drifted off to sleep.

She admired his long dark lashes trailing from his lids, the faint spatter of freckles on the bridge of his nose. She studied him, looking for any sign of Travis, but in her sweet boy's face, she found none. The corner of his mouth twitched, and a soft moan escaped his lips. The skin above his brow creased.

What lay there in his dreams? Did they terrify him as her dreams sometimes did? All this time wondering and now her son, her Bobby, was here, less than a foot away.

Nick brought two cups of coffee and handed her one. "Here, I thought you could use this."

"Thanks." Carrie took the cup and drifted toward the window. Thick, white flakes poured into the silence outside. After her harrowing ride to find her son, she saw the beauty in them again.

Nick snuggled up behind her. "If we're going to trust each other, you need to come clean. I'm sure what Will did upset you, but there's more to it. Isn't there?"

She motioned toward the kitchen. They settled on stools at the island. Carrie set her cup on the dark granite and clasped her hands. She looked into Nick's eyes and hoped he would understand.

"I've come to a conclusion there will never be a good time to tell you this," she said. "Will is my son." Even she found it hard to believe those words.

A stunned silence settled between them for a moment. "Your son?" Nick asked. "But how? When did you...?"

Carrie held up her hand. "I know this comes as a shock. I didn't tell you because I never thought I'd ever see him again. I was fifteen years old when I gave birth to him."

Nick rubbed the back of his neck. "Are you sure Will is your son?"

"Can you tell me his date of birth?"

"Nick took out his cell phone and showed her the birth date Will gave him.

The lump in her throat returned. "That confirms things. Plus, he has a star-shaped birthmark on his right forearm. I've never forgotten it."

"A star-shaped birthmark?"

"Yes. I asked Will about it, he told me his mom, Claudia, called it his lucky star." She wiped at the tears forming in her eyes.

"So, you gave him up for adoption?'

Guilt and shame engulfed her. This would be the hardest part. "No. I ran out of formula and left him with my mother." Bitterness swelled inside her. "One hour, I was only gone one hour. In that time, she sold my son for two thousand dollars.

Nick's brow furrowed "Two thousand dollars?"

"Yes, so she could buy her precious drugs. She sold him to some couple who took him and disappeared. The police never found them." She looked at Nick. "But I just don't get it. I met Claudia, and she didn't seem like the kind of person who would be involved in such a crime."

"You can never really tell what someone is capable of," Nick said. He stretched out his arms, covered her hands with his own. "Carrie, I have to ask. Who is Will's father?"

She removed her hands out from under his and frowned. "Travis—Travis is his father. The son of a bitch didn't stick around. Said they'd put him in jail if anyone found out because I was underage. I never even told my mother about Travis. He came for me after our son was gone. I made the foolish decision of leaving home with him."

Nick stared at her. His face still full of questions.

"I didn't know how to tell you," she said softly.

"Would you have told me if Will hadn't come back into your life?" Anger skimmed his voice. "Well, would you have?" he asked again.

Her answer, though it pained her, was honest. "I don't know."

"What other secrets are you keeping from me?" His eyes narrowed as he searched her face.

Carrie stood up. Her lip trembled. "Don't you dare, Nick. Don't you dare. Not with all your secrets."

Nick slid off the stool. He moved toward her. "I've been honest with you, Carrie."

She stepped away and shot him a look. "What about Travis? He didn't just go away, did he? Travis would never let me go. Not unless he was dead."

Carrie covered her mouth. Her words hung in the air between them. The night Nick took Travis away, and she woke the next morning with a twist in her gut, she knew then, with certainty, Travis was dead.

Nick's green eyes grew dark. "Be careful, Carrie. You won't find comfort in the truth. I never lied to you. I said he wouldn't bother you again and you never asked me what happened."

He reached out, cupped her chin with his hand, and lifted her face. "I did what I had to do for us. And I would do it all over again. I can live with it, and I hope you can, too." The pain on his face evident, he pulled his hand away.

She had to admit Nick was right. He never lied to her about Travis. She chose not to question him that day. She couldn't face Travis's death and what it meant. Her freedom in exchange for his life. And now, an invisible line lay between her and Nick. Everything rested on her. She could cross that line and accept Nick for the man he is or stay on her side and judge him for what he'd done.

Carrie met his eyes. In them, she saw all the unspoken words between them. Her mind cleared, and she knew she'd never turn away. She couldn't imagine her life without him.

"Living with Travis became a nightmare I couldn't wake up from," she began. "I lived in fear each day. He drove me to do unspeakable things. Some of those things I'll never erase from my mind."

She reached for Nick's hands. "My life changed when you came. I'm no longer afraid. And when you hold me, touch me, make love to me, I come alive like never before. I feel things I never thought possible."

Carrie pressed closer to him. "The answer to your question is yes. Yes, I can live with it."

"So, no more secrets between us," Nick said. His voice, thick with emotion, stirred something inside of her.

"No. None."

"And Will?" he asked.

She avoided his eyes. "I'm not sure it's the right thing to do. Besides, he'll hate me when he finds out his suffering was my fault."

Nick shook his head. "You have to stop blaming yourself. Guilt has taken up enough of your life, Carrie. We all make decisions we regret, but that's what makes us human. Unfortunately, we're not perfect."

He stroked her hair and brushed a tear from her cheek.

"I'm no expert, but I'll give you some advice," Nick said. "The longer you wait, the worse it will be. Will's a big boy. He'll handle it … in time. What you tell him about Travis is your choice. Don't make matters worse by hiding this from him like you did me."

"Nick, you don't understand. I was so young. My mother hated me. Travis abandoned me. I didn't tell you because I didn't want you to think less of me."

"Think less of you? Haven't you learned anything about me by now? Carrie, I put my life on the line for you."

Frustrated, he dropped her hands, raked his fingers through his hair, and paced. "Nothing could make me think less of you. It hurts to think how little you trust me. After our talk, I thought at least you'd be honest with me. I meant it when I said you didn't have to be afraid to tell me anything."

"Don't be upset. I do trust you, Nick, but this isn't about you." She lowered her head. "Maybe, I don't trust myself."

"What's that supposed to mean?"

"For most of my life, I've made the wrong decisions. That is … until you. You're my first right decision, Nick. Please don't ever make me regret it."

"I won't." His voice grew tender. He took both her hands in his. "Here's your chance to make another right decision. Tell Will. Tell Will you're his mother. He has a right to know."

CHAPTER 42

CARRIE

Lying in Nick's arms brought Carrie little sleep. She eased out of bed as early morning sun filtered through long shadows still clinging to the walls. While Nick slept, she dressed.

Inside the master, she unzipped her suitcase. Lifting out the small receiving blanket, she held it to her once again. Downstairs, her son lay sleeping on the sofa. Carrie thought about Nick. He was right. She needed to tell Will the truth and face whatever came with it.

The blanket with her, she headed downstairs. Her brain screamed coffee, and she set the blanket down and put the pot on. While the coffee brewed and Will lay sleeping, she placed fresh logs on the hearth and poked at the embers to get the fire going again.

Back in the kitchen, she poured herself a cup of coffee and was about to sit at the island when Will came in. His tousled brown hair hung over puffy, sleep filled eyes.

He stretched, let out a yawn. "Can I have a cup?"

"Sure," Carrie said. She poured him one and placed the cup across from hers. "Cream, sugar?"

Will flopped onto a stool. "Yes, please." He poured in some milk and dropped in two spoons of sugar.

Carrie stared in disbelief at the boy sitting across from her. Her heart thumped faster. She sucked in air, finding it difficult to breathe. All this time, she'd no idea Will was her son, her Bobby. The same child who she imagined in a good home with loving parents, had grown up in unspeakable horror. Lived each day of his young life in fear just as she had.

"How are you feeling?" she asked. She sipped her coffee with shaky hands.

"Much better." Will stirred his coffee and paused. "Carrie, I'm really sorry. I should've stayed on the marked trails."

"It's okay," she said. "How about those coyotes?"

"They scared the hell out of me," Will said. "I didn't know what to do. I set off the flare, and then you found me."

"You did the right thing. We're just glad you're okay."

Carrie rose and inched her way to the other side of the island. *Claudia be damned!* She'd wait no longer.

"Will, we need to talk," she said.

He lifted his cup, prepared to take a sip. "What about?" Curious, he stopped and then set the cup down. Panic lit his face. "Is it my mom? Did something happen?"

"No, no. She's fine."

With one hand, Will swiped his hair away from above his eye. "Something else wrong?"

"This is about me. I'm afraid this will come as a shock, but there is no easy way for me to tell you this," Carrie said. The words caught in her throat. She looked at her son and forced them out.

"Will, when I was fifteen years old, I had a child. The circumstances weren't ideal, leading me to make a foolish decision." Carrie placed a hand on the island to steady herself. "Will, I'm your biological mother."

Will's eyes bore into her. "What are you talking about?"

"I didn't know that you were my son until last night."

Disbelief washed over his face, exasperation tinging his voice. "No, it's not possible."

"Let me show you." Carrie reached for Will's arm. Instinctively he pulled away. "Please, she said, "I'm not going to hurt you."

He hesitated before letting her unbutton his sleeve. Carrie turned up the cuff until his star-shaped birthmark appeared. Gently, she traced her finger across it.

"This mark on your arm, I saw it for the first time on the day you were born and again last night when Nick removed your shirt. I never forgot it. And all these years, I never forgot you. You're my Bobby." Her voice was barely above a whisper. "That was your name."

Will jerked his arm away. His blue eyes watered and he jumped off the stool.

"I don't believe you. You're making it up. You can't be my *mother!*" He continued to move away. "My mother died when I was born. My stepmom told me. She wouldn't lie to me. My biological mother is dead."

Now, it was Carrie's turn to look confused. "Your stepmom?" Was it possible Claudia had played no part in the crime? "I don't understand, Will."

"She married my dad when I was two years old." Will's chin began to tremble. "She told me my biological mom died when I was born. So did my fath…" His eyes grew big. "Was Russ my real dad?"

Carrie's head throbbed. How could she ever explain what happened and not add to his emotional scars? She took a breath and tried to keep her voice steady. "No, Will. Russ was not your biological father."

The color drained from his face. He pointed his finger at her. "You gave me up, didn't you?" He moved further away. "You probably *never* wanted me."

His words were like a punch to her gut. "No, no. Please, don't believe that. I wanted you more than anything in this world. "She—my mother— wasn't well. She did a terrible thing."

Carrie fumbled for the right words. "I needed to get formula, and I left you with her." Her voice quivered. "While I was gone, she sold you in exchange for money to buy drugs."

Carrie's body shook at the look of horror on her son's face. There wasn't any way to make things right. He didn't believe she ever loved him and she didn't blame him.

"Please believe that I've thought about you every single day of my life." She hurried around the island and grabbed the blanket. "This was yours. I've kept it with me all these years while I wondered where you were, what you looked like. I pictured you in a good home with loving parents. It was the only way I could cope with losing you without going mad."

On instinct, Will's hands balled into fists, and he glared at her. "Well, how nice of you to keep my *blanket,*" he scoffed. "Now, let me tell you about those loving parents. From the time I was two years old, his form of punishment was to lock me in the closet under the stairs. My stepmom would cry and beg him to let me out."

He took a step closer, his eyes lit with fury. "When he couldn't stand to listen to her, he hit her. When I was older, he began hitting me, too, on a regular basis."

Her tears blurred his face. His words broke her heart. "Will, I couldn't have known. I had no idea where you were." Pain ripped through her core. Her son had suffered more than she could have imagined.

He stared at her and shook his head. "My grandmother sold me?" His tears fell hard and fast as he turned and bolted from the room. His footsteps pounded on the stairs.

Carrie ran after him. "Wait, please!"

Will reached the top of the stairs and turned. His face flushed a deep red as he stared at her.

"You have every right to be angry with me," Carrie said. "I can't begin to tell you how angry I am at myself for leaving you that day." Gingerly, she advanced up the stairs. "I should never have done that, but you need to understand something. Even if the police had found you, I'm not sure how much different your life would have turned out. My mother, your grandmother, wasn't a good person. She abused me from the time I was a little girl. She was an alcoholic and a drug addict."

Will held up his hand warning her and then wiped at his tears. "What about my father? Where was he when all this happened?"

Carrie paused. Her stomach dropped. If she told the truth about Travis, what then? She locked her eyes on her son's face. One lie, she'd allow herself one lie. She'd lie to her son about his father so as not to cause him any more pain. "He died in a car accident before you were born."

"You didn't answer my question," Will said. He balled his fists. "Did he want me? If he hadn't died, would things have been different?"

Shame and bitterness engulfed her. He was her son. She wasn't able to protect him when he was a little boy, but she'd do it now. "Yes, of course."

"How?"

He was pushing her for the answer he wanted—no, needed to hear. "I would have had someone to help take care of you and me."

He uncurled his fists, and his arms fell limp at his side. An endless flow of tears ran down his face.

"Will, I know this is a lot to take in. I'm not asking you to accept me as your mother, but please, believe me, if I'd known where you were, I'd have given my own life to rescue you from that awful man. I love you. I always have. Nothing will ever change that. It doesn't matter if you can't love me."

Carrie climbed up the steps and faced him, unsure of what to do or say next. "I'm not asking for your forgiveness, Will. I've never forgiven myself. The past will always be there. I hope someday we can move forward and try to help each other heal."

Will pushed past her. The slam of his bedroom door shook her soul. She leaned up against it, wanting to somehow comfort him. She covered her face with her hands and wept. How could she ever make things right? She needed to face reality. Her son might never want her in his life.

That night, as Carrie lay there in the dark, her resolve grew. Finally, her son lay sleeping within a few feet of her once again. Too many years of wondering had gone by to waste any more time on regret. Whatever it took to regain his love, no matter how long or hard, she'd do it.

CHAPTER 43

RICARDO

Ricardo sat, reading glasses on, eyes fixed on the computer screen. He concentrated on the spreadsheet holding the details of his next shipment of drugs, all entered in code, made to look like it belonged to one of his legitimate businesses. His precise nature had led him to his current stature in the drug trade. Harvard educated, with a Master's Degree in Business, he learned early on the real money was made by trafficking drugs from his native Columbia.

Ricardo belonged to a criminal network that operated independently, the BACRIM or *bandas criminales,* a third-generation Columbian drug trafficking syndicate. After a series of murders and captures of those long in control, the door to the drug trade had opened wide, allowing Ricardo to step through and stake his claim.

He removed his glasses and rubbed his eyes. Since his last conversation with Nick, his black mood refused to lift. The man he trusted above all others had betrayed him. Nick destroyed his dream of Carmela safe and happily married to a man he deemed worthy of her. Safe being the operative word.

In most instances, the family was off limits, but there were others out there in the drug trade who didn't hold the same values as he did. Without Nick, he'd have to find other ways to ensure her safety.

A soft tap on the door caught his attention. "Come in, *mi amor.*"

Carmela breezed in wearing her riding clothes. She removed her riding cap, and let it dangle from her hand by its strap. One thick long braid dipped over her shoulder. She unbuttoned her blue blazer, revealing the white shirt underneath. Beige riding pants rose up from her dark boots. She walked toward Ricardo with Chino trailing behind her.

"*Papá,* I want to thank you again for Allegra. I just finished riding, and he's doing much better. He responds to all my commands now. He'll be ready for the Dressage Competition sooner than I thought."

I'm glad you're enjoying him, Carmela." Chino padded around the desk and sat by Ricardo. He reached and stroked the huge head. "Such a good boy," he said.

Carmela tossed her hat on the sofa and studied her father. "Papá, what is it? Something's wrong. Ever since Nick left, you're not yourself."

His body tensed at the mention of Nick's name. He clasped his hands. *"Estoy cansado, mi amor.* Lots of work to be done."

"Tired? You're not being honest with me. It's more than that. I can feel it." Carmela sank onto the sofa. "I don't want you to think I'm disappointed about Nick. We talked before he left. I told you, he wasn't in love with me, *Papá.* I'm okay with it, and you should be too."

"There's more to it than that, Carmela. It's much too complicated for me to explain."

"What is it?" A heavy sigh escaped her lips when he didn't respond. "Look, *Papá,* I'm old enough to tell you what I think. You wanted Nick to marry me so he could protect me from your drug business."

Ricardo frowned and waved his hand at her. "I don't know what you're talking about, Carmela. Stop saying such foolish things."

She cut her eyes at him. "You can deny it all you want, but I know the truth. I've known it for a long time. When I finish school next year, I'll come home for good. Without Nick in the picture and no one you trust to take his place, things will change."

"What do you mean change?"

"Papá, I want you to teach me how to run your businesses, including the drugs."

Ricardo stood up. His posture stiffened. "Stop talking nonsense. I don't have time for it, Carmela." He strode to the bar and seized a tequila bottle. He poured a shot and drained the glass.

Carmela remained resolute. "As you said, one day, you'll be gone. Wouldn't it be wise to teach me so I can protect myself?"

Ricardo faced her. He was no fool. Of course, his bright, young daughter figured it all out. It was useless for him to continue to deny it. He would never have chosen his path for her, but standing here, looking into her eyes, he believed she could handle it.

"I never wanted this for you, Carmela. There aren't many women in the drug trade. And those, who have tried, haven't lasted long."

"No, there aren't any women as smart as me in the drug trade," she corrected. "*Papá,* you're the best person I can learn from. If you teach me, you won't have to worry. I know the majority of your income comes from the drugs.

"And you have no problem with this, Carmela? Drugs are a dirty business."

"I'd be a hypocrite if I did. Of all the things I've been afforded, the majority came from drug money. Your other businesses came way later. The winery and the restaurants are fairly new."

A dull ache formed in his head. He took great care of his other businesses. His winery in the Napa Valley had garnered many awards for its wines. His successful chain of restaurants, aptly named, *Buena Comida,* meaning good food, also brought in substantial revenue. He had hoped Nick would take them over, grow his massive fortune, and keep his daughter in the safety and luxury she deserved.

Ricardo considered Carmela's words. He never thought the day would come when they'd be having a conversation like this. If Carmela were a boy, he wouldn't hesitate to teach a son the business. He folded his arms and paced the room.

His lies had never masked the truth. She was no longer a child. Carmela was a smart, well-educated woman. With the proper teaching, she could very well stand up to the pressure, but giving orders to kill when necessary was another matter. She might even have to have someone close to her, like Nick, eliminated.

"Listen, *mi amour.* I have to take some time and think about this. As your father, this decision is not an easy one. If I do decide to grant your request, you must understand there is no getting out. You stay in until the end."

Carmela stood and faced her father. "I understand. Please consider it, *Papá*. I know you're uncomfortable with this." She kissed both his cheeks and slipped out the door. "Think about it."

Chino remained sprawled on the floor, eyes closed. Ricardo sat behind his desk. He pressed his fingers to his throbbing forehead. Nick was to blame for all of this. He'd never have to consider Carmela's request if Nick hadn't betrayed him. What she said was true. If something happened to him, without the proper knowledge, she'd be exposed to those who would destroy her.

It gnawed at him, this situation with Nick. This feud between them must end, be put to bed so he'd have some peace. Bitter bile rose in his throat. Nick let a woman come between them. This man, who he once thought of as a son, must die. And that *puta,* that bitch, along with him.

His cell phone hummed. The news he'd been waiting for came through from the other end.

"South Dakota," a voice said.

"*Sí,*" Ricardo replied. "Call me when it's done." He placed his cell phone on the desk and sighed. A sense of relief washed over him. Soon, he'd put this ugliness of Nick and the woman behind him.

CHAPTER 44

NICK

R ight before dawn, Nick kissed a sleepy Carrie on the forehead. She stretched cat-like and threw her arms around his neck. He caught the longing whisper inside her and was glad. She had been distant these last few days after her talk with Will.

Every inch of him craved her as he pulled her on top of him. Heat coursed through his body and when she was ready, he slipped inside her.

Their hips fell into rhythm. When he reached the brink, she made him hold on a little longer. She lifted his hands to her breasts, and he traced his thumbs across her nipples. A moan escaped her lips. Her head lolled to the side, and his eyes followed the smooth column of her neck. She arched her back and drove her hips faster. The wave inside him broke, and she held on, rode it with him. His voice, thick and heavy, spoke her name. He shuddered, and his body relaxed.

Their eyes met as she bent her head, her long black hair forming a curtain around them. Her lips teased, traced lightly over his. His arms went around her, and he took full possession of her mouth. His kiss long, slow, deep. Satisfied, she slipped down beside him.

Nick locked his arms around her. "Wow ... and good morning. Thanks for the wake-up call." His voice was husky and warm.

Carrie smiled. "You're welcome. It's the least I can do."

She had created a never-ending need inside of him. No other woman had ever made him want her the way she did. It took all his resolve to leave the warmth of their bed, but Brody had called. The books were ready sooner than expected.

Nick was glad. The faster they left South Dakota, the better. Their safety was always foremost on his mind. He'd drive into Rapid City, see Brody, and pick up a few more groceries. He promised Carrie he'd show off his cooking skills this evening.

Later, he'd confirm the details with Dalton for the use of his private jet out of Sioux Falls. Dalton would take care of getting rid of the guns. He'd also make sure they made it through airport security and customs with the remainder of the money in Sioux Falls and at their final destination.

Nick pulled the Range Rover out of the garage. Brody had agreed to meet him early at the store. Three hundred thousand inside a brown manila envelope lay underneath the seat. Those books were worth that and more.

Since Carrie had come clean with Will, Nick had spied the two of them talking together several times. He quietly bowed out, leaving them alone. Nick assured her, in time, they would make their peace with each other. He sensed they were working on it. The poor kid could use a break, after all he'd gone through. Carrie needed to be patient. Teenagers deal with life on their own terms. They tend to hold grudges longer. It was tough enough just trying to grow up.

He did agree with Carrie's decision to tell Will his father died in a car crash. Nothing good could come from telling him the truth. Just as his not telling Carrie that Travis was her father needed to stay buried. After all, the knowledge that Will was a child of incest would be a bitter pill for either one of them to swallow.

Brody opened the door to the hardware store when Nick arrived and locked it behind them. He led the way downstairs.

Nick handed him the manila envelope. "It's all there."

He tossed the unopened envelope on his desk. "You're one of the few people in this business I trust." He handed Nick three passports. "Take a look. I think it's some of my best work."

Nick flipped through the passports. "I would definitely agree." He placed them inside his jacket pocket.

The two men shook hands and then walked to the door. "Listen, man, anytime you need anything, don't hesitate." He gave Nick a bear hug. "Safe travels."

"Thanks," Nick said and slipped outside.

Nick picked up the groceries for dinner and drove toward the Black Hills. As nice as the past week had turned out, they lived on borrowed time. Ricardo would be pulling out all the stops to find them, and he couldn't let that happen.

Thoughts of Carrie swirled inside his head. Love hadn't entered his mind for a long, long time. He'd loved before, but never like this. His love for Carrie embodied his very being. She became the constant in his life. He couldn't envision a future without her.

If he was honest with himself, the moment she came through the swinging doors of the diner kitchen, his world changed. Up until now, his life played out in black and white. With Carrie, it turned into a kaleidoscope of colors with endless possibilities. She became his heartbeat, the thing that kept him alive. He'd push his past and all his demons aside. All for her. Everything he did from this point on would be for Carrie.

It was mid-morning when he returned to the house. He started up the steps, grocery bags in hand when something hit his back. Teetering on the edge of the step, he almost lost his balance and fell. He spun around, nearly spilling the contents of the bags.

A giggle came from behind the bushes. Carrie appeared, her hands forming another snowball.

Nick grinned and set the bags down. He grabbed a handful of snow and molded it into a ball. "So, you wanna play?" he asked and laughed.

Carrie launched her snowball. Nick ducked as it sailed past his face. He fired one at her and Carrie squealed with delight when it hit her square on the front of her jacket. Both of them gathered more snow, and, within minutes, they had a full-blown snowball fight going.

Carrie dipped left and then right between the bushes while Nick crouched beside the Range Rover.

The front door opened, and Will stepped out.

"Hey, what's going on?" A snowball sailed past his head and hit the door.

Nick popped up from the side of the Range Rover. "Don't look at me," he said, pointing to the bushes.

Will swiped snow from the porch railing and then molded it between his palms. He flew down the steps and ran toward the bushes.

Carrie stood up just in time to get hit in the shoulder. Her face flushed red.

"Hey, no fair. Two against one." She ducked past Will and headed for the stairs. Nick caught her waist, and they both tumbled to the ground in fits of laughter, while Will hurled snowballs at them.

"Uncle," Nick cried. "I give up, Will."

"Me, too," Carrie said.

Nick pulled her to her feet, and they slapped at the snow on their clothes.

"I guess we know who the snowball champ is," Carrie said, her face flushed pink from the cold. "How'd you make them so fast, Will?"

"You forget, I grew up in the mountains. Snow is our thing." He threw the remaining snowball in his hand toward the bushes."

They laughed, gathered up the groceries, and headed inside. They changed into dry clothes, and Carrie helped Nick unload the groceries. Will, as was his habit, retreated to the television in the great room.

Carrie made a cup of tea while Nick prepared to cook. She took her cup and sat opposite him at the island.

He placed a cutting board on the counter and then peeled and sliced an onion. Taking fresh oregano and basil, he chopped and added them to the onion.

"So, that's how an expert does it." She grinned and sipped her tea.

Nick let out a chuckle. "Now, watch a master at work." He plucked a large pot from one of the cupboards, drizzled some olive oil in the bottom and placed it on the burner. Taking a large knife, he peeled fresh garlic cloves, turned the blade, and crushed the garlic underneath it.

He lit the burner on low and tossed all the ingredients into the pot. They sizzled, filling the kitchen with the scent of fresh garlic and herbs. He turned to Carrie.

"That my dear is the start of good gravy."

"Gravy?" Carrie questioned. "You mean tomato sauce?"

Nick gave her a horrified look. "Yes, gravy. Italians never call it sauce."

Carrie patted her chest, pretended to swoon. "I'm so sorry. I wasn't aware of that fact."

"Very funny," Nick countered. He opened several cans of crushed tomatoes and added those to the pot.

Carrie watched fascinated as he seasoned ground beef and skillfully formed meatballs with his palms. He finished, set them in a pan, and slid them in the oven.

"I'll add those to the gravy later." He washed his hands and then reached into the wine cooler.

"Now, for the best part." He winked at Carrie and opened a bottle of wine. Lifting the lid on the pot, he splashed some in.

"Nobody could argue with that," Carrie agreed.

The pot of gravy simmered on the stove for the next four hours. The rich aroma of tomatoes and herbs filled the house.

With dinner almost ready, Nick halved a loaf of Italian bread. He slathered the bread with butter, oregano, minced garlic, and then shoved it in the oven.

It was still light outside when they sat down to an early dinner. Nick beamed over his accomplishment as he filled their plates with pasta, ladling the steaming hot gravy over the top. He sliced the Italian bread and set it in the middle of the table.

Will, head bent over his plate, shoveled food in his mouth. "Man, this tastes great," he said between swallows.

"It's delicious," Carrie agreed. "Your mother taught you well." She twirled her fork and slipped in another mouthful of spaghetti. "You outdid yourself. I could learn a lot from you."

Nick smiled. "I have a lot more up my sleeve besides this. You'll see."

After second helpings for all of them, Carrie volunteered to clean up. She set about gathering up their plates.

"I'll help, too." Will chimed in while he walked his plate to the kitchen.

"I think he's starting to feel a little better," Nick said. He bent and kissed her cheek. "I need to make some phone calls."

"Go on. We'll finish up here."

Nick retreated upstairs and started to dial Dalton's number when his cell phone rang.

"Hey, I was about to—what?" Nick bolted to the window and looked out. "Yeah, got it." He disconnected the call, rushed to the bed, and lifted a corner of the mattress. The silencer already attached he grabbed his 9mm and charged down the stairs. In the kitchen, Carrie stood loading the dishwasher, while Will handed her the dishes.

"Listen, I need you both to go upstairs now. Go to the master bedroom and lock the door."

Carrie's face paled when she saw the gun. "What's going on?"

"Just do it," Nick ordered. "Stay away from the windows. Don't come out until I tell you to. Understand?"

Will stared at the gun and then looked from Nick to Carrie. "What's going on?"

Carrie grabbed Will's hand. "Do what he says. Let's go." They hurried up the stairs.

Nick listened for the lock to turn, and then crept toward the patio slider. His body pressed against the wall next to the slider, he peered out. Moonlight washed over a set of footprints embedded in the snow. The hairs on the back of his neck prickled. Someone was already here. Whoever Ricardo had sent had made their first mistake. Unlocking the slider, he eased it open and stepped out into the empty silence.

Bitter cold brushed his skin as the last of daylight faded. Wind-blown snow formed huge drifts all around the patio. He scanned left, and right, and then crept across the patio. The footprints trailed around the left side of the house. His 9mm clutched tight, he advanced inch by inch in their direction. Snow crunched beneath the weight of his feet. A lone coyote howled in the distance.

He neared the corner of the house. Out ahead, a shadow loomed. His adrenaline surge rushed through him. A familiar feeling as he took aim, ready to squeeze the trigger. His vision focused on the figure about to come into view.

A burst of gunfire hit the night air and echoed off the mountains. Only Nick hadn't pulled his trigger. His silencer would have muffled the noise from a bullet. He recognized the shotgun blast. He inched his way toward the sound, his body close to the side of the house. About to round the corner, he jerked as a lone figure, moaned and toppled face down in the snow a few feet away. A trail of red trickled across the snow. A second figure emerged, its shadow moving toward him from the corner of the house. Nick raised his 9mm again.

"Whoa, hold up." A voice boomed out, breaking the deadly quiet.

Nick squinted, exhaled, and then relaxed. It was Dalton.

"Son of a bitch. I almost shot you."

Dalton pointed his shotgun toward the body lying on the ground. "I got your man. My guys are checking the perimeter. So far it seems he was on his own."

Nick strode over. Dalton bent and rolled the body face up. A considerable blotch of red ran across the man's chest. "Recognize him?"

Nick leaned in, studied the face. "No. He's not familiar at all."

"Means Ricardo is bringing in new blood."

Nick angled his head, nodded in the direction of the body. "He can do better. The guy left a clear trail in the snow. You don't leave warning signs when you come to take someone out."

Dalton slapped Nick on the back. "There's not many ghosts like us, Nick. You know that."

Nick winked. "Sure as hell do." He tucked his 9mm into his waistband.

"I'll drive my truck around," Dalton said. "We'll load him up. There's plenty of land for me to get rid of what's left of the body after the coyotes have at it."

Within minutes, the two men loaded the body onto the flatbed of Dalton's truck. He slammed the tailgate closed and turned to Nick.

"My plane will be fueled and waiting for you tonight. I know it's a drive to Sioux Falls, but the sooner you get the hell out of South Dakota, the better. It's all taken care of. You should have no trouble with customs on either end.

Nick held out his hand. "I can't thank you enough, Dalton."

Dalton brought him in for a bear hug. "You take care of yourself and that pretty lady of yours." Dalton lifted his Stetson and scratched his head. "Hard to figure out where the boy fits in though."

Nick shrugged. "Simple. He's her son. They reconnected under somewhat unusual circumstances."

Dalton laughed and pointed his finger at Nick. "Looks like you got a readymade family out of this deal."

Nick smiled. "Maybe."

Dalton's taillights faded away as Nick turned and headed inside. He froze when he saw a trail of wet footprints across the great room leading up the stairs. He pulled out his 9mm again and crept up the stairs. The door to the master bedroom hung open.

CHAPTER 45

CARRIE

Carrie and Will huddled together in the bedroom. The fear she hadn't known in a long while spiraled up inside of her. She could see now, the future she had chosen with Nick included being held accountable for their past. True happiness might always elude them.

Will moved to the window and peered out. "Will, you heard Nick. Stay away from the windows," she said.

He glared at her. "Nobody ever tells me what the heck is going on. I'm supposed to stay locked up here without a clue?"

Carrie's brows knit together. "Look, I realize you're confused about all of this, but you have to trust us. We need to do what Nick says."

Will's eyes popped wide, and he pointed his finger at her. "I knew it! The two of you did something bad. I was right about the guns and the money. I never believed the phony story Nick told me."

"Will, listen…." Carrie detected a sound. Nervous prickles ran up and down her spine. She glanced at the door. The knob twisted slowly back and forth. She spun around and grabbed Will's arm, leading him into the master bath.

"Hey, what the heck?"

She put a finger to her lips and nodded at the door. "Go inside and lock up."

"But what about you?" Will whispered.

"Don't worry about me. Do it now."

With Will secured, Carrie surveyed the room looking for a weapon. The door jiggled, and she spun around. Something heaved against it, rattling the frame.

She bolted over to the fireplace. Grabbing a metal poker, she dashed to the nightstand and killed the light. She pressed herself close to the wall by the side of the doorway. She gripped the poker with both hands and raised it above her head.

The door vibrated again. She drew a shaky breath and clutched the poker tighter. The frame rattled, and the door flew open. A dark shape burst through.

Carrie swung the poker repeatedly at the figure. It landed twice with a loud crack. Something dropped to the floor. The figure swayed but remained upright.

She thought of her son, locked in the other room, and kept on swinging. No one was going to take Bobby from her ever again. Both of them had only just begun to heal the wounds inflicted upon them from their broken past. She wasn't going to let anyone or anything come between her and her son again.

All her focus on the figure before her she continued her assault, until, its arms flailing at her, it moaned and fell at her feet.

Carrie stepped over the body and switched on the light. A battered and bloody man lay on the floor in a crumpled heap and his gun a few feet away. Still holding the poker, she eased over and snatched the gun away. She set the poker aside and kept the gun aimed at the man. Although she had vowed never to fire a gun again, she wouldn't hesitate to use it to protect her son.

She called out. "Will, I'm fine, but you stay inside there until I tell you to come out."

"What's going on? Why can't I come out?" Will shouted through the door.

"I'm not sure it's safe. Please do as I say." She moved toward the opposite wall. A sound exploded outside making her jump. Her pulse rocketed. If something happened to Nick, hers and Will's life would end.

She heard the faint sound of voices, and a vehicle pull away up the drive. The sound of footsteps breached the hall.

Her hands trembled, and she gripped the gun tighter. She aimed at the doorway, her finger ready to pull the trigger.

Relief washed through her when Nick rounded the frame, and she lowered the gun.

"Thank God, you're okay. I heard a gunshot. I wasn't sure if…"

Nick's mouth fell open. He looked from her to the man lying on the floor. His gun still in his hand, he bent and examined him. "He's out cold."

Carrie dropped the gun and tore toward Nick. She flung her arms around his neck. "Are you sure you're alright?" she asked.

"I'm fine. Nothing for you to worry about." A sly grin spread across his face. "I see you took care of things here. Where's Will?"

"Will, you can come out now," Carrie called out.

Will stepped out of the bathroom and surveyed the scene, a look of disbelief on his face. He gestured toward the man on the floor.

"Who the hell is that? What happened?" He looked at Nick. "Did someone get shot?"

Nick released Carrie. "Yes, a real bad guy." He pulled out his cell phone and punched in a number. "Yeah, another one. No, Carrie took care of him. Yeah, you heard me right. I'll secure the package and leave it for you."

"What now?" Carrie asked.

"Dalton will take care of him. We're leaving tonight. I need you both to pack up while I deal with him." He pointed to the man on the floor.

"Leaving." Will said. "Where are we going?"

"Will look, I know this isn't fair to you, but right now we have to head out of here." Nick said. "I promise, when we get on the plane, I'll be straight with you."

"Plane?" Will said. "I'm not getting on any plane. Not unless it's flying me to Laurel to my M—'' He stopped and looked at Carrie. "I mean, to my house."

"Carrie faced him. "It's okay, Will. Claudia will always be your mom first."

Nick reached out and touched Will's shoulder. "As soon as it's safe, we'll make sure you get to Laurel. Right now, I need you to trust us. You can call her after we land. Okay?" Nick held out his hand. "Shake on it?"

Will wavered a moment before shaking Nick's hand. "Yeah, I guess."

After Dalton left, Nick pulled the Range Rover up to the front of the house. With darkness all around them and bitter cold biting at their skin, they loaded up the Range Rover and left the Black Hills for Sioux Falls.

CHAPTER 46

CARRIE

Lugano, on the border between southern Switzerland and northern Italy, was where they made their new home. The Swiss city, spread across rolling hillsides and surrounded by mountains, contained the largest Italian-speaking majority outside of Italy. And since Nick was fluent in Italian, it suited them just fine. Cradled in the center of town were numerous promenades, shops, and gourmet markets. Along the waterfront, various restaurants stood upon streets paved with pale red bricks.

The house Nick rented for them had terraces with panoramic views of the Swiss Alps and the glacial Lake Lugano. More modern than the house in South Dakota, square in design, it boasted lots of tall windows and straight lines. Bright open rooms filled with light flowed into one another. A massive glass-tiled fireplace soared to the ceiling in the great room. Imported modern German Leicht cabinetry in black and white lined the kitchen walls on either side of a long island in the center. There were six bedrooms, each with its own bath, and a huge master suite with a sitting room and a separate private terrace.

Eighteen months had elapsed since leaving South Dakota on that frigid night. Eighteen months of calm. What Carrie referred to as normal. She relished the three of them getting to know each other, learning to live together day by day.

After the initial shock of finding out she was his biological mother, Will let go of his resentment toward her and he also relinquished his first name. He came to them and asked to be called Bobby, the name she'd given him. Eventually, he changed his name legally. Taking Bobby as his first and since he never knew his biological father, he settled with Carrie's last name of Overton.

Carrie shared stories of her life in Breezy with her abusive mother. And as hard as it was for her to hear, Bobby shared his stories. Although saddened by the fact the two of them had bonded over a history of abuse, she realized she couldn't change the past for either of them.

She cherished her time with him. Though still somewhat shy, her son was growing into a man right before her eyes.

He had flown to see Claudia twice, at Christmas and Easter but was spending his summer vacation with them in Lugano. Carrie accepted Claudia always being his mom before her, so long as she could continue to build a relationship of her own with him. Claudia had been horrified to find out about the crime her dead husband had committed.

And, although none appeared, Carrie still searched for signs of Travis in Bobby. Worried he might morph into a monster like his father, she took great pains to reinforce the tender side of his personality.

Bobby also proved to be pretty smart. So much so, he agreed, with Claudia's okay, to let them enroll him in an elite Swiss Academy.

He slowly let his guard down with Nick. And, as promised, Nick came clean with Bobby about almost everything. He explained how the people he killed were criminals. Nick assured Bobby that he was trying to change his life, except the man he had worked for didn't want him to. He impressed on Bobby how they must still be careful in order to stay safe.

Bobby contemplated what Nick told him, asked questions and seemed satisfied. Said he understood now why they needed to leave America.

It still amazed her how they flew away from South Dakota, not knowing what the future might look like. More amazing, how much happiness this new life with Nick brought her. Regardless of what came before, Nick proved himself to be a good man, and it was all that mattered to her now, and she let him love her the way she deserved to be loved.

Their relationship grew stronger, an unbreakable bond between them. They understood each other, where they had come from, the sins they committed. The rare times they argued, as couples often do, she argued without fear. Nick's hands woke the passion in her, held her, made her safe, but never hurt her. She loved him all the more because of it.

Out in public, Nick was known by the name on his passport, Michael Warren, but at home he was Nick. Her Nick.

This past winter, he taught Bobby to ski. A great bonding experience for them both. Carrie passed on the skiing lessons. She'd promised to learn to ski next winter. In her condition, she didn't want to take chances.

Down to the wire now, the baby was due in two more weeks. Eager to meet the child she carried inside of her, the end of August couldn't come soon enough.

On birth control, a child was the last thing on her mind, but as the doctor told her, it can and does happen. She had waited to tell Nick, unsure of how he would react to the news that he was about to be a father. Under the present circumstances, it was something they hadn't discussed.

They were out to dinner one night at one of their favorite restaurants, by the Cassarate River when Carrie decided this would be the perfect place to break the news.

They loved Cantina Trattoria's rustic charm. Its textured walls, and wood beams overhead giving it a cozy feel. Jars of decorative oils, dried pasta, and hot peppers lined the shelves. A view to the kitchen allowed diners watch the chef prepare fresh ribbons of pasta and house specialties. The scent of garlic, herbs, and sauces mingled together in the air. They sat at the same table they had occupied numerous times before. By the window with a view of the river and the mountains. Nick ordered a bottle of wine, and when the waiter reached over to fill her glass, she covered it with the palm of her hand.

"Just water, please," she had said.

"Water? No wine tonight?" he asked, puzzled.

She locked onto those green eyes. Those eyes that adored and loved her. Finally, she could give him something in return. "Not for the next seven months."

He set his wine glass down. "Are you saying?"

"Yes," she said.

A slow smile played on his lips. His eyes brimmed. He reached across the table for her hand and then pressed her palm to his lips for a gentle kiss. "I love you," he said. And for her, it was enough.

As time slipped by, she found humor in Nick's treatment of her, like a china doll that could break at any minute. Her hormones raging, she surprised him with her fierce lovemaking and had to convince him they wouldn't hurt the baby while making love.

Now, nearing her last weeks, she readied herself. Satisfied and happy with the nursery painted in pale yellow, with furniture in soft greys and Noah's Ark animals marching across one wall, all she wanted to do now was stay close to home and nest.

She refused Nick's offer of a nanny. Having missed Bobby's childhood, her only desire was to spend every precious minute with her little one.

Aunt May would visit after the birth, to help out, and she could hardly wait to see her aunt again. They'd spoken by phone, and Carrie explained as much as she thought was necessary to her aunt regarding her current situation. It would be May's first visit to Lugano and also her first time meeting Nick in person. May was stunned to learn Bobby was Carrie's son but overjoyed they had reconnected.

Carrie never forgot Joann either and all her kindness during her time in Laurel. They kept in touch by phone and Carrie promised to arrange for her and the kids to come and visit once she established a regular routine with the baby.

Today, having slept late, Carrie twisted her bulk and strained to see the clock on the nightstand. "Oh God," she said and let out a moan. It was almost noon.

Carrie showered and chose a pale pink shift, loose enough and comfortable in the warm weather. Attempting to push her swollen feet into a pair of sandals, she gave up and settled for flip-flops. She wobbled into the kitchen.

"Good afternoon, gorgeous," Nick said. He relaxed at the kitchen table dressed casually in jeans and a polo shirt. A newspaper lay open in front of him, and a half-empty bottle of beer sat beside it.

Carrie flinched and rubbed the bottom of her back. "Glad you still think so," she said. She poured a glass of orange juice and sipped. "I've been thinking. I already missed breakfast and since it's such a nice day, why don't I pack some lunch and we can eat it beside the lake."

Nick put the paper aside and chugged on his beer. "Sounds good to me. How can I help?"

"Get a blanket and the picnic basket out of the hall closet while I get started."

He brushed past her, kissing the top of her head. "Sure thing."

Nick set the basket on the counter. Carrie prepared ham sandwiches, then sliced tomato, and added some mozzarella for a Caprese salad. She placed it on a small platter along with some fresh basil leaves and covered it. Sweet melon and grapes completed the meal. Carrie opened the basket. Nick's gun lay in the bottom. Though she didn't think it necessary, when it came to their safety, she'd never second-guess him. He took it with him wherever they went. She positioned a linen napkin over it then set two plates on top.

Bobby bounded into the room all smiles. "Guess what?" he asked.

Carrie couldn't keep from grinning each time she saw her son. Bobby had grown into a handsome young man, not to mention how he towered over her now. She found the slice of dark brown hair that still dipped over his right eye more endearing than ever.

"What?" she asked. "By the look on your face, it must be something good."

"Not good, great," Bobby said. "She said, yes."

Nick raised his hand, and they high fived. "I told you she would. You just have to step up your game a little."

Carrie eyed the two of them. "Who said yes?"

Nick laughed and puffed out his chest. "I gave Bobby some pointers on how to ask a young lady out. There's a particular girl he has his eye on, but he was afraid she'd turn him down."

Bobby beamed at Carrie. "She's just not any girl. She's *the girl*! The most popular girl at school."

Carrie rolled her eyes and giggled. She wagged her finger toward Nick. "You got pointers from him? I remember how nervous he was when he asked me out for coffee." It struck her as somewhat strange how she could recall that day and find humor in it.

"Who, me? Nervous?" Nick asked. "All in your mind." He gave her a quick wink. "You did say yes."

The two of them laughed. Bobby looked puzzled. "What are you two talking about?"

"Someday, I'll tell you that story, Bobby, Carrie said. "We're going to picnic by the lake if you want to come. You can tell me all about this special girl."

Bobby nodded. "Sure, I'll meet you there in a few minutes. I need to change. Might wanna go for a swim." He grabbed an apple from a bowl on the counter and scurried upstairs.

She looked over at Nick. "Come give me a hand."

He helped finish loading the basket, adding another beer for himself and water for her. They strolled to the lake at the edge of their property. Nick spread the blanket out and eased her onto it. He deposited the basket between them.

Carrie fidgeted, unable to get comfortable. "I feel like a beached whale," she uttered.

Nick laughed. "Prettiest one I ever laid eyes on." He drew a sandwich from the basket, handed it to her, and grabbed one for himself. "It will all be over soon, babe."

"Easy for you to say." Carrie grinned and unwrapped her sandwich. Her body jerked as white-hot pain tore through her shoulder and she dropped the sandwich. She shuddered, as something wet traveled along her arm and she looked down. Blood dripped from her fingers and seeped through her pink dress. She reached for Nick.

"I think … I've been shot." She struggled to focus as darkness closed in.

The warmth of Nick's arms wrapped around her as he lifted her and carried her to the terrace at the rear of the house. Through a haze, she watched him crouch, run and grab his gun, and some linen napkins. He set his weapon down and fashioned a tourniquet from the napkins and tightened it around her arm.

He pressed her close while he cradled her in his arms. "Carrie, Carrie," Nick pleaded. "Stay with me. Stay with me."

Bobby emerged from the house and started toward them. Fear gripped his face at the horrifying scene before him. Nick yelled for him to get down. Bobby bent and crawled toward them. He looked down at Carrie and then reached for her hand.

"Mom, it's okay. You're going to be okay. Mom, can you hear me?"

Carrie drifted in and out. Voices rang at her from far away. Only she couldn't understand what they were saying. Images invaded her vision, one after the other. Travis, his face twisted with rage, reached out and tried to latch onto her. Then Carlos appeared, spitting out words at her through the bloody open wound in his throat and finally, her mother, vodka bottle in hand, beckoning Carrie to follow her. She struggled to escape them, her body pushing through a wave of thick syrupy liquid.

It hurt to breathe. Cold seeped in, wrapped itself around her body. Where was the heat? She needed heat. A voice rang out from within the light ahead of her.

'*Mom, Mom*' it called out. She smiled, ran toward it, and away from the darkness. Away from those images and into the light.

CHAPTER 47

NICK

Nick stared into the vast open sky outside the window of Dalton's Gulfstream G550. Dalton had sent the jet after Nick's phone call, without him having to ask. He checked his watch. In another half hour, he'd land in Rapid City.

He declined the wine, and assorted liquor the flight attendant offered him after his meal. He'd drink water until he finished the job. He needed to stay sharp, on point.

The Black Hills appeared on the horizon, dressed again in their vibrant hues, but all he could think of was Carrie, and the first time they made love. It wasn't just sex. Not to him or her. The raw hunger inside of them ran much deeper. Both of them empty wells, feeding off of one another.

He'd gotten lost looking into those violet-blue eyes. In them, he saw everything she had been and all she was meant to be. Nick looked down at his hands where her long dark hair, like black velvet, would slip through his fingers when they made love.

He gazed at the far mountain tops; their peaks dusted white and remembered how he watched her delight in her first snowfall. He could almost feel her arms around him as she clung to him on the back of the snowmobile. The image of her standing at the stove, cooking their first meal, and their silly snowball fight. He was filled with memories of her.

He pushed hard against the ache inside that wouldn't go away. He had failed her, broken his promise to protect her. How foolish he'd been to think leaving the country would keep them safe from Ricardo. Like an octopus, his tentacles reached far and wide. The only thing left to do now was cut off its head.

Night had fallen by the time the jet's wheels touched down and glided over the tarmac. Nick grabbed his bag. He pulled the zipper up on his tan jacket and stepped out. Fall kept a chill in the air in South Dakota. Dalton exited a limo and waited at the bottom of the stairs.

"I'm so sorry. I hardly know what to say." Dalton gripped him in a bear hug.

Nick stepped back and looked into the big man's eyes. "You're being here is enough." He glanced around.

"What, no pick-up truck?" Nick teased.

"Not this time, partner. You deserve a decent ride to the ranch after that long trip. We do have a ways to go. Might as well be comfortable."

Nick smiled. People always made the mistake of pegging Dalton as a simple rancher, which he was, among other things. The jet became his necessary luxury when he traveled to complete a kill. The rest of his time was spent at the ranch he loved so much.

"I'll tell you what I heard," Dalton said after they settled in. "Word is Ricardo's been teaching Carmela the business."

Nick laughed. "I think you heard wrong. He'd never do that. He made it his mission to keep her far away from the drugs."

"I got it from a good source. And my sources are rarely wrong. So, you can do with that information what you will, buddy."

"Look, I'm not saying your sources are all wrong," Nick said. "I'm a bit skeptical, that's all."

When they reached the ranch, Dalton showed him to his room and told him a late supper waited downstairs when he was ready.

"I'm ready now," Nick said. He followed Dalton to the dining room. The simple ranch house was much smaller and more understated than his other home. Dalton used the timber and stone house for entertaining guests and when he found it necessary to impress a lady or two.

His ranch home held a large living room with a brick fireplace and dining room beside a simple kitchen. The master was on the main, with two more bedrooms upstairs.

They dined on a simple meal of steak and potatoes, the meat courtesy of one of Dalton's Black Angus cows. They ate their meal almost in silence and then retired to the living room.

Dalton lit a fire, and the two men settled into the leather chairs facing the fireplace.

"I've been meaning to ask you," Dalton began. "What about Bobby? How's he holding up?"

He looked away from Dalton and studied the fire. "Bobby practically witnessed the whole thing, took it pretty hard."

"Is he still at the house?"

"Yes. He wanted to stay."

Dalton looked surprised. "You let him? After what happened."

"He's well protected," Nick said. "Marco Valletta is there with a couple of guys. I trust him."

"Marco's a good man. Almost a ghost," Dalton said. He shifted uneasily, turned his head toward Nick. "Any way you want to play this, Nick, I'm there."

Nick shook his head. "You've done enough. I'll handle this one on my own."

Dalton sucked in his breath. "Now, you listen to me. There is no way I'm going to let you go up against Ricardo alone. The odds aren't stacked in your favor, and you know it."

Dalton spoke the truth, but he didn't feel right asking for Dalton's help. He had nothing to do with the rift between him and Ricardo.

"Dalton, this is my fight, and I need to see it through alone."

Dalton's eyes blazed almost as bright as the fire. He pounded his fist on the arm of the chair. "I don't think I made myself clear enough. If I have to keep you here until you agree, I'll do it."

Nick studied him. A slow grin spread across his face. "Keep me here?"

"You heard me," Dalton shot back. "And don't think I won't do it."

Nick couldn't keep from laughing. "You could try."

He recognized how important Dalton was to him. After Carrie, he couldn't handle losing him, but Dalton had made it clear he planned on going with him.

"Look," Dalton said. "The kill shot is yours. I won't take that satisfaction away from you. Let me and some of my guys work the perimeter. Clear a path, so to speak."

Nick leaned toward the fire, hands locked together in his lap. Dalton was right. His chances were better with him on board.

"Okay. You clear me a path to the son of a bitch, and I'll finish him."

"Now you're talking," Dalton said. He rose, poked the fire and tossed another log on. "Tomorrow, we'll get all the gear together. You choose which weapons to take. My plane will be ready."

"Ricardo will be in Napa at his vineyard," Nick said. I have a map marking the perimeter from when I helped him set up security years ago. Two guards flank each perimeter, north, south, east and west. The workers are off on Sunday, so tomorrow is our target date. "Your men will need long range rifles."

"And you?" Dalton asked.

Nick looked Dalton in the eye. "I'm going to get up close and personal."

Later, upstairs, Nick readied himself for a sleep he knew wouldn't come soon, if at all. He counted on this next kill to bring him some peace. Ricardo must die for this madness to end. As long as he lived, no place on earth would be safe.

Tomorrow, he'd face the man who saved him all those years ago. The man who at one time, trusted him above all others. That trust long ago broken. A betrayal one man couldn't forgive, leaving the other no choice but to seek revenge.

Nick shivered in the early morning sun as he ascended the steps to Dalton's private jet. At least, Napa would be warmer. Along with Dalton and five of his men, Nick helped load all the gear onto the aircraft. Each man, including himself, would have an LR1000 long range rifle. Nick chose the LR1000 for its low recoil, accuracy, and ability to shoot up to a thousand yards. All of the rifles were equipped with suppressors to reduce noise and ground signature which could give away their location. Besides the rifle, Nick would also have his 9mm.

Ricardo's vineyard encompassed two hundred acres. He'd have men posted along the perimeter for sure. Each of them would take out one guard apiece, except for Nick. He insisted on taking out two. This gave Nick a clear route to Ricardo's house.

Three hours later, Nick, Dalton and his men exited the plane in Sacramento. They piled into a black van waiting to take them to the Napa Valley. Nick spread out a map in the rear of the van and reviewed each man's positions. The men donned headsets and secured their weapons.

The van dropped each man at their specified location above the vineyard. They'd make their way through some woods to the vineyard below and communicate after each kill shot.

Nick took the north perimeter, the one closest to the house. He crept through the thick brush and, within minutes, he spotted his first kill.

He pulled on his black leather shooting gloves, then lay down in a prone position, the stock of his rifle pressed between his shoulder blade and cheek. The familiar adrenaline rush pumped through his body, and he took aim. He scoped his target and squeezed the trigger twice. The man fell to the ground and lay still. One more and his perimeter would be clear.

Nick crept further along and spotted a lone figure, straw hat on his head, standing at the edge of a row of vines, firearm clearly in view. He lay down again and scoped his target. Nick was about to release his second series of shots when the figure turned and removed his hat. He pulled out a bandanna and wiped sweat from his brow.

Nick swallowed at the hard pulse in his throat. His stomach muscles coiled. For the first time ever, he hesitated. The man at the end of his line of fire was Ernesto Bario. What cruel twist of fate had brought Ernesto here? Ernesto's main post was in Miami.

He watched Ernesto place the hat on his head again, knowing if their roles were reversed, Ernesto wouldn't hesitate to blow Nick away, but it still didn't make killing him any easier.

He reclaimed his position and scoped his target. His adrenaline surged, and he released two shots to the head, killing Ernesto instantly. Another demon he'd have to live with.

Nick waited in the brush. A half-hour later the message came through his headset. The full perimeter was clear. He pulled a cloth from the pocket of his jeans, wiped the rifle clean in case it caught any prints, and laid it on the ground. He removed his headset and did the same.

Cautious, his senses heightened, Nick made his way through rows of green leafy vines tethered to wooden posts. Hard packed brown earth stretched out before him. The pungent odor of ripening fruit filled his lungs. Starlings sailed high above his head, oblivious to the bloodbath below.

The rooftop of Ricardo's house came into view. Nick darted among the last row of vines nearest the house. He could hardly believe his luck when Ricardo emerged from the back door. The bitterness inside Nick wrapped itself around his core. His pulse spiked, and his blood surged, roaring in his ears almost making him lose control.

He watched Ricardo walk from the house toward the vault where the wine was processed. He waited until he disappeared through the door before heading for the vault. Pulling out his 9mm, he attached the silencer, then eased the door open.

Nick scanned the area. Rows of aging wine barrels lined the cement floor. Florescent lights hung from the ceiling along the length of the room. Footsteps echoed, and he followed the sound. He continued on, the soft soles of his shoes silent. The scent of oak from the barrels permeated the room. Nick rounded the corner. Ricardo headed toward the processing room. Inside the room, he checked a gauge on one of the many stainless-steel vats.

Nick crept up behind him. He pressed the barrel of his gun firmly against Ricardo's head. All the sorrow of the past few weeks rose up inside of him. The air thinned, and his mouth went dry. Seconds ticked by. He could sense Ricardo's fear as he raised his hands in surrender.

"So, *Amigo*, this is how it is to be? A bullet from you with my back turned. I thought you were more of a man than that."

"Suit yourself," Nick spat. "Turn around." Nick took a step back, keeping his gun trained on Ricardo.

Slowly, his hands still raised, Ricardo turned. "How could you let things come to this, Nick?"

A razor-sharp spasm crossed Nick's gut. A profound sense of loss for what might have been. All he had wanted was peace between them. He'd wanted that more than anything. It pained him to look into Ricardo's eyes and see himself reflected there.

"I'm not the one responsible, Ricardo. You're the one who started all this."

Ricardo lowered his hands. "Me? No, no it wasn't me. You made a choice, Nick. And you paid the price for it."

"And now I've come for my refund."

"You were a foolish man to give up the life you could have had with Carmela for that woman."

"I'm not here to debate things with you, Ricardo. I'm here to put an end to all of this. I know full well, if I don't kill you now, you'll never stop. It's not in your DNA."

Darkness crossed Ricardo's face, the lines around the corners of his eyes creased. His hands clenched into fists at his side. He took a step forward. "I loved you like a son, Nick. Like a son!" The vein on his forehead pulsed.

Nick raised his weapon, pointed it at Ricardo's forehead. "No. You're wrong, Ricardo. If you loved me like a son, I wouldn't be putting a bullet in your head."

Ricardo raised his hand and shook his fist. "Where is your honor, Nick?"

Nick's body tensed at Ricardo's words. "There is no honor in killing, Ricardo. A lesson I learned firsthand from you."

There were no words left to say. He wouldn't stand here any longer and debate with a man determined to ruin his life. He'd keep things professional just like Ricardo had always wanted him to do. Nick gripped the gun tighter. His adrenaline rush surging so strong, it almost overpowered him. It hit every single nerve and roared in his ears. His heart nearly exploded inside his chest. He looked into the darkness of Ricardo's eyes and squeezed the trigger.

Ricardo's shocked expression lasted mere seconds as the bullet sped through the chamber and hit him dead center in the forehead. Nick watched the man who once saved him, the man whom so many feared, collapse and lie still. It was over. He was free.

Then it came. A scream so loud, so terrible, echoing off the cement walls. Nick spun around. Carmela rushed past him with Chino keeping stride.

She collapsed to the floor, cradling her dead father's head in her lap. "No, no," Carmela wailed. "*Papá,* please, please." Blood from Ricardo's wound stained her white silk blouse. She looked up at Nick through her tears. Confusion and fear on her face.

"Why, why? How could you do this?"

Nick stood, unable to move, his heart breaking at the sight of Carmela holding onto her dead father's body.

"Carmela, I never wanted this. You have to believe me. Your father left me no choice."

Chino scampered over to Carmela. He began licking Ricardo's limp hand and whimpering.

She lifted her father's head from her lap and gently lowered it. She stood up, lunged toward Nick, arms flailing, her dark eyes raging. She pounded his chest. "I hate you. I hate you." She tried to grab his gun. "I'll kill you for what you did."

Nick dropped his weapon and gripped both her wrists. "Carmela, listen, let me explain."

"No, no Nick. Nothing you say can ever make this right. I mean it, I will kill you for this." She struggled against him, her face red with rage.

Nick realized nothing would make sense to her. She had just lost the person she loved the most in the world. He let her go, retrieved his weapon from the floor, and backed away.

"Ataque!" Carmela screamed at Chino.

Chino looked from Carmela to Nick but didn't move.

"Atague, Chino!" Carmela shouted at the dog again.

When he failed to obey, Carmela kicked him in his hind leg. Chino yelped, backed away, and hung his head.

Carmela scowled at him. "You useless thing!"

Nick turned and walked toward the door. He couldn't stay any longer to witness her pain. He fought the tears gathering at the corners of his eyes as Carmela continued to scream.

"I promise you," she shouted after him. "You will die for this. He taught me all about his business. I won't stop until you're dead. Do you hear me? Not until you're dead!

Nick froze at Carmela's final words. He turned and stared down the rows of barrels filled with fermenting wine to the small figure raging at him. At that moment, he knew what he had to do. Nick raised his arm and aimed his 9mm for the last time.

Exhausted, Nick reached Lugano and lumbered up the stairs to the master bedroom. Thoughts of Ricardo, Ernesto, and Carmela had accompanied him on the long flight home. More demons added to his long list. He'd bury them along with all the others.

He approached the top landing. A soft cooing sound drifted toward him from the hall. He walked to the doorway of the nursery and stopped.

A veil lifted from in front of his eyes and his lungs filled. It happened every time he saw her. His world fell into place. It was there, always that bond between the two of them, like a sixth sense.

Carrie sat in the rocker, a small bundle in her arms. She looked up and smiled. "Welcome home. Come meet your daughter."

CHAPTER 48

CARRIE

Wearing a beige dress trimmed in lace, Carrie stood at the altar with Nick. Handsome, in a navy-blue suit, he fidgeted with his tie. She laughed to herself knowing how much he hated wearing a tie.

Excited to be his best man, Bobby, also in a suit and tie was stationed next to Nick. Carrie still grappled with the fact that this attractive young man was her son.

When she spotted the little church in the hills near their villa, she found it perfect for the small ceremony. Though neither of them was religious, she rejoiced when Nick agreed.

The move from Lugano to Tuscany, Italy suited them. Villa Tranquillo became their new home. Tranquillo meaning peaceful or quiet in Italian held special meaning for them all.

The walled compound contained seven bedrooms. Its long wide terraces looked out over the vast pastures below. The property itself boasted stunning gardens and a private courtyard off the master suite.

Two living rooms, a winter dining room, a summer dining room, and kitchen completed the main floor. The beamed ceilings and original woodwork were complemented by intarsia inlay doors, with exquisite carvings that warmed the inside. The remaining bedrooms and bathrooms graced the upper level.

Looking out at the rows of dark mahogany pews warmed her heart. The people that meant the most to her were all present. Aunt May held little baby Isabelle. Joann sat beside her with Veronica and Justin. Nick's sister Marie, her husband Dario and their three children were also there.

The corners of Carrie's mouth edged up in a smile when she looked at the end of the aisle by the doors to the church. There sat Chino, the latest addition to the family. Nick never gave her an explanation when he returned home to Lugano with Chino, but it didn't matter. Chino soon earned their love and respect.

Carrie never imagined her life the way it was now. Memories of Breezy, her mother and Travis were all but gone and along with them, her nightmares.

Now, she had a son and a daughter to cherish. A man who loved her more than any man ever could. Who would have thought all this possible when just six months ago she had almost died from a gunshot wound?

Carrie forgot most of what happened the day of the shooting, except for the searing pain and Nick's arms around her as he carried her to safety, but more importantly, she had learned, later on, the voice that cried out and called her mom, belonged to her son. She believed with all her heart Bobby's voice helped save her.

When Nick was reassured that she and their unborn baby would survive, he left. Carrie understood he'd do whatever was necessary for their safety. She worried herself sick about him, but she trusted him and his promise to return.

Carrie never questioned Nick as to where he had gone nor asked what he had done because, in her heart, she knew. All she cared about, and rejoiced in, was his coming back home to them.

She gave birth to their daughter without Nick by her side. When they handed the baby to her, the terror inside her faded. Isabelle belonged to them and was physical proof of their love for each other.

The day he returned and met Isabelle would always remain one of the best days of her life. Tears fell from his eyes when he held his daughter for the first time. Izzie, as Carrie fondly called her, was the light of their world. What Nick had given her, she failed at times to find words for. Her children, and now her soon-to-be husband were all she needed.

With Isabelle's birth, she decided to end the lies between herself and Aunt May. Nick flew May to the house in Lugano. Without mentioning his name, Carrie told her how awful the man she'd run away with treated her. How he forced her to defend herself during the robbery and murder.

She explained how Nick had saved her life, but she left out the part about how Travis died.

Aunt May, shocked at first, was heartbroken to hear of the trauma Carrie had gone through, but in the end, she was grateful to Nick for loving Carrie and giving her a new life.

She also came clean about her life to Joann, and she wanted her to know how much her friendship meant. At first, she worried she'd lose Joann as a friend, but it only served to draw the two women closer.

And with Claudia's sudden death a year ago, Nick took extra care to spend more time with Bobby. He wanted to teach him what it meant to be a good father and how much he cared about him.

Two weeks ago, they solidified their relationship when Nick officially adopted him and gave him his last name. From that day on, Bobby D'Angelo slept without a light on.

Not long after, Nick got down on one knee and offered her a six-carat diamond ring, which she refused to accept. Carrie wanted the ring to symbolize what they meant to each other. Instead, she delighted in a simple thin pavé diamond platinum eternity band.

For Nick, they chose a gold band with four small diamonds to represent her, Nick, Bobby, and Isabelle. It touched her heart when he insisted on adding a fifth diamond. There would no doubt be another little D'Angelo in the future.

Although she feared it, it wouldn't change her feelings if Nick became a ghost again. The man who rescued her and loved her without judging her many faults was the man she'd love until her last breath on this earth. Nothing could ever change that.

Nick had given her so many firsts. Her first snowfall, her first real home, and her first true love. And of course, his greatest gift, Isabelle.

Carrie looked into Nick's eyes as he slipped the eternity ring on her finger. She had always wanted her freedom and a safe place, a real home, a place without fear. In the aftermath of all that had transpired came the realization what she needed most was to be loved. It made no difference where she lived. Her real home was in the arms of the man she loved.

The ceremony finished, and Carrie D'Angelo stepped down from the altar. Aunt May placed Isabelle in her arms and Carrie walked out of the church and into the sunlight with her husband and son at her side.

EPILOGUE

CARMELA

Carmela Santiago sat behind the desk in the burgundy leather chair in what was once her father's study. Her dark eyes trained on the computer screen. The next shipment of drugs was due to arrive the day after tomorrow.

Her father had taught her well. Carmela ran her father's empire as if it had been her own all along. She surrounded herself with people she trusted. And, like her father, demanded loyalty. Those who did not comply were simply removed.

Carmela's mourning for her father did not last long. With businesses to run, there wasn't much time to mourn, but she kept his memory close to her heart and would always appreciate the life he'd given her.

Feeling the strain of staring at the screen for hours, Carmela blinked and turned her head away. She rose from the desk and poured herself a shot of AsomBroso Tequila. Lifting the glass to her lips, she downed the warm liquid in one swallow.

Carmela set the glass on her desk and stepped to the window. She stared out at the vast gardens before her and beyond. Her eyes rested on the pasture below.

Memories of Nick and the day she showed him Allegra, surfaced once again. What was it he said? 'Don't ever let anyone tame you. Put out that fire inside.' Yes, she remembered it well.

That and the image of Nick, standing over her father in the winery, would never leave her. Her heart lurched each time she thought about that day. Regardless of what had happened between the two men, what Nick did was unforgivable.

Her threats and screams as Nick walked away were among the things keeping her sane. She recalled the look on his face when he turned and raised his gun.

Nick should have shot her that day and ended it all. Instead, he had lowered his gun and, without another word, turned and walked away.

Chino continued to ignore her orders to attack him. Having no use for such a disobedient animal, she didn't care when he followed Nick.

Carmela walked to her desk and opened up a folder. She studied the picture inside. A handsome young man with blue eyes stared up at her. They were not as violet blue as his mother's eyes, but in them, she saw many things.

"Don't worry, Nick," she said. "No one has put out the fire in me. And one day, it will rain down on all of you. I promise."

Stephanie Baldi grew up in the Brooklyn neighborhood of Gerritsen Beach. Her love of writing began during Saturday trips with her mother to the small local library where children gathered to hear a story read by the local Librarian. When the story ended, Stephanie would pick out a book to take home and read.

But it was not until years later after a career in Patient Accounting and a stint as a Licensed Realtor that her dreams of becoming a writer flourished with a move to the Pocono Mountains in Pennsylvania. It was there that her first novel, *Redemption* was conceived. But family trials and tribulations forced her to abandon the manuscript for a time until her move to Georgia to be closer to her family.

As a writer, Stephanie is dedicated to giving her reader's fast-paced, high stakes, page-turning stories that keep you on the edge of your seat and are full of surprising twists. She resides at her lake home in Villa Rica, Georgia with her husband and two cats. Stephanie is currently at work on the final installment of this trilogy titled *Reckoning* which is slated for release in 2020. She is thrilled to have been nominated for Georgia Author of the Year for *Redemption.*

You can find her online at www.stephaniebaldi2.com. Or follow her on facebook.com/sbauthor7 and Twitter at sbauthor7

Coming 2019

RETRIBUTION

Excerpt CHAPTER

CARMELA

Carmela Santiago reveled in the power beneath her. With both her legs in a neutral position, she concentrated, applying equal pressure against Diablo's sides to increase her horse's speed. Hot wind swept past her face. The pounding of his hooves surrounded her, their rhythm a beating heart. She gripped the reins as they approached the first hurdle. Leaning forward, she held on, clearing the fence with ease. Her long, dark braid sailed out from under her riding cap. A smile spread across her lips. She patted Diablo's side in appreciation.

An hour later, with Mateo's help, she transferred the horse into the trailer. Diablo, given to her as a peace offering from one of the many drug cartels she dealt with, trained well. The world-class Arabian's stamina outdid Allegra's. But Allegra, a precious gift from her father, Ricardo, held a special place in her heart. While Allegra's performances at Dressage Competitions were outstanding, Diablo had neither the temperament nor patience to parade around a ring. He preferred the challenge of the jump, just like his master. Carmela rode both horses with pride.

She found it hard to believe almost six years had passed since Ricardo's death. The relentless ache inside her burned as she recalled how his life ended from a bullet to his brain, courtesy of Nicholas D'Angelo, the one-man Ricardo had trusted above all others. So much so, he'd wanted a marriage between Nick and his only child.

Carmela reflected on how her future might have gone if Nick hadn't betrayed them both. Her admiration developed from a child's crush into the cravings of a woman, but she never let her emotions show after discovering he wasn't in love with her. He'd fallen for someone else. Carrie Overton stole Nick away, turning him against her father.

She swallowed hard and chewed her lower lip. Carrie, now Mrs. D'Angelo, stood in the place belonging to her.

She'd found out, besides Carrie's son, Bobby, they had two children together, Isabelle, a five-year-old girl, and Michael, a two-year-old boy named in memory of Nick's deceased brother.

Thinking about those children set off thunderstorms in her mind. They were the children she should have borne him. Her teeth clenched, producing the familiar ache in her jaw. Taking several deep breaths, she tried to calm herself.

The past years had given her the freedom to continue to build her father's businesses into an empire fueled by a steady stream of drug money. She liked to think how proud he'd be to see how much she'd accomplished.

A silver Lincoln sedan drove up, and she climbed into the rear seat.

"You were amazing out there." His voice, smooth as silk, washed over her while his dark eyes caught hers in the rearview mirror.

"Gracias, Diego." She sank into the soft leather and admired his jet-black hair dipping below his collar. Her desire rose. She smiled knowing soon they'd satisfy it.

Diego Silva, her most trusted bodyguard, had also become her lover. Not a wise choice, but running her drug business left little time for vetting suitors.

They drove to the stables behind the vineyards in Napa. The winery where her father died became the place to which she devoted most of her life. No one understood her attachment, but she stayed because she needed to keep the memory of his death close. Satisfaction would never come until she avenged his death.

Carmela followed Mateo to Diablo's stall while Diego leaned against the Lincoln. A musky scent emanating from the horses greeted her and mixed with the sweet-smelling hay. Hooks, hanging from the rough wooden walls in the tack area, held bridles, leads, curry combs, and other equipment.

She rubbed Diablo's muzzle before turning to Mateo. "Make certain you curry him before you brush him. Pick out his hooves. Check his eyes and nose—''

Mateo held up his hand. He tipped back his large black Cattleman's hat. The dark skin between his brows wrinkled. "*Señorita,* I will take good care of him…as always."

She shook her head and smiled. "I'm sorry, Mateo. I know you are as devoted to him as I am."

A loud whinny came from a stall to behind her. Allegra pushed his head through the opening in the gate and whinnied again. She grabbed a carrot from a feedbag hanging outside the stall and presented it to Allegra. He chomped it down in two bites, then nuzzled her empty palm, his bristles tickling her skin.

"Mateo, turn Allegra out in the pasture. He seems restless."

"*Si, Señorita*

She left the stable, and Diego held the car door open. They drove, in silence, to the spacious mansion. She climbed the stone steps and hurried inside.

The Napa house, larger than the one in Miami and as well-appointed, boasted imported tile plus custom woodwork throughout. Massive windows framed grand views of the gardens and vineyards. Various rooms contained priceless art displayed according to their form, the collections here superior to the Miami artwork.

Her butler, Armando, greeted her in the marble foyer. Dressed impeccably in a white shirt with Windsor cut collar, grey tie, black jacket and trousers, he stretched out his arm.

"*Buenas tardes,*"

Employed by her family since her childhood, she was grateful when he agreed to stay on after her father's passing.

She removed her cap and coat and handed it to him. "Thank you, Armando."

He bowed and smiled. "Can I bring you anything, *Señorita?*"

"No, thank you. Maybe later."

With each step up the large winding staircase, her heart beat faster. Within minutes, Diego would climb these same stairs to her bedroom.

Carmela closed the door. She pulled off her riding boots and unbraided her hair, letting it fall in waves down her back, the ends dipping below her waist. Stripping off her clothes, she admired her caramel-colored skin in the full-length mirror.

The bedroom door opened. Diego rushed in. He removed his coat, then his shoulder holster, dropping them to the floor. Continuing to peel off his clothes, he shook his head. "My God, you make a grown man weak as a kitten."

The corners of her mouth edged up into a smile, her skin tingling at the sight of his naked body. "And you make a grown woman blush."

Diego pressed up against her, easing her onto the bed. He stroked her face and whispered, "Carmela, I love you. I have never felt like this before."

Her body went stiff, and she frowned. "Why do you have to spoil things?" She moved away and rose from the bed. Grabbing her robe from the pale blue tufted bench at the foot, she slipped it on. She didn't want to hear his foolish talk about love.

"Carmela, why do you act this way?" His voice held a twinge of anger. "Come back to bed."

She scowled at him. "Diego, we have gone over and over this a million times. I'm not looking for love. Not now, not ever."

Diego cursed under his breath. He jumped up and gathered his clothes. "What is this obsession you have? I'm warning you, if you pursue your crazy revenge, it will not end well. These things never do. You need to let it go, Carmela."

She crossed her arms and stuck out her chin. He could never imagine the scene she'd witnessed. Otherwise, he'd agree with her plans.

"This crazy revenge, as you call it, is not something I can let go. My father is dead!" A single tear erupted from her eye.

Diego moved closer. "I know how much you hurt," he soothed. "But this idea of yours may get you killed." He wiped the tear from her cheek.

Carmela brushed his hand away. She secured the sash on her robe. "You don't understand. It is my duty to make his assassin pay. My heart knows he will never rest in peace until I do." She rushed past him and ran downstairs to her study.

Turning the lock, she collapsed into the leather chair behind her desk. She removed a photograph from the drawer. Her pain still palpable, she studied the faces inside the frame. Nick stood beside her, his arm draped around her shoulder. They smiled into the camera. What a charade. Now, she could see right through his false smile, the too casual way his arm rested upon her. What she once perceived as love meant nothing more to him than a caring friendship. While his feelings floated above the surface, hers ran much deeper.

As an awkward young girl in middle school, she dreamt of a future with Nick. Something she had never admitted to anyone. If Nick had complied with her father's wishes to marry her, she wanted him to do it because he loved her and not out of obligation.

Those dreams of hers turned into a nightmare after Carrie stole Nick from her. Carmela's malice twisted itself around her gut, forming a deep chasm nothing could fill until the day she made Nick pay. The desire she once felt for him grew into a bitter hatred, encompassing all those he cared for.

Placing the photograph inside the drawer, she fingered a folder lying on her desk and flipped it open. She stared at still shots of Carrie D'Angelo and another man. She studied his features. His appearance proved him to be much older than her. Below the man's photo, written in her father's handwriting, she read the name, Travis Montgomery. Besides being the thief Nick executed for him, what was his connection to Carrie? The time to find the answer had come.

Sweeping the two photos aside, she picked up another one. She recognized the two men lying in pools of blood. Carlos and Eddie once worked for her father. Carrie Overton along with Travis Montgomery had shot them to death. Nick, given orders by Ricardo to find and kill them, deviated from his assignment by killing Travis and allowing Carrie to live.

In teaching her the business, her father had taken off the blinders, making it clear what kind of work Nick performed. He made sure she understood in the drug trade someone like Nick became a necessity.

Since her father's death, she acquired her own person of necessity, Miguel Medina. Whenever the need arose to eliminate someone, she called Miguel. Trustworthy and efficient, she relied on him to take care of the ugly side of the business. She could have ordered him to kill Nick and his family long ago, but she wanted more. They needed to feel her suffering.

She examined the photos again before sweeping them aside. Underneath them lay a newspaper clipping. Bobby D'Angelo's smiling face stared at her. The headline read, 'Young Art Dealer to Show Premier Collection at New York Gallery.'

Carmela pursed her lips and continued to stare at the newspaper. She reached for the phone.

"Bernardo, get my private jet ready. I need to fly to New York tomorrow." Carmela set the receiver down and closed the folder. She rose and wandered to the window.

"*Papi,*" she said. "I am listening to you. I hear you crying out from your grave. It has taken me a while, but I will make those words I said to Nick become a reality. I won't stop until he's dead. I won't stop until they are all dead."